Does the captain think I have ulterior motives?

It was hard for Burnham not to feel as if she were on trial. "I need an investigative partner," she said to Georgiou. "One whose training, mental discipline, and foundations in logic are comparable to, and compatible with, my own."

"Why not Pike's first officer? I hear his Number One is no slouch, in any regard."

A polite nod of demurral. "While I have the utmost respect for Commander Una and her Illyrian mental conditioning, I think I will find it easier to build a working relationship quickly with someone of a more . . . *Vulcan* temperament."

"I see." Georgiou stood and circled her desk to stand in front of Burnham. "I'm going to take your word for this, Michael, because we don't have a lot of time. If I approve this meeting of the minds, are you sure you can find a solution in under three hours?"

"No," Burnham said, unwilling to lie to her captain and friend. "But I *am* certain that thousands of innocent lives will be lost if we do *not* attempt this."

Georgiou's grim resolve turned to a look of quiet hope in the face of impossible odds. "All right, then. Good talk, Number One." She lifted her chin toward the door. "Get to work."

"Aye, sir." Burnham accepted the informal dismissal and escaped to the bridge, then to the turbolift, before Georgiou had time to reconsider.

Burnham headed for the transporter room, where her next official duty would be to welcome to the *Shenzhou* the one person in the galaxy she had hoped never to see again, and who would now be coming aboard at her invitation.

I get the distinct impression this constitutes a working definition of irony.

STAR TREK®
DISCOVERY

DESPERATE HOURS

DAVID MACK

Based upon *Star Trek*®
created by Gene Roddenberry
and
Star Trek: Discovery
created by Bryan Fuller & Alex Kurtzman

G

GALLERY BOOKS

New York   London   Toronto   Sydney   New Delhi   Sirsa III

G

Gallery Books
An Imprint of Simon & Schuster, Inc.
1230 Avenue of the Americas
New York, NY 10020

First Gallery Books trade paperback edition September 2017

GALLERY BOOKS and colophon are registered trademarks of Simon & Schuster, Inc.

For information about special discounts for bulk purchases, please contact Simon & Schuster Special Sales at 1-866-506-1949 or business@simonandschuster.com.

The Simon & Schuster Speakers Bureau can bring authors to your live event. For more information or to book an event, contact the Simon & Schuster Speakers Bureau at 1-866-248-3049 or visit our website at www.simonspeakers.com.

Manufactured in the United States of America

10 9 8 7 6 5 4 3 2 1

ISBN 978-1-5011-6457-6
ISBN 978-1-5011-6461-3 (ebook)

for those fighting to keep the dream alive

Historian's Note

The events of this story take place in May 2255, approximately one year before the *Shenzhou*'s historic mission to the binary stars, and one year after the *Enterprise*'s first mission to Talos IV.

Justice and judgment lie often a world apart.

—Emmeline Pankhurst, British suffragette
My Own Story (1914)

1

Goddamn it. What now? Jon Bowen took the steps two at a time, climbing the switchback staircase as if it and his ass were on fire. The operations level was four flights up from his quarters, but he was winded after only two. Most days he would have waited for the lift, but most days the Arcadia Explorer platform wasn't being hammered by a Sirsa III tropical maelstrom that caused its underwater drill to spew a flood of alarms.

A trio of mechanics barreled past Bowen on their way down the stairs. He put his back to the wall to let them pass, since they were burdened with tools, cables, and bulky emergency gear. None of the tool-pushers acknowledged him as they ran by. That suited him fine. Beads of sweat rolled from under his thinning blond hair and down his forehead while he caught his breath. As soon as the stairwell was clear, he continued his climb, swearing under his breath at the aching in his lower back, the cramping muscles in his thighs, and the lightness in his head.

The closer he got to the top of the stairs, the more clearly he heard the platform's alert siren, a buzzing sonic assault that had been optimized by acoustic engineers to cut through the roar of howling winds and crashing waves. The deck was wet near the door that led outside, and the corridor to the operations center was steeped in the white noise of rain lashing the platform's exterior. Ignoring the flashing orange lights and continuing sirens, Bowen hurried down the narrow passage into the crowded confines of ops.

Blue light from banks of displays contrasted with amber flashes from the emergency lights overhead. Crew members manned every duty station, a rarity in the middle of the night. Bowen headed for the center situation table and shouted, "What the hell's going on?"

The night-shift supervisor, Lewa Omalu, yielded her place at the situation table to Bowen, handing him the coordinator's headset as she stepped aside. "The drill hit something."

"That's what it's for, isn't it?"

Omalu pointed at a flashing error indicator on the master systems display. "It's stuck."

"Sonofabitch." Bowen grumbled harsher profanities under his breath as he magnified the sensor image from the bottom of the drilling shaft. "What the hell stops a plasma drill?"

"The same duranium-rich composite that drew us here in the first place." She pointed with one dark-brown finger at a cross-section image of the seabed. "We'd just broken through the last sedimentary layer when the drill stopped dead."

None of the numbers in the display made sense to Bowen. "So pull it out."

"What part of 'stuck' did you not understand?" Omalu noted Bowen's sharp glance and pulled back on the reins of her temper. "I've got every tool-pusher I can spare patching in backup power now. As soon as we reverse the drill free, I'll pull it up for a damage check and send down a probe to see what we've got."

"Sounds good." Bowen let go of his own bad mood. This was just another night on the job, another routine SNAFU—nothing to get worked up about. "Will the storm be a problem?"

Omalu glanced toward the wide transparent-aluminum window at the south side of ops, noted the lightning-strobed barrage of wind and rain that pummeled the Arcadian Explorer, then threw a skeptical look at Bowen. "You're kidding, right? It's just a rainstorm. I used to sail through worse every summer when I was just a girl in Lagos."

"That's what I thought. Just wanted to check." He wondered if he would be able to get back to sleep if he returned to his quarters now, or if he should stay awake since daybreak was only a couple of hours away. He asked Omalu, "Any coffee left in the kitchenette?"

"What do you think?"

"I think people on this rig need to learn that when you kill the joe, you make some mo'. It's just common goddamned courtesy. You know what I'm—" The overhead lights went out as the deck heaved and pitched, throwing Bowen against the situation table. Omalu and half a dozen other members of the operations team tumbled and collided with one another against a bank of consoles. The buzzing alert was replaced by a whooping siren, and in an instant nearly every indicator on the master systems display turned condition-critical red.

Outside the southern window, a fireball erupted from one of the fuel pods, and a cargo crane swung away from the platform and plunged half its length into the sea.

Bowen reached across the situation table to open an internal channel. "Engineering, this is ops! Status report!" All he heard was static. He switched to a different channel. "Drill team, ops! Report!" Dead silence.

Omalu clawed her way back to Bowen's side. "Did something hit us?"

"How should I know?" Bowen struggled to make sense of the chaos unfolding on all of the platform's situation monitors. "We've got fires on sublevels six and seven. No readings at all below that." He pivoted toward the drilling supervisor. "Ramayan! What's happening?"

"Seismic activity directly beneath us," said the Mumbai-born drilling supervisor, his voice pitched from shouting over the din of alarms and an ominous rumbling that resonated through the platform's superstructure. "Rapid rise in the seabed! It's pushing the drill back up into—" His report was cut off by another explosion outside the window. The bent and fractured drill housing shot up through the platform, erupted from its roof, and triggered a cascade of structural failures. Bowen watched in horror as the center of the Arcadia Explorer vanished into the fresh cavity wrought by the expulsion of the massive drill assembly.

"Holy shit," Bowen muttered. Louder, he demanded, "Damage reports! Now!"

First to respond was Omalu. "Rising seabed confirmed. All of our support pylons have fractured." She patched in a feed from one of the exterior safety sensors. An image of the platform appeared over the situation table, revealing that the massive facility's two lowest levels had already collapsed and vanished into the churning water below—taking with them more than two hundred personnel, including most of the engineers. The image tilted as the platform lurched again, knocking Bowen off his feet. Omalu white-knuckled the center table. "If this rig shifts more than six meters in any direction, it's gonna sink."

Terror made a jumble of Bowen's thoughts. The Arcadia Explorer stood on pylons of duranium-reinforced thermoconcrete. They should have been impervious to any natural disaster this planet could dish out. Now the entire facility was moments away from vanishing beneath 2,400 meters of water.

There was no time to effect repairs, and with most of the engineers already gone there was no one to make them. Bowen had no choice. He pressed his palm against a biometric pad on the master systems display. "Computer, sound the evacuation order, all decks!"

"Confirmed," the computer replied in a masculine voice with a dry London accent.

Bowen turned from the console and stood tall. "Everyone, get the hell out of here! Get to a pod, a shuttle, anything! Move!" The room cleared within seconds. Bowen had to nudge Omalu to get her away from the systems display. "It's over, Lewa! We gotta go! Now!" They nearly fell over each other on their way to the nearest exit, and Ramayan Chandra was right behind them as they left ops and charged outside into the storm.

Omalu froze at a T intersection in the catwalk. Bowen started to point her toward the right, but then Chandra pulled them both in the opposite direction. "This way!"

Bowen protested, "But the pods—"

"Are too far," Chandra said. "The shuttle's closer! Come on!" The slender engineer took the lead and guided them through blinding sheets of rain that stung Bowen's face.

Just as Chandra had promised, around the nearest corner was a narrow bridge to a landing platform where a shuttle was parked.

The three of them ran toward it and fought to keep their footing as the rig shifted again. Omalu's feet slipped on the wet metal bridge, and she nearly plunged over the

railing into a jumble of broken metal beams above a churning mass of black water. Bowen grabbed Omalu's shirt
and pulled her back onto the bridge. "You all right?" Rain
pelted her face as she nodded. He pulled her into motion
and they resumed their run toward the shuttle.

Chandra reached the small craft first and threw himself
into its pilot's seat. Omalu stayed behind to seal the hatch
while Bowen strapped himself into the shuttle's command
seat. "Get us in the air," he snapped at Chandra, "before
this—"

Calamity preempted his warning. With a sound like
thunder the rig slid off its shattered pylons and tilted
toward the sea. Outside the cockpit canopy, a nightmare
unfolded. Entire sections of the rig sheared apart, spilling
metal and bodies into the ocean.

On other landing platforms, shuttles and other small
spacecraft slid over the edges and sank into the raging sea.
Feeling gravity take hold of his own shuttle, Bowen realized
he was very likely witnessing a preview of his imminent fate.

"Ramayan—!"

"I know, Jon! Shut up!"

Chandra cold-started the engines and fired the maneu-
vering thrusters. Bowen clutched the shuttle's console as
the tiny craft shot toward the water—and then he gritted
his teeth as Chandra pulled up on the controls, forcing the
craft into a high-g climb. Its belly and port stabilizer grazed
the waves, kicking up spray in their wake.

Then Bowen and Chandra saw the bulk of Arcadia
Explorer collapsing toward them. Time seemed to slow
as Chandra made a gut-twisting turn coupled with acceleration and a barrel roll, and guided the shuttle through a
ragged gap in the rig's broken superstructure, like a fragile
thread passing through a needle made of death. Lightning

bent across the black sky ahead of them, and for half a breath Bowen thought they had exploded—

Then the glare abated, his vision adjusted, and he knew they had made it out alive.

As the shuttle banked into a steep turn, Bowen looked down to see the last of the rig splinter apart and vanish in a series of fiery blasts that within seconds were swallowed by the sea. Oily clouds lingered over the froth-capped waves where the rig had stood just minutes before.

The water churned—then parted to reveal a massive form, one alien and monstrous, like some terrible leviathan of ancient myth, newly free of the ocean's embrace. Segments of the rig tumbled off its curved back and slid once more into the briny depths.

"My God." Bowen pointed down at the monstrosity. Chandra regarded it with confusion and amazement; Omalu's reaction was one of abject horror. Before they had a chance to study its details, the storm head swallowed their shuttle, which hurtled away from the disaster shrouded in darkness, thunder, and scouring rain.

Omalu slumped to the deck between Bowen and Chandra. "What was that thing?"

"I have no idea," Bowen confessed. "But we'd better have a good answer to that question before we face the governor, or we're all gonna be screwed."

2

It was a commanding officer's privilege to be fashionably late, and tonight Captain Philippa Georgiou was making the most of that perquisite. On some level, she knew her fastidious preparation of her dress uniform had been an act of procrastination, one born out of a desire to avoid a circumstance about which she was still in denial. The same had been true of her languid pace as she left her quarters and boarded a lift to the officers' lounge, which was located on a lower deck, on the other side of the *Starship Shenzhou*'s saucer section. Now she approached the door to the lounge and found each step more difficult to take than the one before.

Then the portal parted ahead of her, and an up-tempo jazz melody of piano, clarinet, bass, and wire-brush percussion flowed into the corridor, along with a low murmur of many voices in polite conversation. Enlisted personnel from the ship's services division roamed with trays of drinks and appetizers, attentive to the appetites and needs of their guests. It was an upbeat but dignified soiree, one befitting its guests of honor and the occasion.

Georgiou noted that most of the other officers already held flutes of Champagne, so she snagged one off a tray as she passed by, and thanked the server with a smile.

She turned and took in the room. Off to one corner, the ship's new communications officer, Ensign Mary Fan, was demurely enduring the flirtations of the lanky chief engineer, Lieutenant Commander Saladin Johar. Across the room, near the viewports that looked out upon the dusky northern hemisphere of Ligot IV, some manner of good-humored debate was unfolding between junior tactical officer Lieutenant Kamran Gant, conn officer Ensign Keyla Detmer, and operations officer Lieutenant Belin Oliveira. Whatever point Gant was making, it had the two women alternately shaking their heads and breaking out in peals of laughter.

Through the milling camouflage of junior officers Georgiou spotted the ship's soft-spoken chief medical officer, Doctor Anton Nambue, making small talk with senior tactical officer Lieutenant Michael Burnham. It struck Georgiou as peculiar that the normally taciturn Burnham—whom Georgiou had treated as her protégée ever since Ambassador Sarek had talked the Vulcan-educated human into accepting a Starfleet officer's commission six years earlier—was engaged in jovial banter with the good doctor. *Maybe she's finally learning to loosen up a little,* Georgiou hoped. *That would be a miracle long overdue.*

At the far end of the room from Burnham stood her longtime professional rival and rhetorical foil, Lieutenant Saru. The Kelpien science officer's impressive height—just over two meters—ridged skull-like visage, and mildly awkward backward-leaning posture made him hard to miss, even in a crowd. Saru seemed determined to monopolize the attention of the party's two guests of honor, first officer Commander Sonnisar ch'Theloh and second officer Lieutenant Commander Itzel García. The Andorian's smile was betraying signs of strain, and García's focus volleyed between Saru's steady prattle of polite banalities and the empty chasm of her glass.

Looks like a rescue mission is in order, Georgiou realized.

She snagged another glass of Champagne on her way across the lounge, and with confidence and grace insinuated herself between Saru and his conversational hostages.

"So as one might imagine," Saru said, not yet having noted Georgiou's presence, "my decision to apply a Kelpien design aesthetic to diplomatic quarters intended for the Pahkwa-thanh ambassador was met with a less than enthusiastic . . ." His anecdote trailed off as he observed the shifts in ch'Theloh's and García's attention. He pivoted to glimpse Georgiou, then recoiled with a subtle jolt. "Captain! Forgive me, I didn't realize you'd joined us."

"It seemed the merciful thing to do." She handed her extra flute of Champagne to García. "You looked like you could use another."

García set aside her empty glass and accepted the fresh drink with a grateful nod. "Too kind, Captain." After a sip, she asked, "Time for your big speech, then?"

"Am I supposed to give a speech?" Georgiou feigned surprise, but ch'Theloh's and García's smirks of amusement made it clear they weren't buying her charade. Saru, however, met the moment with his typical blank expression, as if he couldn't laugh without express permission or a direct order. "Fine," Georgiou said, moving past her two senior officers so she could put her back to the wide viewport and address the entire room. She picked up a teaspoon from a nearby table and tapped her glass with it.

Its bright chiming silenced most of the room, except for a small pocket of junior officers in the back, who were too busy laughing to note the signal. It was an oversight Lieutenant Saru addressed without delay. He faced the clutch of freshly minted officers, struck an imperious pose, and barked, "Ensigns! Be quiet! The captain wishes to speak!" His order stifled the jocularity in the corner—and chilled the mood in the rest of the room to boot.

Georgiou masked her discomfort. *Worst opening act ever.*

She put on a smile to ease the tension. "First, thank you all for coming out this evening. As I'm sure you all know by now, we've gathered to bid a fond farewell to our esteemed first officer, Commander ch'Theloh, who's leaving us to accept his own first command, on the *Starship Tereshkova*. And, as if being deprived of my trusted Number One of four years wasn't painful enough, he's gone and poached our second officer, Lieutenant Commander García, to serve as his Number One." She faced ch'Theloh. "Sonny, you've been a superb second-in-command, and you've been a good friend. As much as I hate to see you leave us, it makes me happy to know that the *Tereshkova* is going to have such a fine commanding officer." Pivoting toward García, she continued, "Itzel, you've come such a long way in so short a time. At sixteen you left your small village in the Yucatán for Starfleet Academy. And it seems like it was only yesterday when you transferred aboard the *Shenzhou* as a relief operations officer. Now you'll be second-in-command on one of the fleet's most storied vessels. I couldn't be prouder of you." Glancing at ch'Theloh, she added, "Of both of you." She lifted her glass high, and the other officers in the room mimicked her gesture. "Our loss is the *Tereshkova*'s gain. Join me in wishing *Captain* ch'Theloh and *Commander* García many years of boundless wonder as they embark on their next great adventure together. Cheers!"

From the crowd came back a resounding chorus of "Cheers!" Then glasses tipped upward as the officers of the *Shenzhou* drank in salute to their departing shipmates.

Satisfied that her obligations were fulfilled, Georgiou drifted back into the crowd to mingle and be sociable. She spotted Burnham standing alone and moved toward her. Just as she reached the younger woman's side, Saru emerged from the crowd and situated himself between them. "A stirring encomium, Captain," the Kelpien said. "A most fitting valediction."

Burnham raised one eyebrow at Saru. "Indeed. And her accomplishment is all the more notable for having been compelled to follow your own rousing call to arms."

Saru tensed and regarded Burnham with barely veiled contempt. "Meaning what?"

"Only that I hope never to contend with such a *memorable* introduction."

"I doubt you will ever merit one," Saru said.

"Kind of you to say so, Mister Saru."

It took Saru a moment to realize he had been insulted twice in a matter of seconds. He clenched his fists and trembled like some overly anxious breed of small dog. Georgiou took his flustered reaction as a sign that it might be a good idea to separate him and Burnham before they caused another of their infamous scenes in the midst of an otherwise pleasant *bon voyage* party.

She guided Burnham toward the exit with a gentle touch on her upper arm. "Walk with me, Lieutenant. There's something we need to talk about."

"Of course, Captain." Over her shoulder Burnham fired a parting shot at her rival. "Stay sharp, Saru. I think one of the guests is stealing cutlery."

Saru pivoted quickly to either side as he searched the

room for the alleged culprit, only to realize Burnham had duped him for the umpteenth time.

Georgiou knew that Burnham's mockery of Saru might be classified by the Starfleet Code of Military Justice as "conduct unbecoming an officer," but even more so would be the captain's own laughing at Saru's disgruntled scowl, which haunted the two women all the way across the lounge as they escaped the celebration for the empty corridor beyond.

One of the most difficult lessons Michael Burnham had absorbed during her years of education on Vulcan was to curb her desire for instant gratification of her curiosity. Whenever she found herself confronted with new information or a new question, she yearned to plumb its truths without delay. It had taken her effort and time to learn that, in some circumstances, it was wiser and more productive to be patient and allow the facts to reveal themselves in their proper context.

That hard-won bit of wisdom was in the forefront of her thoughts as Captain Georgiou led her out of the officers' lounge and down the *Shenzhou*'s curved corridor. The captain's invitation had been proffered almost immediately after Burnham's verbal parry-and-thrust with Lieutenant Saru. Did that mean this conversation would be about that?

Tonight had not been the first time Burnham and Saru had sparred with rhetoric. However, she had been told by several of her shipmates that she was, on occasion, capable of transgressing against the decorum expected of Starfleet officers. Some of her peers had attributed her shortcoming to the fact that she had not attended Starfleet Academy, but rather had received her commission after graduating from the Vulcan Science Academy. The truth, however, was that Burnham had lived most of her life among Vulcans. As a consequence, human culture and customs often felt alien to her—a social hurdle that Captain Georgiou had spent the past six years working to help Burnham overcome. *With mixed results,* she admitted to herself.

When they reached the bow of the ship, Georgiou stopped in front of a wide viewport. The captain stood at ease, her hands folded at the small of her back, and stared out at Ligot IV. "In less than ninety minutes, the *Tereshkova* will join us in orbit, and ch'Theloh and García will beam over and assume their new command billets. Which means I have a choice to make."

"A choice, Captain?"

"A rather important one." Georgiou studied her with a sidelong look. "Nature abhors a vacuum. Apparently, so does Starfleet Command." A sly smile. "Admiral Anderson has named you the acting executive officer of the *Shenzhou,* effective immediately."

Burnham considered the captain's words. "*Acting* executive officer? Should I interpret that to mean the promotion is temporary?"

"Not necessarily," the captain said. "I would say the billet is . . . conditional."

It was unlike Georgiou to speak in evasions. That made Burnham wary. "Might I ask: Conditional upon what factors?"

"That's entirely at my discretion. Though I suppose the first criterion I might consider would be whether, in fact, you actually want the job."

Why would she ask me that? Burnham reflected upon the six years she and the captain had served together, the numerous crises they had endured, and all of the patient wisdom the captain had shared with her. Her mentorship had picked up where Sarek's had left off, and in many ways had proved the more challenging to master. *But does she still doubt me?*

Not wanting to appear overeager or dismissive, she fished for more information. "Why would you think I wouldn't want to be first officer?"

Brow furrowed, Georgiou thought about her answer. "To be honest, Michael, you've never struck me as particularly ambitious. That's not to say you've ever been less than excellent in any role I've ever asked of you. But every promotion you've had since you came aboard was the result of Commander ch'Theloh's recommendation or my own."

"Do you think you might have erred in promoting me?"

"Not at all. I'm merely pointing out that you've never applied for a promotion. Never sought the kind of career advancement that most of your peers shamelessly pursue."

Burnham nodded. "True."

Despite the years Burnham had spent aboard the *Shenzhou*, she still felt alienated from its predominantly human crew and their emotional decision-making. Weary of her constant isolation, she had investigated the viability of a transfer to the *Starship Intrepid*, which now had an all-Vulcan crew. That query had backfired, of course. The commander of the *Intrepid* had made clear she would not be welcome aboard, no matter how much she insisted on identifying herself as "culturally Vulcan." Unwelcome among the people she understood, she found herself condemned to serve in exile among people who would never comprehend *her*.

Georgiou continued, "So you understand my apprehension? A first officer is responsible for more than just the management of the ship and its crew. The XO is in charge of crew morale, and has to be ready to assume command should something happen to the captain. It's not a position to be accepted lightly." Concern crossed the captain's face like a shadow. "On the other hand, there are those who would say anyone who would aggressively seek the job is very likely not the sort of person one would want to give it to."

The subtext of Georgiou's remark seemed clear to Burnham. "Technically, Lieutenant Saru does have seniority, Captain. Furthermore, unlike me, he attended Starfleet Academy."

"And yet," Georgiou said, "Admiral Anderson recommended you for the position."

"Did he say why?"

"It's not my place to question an admiral's rationale." The captain faced her. "My role is to decide whether this new billet fits you or not. If it does, I'll make it permanent. If not—" She mustered a regretful frown. "You'll have to curb your abuse of Mister Saru."

Answering to Saru as the first officer was a grim notion, one that made Burnham see this change of circumstance as the opportunity it was. She faced the captain. "I won't let you down."

"That's what I'm counting on." Georgiou reached out and gave Burnham's biceps an encouraging gentle squeeze. "Make this stick—*Number One*." She let go of Burnham, took a step back, and smoothed the front of her uniform tunic. "Now, if you'll excuse me—" She turned and walked back the way they had come. "I need to go have a far more awkward version of this conversation with my new second officer."

—

The farewell party had still been going strong when Lieutenant Saru excused himself. No one had stopped him as he crossed the room. No one had called after him or had tried to pull him into their closed rings of conversation. His fellow officers had simply ignored his departure.

The decision to leave the party had been an easy one for Saru. After the captain and Burnham had slipped away to the corridor, he had known it was time to go. As a member of a prey species, Saru sometimes found that large gatherings could be a comfort to him, because they reminded him of his people's tendency to cluster for mutual defense. But all too often he found himself relegated to the perimeter of social gatherings—and his Kelpien instincts told him that it was from the fringes that predators culled the weakest members of a herd.

That's what I get for trying to socialize with the hunters, he brooded on the walk back to his quarters. Not all of his shipmates acted like apex predators, of course, but it was a dominant trait in most of the crew. He treasured the rare exceptions among the *Shenzhou*'s crew: an aura of peacefulness informed Doctor Nambue's every action, and there was a gentle quality to operations officer Belin Oliveira—an affect that Saru suspected came from the human woman's strict adherence to a vegetarian diet.

And then there was Burnham.

She was an enigma to Saru. Human by birth, but educated for most of her life by the Vulcans, Burnham adhered to a vegetarian diet like most Vulcans, and she revered their mental discipline and generally nonviolent nature. She was the sort of person he had expected would put him at ease. Instead, she had been a thorn in his side since the day she came aboard, a newly commissioned ensign safe under the captain's tutelage. For years she had nipped at his heels, dogged him up the chain of command, and bested him with cold logic and merciless reason.

Less than a year had passed since she had caught up to him in rank. He had taken solace in the notion that he remained above her in the chain of command, by virtue of his being the senior officer of the ship's sciences division. Then had come Burnham's promotion to senior tactical officer. He had congratulated her, of course, because that was only proper. But to acknowledge her as his equal had galled him.

Now he felt a change in the air, and he knew bad news was in the offing. His threat ganglia emerged from just above his ears and tasted the electric scent of imminent danger.

It was a gift—or perhaps a curse—of his species to be able to sense peril. On his world such a deep blooming of dread would be cause to run for cover, a cue to take shelter because the predators were on the hunt. But here, in the relative safety of the *Shenzhou*, that instinctual perception of disaster warned him of a threat that was not existential but professional. He reached up and gently nudged the sensitive branchlike filaments until they retracted.

There was nothing left to do now but wait for the killing stroke to fall.

He sat alone at a table beneath an angled viewport in the main room of his quarters. On the table stood his three-level chess board. He thought of all the years he had spent mastering the game, first at the Academy and continually in the years since his commission. All that time spent learning the difference between strategy and tactics; all the effort he had made to understand a game of staggering complexity bundled in a martial metaphor. Now it was just a collection of figurines on checkered boards connected to an arched stand, a pointless diversion.

The door signal buzzed. He knew who it had to be.

Saru heaved a sigh, then called out, "Come."

The door slid open, and Captain Georgiou entered. "You didn't enjoy the party?"

He couldn't make eye contact with her. "I didn't see any point in lingering."

The captain walked toward him, and the door closed behind her. She sat down across the table from him and nodded at the chess set. "Who's your opponent?"

"It no longer matters. The victor is decided."

Georgiou studied the deployment of pieces on the boards. "Perhaps not. From what I see, this match is barely in its middle game. There are any number of—"

"Captain, please." Saru was too tired to endure one of the captain's trademark digressions. "We both know why you're here."

She tried to maintain a stoic front. "Do we?"

"Burnham is being promoted ahead of me."

The truth spoken aloud drew a grimace from Georgiou. "Yes."

"In spite of my seniority. And my command training at the Academy."

Now it was the captain who evaded eye contact. "Yes."

Bile crept up Saru's throat, and his muscles tensed. Every part of him wanted to run, to retreat. But there was nowhere to go, no place any better than where he already was—and that truth only made him all the more anxious. "May I ask why?"

"I honestly don't know what to tell you. The decision came from Admiral Anderson."

"Did it?" He bolted from his chair, his resentment and

wounded pride spilling out of him like a flood through a broken dam. "No doubt Ambassador Sarek had a hand in that."

The captain met his accusation with anger. "Unless you have proof, I suggest you keep that notion to yourself, mister."

"How could he not? What other explanation makes sense?" He paced, feeling as if he had been caged. "Look at my record, then look at hers! My fitness reports have been exemplary!"

"They have," Georgiou said.

"Hers is riddled with reprimands. Clashes with superior officers, with her peers—"

"But also great achievements," the captain said. "Moments of intuition. Acts of bravery. I'm sure the admiral took those into account."

Saru ceased his pacing. "Did you have a say in the decision?"

"I get to decide if it's permanent. For now, she's the acting first officer."

He could hardly believe it. "First officer! Do you think she's suited to the job?"

"I do."

"Why?"

Georgiou considered her answer. "I think she has the makings of a great command officer. Not just technical skills, but good intuition, not to mention confidence."

"Are those qualities you think I lack?"

"Not at all, Saru. But sometimes these evaluations are, by necessity, subjective."

He shook his head. "It's not fair. Counting my years at the Academy, I've served in Starfleet nearly twice as long as she has."

"That's true. But I think you're focusing too much on the negative."

"Am I meant to see something positive in this?"

The captain stood. "You're also being promoted. To acting second officer."

He froze and willed himself not to roll his eyes in contempt. "Forgive me, Captain, but I find that to be cold comfort."

She adopted a conciliatory tone. "I understand your disappointment, Saru. I had to endure it myself, once, and I know it won't be an easy thing to accept." She moved closer. "But if I might offer you some advice, as your captain?"

Putting on his best air of calm, he said, "Of course."

"None of us can control the hand of Fate, or the actions of others. The only thing we *can* control is how we choose to react. And that's what I need you to do now, Saru. When you're alone, in the privacy of your quarters, take the time you need, and find a constructive way to purge yourself of this anger and disappointment." Her soothing manner turned sharp. "But don't bring a single shred of it with you when you're on duty. Do I make myself clear?"

Cowed, he lowered his chin and looked at his feet. "Perfectly, Captain."

"Very well." She moved past him and headed for the door. "Good night, Lieutenant."

He stood like a statue, not looking up, until he heard her exit and the door shut.

Her words festered in his memory, and her warning roiled in his stomachs. Nothing she had said had been untrue, but none of it had granted him any solace. He had only the deepest respect for Captain Georgiou, a feeling that bordered on reverence. That was what had made her constant attention to Burnham so vexing. Even though Burnham was quite possibly the smartest officer Saru had ever met, she seemed to be in constant need of the captain's attention—to the point that Georgiou had never seemed to have a moment left over for Saru.

All I ever really wanted was for the captain to reciprocate even a fraction of the admiration I have shown her all these years. Revisiting bitter memories felt like walking on broken glass. *If only she had mentored me the way she fawns on Burnham . . . !*

Saru pivoted toward the table and with one sweep of his arm swatted his chess set across the room. The fragile curve that linked the three boards broke in half as it struck the bulkhead, and the pieces scattered across the floor. He watched a rook rebound and roll under his sofa; a bishop ricocheted around a corner and vanished into his lavatory.

Standing above the damage he'd wrought, he arrived at a glum conclusion: *I still feel terrible, and now my quarters are in disarray.* Dejected and feeling not unlike a fool, Saru set himself to work picking up this latest mess of his own making.

3

Two armed guards in crisp uniforms and a governor's aide attired in a rumpled suit led Bowen, Omalu, and Chandra down a drab corridor inside the Executive Complex. Like the rest of the settlement on Sirsa III, the seat of the colonial government headquarters was only a few years old. In that time, no one had yet seen fit to decorate it; the only adornments on its walls were generic signage indicating floor numbers and room designations.

Bowen thought it had all the charm of a prison.

The aide opened a door to a conference room and stepped aside. He ushered the trio inside. "Please take a seat. Governor Kolova will be right with you."

"Thanks," Bowen said. He led his colleagues into the conference room. The aide closed the door after them. Bowen paused to listen for the sound of a lock being turned, but heard none.

A cheap rectangular table dominated the space. It was ringed by twelve uncomfortable-looking chairs, five on either long side and one at each end. Along the wall opposite the door, a row of windows looked out on the city of New Astana, the capital of the Sirsa III colony. Like most planned colonial cities, it was laid out with the government buildings around its central hub, from which major thoroughfares radiated like spokes on a wheel. The majority of its structures were prefabricated units, shipped in pieces and hastily assembled on-site above a network of utility and maintenance tunnels. It wasn't pretty, but it was efficient.

Omalu eyed the room with suspicion, then with irritation. "They could have at least set out some water."

"That would require them to care about us," Chandra said.

Omalu moved to stand with Bowen in front of the windows. "I still think coming here was a mistake." She dropped her voice, as if she were worried they were being spied upon. "Our first call should've been to the company, not the government."

"Really?" Bowen wondered if Omalu had thought through their current predicament. "You think we'd be better off going *mano a mano* with the company? Thanks, but no."

Chandra settled into a chair behind them. "And what do you think Kolova can do for us?"

"If we get her on our side," Bowen said, "we'll have a government report that says the rig was sunk by force majeure. That'll protect us from getting charged with negligence and keep the company from voiding our contracts."

"I don't think it matters who breaks the news to the company," Chandra said. "Once they learn we've lost the rig, we're all as good as blacklisted."

"Not if Kolova backs up our story," Bowen said. "We just—" He was cut off by the opening of the door, followed by the entrance of the governor and her retinue.

Governor Gretchen Kolova was a statuesque woman. Her platinum hair was pulled tight into a knot at the back of her head, and her countenance was as sharp as her stare. She walked in proud strides and took her place at the head of the table. Her security detail fanned out into the room as her entourage settled into the other chairs around the table—a collective action that Bowen and his crewmates took as their cue to be seated, as well.

"Mister Bowen," Kolova said. "Ms. Omalu. Mister Chandra. Thank you for waiting." She gestured toward an older, balding man sitting to her right. "This is my chief of staff, Tojiro Ishii." A quick wave toward the younger man sitting across from Ishii: "And my science adviser, Hamid Medina." Folding her hands in front of her, Kolova leaned forward and fixed Bowen with a probing stare. "If you'd be so kind, Mister Bowen: tell us again what happened to your rig."

"A little after four this morning, our drill hit something under the seabed."

Medina cut in, "This was at the drill site you were licensed for last spring?"

"Yes," Bowen said, eager to continue. "Our drill head became stuck, and we initiated emergency recovery efforts. But before we could free it, something—" He tripped over the outrageous nature of the truth, as if he realized for the first time that saying it aloud sounded more than a smidgen insane. "Something rose up from the seabed beneath us."

Dubious looks from the politicos greeted Bowen's report. Ishii asked Omalu and Chandra, "Do the two of you wish to corroborate this account of the incident?"

"It's what happened," Omalu said, her tone suddenly defensive.

Chandra didn't answer Ishii. Instead he told Bowen, "This is a frame-up."

Only then did Bowen notice that the mood in the room was more confrontational than he had expected it to be. "Hang on just a—"

"Mister Bowen," Medina said, "when was Arcadia Explorer's last safety check?"

They had to be kidding. "You're not trying to blame this on us? Listen to what we're telling you: something huge, like a giant bug or a reptile, came up out of the seabed, forced our drill shaft up through our superstructure—"

"In fact," Medina continued, "your rig was three months overdue for a routine safety inspection, wasn't it, Mister Bowen?"

They were attempting a classic blame shift. Bowen wasn't having any part of it. "Don't act like that's something strange. Your people schedule those inspections, not ours." To Ishii he added, "And this was no mechanical malfunction. I'm telling you, something destroyed our rig, and whatever it was, it was huge. As in, at least a couple kilometers long. You get me?"

It was clear that Ishii and Medina were not convinced.

The chief of staff sighed. "Look at it from our perspective. Your rig went down ten hours ago and took almost nine hundred people with it. We can't find its emergency data core, and there are no clear visual records of what happened." He shrugged and held up his hands, as if to signify his powerlessness. "If you were in our place, what would you think of this?"

Chandra replied, "I'd think that a gravity-based condeep rig with a mass greater than most starships doesn't fall over and sink because of a drilling mishap." He met Medina's stare. "Use your head. Rigs like the Arcadia Explorer have been hit by icebergs and not budged an inch. They're made to survive earthquakes. This was no equipment failure. Something *hit* us—and if I were you, I would be hauling ass to find out what it was."

Ishii bristled. "Are you threatening us, Mister Chandra?"

Bowen said, "No. If we were threatening you, we'd bring up a rather touchy subject and remind you that if you try to make us take the fall for the rig, a data file full of ugly truth will get sent to the Federation Council." In unison, Kolova, Ishii, and Medina leaned back from the table and tensed, making clear that they had understood his meaning.

Better than garlic against vampires, Bowen gloated.

"I think it would be best," Ishii said in a carefully neutral tone, "if we all took care at this juncture not to say anything that would inflame this—"

A distant explosion rumbled the building and shook the windows behind Bowen. He and everyone else faced the windows, through which they saw a small flying craft, one with a bizarre insectoid quality to its design, swoop around the perimeter of New Astana. In the middle of the capital, not far from the Executive Complex, smoke and flames rose from a building that had just been attacked—and the small alien ship was coming back for another pass.

Kolova glared at the fast-moving threat vessel. "What is that?"

"If I had to guess," Omalu said, "I'd say it was sent by the same thing that sank our rig."

One of Kolova's security personnel pressed a finger to his ear, then rushed to the governor's side and whispered to her. She listened, then replied, "Knock it down." As he stepped away to relay her order, Kolova told the rest of the room, "It's a drone. No one on board."

Outside, the drone shot past in a gray-green blur, laying down a barrage of fire in its wake. The Executive Complex shook, and the lights overhead stuttered and went dark.

A female security guard announced, "The complex has been hit, and power's out." She moved to Kolova's side.

"Madam Governor, we need to get you to the bunker, right now."

"Fine." Kolova pointed at Bowen, Omalu, and Chandra. "Bring them."

The agent nodded. "Yes, ma'am." Raising her voice, she shouted the rest of the room's occupants into motion. "Everyone, out! We're going down the hall to the left, then we'll take stairwell B down six levels. Hustle, people!"

Herded into a loose single-file line, the colonial officials and the rig survivors scrambled out of the conference room and followed the governor's protection detail down the corridor to the stairwell. As they navigated the switchback flights to the lowest sublevel, Bowen said to Kolova, "Thanks for not leaving us behind."

"Don't thank me," she said. "This isn't charity. I need you alive until we find out what the hell that thing is—and what you did to piss it off."

Chandra was right, Bowen stewed. *One way or another, they'll blame this on us.*

Holy shit, this thing is fast. In the fifteen years Mikki Bolander had been flying interceptors for colonial civil air patrols, she had never seen anything that moved like the alien drone buzzing New Astana. The uncrewed ship banked and turned in ways she couldn't hope to match, not even with the protection of inertial dampers. Every time she started to line up a shot, the drone made an abrupt change of heading and evaded her interceptor's targeting computer.

She keyed her flight helmet's transceiver with a tap on its side. "All wings, this is CAP Leader. Anybody got a shot on this thing?"

Outside her canopy the cityscape blurred and the horizon rolled as she chased the drone through a spiraling turn and climb, falling farther behind by the second.

"CAP Leader, this is CAP Three. Almost had a lock, then I lost it."

"This is CAP Two. I can't even see you, CAP Leader."

"We're in the clouds, CAP Two." Bolander forced herself to keep her eyes on her instruments. Trying to pilot by visual clues in a cloud bank was a recipe for disaster, even for the most experienced of rocket jockeys. She was out of range for a clean firing lock on the drone. "We're coming around at bearing three-eight mark four—high on your ten o'clock."

The drone cut a sharp turn into a dive, and then it and Bolander's interceptor arrowed out of the clouds, screaming straight toward the planet's surface.

A storm of charged plasma converged on the drone as CAPS Two and Three both did their best to turn the alien ship into slag. Instead, the agile, beetle-shaped killing machine barrel-rolled through their baptism of fire, then went ballistic, executed a graceful turn during a midair stall, then shredded CAP Two with a flurry of bluish-white energy pulses.

"CAP Two is down," Bolander said, for the benefit of whoever was tracking and logging the dogfight back at CAP Command. "CAP Three, break hard left, and—" She watched the drone pulverize her second wingman in a high-speed blur.

Time became elastic, stretched by grief and fear, as Bolander watched two jumbles of smoking wreckage twist their way toward the ground and explode on the outskirts of the city.

"Command . . . CAP Three is down."

Jae Barnes, the flight coordinator, sounded panicked.

"Disengage, CAP Leader. We're launching CAPS Four and Five now. They'll be with you in three minutes."

Bolander tracked the drone through another turn and quickly deduced the targets of its next attack run, which was only seconds away. "I don't have three minutes. And two more wings won't make any difference up here. Tell Four and Five to stand down."

"That's not your call, Mikki."

"The hell it's not, Jae. I'm gonna take this thing down, or die trying. But you keep Ling and Sogobu on the ground. CAP Leader out."

All she heard from Jae before she turned off her interceptor's comms was, *"Dammit, Mikki, don't—"* She knew what the rest would be, and she had no time for a debate.

The drone was lining up for its next pass over the center of New Astana.

Gonna have to eyeball this, Bolander realized. The interceptor's tactical system was based on computer-assisted targeting of its charged plasma cannons. Any tactic that deviated from that mode was beyond the fighter's ability to assist.

Several hundred meters below her, and a few kilometers east-northeast, the drone settled into its attack pattern and accelerated to full speed. Bolander made her best guess for the timing of her attack—then she pushed her interceptor into a dive and forced its throttle fully open.

Acceleration crushed her back into her seat. She felt her head swim from the g-force, but she couldn't afford to relent. If she wavered . . . if she was weak . . . she would miss.

She wasn't going to miss. She refused to.

At six g she could barely breathe. At eight she stopped trying. At ten she was sure her eyeballs were about to pop inside her skull, and her skeleton was going to shatter.

Then the drone came into view, for just a split second.

It was so close she felt as if she could reach out and touch it.

Ramming speed!

Victory was almost hers—

Then came a burst of blue, and she felt her world rip into shreds, revealing the void that yawned between every particle of being, the great entropic nothing that hid behind the fragile disguise of time and space. Within that momentary flash, Bolander knew she had failed—but she also knew she had kept her promise, and even the darkness at the end couldn't take that away.

It was a catastrophe. Smoky spires twisted up from the ravaged streets of New Astana, and Governor Gretchen Kolova felt sick to her stomach. She watched the alien drone make another pass over the capital. The tiny ship seemed unbeatable. There had to be some way to stop it, but none of the defenses at her colony's disposal had been equal to the task—a fact that left the insectoid killing machine free to wreak havoc.

She aimed a scathing look at her chief of staff. "Dammit, Tojiro, there has to be something we can do." Together they gazed in dismay at the bank of screens that covered one wall of the emergency bunker. "How do we bring it down?"

Ishii shook his head. "I wish I knew, Governor."

Medina left a huddle on the other side of the bunker's command room and returned to Kolova and Ishii. "Governor, we've confirmed at least part of Mister Bowen's report. There is some type of alien juggernaut floating at the Arcadia Explorer's registered coordinates."

Kolova latched on to the news, as if it might provide some clue to their salvation. "What else can you tell me about the Juggernaut, Hamid?"

"It's quite large," Medina said. "A few kilometers long, give or take. And its general configuration looks similar to the drone buzzing the capital, so it seems likely to be the drone's parent vessel. Still no idea if there's a crew aboard the Juggernaut, though."

The chief of staff struck a dubious note. "Juggernaut? Is that what we're calling this thing? Officially, I mean?"

"Until we come up with something better," Kolova said, settling the question. She prompted Medina, "Anything else?"

"It's emitting a series of pulses on numerous frequencies. Some follow a repeating pattern, which suggests communication, but others have been analyzed and seem to constitute a countdown, which could suggest it's preparing to launch one or more additional drones."

From across the bunker's command center, Bowen, the rig commander, aimed at Kolova an accusatory stare that simply screamed, *I told you so.*

"I want to know our options, all of them," Kolova told Ishii.

The frazzled older man shook his head. "I don't know that we really have any, Governor. Civil Air Patrol admits that it's outmatched. And the first thing the drone did was neutralize our automated defense batteries. The only reason the city hasn't been reduced to rubble already is that it only seems to fire when it has a moving target or identifies a structure of value."

"What about handheld surface-to-air defenses? Do we have anything like that?"

"Sorry, Governor," Ishii said. "That kind of tech is restricted to Starfleet—and we were quite specific in our application for a colonial charter that we didn't want Starfleet personnel on the surface or in orbit. Which means our defensive options are equally limited."

Desperate but still hopeful, Kolova looked to Medina. "What about a nonmilitary solution? Can we generate a field that might disrupt the drone's control systems?"

"You mean like an energy dampener or a weaponized electromagnetic pulse?" The science adviser shrugged. "Maybe, but there's a good chance we'd frag our only fusion reactor, and no guarantee the drone would even be vulnerable to the attack."

It was so ridiculous. What problem had no solution? Kolova was determined to reason her way out of this mess, no matter what it took. "How about if we surrender? We wouldn't have to mean it, exactly, but maybe if we wave the white flag, it could buy us some time."

Her suggestion attracted the input of Cameron Le Fevre, the capital's chief of police. The thin, clean-shaven man adjusted his wire-frame glasses. "That's not a bad idea, Governor, but if I might inject a bit of pessimism into the mix, we've no idea if this alien contraption even speaks our language, or if it would respect our surrender if it did. Of course, that's no reason not to try, mind you. But perhaps we should ready ourselves for a protracted siege."

Kolova turned once more to Ishii. "How long can the capital hold out?"

"If the reactor and municipal infrastructure don't fail? A week, maybe."

"And if we lose the reactor?"

"Then we're screwed," Medina interjected. "Reserve batteries will run out in two days. After that, water distribution stops, along with sewage removal. Plus, we'll lose

comms—assuming the drone doesn't hit the subspace an-
tenna at some point."

Bowen and his two colleagues from the rig approached
Kolova's circle. "Governor? If we might make a suggestion?"

Ready to entertain any notion that might help, Kolova
welcomed the rig engineer and his friends with a wave. "I'm
all ears, Mister Bowen."

"Have you considered ordering an evacuation?"

So much for the notion of there being no stupid ideas.

"Yes, we did. But in case you haven't noticed, that
drone is shooting down armed high-speed interceptors.
What chance would a slow personnel transport have?"

Medina added, "Not that it would matter, since there
are more than three hundred sixty thousand people on this
colony, and fewer than a couple dozen working transport
ships with a capacity of a few hundred people each. Or did
you forget we dismantled our main colony ship to build the
capital and other key settlements?"

Bowen nodded, chastised. "All right. So we're not running, but we're in no shape for a stand-up fight, either. So
what're we supposed to do now? Lock arms and sing 'Kum-
bayah'?"

"Couldn't do much worse than we have so far," his as-
sociate Chandra mumbled.

This was exactly the sort of situation that Kolova and
her senior advisers, not to mention most of the major
stakeholders in the Sirsa III colony, had long hoped to
avoid. They had known that increased independence from
Federation oversight would carry heightened risks, especially in the event that something went catastrophically
wrong. Now the question of whether that had been a bad
judgment would be brought to the fore—assuming any of

them lived long enough to confront the consequences of their choices.

"I think we need to face the truth," Kolova told the room. "Whatever this thing is, it's not something we're equipped to fight on our own. And the longer we wait to ask for help, the greater the chance that it'll kill us all and raze our colony to the ground."

Ishii and Le Fevre both tensed. The chief of staff said, "Governor, please tell me you aren't suggesting what I think you are."

"I'm sorry, Tojiro, but I just don't see that we have a choice now. We'll do whatever is needed to mitigate the damage . . . but it's time to send out a distress call. And to pray that Starfleet has a ship close enough to respond in time."

4

Georgiou was sure she must have misheard the woman whose holographic avatar stood in front of the *Shenzhou* bridge's center viewport, beyond which twisted a tunnel of warp-distorted starlight. For the sake of decorum, however, the captain kept her tone neutral in front of her bridge officers. "Could you repeat that, please, Governor?"

"It came up from under the seabed." Kolova had been on edge at the beginning of the conversation; the longer it continued, the greater her dismay became. *"We had a drilling rig out there looking for valuable mineral deposits. The rig manager says the drill head hit something and got stuck. When they tried to pull it free—"*

"It sank the rig," Georgiou said, finishing the governor's thought. "I see now, thank you. How long after the incident at the rig did the attack on the capital begin?"

"About ten hours." A muted rumble was followed by a rain of dust on Kolova's head. *"The drone's been hammering us for over an hour now. If we don't do something soon, it might pulverize the entire capital."* Another distant boom flickered the lights and momentarily garbled the subspace signal from Kolova's bunker. *"How soon can you reach us, Captain?"*

"Very soon." She glanced at Detmer, who, without looking up from the helm, signaled to Georgiou the ship's ETA with hand gestures. "Roughly three hours."

She had considered that good news, yet Kolova grew more frantic. *"Three hours? With this thing raining fire and brimstone on our heads the whole time? Are you serious?"*

"Governor, be calm," Georgiou said. "We've reviewed your sensor logs and analyzed the drone's attack behavior. It might inflict some additional property damage before we arrive, but nothing we can't help you fix. As long as your people stay in shelter, you should all be fine."

Out of the corner of her eye, Georgiou saw the look on Burnham's face that suggested her new acting first officer was about to say something unhelpful. Low at her side, below the perception of the viewscreen's sensor, Georgiou tensed her hand and pointed it toward Burnham, staving off whatever impromptu remark the younger woman might have been concocting.

Then, from the post to Georgiou's right, Lieutenant Saru opined, "Unless the drone decides to target the capital's fusion reactor plant. Then the impact to the—" The Kelpien curtailed his grim speculation when he noticed Georgiou's poisonous stare in his direction.

Hoping to bury her subordinate's verbal blunder, Georgiou put on her most reassuring countenance and adopted a soothing, almost maternal tone of voice. "Stand strong, Governor. My ship will arrive in three hours' time, and we will do what is necessary to ensure the safety of your colony and its people. You have my word."

"Thank you Captain." Another blast, closer than the ones before, shook Kolova's bunker and limned her with gray dust. *"We'll try to keep our heads down until then. Kolova out."* The governor's hologram disappeared.

Georgiou stood from her command chair and moved

forward to stand behind and between Detmer and Oliveira. "Keyla, how soon can you get us to Sirsa III?"

The red-haired Dusseldorf native checked her console. "I might be able to shave a few minutes off our trip." A sly smile. "Maybe more—if I bend a few rules."

"Bend away, Ensign." To the ops officer, Georgiou said, "Belin, as soon as we deal with the drone, I want all departments to analyze the Juggernaut that launched it."

Oliveira nodded. "Understood, Captain. I've already cleared the schedule for the main sensor array, and I've placed all forensic teams on standby."

"Well done." With the fundamentals under control, it was time for Georgiou to focus her chief assets on the main objective. "Number One, Mister Saru: my ready room, please. Lieutenant Gant, you have the conn." The captain walked aft, to her private office. Gant, the *Shenzhou*'s new senior tactical officer, handed off his post to a relief officer, then moved to the command chair. Burnham and Saru exchanged wary looks, then followed Georgiou.

Inside the ready room, Georgiou settled into the chair behind her desk. Burnham and Saru stood on the other side, both at attention. Georgiou let them stew for a few seconds. Had she desired a less formal conversation, at the far end of the room there was a meeting table just large enough to seat six people. But she knew that Burnham and Saru were both the sort of officer who responded favorably to a degree of formality. *Have to go with what works.*

"We have a crisis ahead of us," Georgiou said. "And not much time to prepare."

"And not much to go on," Saru cut in. "The sensor logs of the drone are scrambled, at best. And the colony's intel regarding the entity it calls 'the Juggernaut' is quite sparse."

A stern look by Georgiou silenced Saru. Satisfied she once again had the floor, she continued. "We are the closest Starfleet vessel to Sirsa III, and those people are counting on us. I, in turn, will be counting upon both of you to make certain we find a swift and successful resolution to this mess. Do I make myself clear?"

Two nods. That was reassuring—until Burnham spoke. "Might I inquire, Captain, why Starfleet is so eager to assist a colony that went to such great lengths to keep it at a distance?"

"Because no matter what the political preferences of any given colony might be, Number One, Starfleet doesn't play politics when lives are in danger. To be honest, I wouldn't care if the colony had declared its independence. All I care about is that there are people at risk, and we are their best, closest chance for help. Does that make sense to you?"

Burnham lowered her chin, a sign of both acknowledgment and humility. "Yes, Captain."

It was to Saru's credit that he read the moment better than Burnham had. "Assuming Lieutenant Oliveira is coordinating our shipboard resources, would I be correct to deduce that you wish me to make a detailed analysis of all sensor data related to the drone and the Juggernaut, and to cross-reference analyses by all of our science specialists?"

"You read my mind, Mister Saru." To Burnham she added, "Number One, make sure sickbay and engineering are ready for battle. Then have a look at the drone's combat behavior and work up a tactical-response profile. I want to be ready to engage that target as soon as we make orbit. Understood?"

"Aye, sir."

"Keep each other apprised of your efforts. I'll want your

status updates in two hours." As soon as she noted their nods of confirmation, she added, "Dismissed."

Burnham and Saru left the ready room quickly, each without saying a word to the other. Georgiou could only hope their chilly détente would not be a harbinger of the pair's working relationship in the years to come. *Getting them to function as a unit won't be easy,* she mused. *I just hope I don't end up having to transfer one of them.*

She noted the dwindling time remaining to the *Shenzhou*'s arrival at Sirsa III and switched on her desk's computer. Just as her senior officers had their preparatory tasks, she had hers—one she would gladly have traded with any of them, if only it were an option.

Her job was to explore any and all options for a diplomatic solution to this fiasco—not just with the Juggernaut, but with the colony itself. It was not a mission to which she looked forward, because her years in Starfleet had taught her there were few things as dangerous as a proudly independent colony being forced to seek help from the government it had left behind.

Too late now, Georgiou imagined telling Kolova and her people. *You asked for help, and now you're going to get it— whether you like it or not.*

An automated alert had roused Captain Christopher Pike from a sound sleep. It was the middle of the night according to the ship's onboard chronometer—gamma shift according to the duty roster—but as Pike stepped out of the turbolift onto the bridge of the *Enterprise*, he found its atmosphere of keen readiness no different from that of his normal alpha-shift cycle.

His first officer, Commander Una, was already there,

moving from one duty station to the next, gathering intel. As the statuesque, dark-haired Illyrian woman left the communication officer's side, she noted Pike's arrival and straightened her posture. "Captain on the bridge!"

"Skip the protocol, Number One," Pike said. "What's happening?"

Una met him at the command chair and stood aside as he pivoted into the center seat. "Distress signal, sir. Priority one. Origin, the Sirsa III colony."

Priority one meant the colony was under attack, which explained to Pike why the ship's computer had awakened him upon receipt of the message. "What do we know so far?"

Una nodded at the tactical officer, who relayed a sensor feed to the main viewscreen. Pike watched an insectoid craft buzz a prefab-looking colonial capital and harass it with barrages of charged plasma. As the transmission continued, it showed interceptor craft being destroyed when attempting to engage the alien vessel.

He leaned forward, his mind focused, his instincts to defend and avenge aroused. "What do we know about the attacker? Origin? Demands? Capabilities?"

"Not much," Una said. "The colony's report suggests the attacker is a drone launched from a larger vessel that surfaced at sea beneath a geological exploration rig."

"Do we have any intel on the parent ship?"

Lieutenant Spock swiveled his chair away from the sciences console to respond, "None so far, sir. The colony's drilling rig was lost, along with all of its sensor logs, approximately twelve hours ago." The half-human, half-Vulcan science officer relayed some data from his console to the main viewscreen. "Analysis of the drone attacking New Astana has yielded no matches in our memory banks for either its hull configuration or its energy signature."

Pike asked Spock, "How much of a punch does that drone pack, Lieutenant?"

"Its primary charged-plasma emitter is capable of inflicting significant damage on unshielded structures and lightly shielded civilian patrol vessels. However, my analysis of its deflector geometry and overall power level suggests it will pose little threat to the *Enterprise*."

"Good to know," Pike said. "Helm, how far out of our way is Sirsa III?"

"Just over ten hours at warp six," said Ensign Datlow.

Una leaned in to confide to Pike, "Sir, the *Shenzhou* has already confirmed it's en route to Sirsa III and will arrive less than three hours from now. Shall I inform Captain Georgiou that we're en route to provide assistance?"

His first officer had posed the question with what Pike recognized as exquisite political finesse. She had not gainsaid his anticipated order of diversion to the beleaguered colony, nor had she assumed it to be a foregone conclusion. She had presented her information in a neutral manner, while subtly implying the redundancy of effort that would occur as a consequence of their uninvited involvement in the situation, and reminding Pike that Captain Georgiou was a starship commander whose seniority and experience far outstripped his own.

It was an easy decision to make, but he let the question linger for a few seconds, to convey the impression that he was weighing the matter in earnest.

"Helm," Pike said at last, "maintain current heading and speed. Number One, instruct all departments to analyze the sensor data from Sirsa III and to prepare response plans, just in case they're needed. Ensign O'Friel, contact the *Shenzhou* and let them know we'll be standing ready in case they need assistance. Mister Spock, monitor the situation at Sirsa III, and notify me of any significant changes in the situation that might demand our involvement."

He stood and headed toward the turbolift, expecting Una to take his place in the center seat. Instead she followed him and caught up to him as he reached the call button for the lift. "Captain, might it not be prudent to adjust our course to reduce our response time to the colony, just in case the *Shenzhou* requests backup?"

"I'm sure Captain Georgiou has the matter well in hand, Number One." He pressed the call signal for the lift. "She was commanding a starship when I was still a deck officer."

"Be that as it may," Una said, "this is a priority-one distress signal. And if the data concerning the drone's parent ship proves to be reliable, this crisis might demand the attention of more than one starship."

Pike nodded but was not persuaded. "Perhaps, Number One. And if Captain Georgiou asks for our help, she'll have it. But she's already called the ball on this one."

" 'Called the ball,' sir?"

He wondered whether Una had really never encountered that bit of sports-inspired jargon during her time at Starfleet Academy, or if she was merely latching on to it as a means of questioning his judgment. "Once a Starfleet vessel has confirmed its response to a crisis such as this, even to a matter as serious as a priority-one emergency, there is no need for other ships to divert." He narrowed his eyes at her. "But I don't need to tell you that, do I, Number One?"

His criticism seemed to make Una uncomfortable. "You might think me foolish for saying so, Captain . . . but I get the feeling this situation is different. That we need to go *now*."

"I'll take that under advisement, Number One." The

turbolift doors parted ahead of Pike, who stepped in, then pivoted to face Una. "Apprise Starfleet of my decision."

"Understood, sir."

The lift doors closed, and Pike took hold of the control lever. "Deck five," he said. There was almost no sensation of motion, but the turbolift accelerated down into the *Enterprise*'s saucer with a rising hum of auditory feedback, then shifted onto a lateral track for its circuit around the core to the section nearest Pike's quarters.

Alone with his thoughts, Pike was troubled by Una's warning that there was something different about this emergency. On its face it was just a routine distress call, one that had been handled by a closer Starfleet vessel, and that no longer merited his attention.

But even as he collapsed back into his bunk for some desperately needed rack time, Pike was haunted by a nagging sensation that he had not heard the last of the crisis on Sirsa III.

Above all, Michael Burnham strove to be thorough in her work. Attention to detail had been drilled into her during her childhood, thanks to the rigors of instruction in the Vulcan Learning Center of ShiKahr. Incomplete answers were anathema to the Vulcans. Her mentors and tutors had trained her to be ready to offer up her calculations on a line-by-line basis, or to cite her sources for all answers she proffered during an exam. There had never been any way to know which of her answers would be challenged, so Burnham had learned from a young age to be ready to defend all of her conclusions with precision and tenacity, lest her logic or her intellect be called into question by the criticism of her Vulcan peers.

She approached her duties as a Starfleet officer with the same conviction.

Just as Captain Georgiou had ordered, she had worked with the ship's department heads to prepare response plans for the Sirsa III emergency. Doctor Nambue, the chief medical officer, was briefing teams of combat medics and nurses, in the event that there were numerous wounded in the capital. Lieutenant Commander Johar, the chief engineer, was already setting up technical teams to conduct forensic analyses of the drone and any other alien technology that might be acquired during the course of the mission. Meanwhile, on the bridge, Lieutenant Gant had tested half a dozen tactical-response scenarios, half of which had been created by Burnham months earlier during her tenure as the ship's senior tactical officer.

All of which left only the singularly unpleasant task of assessing the readiness of the sciences department, which was under the supervision of Lieutenant Saru.

Ever since accepting a commission in Starfleet, Burnham had done her best to uphold the Vulcan ethos of unemotional logic. She knew this had made her a peculiar specimen among her peers. The fact that she had garnered the favor of Captain Georgiou also meant she had drawn the ire of Saru. From her first step aboard the *Shenzhou*, Burnham had felt as if Saru held her in disregard on her best days, and in contempt on all the others. They had been rivals for the same opportunities, the same promotions, and the same honors, at every step.

Now it was Burnham who held the position of acting first officer, and Saru who had to answer to her authority. In a way, Burnham almost envied the Kelpien. He would not bear the blame, should their working dynamic falter. If he proved resistant to Burnham's style of leadership, the onus of responsibility would fall upon *her* shoulders, not his. She wondered if he even realized that, having been denied the promotion he sought, he now held more influence over Burnham's fate than he could possibly appreciate.

She found him in science laboratory 3, surrounded by a curve of viewscreens flooded with sensor data and annotated reports from his subordinates. He appeared, for a change, to be in his natural environment—swimming in knowledge, safely hidden in the shadows. It seemed to Burnham a shame to disturb him, but duty compelled her.

"Ahem," she said, clearing her throat.

He tore his focus from the viewscreens to assess her with a half-lidded glare of contempt. "Oh, it's *you*." Swiveling back toward his wall of raw data, he asked, "What do you need, *sir*?"

Had he always been so disrespectful? She let it go. "Your summary report of the science department's findings vis-à-vis the alien drone and its possible parent vessel."

He gestured with spread hands at the avalanche of raw intelligence on his screens. "We have tons of input. I regret that none of it as yet seems to point to any reasonable conclusion about the origin or specific capabilities of the threat on Sirsa III."

Burnham felt Saru's antipathy. It poisoned every word he said to her. She did her best to stay professional. "Can you make any recommendations with regard to neutralizing the drone?"

"Nothing beyond what Lieutenant Gant has already suggested."

It would not be productive, Burnham knew, to let the animosity Saru felt for her linger unchecked. She needed to overcome it, and what she knew of Kelpiens as a species and of Saru as an individual suggested the best way to do that was to enlist him in common cause. "Mister Saru, I value your input as a department head. What method of engagement would you advise we pursue with the drone and its parent ship once we reach the planet?"

Saru looked up from his console, then turned slowly to face Burnham, as if he expected her query to be little more than preamble to a rhetorical snare. "Are you implying that you might actually consider my input without prejudice or favor before making your recommendation to the captain?" He stood and towered over her. "Or is this just some empty gesture to win my trust?"

"As long as I have your cooperation," Burnham said, "your trust is immaterial."

He bristled at her truthfulness, then straightened his posture so that he stood even taller. "Based on what I have seen so far of the drone, I would recommend a swift and overwhelming attack against it and its parent vessel, at our earliest opportunity."

"Curious," Burnham said. "That is not the action I expected you to endorse."

"Why? Because I'm a Kelpien? A natural prey species? You think that means I'm just a helpless naïf, awaiting the cold kiss of Death?" He stepped closer and intruded upon her personal space. The fact that her eye level aligned with the bottom of his chest made his presence more than a little intimidating. "Just because my people evolved as victims of the hunt, that doesn't mean we won't defend ourselves."

It was a fair point, and Burnham conceded it with a lowering of her chin. "You're right, Lieutenant. And I accept your recommendation as a valid one—though I do not share it."

Saru's countenance darkened. "Why not?"

"Please don't misunderstand me," she said. "The drone

is an exigent threat and must be dealt with accordingly. The parent ship, however—its status and motivations are unknown. It might be in our best interest to take a diplomatic approach, at least at first, to try to establish contact with it. If we can avert further violence through—"

"Are you deranged?" Saru had abandoned all semblance of deference, an act that Burnham had long suspected was one the Kelpien reserved for use in front of Georgiou. "The drone has taken multiple lives in the capital, and its parent ship destroyed an offshore rig with over nine hundred personnel on board—most of whom didn't live to tell the tale. These things are clear and present dangers, and they have to be destroyed with all due haste!"

Burnham absorbed Saru's rebuke but remained detached from any emotional reaction to it. "You seem to forget, Mister Saru, that the motive for the Juggernaut's action against the rig remains unknown, as does the drone's assault on the capital. This entire situation might be the result of a miscommunication. The rig's foreman admitted that shortly before the Juggernaut rose and sank his platform, their drill head had become stuck in something. It seems likely that the drill hit the alien vessel's hull—an impact that it might have misinterpreted as an act of aggression. If so, we should not be so quick to rush to judgment—not when there might remain a possibility of establishing peaceful contact with a previously unknown alien intelligence."

Saru reached back, shut off the viewscreens surrounding his workstation in the lab, then regarded Burnham with a sour look. "That's a rather forgiving assessment." Wearing his disgust as a badge of honor, he added with grim sincerity on his way out of the lab, "I wonder if you'll still feel that way after it tries to kill us."

5

A few hours under siege had given Jon Bowen a new appreciation for the peace of his life at sea, a pleasure he had taken for granted right up until the moment it had been ripped out from under him. He, Omalu, and Chandra huddled like fugitives in a corner of Governor Kolova's bunker, surrounded by a couple of dozen strangers whose furtive looks and conspiratorial whispers had started to worry him. His gut told him to get himself and his people out of here. But there was nowhere to go as long as the alien drone continued its strafing runs over the capital.

Omalu checked the room's bank of synchronized chronos. "How long until Starfleet gets here and gives us some damn help?"

"Soon," Chandra said. "Any minute now."

Erratic detonations from the surface trembled the bunker and opened a narrow fissure across half the ceiling. Dust fell from the hairline fracture. It wasn't a large rupture, but the fact that it existed at all drew nervous looks from Kolova and the rest of her people, as well as from Bowen and his. Whatever protection the bunker offered, it was far from absolute. Given enough time, or perhaps just one direct hit, the drone might reduce it to rubble.

Bowen tossed a fearful look at Chandra. "At this rate, there won't be anything left for them to save."

Kolova, Ishii, Medina, and a handful of city-government types surrounded the room's central situation table, which projected a miniaturized holographic representation of the capital. Every few seconds another section of it would flare red, then continue to blink—an indication of the drone's latest attack. The latest alert drove Kolova to pound the side of her fist on the table. "Dammit! Now the drone's shooting our firefighting teams!"

"It's not being malicious," Bowen offered. "At least, I don't think it is." He moved toward the situation table, ignoring the resentful glares his move prompted from the politicians. "It's just shooting at anything that moves, preferably things with biological sensor profiles."

Ishii gesticulated in frustration at the map. "So what do you recommend we do, Bowen? Sit back and just let the city burn? How'd that work out for your drilling rig?"

It was a cheap shot, one that left Bowen too enraged to think of a response that didn't involve his fist flattening Ishii's nose.

As Bowen and Ishii stared each other down, Le Fevre, the police chief, stroked his chin while eyeing the map. "Interesting that the drone chose to hit New Astana instead of one of the less defended coastal settlements, isn't it?"

His observation silenced the room and made him its focus.

Betraying equal measures of curiosity and suspicion, Kolova asked, "Why interesting?"

Le Fevre shrugged. "Three hundred sixty thousand people on this rock. Six major population centers and a dozen or so smaller farming collectives, not to mention half a dozen mobile drilling rigs at sea. Plenty of targets to choose from, including several that are closer to the Juggernaut than we are. So why is the drone buzzing us?"

The governor reacted as if the answer were obvious. "Because this is the capital."

"But does the drone know that?" Le Fevre faced Medina, the science adviser, as he continued. "New Astana isn't significantly larger than the other five major centers we built. And since all our cities were created around the same time, using the same infrastructure template and prefab housing modules, there's no appreciable difference in their ages or configurations." He waved at the hologram. "For crying out loud, we don't even fly a flag!"

Slowly, then with greater enthusiasm, Medina started to nod. "Yes, you're right." He punched in some commands to the situation table, and the hologram of New Astana was replaced by an image of Sirsa III, slowly turning. "Given the speed of the drone, it could've circled the planet several times over by now. If it had wanted to hit any of our other cities or platforms, it could easily have done so. But for the last three hours and counting, it's harassed only us."

"Which brings us," Le Fevre said, "to the question of . . . *why?*"

The police chief let the question linger, as if to enable the others in the room to reflect upon it and reach their own conclusions—but Bowen knew a trap when he saw one being sprung. He shook his head at Le Fevre. "I see what you're doing, Chief, and I don't like it."

Le Fevre turned to plead his argument to Kolova. "Governor, think about it. The first incident with the Juggernaut was triggered by Bowen's rig. All but a handful of his crew went down with the platform, but Bowen and his two senior people escaped—and came directly to us. Can it really be a coincidence that the Juggernaut's drone is focusing its attack here?"

"Even if you're correct," Kolova said, "what difference does it make?"

"Perhaps there's a way to halt the drone's attack," Le Fevre said. "Maybe the reason it won't relent or move on—" He aimed a meaningful look at Bowen, Omalu, and Chandra. "Is that it hasn't found the targets it's looking for."

Chandra and Omalu moved closer to Bowen, who lifted his hands in a defensive gesture at the city folk. "Hang on just one goddamned minute. Is this chucklehead actually suggesting that I and my people be thrown out to the drone, like chum to a shark?" To Kolova he added, "Tell me that's not gonna happen." To his dismay, she hesitated to answer, which was tantamount to a confirmation of this rapidly unfolding nightmare. He shifted his attention to Le Fevre. "Has it occurred to you that maybe the drone just wants our shuttle, not us?"

"Yes," the chief said. "I had considered that possibility. But I believe in being thorough."

Omalu snapped, "And if it kills us, then continues attacking the city? Then what?"

Le Fevre's shrug telegraphed indifference. "At least we will have eliminated one set of variables from our presently dire equation."

Around the edges of the room, uniformed security personnel started inching their hands toward the grips of their stun batons. Bowen had no intention of waiting to be swarmed. He marched straight at Le Fevre and clenched his fist. "The only thing getting eliminated today is your teeth, you sonofa—"

From overhead came a thunderous roar of explosion, one that browned the lights inside the bunker for half a second. When full power returned, Ishii reverted the situation table's hologram to the image of the city—which no longer was haunted by the circling specter of the drone. Then a woman's voice crackled from the table's blast-addled speakers:

"Attention, Governor Kolova. This is Captain Philippa Georgiou, commanding the Starship Shenzhou. *We have neutralized the drone that was attacking your city. What is your status? Please respond."*

Kolova pressed the reply switch. "Captain, this is Governor Kolova. My staff and I are unhurt, but there's extensive damage in the city, and an unknown number of casualties. Also, most of our emergency first responders were killed and their equipment destroyed in the attack."

"Understood. Stand by to receive emergency medical and engineering teams, and be advised that I will be sending down a landing party to investigate the Juggernaut."

"Acknowledged, Captain. And before I forget: thank you."

"All part of the service, Governor. Shenzhou *out."*

The channel closed with a soft *click*, and relieved applause filled the room.

Bowen turned, rounded up Omalu and Chandra, and guided them toward the exit. "Let's get the hell out of here, on the double."

Chandra asked under his breath, "Before they change their minds about us?"

"No," Bowen said, "before I change my mind about remodeling Le Fevre's face."

Doctor Anton Nambue had a few dozen critical tasks he needed to address before he beamed down with medical relief teams to Sirsa III. Assuaging the neurotic demands of one of his less-than-essential personnel would not normally have been one of them, but Doctor Gregor Spyropoulos had grabbed Nambue by the front of his uniform.

"Please!" Spyropoulos said, almost manic.

Nambue tried to free himself, but the older man's grip was viselike. *I'll have to reason with him.* "Greg, I'm sorry, but you're not on the roster this time."

"I'm *never* on the roster," Spyropoulos said. "That's what I'm trying to tell you! Three years I've been on this ship, and not once have I ever been on a landing party."

"Of course you haven't," Nambue said. "You're a *dentist.*"

That declaration only made Spyropoulos more upset. "So? I know I'm a goddamned dentist. That doesn't mean I can't be useful on a landing party. I have medical training."

"Certification in oral surgery doesn't really qualify as 'medical training,' Greg." Nambue picked up his white field satchel and shrugged under its strap, which landed diagonally across his torso, while the medkit sat comfortably at his hip. "Look. Speaking as someone who's been on more landing parties than I can count, let me assure you: you're better off here on the ship."

Spyropoulos looked so frustrated, Nambue thought the balding man might spontaneously combust right there in the middle of the *Shenzhou*'s antiseptically pristine sickbay. "I don't want to be *better off*, Anton! I want to be *promot-*

able. You know as well as I do that experience on landing parties carries a lot of weight during personnel reviews. I've been in Starfleet for over sixteen years, and I'm still a damned lieutenant. If I ever want to get my O-4 grade, I've got to do something to get noticed. Like be part of a high-profile colonial medical-relief team."

"You are aware that the capital has more than two hundred dentists of its own, right? So unless every single one of them is busy when someone needs an emergency root canal—"

"Don't mock me, Anton. Give me scut work. Make me a paramedic trainee. I don't care what I'm doing, as long as I get to be part of the effort."

Ninety seconds of arguing with Spyropoulos had left Nambue feeling as drained as he often did by the end of a long day. He needed off this carousel, and acquiescence seemed the fastest and least problematic way to extricate himself from this emotional tug-of-war.

"Fine, go pack a field kit."

Spyropoulos clapped his hands, then grinned. "Thank you!" The dentist sprinted toward the double doors of sickbay's main entrance.

"Report to the transporter room in ten minutes," Nambue called after him.

"I'll be there in five! You won't be sorry, Anton!"

Nambue waited for the doors to close, then he sighed. "I seriously doubt that."

"Secure from red alert," Georgiou said, "but maintain yellow alert until we've retrieved the probe." She turned her chair toward her new senior tactical officer. "Good shooting, Lieutenant."

"Thank you, Captain," Gant said with a smile, then lowered his dark eyes in humility. "But the targeting computer did most of the work."

"Nonsense. I've watched veterans miss easier shots. Learn to take a compliment."

"Aye, sir." Nods of congratulation came to him from around the *Shenzhou*'s bridge.

"That being said, I hope for your sake the drone really has been neutralized."

"Oh, I guarantee you, Captain," Gant said, "that thing is toast."

Georgiou stood from her command chair and moved forward, toward the three broad center viewports that looked out upon Sirsa III. She had always admired the vantage point of the *Shenzhou*'s underslung bridge. Being situated on the underside of the *Walker*-class vessel's saucer-shaped primary hull gave the bridge an unobstructed view of the space beneath the ship. That position had always conjured for Georgiou the illusion of standing astride the cosmos rather than just gazing up at it, as one would from a bridge on the dorsal side of a starship.

Now she gazed down upon the seemingly placid face of a world barely touched by sentient habitation. Even when she strained, she was unable to pick out the colony's capital of New Astana from the more dramatic natural features on the planet's surface. "Ops, do we have a fix on where the alien probe went down?"

"Affirmative," Oliveira said. "Thirty-nine point three kilometers south-southeast of the capital, in an unpopulated stretch of flood plains near the coastline." The Lisbon native looked over her shoulder at Georgiou. "I can magnify it on-screen, if you like."

"That won't be necessary. Scan to make sure it's stable, then use a cargo transporter to beam it into our main hold. If you detect any sign of toxic or radioactive material—"

"Quarantine the hold and advise all forensic engineers to follow hazmat protocols."

"Thank you, Belin," Georgiou said, her hand alighting for a moment on the younger woman's shoulder, a fleeting gesture of praise. Then Georgiou returned to her command chair and used its armrest panel to open a channel to main engineering. "Mister Johar. Ensign Oliveira is about to send something your way. Is your team ready?"

"Champing at their bits, Captain," Johar replied over the comm.

"Glad to hear it. As soon as we get the drone wreckage on board, I want you and your people to rip that thing apart and tell me everything there is to know about it. What makes it tick, where its parent ship came from, whether we could face several at a time—everything."

"Understood. If I have to, I'll go up its afterburner with an electron microscope."

"Thank you, Commander. I'm sure that mental image won't haunt me for days to come. Bridge out." She closed the channel and looked around for her two senior officers. Given their history of contention, she had expected to see them at opposite ends of the bridge. Instead, they were side by side, hunched together in front of an auxiliary tactical display near the back of the bridge. Curious to see how the pair was working together on their first day after promotion, she drifted up behind them like a ghost and lingered at their backs while she eavesdropped.

"I'm not hearing anything but a countdown to more trouble," Saru said.

Burnham was cool but firm in her reply. "That is clearly a signal from the Juggernaut."

"A signal, yes. But that doesn't mean it's trying to communicate. Pulsars emit regular repeating signals, but they aren't known for being clever conversationalists. The universe is awash in coherent signals of no meaning or consequence."

"Much like this debate," Burnham said with dry contempt.

They're getting on as well as ever, Georgiou realized, to her mild disappointment. She stepped forward, alerting the pair to her presence. They parted as she said, "What can the two of you tell me about the Juggernaut?"

"It remains at sea," Saru said, "floating at the same coordinates where it surfaced and disrupted the drilling platform Arcadia Explorer." He spoke quickly, as if he feared interruption. "It is emitting unusual sonic and electromagnetic pulses. The colony's sensor logs confirm the pulses began as soon as the vessel surfaced. A cursory analysis of the pulses suggests they represent a countdown, possibly to the launch of another drone, or to its own deployment."

Georgiou nodded, then looked to Burnham. "Where did it come from?"

"Beneath the ocean floor, as the rig foreman alleged." Burnham called up some sensor images of the seabed under the Juggernaut. "The drill head penetrated the sea floor here. At a depth of roughly six hundred eleven meters it struck and was resisted by the hull of the Juggernaut, which then surfaced, destroying the rig platform."

It wasn't like Burnham to be so maddeningly literal. "I

meant, Number One, where did it come from originally? I'm assuming it's not indigenous."

"That does seem unlikely," Burnham said. "None of our files on Sirsa III indicated any sign of inhabitation prior to the founding of the colony. However, the configuration and hull composition of the Juggernaut and its drone are both unknown to us. Neither matches any profile currently found in our memory banks."

"Which brings us," Georgiou said, "to the matter of what to do next."

Saru stood tall. "In light of the fact that the Juggernaut has already destroyed an ocean platform, resulting in the loss of over nine hundred lives, and has launched a drone that has killed an unknown number of civilians in the capital, and seems poised to do so again, my advice would be to strike now, while we possess the advantage, and destroy it."

It was an impassioned plea, one more strident than Saru had been known for. Georgiou nodded once. "A prudent suggestion, Mister Saru, but perhaps premature in its resort to violence." She faced Burnham. "I heard you tell Saru that you think the Juggernaut's signal emissions might be an attempt at communication. How likely is that?"

"I'm unable to say, Captain. Mister Saru is correct when he says the signals could be natural byproducts of other processes taking place inside the ship. However, if they do represent an opportunity to make contact, we would be remiss not to investigate it more closely."

Saru stepped forward. "Captain, please—the time to destroy this threat is now, before it has another chance to attack the colony—or perhaps even us."

Georgiou felt trapped between idealism and pragmatism. In her decades of Starfleet service she had seen too often, and far too intimately, the nightmarish tragedy of war and thoughtless conflict. She wanted a reason to choose the less aggressive course of action, and she was counting upon Burnham to provide it to her. *Michael has never had trouble arguing her opinions before; what's different about this mission? Or is it Michael that's different?*

The discussion was interrupted by an update from Oliveira. "Captain? Doctor Nambue and his medical team are ready to beam down."

"Is their security escort with them?"

"Aye, sir."

"Then beam them down and notify Governor Kolova of their arrival." Georgiou turned back toward Burnham and Saru. "I don't want to fire weapons at the Juggernaut until we know more about it. Its hull resisted an industrial drill. Let's find out what it's made of before we commit to a grudge match. Number One, put together a landing party and go check it out."

"Aye, sir. Saru, Gant, you're with me. Oliveira, have two armed security officers meet us in the transporter room in three minutes." She moved at a quick step toward the turbolift. Gant fell in beside her as she passed his station, but Saru seemed stuck in place where she had left him. "Pick up your feet, Mister Saru," Burnham said as she and Gant headed to the turbolift. "Time, tide, and transporters wait for no one."

Shocked into motion, Saru hurried after Burnham and Gant. The lift arrived as he reached them, and the trio stepped inside. Then the door closed and they were gone in a *thrum* of electromagnetic propulsion.

That was more like the Burnham I expect to see, Georgiou mused. *But why does it suddenly feel like she's holding back? What's she waiting for?*

Those, Georgiou feared, were mysteries whose solutions would have to wait for another day.

6

Unlike some of his peers in Starfleet, Saru enjoyed the sensation of being beamed. As he stood on the platform in front of the energizer array in the *Shenzhou*'s transporter room, the pressure of the annular confinement beam had a calming effect upon his oft-frazzled nerves. When he felt himself vanish into the dematerialization sequence, he imagined himself becoming invisible . . . intangible . . . untouchable. For the briefest of moments, he was hidden beyond reach.

He felt safe.

Then came the sensory overload of materialization. Scintillating light, coupled with a musical wash of noise. Sensation returned as his surroundings appeared, bright and unfamiliar, and he found himself with the rest of the landing party, once again solid and utterly exposed.

Vulnerable.

Over the years Saru had taught himself to hide his anxiety. He lifted his tricorder from his hip and switched it on. Pivoting in a slow circle, he ran the standard battery of recommended scans. "Air temperature and quality register normal and free of toxins," he declared, though no one had asked. Aside from the landing party—which consisted of himself, Burnham, Gant, and security officers Temkin and

Rogers—he detected no life signs on or inside the Juggernaut. "We appear to be alone out here," he said to Burnham. "No evidence of sapient life other than us."

The acting first officer nodded. "Very well. Mister Gant,
conduct a detailed study of the vessel's hull. If you can, try
to obtain a sample of this material."

"Aye, sir," said Gant, who filled a small vial with sea-
water and grit collected from an indentation on the back of
the vessel. Noting Saru's stare, he said, "For my collection."

"I wasn't going to ask." Saru watched as Gant, self-
conscious, tucked away the vial.

As Gant walked toward one end of the Juggernaut,
Burnham caught the eye of one of the security officers.
"Temkin, go with him and stay alert." To the other she
said, "Rogers, stick close to Saru." Then she turned toward
Saru. "Make a new scan of the sonic and electromagnetic
signals being emitted from the Juggernaut." Her brow
creased while she entertained a thought. "Add a filter
to simulate how those signals would propagate and be
received underwater in this sea, taking into account its
specific density, salinity, depth, and water-temperature
variations."

"Yes, sir." It was an eminently sensible request. As Saru
made the necessary adjustments to his tricorder, he felt
vaguely annoyed that he hadn't thought to suggest it first.
I'm the senior science officer, he chastised himself. *I should
know to account for local conditions in my study.*

He looked up to see Burnham had already moved off
on her own, toward the end of the Juggernaut opposite the
one being investigated by Gant. Though she carried a tricorder, she didn't appear to be using it. Instead she was re-
lying, as she so often did, on her senses and Vulcan-trained
memory. Her mental acuity never ceased to impress—and

intimidate—Saru. He both admired and resented her for it, as he did for so much else.

Shadowed by security officer Rogers, Saru limited his perambulations to the middle region of the Juggernaut's back. He squinted against the glare of sunlight sparkling across the sea. His eyes roamed the waves in a futile search for any signs of the demolished drilling platform. *What did I expect to find in water this deep?* In his imagination he had seen pools of burning fuel slicked across water littered with flotsam and debris. Instead, there was only the Juggernaut, surrounded by a seemingly endless expanse of sea and sky, an unbroken horizon. A stiff breeze fluttered the fabric of Saru's uniform and kissed his face with a spray of salt water.

Focus on the mission. He finished his adjustments to his tricorder. The scan and simulation ran while he conducted a new test: he programmed his tricorder to emit sonic pulses of its own, in configurations that would echo those of the Juggernaut.

Less than four seconds later, his improvised message garnered a response.

He couldn't hear it, but he felt it—in the soles of his feet, in his bones, his spine, his teeth. Infrasonic pulses, too low to be audible but strong enough to quiver his organs. It triggered a memory older than him, one ingrained into Kelpien DNA, to fear the thundering tread of great beasts, to know that wherever that tremor occurred, death was not far behind.

His threat ganglia emerged in frantic motion. He retracted them by sheer force of will.

Each reverberation in the Juggernaut's hull escalated Saru's anxiety. His breathing turned shallow. His pulse raced—he felt it in his temples and his wrists. Within seconds his mouth was drier than Burnham's sarcasm, and his throat twisted tighter than a tourniquet. He wanted to cry out, to send up an alarm, but his limbs refused to obey him. Stiff as a statue, he fought to turn his head. When he did, he was dismayed to see that none of the others seemed to have even noticed the harbingers of doom being telegraphed by the alien vessel under their feet.

Ensign Rogers stepped toward him, her manner curious. "Sir? Are you all right?" When he failed to answer, she moved closer. The lithe human looked him up and down, growing more alarmed as she did so. She stepped in front of him. "Lieutenant Saru? Is something wrong?"

Saru struggled to force out a whisper. "Don't you *feel* that?"

She shook her head. "Feel what?"

Another series of pulses rattled Saru's teeth. "That!"

Confusion beetled the woman's brow. "You mean that mild vibration?"

"No," he said, at a loss to explain his agitation. "It's more than that. I—It—"

"Sir, maybe I should get the XO." Rogers turned to shout toward Burnham.

Desperation overcame fear: Saru reached out in a blur and set his hand on Rogers's shoulder. "No, Ensign. That won't . . . won't be necessary." He forced through his rising tide of panic to put on a mask of composure. "Resume your patrol. I am fine."

Apprehensive, Rogers stepped away to give Saru his space. He turned his back to her and pretended to fine-tune the settings of his tricorder while he collected himself.

Can't let them say I panicked, he realized. *If I lose my calm, I'll never be considered for first officer, on this ship or any other.* He finished his pantomime of tweaking and returned the device to its place at his side. *A few more min-*

utes and we'll be back on the ship. A deep breath did little to soothe his mounting fear. *Once we're safe, I just need to find a rational argument for why this thing is a nightmare that will try to kill us all.*

Lieutenant Commander Saladin Johar stood off to one side against a towering bulkhead in the main cargo hold of the *Shenzhou*. In front of the chief engineer and a team of his best forensic technology specialists lay a sprawl of burnt, twisted wreckage from the alien drone shot down only minutes earlier above the capital of Sirsa III. A few pieces still smoldered, and at least one glowed red-hot. He shook his head and looked askance at operations officer Oliveira, who had ventured belowdecks to help him coordinate the reassembly and analysis of the drone.

"I suppose it would've been a bit much to ask that it be captured intact, wouldn't it?"

She pursed her lips. "Gotta give Gant credit—he's a hell of a good shot."

Several meters away, the shimmer of the cargo transporter's wide-field beam heralded the arrival of the last swath of debris found on the surface. Everything had been beamed up and materialized inside the cargo hold based on grid references, so that it would preserve the relative positions of the drone's parts. The advantage to that method was that it facilitated a study of how durable the drone's remains were upon crashdown. The disadvantage was that it took up a lot of room in the cargo hold, and brought up half a meter of soil under each grid.

I pity the crewman who has to swab this deck tomorrow, Johar thought.

Chief Petty Officer Shull—a stocky and balding cargo-transporter operator—shut down his console and called over to Johar, "That's the last of it, sir."

"Thanks, Chief. You're dismissed." As Shull lumbered away, Johar reached over to a panel on the bulkhead behind him and opened an intraship channel to the next cargo hold. "Time to get started." He thumbed the channel off without waiting for a reply.

Broad, tall doors that separated the main hold from the next one aft parted with a gasp of hydraulics and a hum of servomotors. As they slid apart, a team of seven forensic engineers and mechanics entered, all walking side by side in a long line, toting their gear like weapons of war.

Oliveira noted their arrival with a smirk and nudged Johar. "Three guesses who's been watching old astronaut hero-vids in the rec hall."

"If *that's* what the right stuff looks like now, we're in deep trouble."

The pair walked to the middle of the hold to greet the arriving specialists. "Good afternoon, my friends," Johar said. "Around you are the remains of an alien attack drone, origin unknown." He gestured at the scattered squares of debris, which stretched across nearly the whole length of the hold. "I hope you don't mind that we've presented it in an *exploded* diagram format." He waited for them to get the gag. None of them reacted, not even with a ghost of a smile. Johar scowled. "Oh, *come on*. That was a quality pun, folks. That's as good as it gets."

"I think that's what they're afraid of," Oliveira confided.

Pearls before swine, he lamented in secret. "So be it. Listen up for your duty assignments. Esposito, catalog this stuff, every last chip and cable. Payne, Reddick: materials analysis. What are its parts made of, and where did that stuff likely come from? Coniff, you're on provenance. Is this thing native to this rock, or did it drop in from someplace else? Find out. Wierzbeski, reverse-engineer an internal schematic for this thing. I want to be able to build one from scratch out of spare parts if we have to. McShane, Bloom: What frequencies does this thing work on? Is it autonomous or remote-controlled? If it's a remote, can we jam its signals? If it's a hybrid system, can we jam and then disrupt it?" He met the team's cool, professional stares. "Questions? No? Then get to work—and let me know the moment you find *anything*."

The specialists fanned out and picked their way through the assorted piles of broken alien machinery. Soon the hold resonated with the oscillating tones of multiple tricorders.

Oliveira and Johar walked past a large chunk of the drone whose internal mechanisms were exposed but still in place. "This thing looks pretty sophisticated," Oliveira said. "Would you rate it as less advanced, more advanced, or roughly on par with our own tech?"

"Until we know more about it, I really couldn't say." Johar kicked a chunk of hull debris out of his path as they strolled along. "It's fast and maneuverable. Good enough to take out civilian interceptors. On the other hand, we picked it off from orbit in a single volley."

"So, it's good in a dogfight, but not tough enough to take a hit from our phasers. Seems like a toss-up."

"Maybe," Johar said, "maybe not. Some ion drives can haul ass and turn on a dime, which is great in an air battle, but they can't maneuver to save their lives in vacuum. And for all we know, the fault might be in the drone's command-and-control system. If it's a dumb attack dog, executing a limited range of tactical responses, it might have been configured to cope with the colony but not a starship. If the Juggernaut that launched it can reprogram these things, then who's to say it won't equip its next drone for combat with the *Shenzhou*?"

Oliveira nodded. "I see what you're saying. The Juggernaut might adapt its drones to match new threats, like pods from a Sibellian hunting tree."

"Exactly. But without the nasty-smelling sap. I hope."

He was about to suggest that they continue their conversation over lunch in the officers' mess, when Ensign Coniff came jogging after them. Coniff waved one brown hand to catch Johar's attention. "Sir! I think I have something."

"Already? That was quick."

"Well, it's only a partial finding," the eager young officer said. "But have a look at this." He turned his tricorder so Johar and Oliveira could see its display. "To address the question of provenance, I decided to see if I could determine how old it is, and then to see if there was a difference between its likely age and that of the seabed from which it emerged. Based on half-life decay in several of the elements I found in its hull, and some fragments of sediment that I suspect it accumulated while submerged in a nonwatertight compartment on the Juggernaut, I'd estimate this drone is approximately nine million years old. Which means this thing was waiting down there for a *really* long time. And—" He switched to a new set of data and handed the tricorder to Johar. "Last but not least, compounds in its hull contain elements that don't exist on Sirsa III, so it's almost certainly not native to this world."

"Good work, Ensign." Johar handed back the tricorder. "Upload those scans to the main computer, on the double."

"Yes, sir."

As Coniff stepped away to resume his work, Johar

turned to Oliveira. "Compounds that exotic would be hard to miss during a detailed planetary survey, wouldn't they?"

"Almost impossible," Oliveira said.

Dark clouds of suspicion gathered in Johar's thoughts. "We should tell the captain. Call me crazy, but I think she'll want to look into this."

As many times as Georgiou had heard the expression "like trying to take blood from a stone," she had never understood it so well as she did now that she was trying to extract the truth from the appointed head of Sirsa III's colonial government. "Governor Kolova, my team has checked these scans multiple times. There's no doubt the Juggernaut has been lying dormant under this planet's sea floor for more than nine million years."

The stern-faced, platinum-haired woman's image was holographically projected in front of the *Shenzhou* bridge's center viewport, magnified in unforgivingly revealing high resolution. *"So you said, Captain. But I think the most important word here is 'dormant,' don't you?"*

"I'm not interested in parsing word choices with you, Governor. This planet was supposed to have undergone an exhaustive search for any signs of precursor civilizations or sentient life prior to the establishment of a colonial presence."

Kolova rolled her shoulders in a dismissive shrug. *"It was."*

The more cavalier the governor's manner became, the closer Georgiou's temper came to slipping its reins. "And full subsurface imaging was required before any permits were issued for mining, either on land or at sea. Yet one of your platforms sunk its plasma drill into the hull of what appears to be an ancient starship lurking beneath the sea floor.

Did your survey scans miraculously miss that enormous starship? Or was evidence of its presence concealed?"

Confronted with a clear accusation, Kolova turned defensive. *"I assure you, Captain: Neither I nor anyone in my office concealed any such thing. We had no knowledge that any past intelligent life-forms or civilizations ever existed on Sirsa III. But if we had, we would have notified the Federation Council, as required by law."*

Georgiou was sure she heard a note of falsehood in Kolova's melody of virtue. "And just how many of the planetary surveys did you or members of your office review before they were submitted for approval?"

"None of them—but only because the surveys were done long before I was appointed to this office." Perhaps noting Georgiou's suspicious reaction, Kolova added, *"All of the surveys were conducted by agents of the Kayo Mining Consortium, roughly five to six years ago."*

That was a new detail, one that reinforced Georgiou's perception that something was seriously amiss with this colony. "Excuse me a moment, Governor." She looked back at her communications officer, Ensign Mary Fan, and, with a subtle gesture below the frame of the image they were sending to Kolova, signaled that she wanted the channel muted.

A flick of a switch later, Fan said, "Muted, sir."

Pivoting to starboard, Georgiou found her new yeoman, Ensign Danby Connor. The young, curly-haired force of nature noted her searching look out of the corner of his eye and turned to give her his full attention. "Sir."

"Connor, pull the colony's files from our memory banks. Show me everything from their application for a colonial permit. Put it on the starboard viewer. Our eyes only."

"Aye, sir." Connor quick-stepped to the nearest duty

station and summoned the colony's information with such speed that Georgiou realized he must have anticipated her request hours earlier and had the data on standby. Before she could compliment him on his preparedness, he had projected the information over the viewport to the right of the center screen. What she saw confirmed Kolova's version of the facts—but it also raised new questions.

Another look in Fan's direction. "Reopen the channel." Fan restored the two-way connection, then nodded at Georgiou to confirm it was ready.

"Governor," Georgiou said, "your colony's application file is rather incomplete."

A sage nod from Kolova. *"It's my understanding that KMC was eager to secure the license ahead of a competitor, so they submitted a partial application with a request for expedited approval. The remaining planetary survey scans were delivered later, directly to the Colonial Authority office in Beijing, on Earth."*

"That's a rather serious break from protocol," Georgiou said.

"It's all completely legal, Captain. The necessary waivers were filed and approved."

It was an evasive reply, but when Georgiou looked at Connor, he frowned as he nodded in confirmation of Kolova's claim. "Be that as it may," the captain said, "we still need to see the complete planetary survey files. Please transmit them to us as soon as—"

"I'm afraid we don't have them," Kolova said.

That sounded like a lie to Georgiou. "How can you not have a copy of the survey files? How do you manage your mining operations without them?"

"The miners drill and dig where KMC tells them to." Kolova paired an insincere smile with a dismissive lift of her

brow. *"The price we pay for political autonomy. Now, if there's nothing else . . . ?"*

"We're done—for now. *Shenzhou* out." The channel closed, and the holographic image vanished from in front of the center viewport, leaving only the majestic curve of the planet falling away beneath the *Shenzhou*'s bridge.

Georgiou had been stonewalled more than once in her many years of service to Starfleet. She detested it as much now as she had when she had been a junior officer—but now, as a captain, she finally had the authority to do something about it. "Mister Connor!"

Her yeoman snapped to attention. "Sir."

"Get on the horn to the FCA—use the priority subspace channel. Tell them I want every bit of data they have on the Sirsa III colony, and I want it *right now*. If anyone gives you the runaround, tell them the next person they'll be hearing from is Admiral Anderson."

"Aye, sir." Connor pivoted back to his station and set to work with a youthful energy and singularity of focus that Georgiou secretly envied, just a little.

Just as Georgiou settled back into her command chair, relief operations officer Ensign Troy Januzzi—who pronounced his surname "Yanoozi," thanks to an arcane bit of language drift—swiveled from his station to face her. "Captain, we've completed a sensor sweep of the Juggernaut. All data has been routed to the science labs for analysis."

"Good work, Mister Januzzi." A notion occurred to Georgiou. "Transmit our sensor data to Starfleet Command. Maybe they'll see something in it that we don't."

"Never hurts to have a second set of eyes, eh, Captain?"

"No, it doesn't, Ensign. And if there's one lesson I've learned that never seems to go out of style, it's this: *Take all the help you can get.*"

—

Few errors of courtesy in Starfleet carried graver penalties than keeping a flag officer waiting. Neither the offense nor its repercussions were the least bit official, of course. It was just one of many facts of life implicitly understood by those who made a career of service in Starfleet: wasting an admiral's time was a surefire way to get saddled with the worst assignments.

In his time, Captain Christopher Pike had endured his share of scut jobs; he was not about to subject his ship and crew to such an iniquity, not if he could help it. So it was that he found himself charging down the corridors of the *Enterprise* in a mad rush to reach his quarters.

Unlike many other types of starship in the fleet, *Constitution*-class vessels had no ready rooms for their captains. Most days, Pike didn't miss having a ready room—except for those occasions when he received a classified transmission above the security clearance of his bridge crew, compelling him to return to his quarters to receive it.

Today he had the bad luck of being on the receiving end of one such message that was being tendered in real time, from the admiral in charge of this sector—and finding his route to his quarters hampered by a sluggish turbolift and dense foot traffic in the corridors.

Pike's door slid open ahead of him, and he darted inside his quarters. Without pausing to switch on the lights he moved to his desk and powered up his secure terminal. After taking a moment to recover his breath, he thumbed open a channel to the bridge. "Chief Garison, patch that signal through to my quarters."

"Aye, sir," his signals officer replied. *"Stand by."*

The screen of Pike's desktop terminal snapped to life,

revealing the strong features of Admiral Brett Anderson, a man whose lantern jaw and piercing eyes were accentuated by a creased forehead that hinted at his decades of service. His short thatch of golden hair was his last bastion of youthfulness. *"I was starting to think you'd forgotten about me, Captain."*

"Sorry for the wait, Admiral."

"Are you certain this connection is secure?"

He checked the channel's status. "Yes, sir. What can I do for you?"

"Analysts at Starfleet Command just got a look at some sensor data the Shenzhou sent over from Sirsa III. In a word, it's a nightmare."

Hyperbole had never sat well with Pike. "Can you be more specific, sir?"

"I'm sending you the original data now, plus our analysis. Review it with your XO and science officer immediately, and set your ship's course for Sirsa III at maximum warp. We need your ship in orbit there as soon as possible."

That sounded ominous. "May I ask for what purpose, Admiral?"

"I need you to perform a mission to which I suspect Captain Georgiou will . . . object."

Cold wind blew in off the sea, stinging Burnham's face like needles of ice. Pacing along the dull, pitted black surface of the Juggernaut's dorsal hull, she was reminded of ancient human myths—tales of a beast known as a kraken, a leviathan the size of an island. A monster that could rise from the depths and leave mariners stranded, their vessels beached upon its back. Like so many other tales of the ancient world, yarns of the kraken had, to Burnham, always seemed absurd and beyond belief. But now she was forced to wonder whether a vessel such as this one might once have crested the waves of a Terran sea, birthing a legend that refused to die.

Most of the Juggernaut's visible exterior was unremarkable, but its few notable features were, Burnham noticed, symmetrical and dual in nature. Each major deviation from the hull's smooth surface either had a matching counterpart in mirror image on the other side of the vessel, or was irregular enough to be discounted as damage. Whatever else she might deduce about the Juggernaut's makers, she was willing to surmise they came from a species that either exhibited bilateral symmetry—like so many other intelligent species known throughout local space—or they revered the concept of symmetry in their designs.

A soft chirrup from her tricorder drew her attention. The device had completed its passive multispectral scan of the Juggernaut while she walked its length. Now she would have a trove of raw information to study after she and the landing party returned to the *Shenzhou*. She dismissed the alert, then looked back the way she had come, toward the rest of her team.

At the far end of the Juggernaut from her were Gant and Temkin. The security officer was anchoring Gant, who had descended the sloped hull of the Juggernaut almost to its waterline and was crouching while he reached with one hand into the water lapping at the alien vessel's dark hull. *He must be filling another vial for his collection*, Burnham realized.

Since the earliest days of Gant's Starfleet career, he had made a point of collecting water or soil samples from every alien world he visited. Once each sample was cleared through the *Shenzhou*'s quarantine protocol, it was afforded a place inside a vacuum-sealed, padded display cabinet in Gant's quarters. His hobby struck Burnham as silly and sentimental, but she couldn't deny that it seemed to make him happy, and the case itself made for a unique conversation piece.

Near the middle of the gargantuan ship, close to the party's original beam-down point, stood Saru and Rogers. The pair were a few meters apart and seemed to be avoiding not only conversation but eye contact. While Saru busied himself fiddling with his tricorder, Rogers passed the time staring at the horizon while keeping one hand on the grip of her phaser.

Burnham trudged back toward the middle of the Juggernaut. She pulled her communicator from her hip and flipped open its grille with a flick of her wrist. A quick tweak with her thumb set it for the limited-range shore-personnel frequency. "Burnham to landing party. I've finished my survey. Prepare to regroup for beam-up."

In the distance, she saw Saru flip open his communicator. His voice issued from her comm, creating a peculiar sensory disconnect. *"Confirmed, sir."*

At the opposite end of the Juggernaut, Temkin pulled Gant back up from the waterline onto the mostly level crest of the ship's dorsal hull. Once they were both steady, Gant flipped open his own comm device, and his transmitted voice spilled from Burnham's communicator. *"Copy that, sir. Heading back now."*

Burnham reached the middle of the Juggernaut well ahead of Gant and Temkin. There she found Rogers keeping her distance from Saru, who seemed to exhibit a skittish alertness to every minuscule shift in the environment. Under normal circumstances she would have written off Saru's agitation to his species' innate talent for finding threats in the most innocent of situations, but something about his apprehension felt different this time.

His anxiety was not unreasonable, in Burnham's opinion. After all, the Juggernaut had obliterated a drilling platform and snuffed out some nine hundred sentient lives in the process. But as she moved closer, she saw Saru was more than just guarded; he seemed afraid.

She sidled over to him but stopped short of making contact. *He's already on edge. Might be best not to do anything to spook him.* Modulating her voice into a lower register, she said in a soft tone, "Saru? Are you all right?"

The Kelpien turned toward her, his dilated pupils betraying his alarm. "I'm sorry? What?" After a moment's pause, he mentally regrouped. "Yes, sir. I think so."

"You *think so*?" Burnham checked to make certain that Rogers wasn't eavesdropping on the two of them. Then she confirmed that Temkin and Gant were still too far away to hear or discern what was transpiring between her and Saru. "Lieutenant, what are you sensing? Is there something about this ship, or this place, that's giving you reason for concern?"

Saru looked at her with mistrust, as if he thought she might be goading him into a trap. Burnham chided herself: *He thinks this is a ruse, that I'm trying to embarrass him.*

She inched closer to him and took care to keep her voice low and even. "Saru, I need your input. I'm asking you, as first officer to second officer, to tell me what you sense."

He drew a deep breath through his long nostrils, then closed his eyes. Was he gleaning something from scents in the air? Or just oxygenating to clear his thoughts? Burnham wasn't sure, and she didn't particularly care, as long as Saru focused and told her something useful.

"Vibrations," he said. "Infrasonic. At regular intervals. Something big is coming."

Burnham tried to pick up on what Saru described, but she lacked his species' knack for sensing low-frequency pulses. It was one of the first times she had envied an ability of the Kelpien officer, though she had often desired the superior high-frequency hearing of Vulcans. "When you say 'something big is coming,' Saru, do you mean from inside the ship?"

He nodded. "The intervals are decreasing. And the intensity is increasing. It's close."

"Can you describe more precisely what—"

An eerie droning filled the air, and a strange oscillating whine resonated through the hull of the Juggernaut. The entire vessel juddered beneath Burnham's feet, and she and Saru fell against each other as the massive ship lurched. Several meters away, Rogers, Temkin, and Gant tumbled apart, and then each of them grasped for handholds on the ship's hull.

The waves to one side of the Juggernaut frothed with gray foam, then erupted in a wall of spray and hot vapor as the eerie noise from inside the ship broke free to the air outside of it. Three shapes, long and dartlike, shot upward through the sudden fog engulfing the landing party and soared skyward. Eager to see from where they had emerged, Burnham scrambled across the top of the Juggernaut just in time to see three previously nonexistent apertures in the hull constrict and seal themselves, leaving behind no seams or evidence.

She turned toward Gant. "What were those?"

Gant was already reviewing data from his tricorder. "Three more drones, sir." He lowered the device and shot a fearful look Burnham's way. "And they're headed for the *Shenzhou*."

Burnham looked upward. The drones had already vanished above the cloud cover on their way into orbit. She
pulled out her communicator and flipped it open, then set it
for ship-to-shore.

"Burnham to *Shenzhou*, priority one!"

Captain Georgiou responded, *"Go ahead, Number One."*

"Raise shields, Captain! You're about to have company."

7

"Red alert," Georgiou declared, taking her place in the bridge's command seat. "Raise shields, arm all weapons." She used her chair's armrest control pad to open a public-address channel inside the *Shenzhou.* "Attention, all decks. This is the captain. All hands to battle stations. This is not a drill. Firefighters and damage-control teams, stand ready." She switched off the channel and turned her attention to the three drones being tracked by the ship's tactical system and represented as highlighted points holographically super-imposed on the center viewport. "Tactical, report!"

Ensign Troy Januzzi had taken over Gant's post at tactical. A sheen of perspiration glistened on the trim young officer's shaved brown head. "Three bogeys inbound, Captain. They're at one-quarter impulse and accelerating." He muted a warbling alert from his console. "Their headings are diverging. One bogey still on intercept, the other two are trying to flank."

"Helm, evasive. Break orbit, get us some breathing room."

"Aye, sir," Ensign Detmer confirmed. The young German woman piloted the *Shenzhou* away from Sirsa III. "Increasing to half-impulse, going evasive."

Oliveira turned away from the operations console to

face Georgiou. "Captain, if we break orbit, we'll be leaving the landing party behind on the Juggernaut."

"I know that, Lieutenant. But for now we need to face the threat in front of us." Georgiou checked the tactical data projected on the portside viewport and kept to herself the fact that she had effectively abandoned the landing party the moment she had ordered the shields be raised. With the shields up, there was no way to transport Burnham or the others back aboard.

"Drones continuing to increase speed," Januzzi said. "The flanking units are adjusting course, starting a pincer attack."

"Suppressing fire, Mister Januzzi," Georgiou said. "Detmer, all ahead, full impulse."

"Full impulse, aye." Detmer pushed the *Shenzhou*'s impulse drive to its rated maximum, and the pitch of its droning rose steadily as the ship raced into combat maneuvers. Outside the center viewport the cosmos wheeled with dizzying speed and randomness, the result of Detmer's wild corkscrew turns and bizarre x-axis flips of the massive starship.

Georgiou decided to test a hunch. "Fan, are you reading any signal traffic between the drones and the Juggernaut? Any sign that they're being remotely guided?"

Ensign Fan checked the readouts on the communications panel. "None, Captain."

"What about signals moving among the drones themselves?"

Once more Fan queried her signal-intercept software. "Negative, sir."

"So much for taking them down without a fight," Georgiou said. "Tactical, lock and fire."

Januzzi keyed in the command. Targeting sights appeared on the viewport, wedded to the icons representing the drones. "Phasers locked. Five seconds to optimal firing range."

"Fire when ready." Georgiou drew a breath and waited to see the drones blasted into scrap and free radicals by the *Shenzhou*'s computer-assisted fire-control system. In her head she counted down their final seconds: three . . . two . . . one . . .

"We've lost the targeting lock," Januzzi said, his efforts at the tactical console turning frantic. "Reacquiring." Within a few seconds it was clear that he had promised more than he could deliver. "Sir, they're generating some kind of scrambling field that blocks our targeting scanners. Should I switch to manual?"

Detonations rocked the *Shenzhou* from either side as the drones peppered it with fire. Georgiou gritted her teeth as she listened to the rattling of her starship's spaceframe. "Do what you have to, Ensign."

"Aye, sir."

Two more salvos hammered the *Shenzhou*, then two of the drones shot across the main viewscreen, fiery blurs against the curtain of night. Then came a third punishing barrage that dimmed the lights and stuttered consoles all over the bridge.

"Damage report," Georgiou said.

"Power relays overloading below deck three," Oliveira said, reviewing new intel on her operations console. "Minor casualties on the engineering decks."

From the engineering station, Ensign Britch Weeton reported, "Captain? Main power is down ten percent, shields are down forty percent. I'm patching in emergency backups."

It was becoming clear to Georgiou that this new trio of

drones would not be so easy to destroy as their lone prede-
cessor had been just an hour before. "Mister Januzzi—?"

"Almost," was all he managed to say through teeth gritted with effort. Then he triple-tapped a firing pad on his
console and unleashed a furious storm of phaser blasts.

Georgiou looked toward the center viewport and
watched the first barrage force a drone into a turn; the
second corralled the alien attacker into a last-second course
change; and the last skewered the drone through its core
and blew it to bits.

Oliveira grimaced in disappointment. "So much for cap-
turing one intact."

"Sorry," Januzzi said.

"Don't be sorry," Georgiou said. "Repeat as necessary.
There are still two drones left out—" The ship lurched from
another hammering blast, which delayed the rest of Georgiou's reply. "Out there. Take them down any way that
works, Ensign."

"Aye, sir," Januzzi said. He plotted a new firing solution and resumed his hunt.

Stars whirled across the main viewscreen as Detmer piloted the *Shenzhou* in mad spirals punctuated by abrupt rolls
and tumbles. Every high-stress maneuver the daring young
conn officer forced the ship to endure left its keel and
spaceframe groaning like an old house buffeted by a storm.

The two remaining drones appeared in the center of the
forward viewscreen, their nose-mounted weapons charged
to a blinding white. Then a majestic curtain of phaser fire
swept over the drones, rendering them into glowing debris
scattered on a thousand vectors. Georgiou heaved a sigh of
relief. "Good shooting, Mister Januzzi."

"Thank you, Captain."

"Secure from red alert," Georgiou said, canceling the

alert status from her armrest. "Helm, take us back into orbit, geosynchronous position above the Juggernaut. Tactical, lower the shields, set weapons to standby." As soon as she heard her orders acknowledged, she stood and moved to stand behind Oliveira at ops. "Was it my imagination, or were those drones tougher than the one we shot down over the capital?"

"Definitely tougher." Oliveira called up a screen of combat stats about the drones, based on data compiled by the computer during the battle they had just waged. "Average speed, maneuverability, shield power, hull strength—all significantly higher than last time."

"Analysis?"

"Either the Juggernaut carries different classes of attack drone for engaging different types of adversaries," Oliveira said, "or it customizes its response based on perceived challenges and the failures of previous drones. Assuming it's not done with us yet—"

"Which is where the smart money is right now," Georgiou interjected.

"—we should assume its next wave of drones will be faster, more numerous, better armed, more robustly shielded, and more tactically adept," Oliveira finished.

Troubled by the implications of that report, Georgiou asked, "How long could the Juggernaut keep throwing new-and-improved drones at us?"

"Hard to say. Depending upon its resources, it might be done already—or it might be able to hound us until Judgment Day. But I'm willing to stake my reputation that the longer this situation lasts, the more powerful those drones are going to get. And sooner or later—"

"They'll get the best of us," Georgiou said, arriving at the grim but inevitable conclusion. She steeled her will for what likely promised to be a long and perilous fight against ever-less-favorable odds. "In that case, Lieutenant, I suggest you send this intel down to Mister Johar—because I get the feeling we'll need a miracle before this is done, and those are what our chief engineer does best."

8

In Georgiou's experience, it was a bad idea for a captain to appear distracted on the bridge. The officer in charge needed to be attuned to the ebb and flow of information and to the mood of the crew. It could harm morale for junior officers to see a captain caught unawares, no matter how reasonable such a reaction might be. This tended to discourage Starfleet captains from multitasking in the center seat, for the sake of perception if for nothing else.

Thus had Starfleet adopted the tradition of a captain's "ready room." Though not all ships of the line had incorporated the concept, many had, and they were proving to be increasingly popular with commanding officers throughout the service. Georgiou was one of them.

Up to her neck in damage reports and repair estimates, she had left *Shenzhou*'s bridge in Lieutenant Oliveira's hands and retired to her ready room, a curved compartment directly aft of the main bridge. Over the past hour, each department's ranking officer had updated their reports at least twice. Each time Georgiou thought she had reached the end of the virtual paperwork, more arrived. Now, as she signed off on the latest numbers from engineering, she was certain she had earned a respite—only to see Doctor Nambue's updated casualty report arrive in her queue.

Angels and ministers of grace defend us. . . .

Her door signal buzzed. Eager for relief from the monotony, she said, "Come."

The portal slid open, and Burnham entered, followed by Saru. They planted themselves in front of Georgiou's desk. She expected Burnham to just start talking, but instead her two senior officers both stood before her, apparently awaiting their captain's invitation to talk.

"Welcome back, you two. What did you bring me?"

The pair traded confused looks. Burnham asked, "Bring you, sir?"

"Just a bit of mirth, Number One." She let the awkwardness linger a moment, then prompted Burnham, "Report. What did you learn about the Juggernaut?"

"We were able to confirm its age, based on sediment samples clinging to the hull," Burnham said. "Its exterior design suggests its creators had a strong affinity for bilateral symmetry. And its hull appears to be composed of a smart metal that can shift between solid and fluid states to create apertures and then seal them without leaving any trace of a seam."

Georgiou nodded. "I see." She looked at Saru. "Anything to add?"

"Patterns of infrasonic vibrations generated inside the Juggernaut appeared to correspond with its deployment of new attack drones. Before we beamed up, I detected a new cycle of vibrations—these being longer and more complex than the ones before. My analysis suggests the vessel will be ready to launch more drones in approximately three to five hours."

"Then we'd best move quickly to find a solution to this crisis." Georgiou turned her gaze back toward Burnham. "Number One, what's your tactical recommendation?"

"I'm not sure I possess enough information to render one, Captain."

That was not the answer Georgiou had expected. It was unlike Burnham to be at a loss for a plan of action, even a simple one. "Well, we need to do something."

"Perhaps if we could get inside the Juggernaut," Burnham said, "I might be able to glean some insight concerning its purpose and functions. Then I could formulate a tactical response."

Saru met the first officer's idea with shock and dismay. "Inside? Are you out of your mind? That entire ship resonates with death, and you want to plumb its innards? Putting aside the madness of that notion, how would you gain ingress? We mapped its entire hull, above and below the waterline, and found nothing that even slightly resembles an entry."

"I have a hunch," Burnham said. "One I'd like to test."

That sounded more like the adventurous young officer Georgiou had come to know over the past six years. It also sounded unwise. "Number One, are you sure that'd be safe?"

"Not at all, Captain. However, I think it might be the most effective path of action."

"I'll need more to go on than your 'hunch' if I'm—"

Oliveira's voice over the comm interrupted her. *"Captain, we need you on the bridge."*

"On my way." Georgiou stood and strode toward the ready room's door, with Burnham and Saru right behind her. As soon as they stepped onto the bridge they parted ways: Saru and Burnham moved to their duty stations, and Georgiou proceeded to her command chair. Oliveira vacated the seat and held it while the captain took her place. "Report," Georgiou said.

"Sensors have detected a massive power buildup inside the Juggernaut." Oliveira nodded to the relief officer at ops, who put the new sensor data on the starboard auxiliary viewscreen. "The energy waveform suggests the power source is either a matter-antimatter reactor, or possibly something more advanced, such as an artificial singularity. Its power output is rising, which suggests the Juggernaut is gearing up for something big."

Burnham asked, "As in, 'direct assault on the *Shenzhou*' big?"

"No, sir. More like 'lay waste to the entire planet' big."

"Thank you, Lieutenant," Georgiou said. "Resume your post." Oliveira returned to her station at the front of the bridge, and Georgiou looked toward Burnham. "If the Juggernaut is gearing up to do something apocalyptic, we need to preempt that action. Suggestions?"

"I think it's too soon to rule out a diplomatic solution, Captain."

Georgiou was sure she had misheard. "A *diplomatic* solution?"

"I share your incredulity, Captain," Saru said. "I have no doubt the Juggernaut poses an imminent threat to the colonists and other life-forms on Sirsa III."

Burnham absorbed Saru's criticism with graceful calm. "There is no way we can know that based on the limited and tainted information we now possess. It is possible that whatever intelligence or program guides the actions of the Juggernaut, it has perceived the colonists, and now us, as aggressors. If so, it is incumbent upon us to seek a peaceful resolution."

There was logic in Burnham's argument; Georgiou would have expected nothing less. But she wondered whether something else was behind Burnham's new attitude of caution. "Number One, while I appreciate your commitment to the—"

"Captain!" interrupted Ensign Fan. "Priority signal from the *Starship Enterprise*!"

What fresh hell is this? Georgiou nodded at Fan. "On-screen."

In front of the bridge's forward view of Sirsa III appeared a life-sized hologram of the commanding officer of the *Enterprise*. A grave expression darkened the human man's youthful, chiseled features. *"Captain Georgiou. I'm Captain Christopher Pike."*

"To what do I owe the pleasure, Captain?"

"We're joining you at Sirsa III and bringing new orders from Starfleet Command."

Georgiou bristled; this had *bad news* written all over it. "Why am I receiving orders through *you*, Captain? Why not directly from Starfleet?"

"You'll have to ask Admiral Anderson if you want an answer to that."

Gant looked up from the tactical console. "Sir, the *Enterprise* is dropping out of warp and moving into orbit, five degrees behind us."

She trained an accusatory stare at Gant. "And I'm learning of their approach only *now?*"

Abashed, Gant looked at his panel, then at junior tactical officer Narwani, and finally back at the captain. "All our attention was on the Juggernaut, Captain."

"Tactical awareness means paying attention to the entire theater of operations, Mister Gant. Do try to remember that going forward."

"Aye, Captain."

It was a bit unfair, she knew, to lay all the blame on Gant. Responsibility for monitoring the wider theater of operations was actually the duty of Narwani, the junior tactical officer, whose head was encased in a gleaming metallic VR helmet designed for that task. But it was Gant's job to work with Narwani and to supervise her, and in that role he'd just failed.

Georgiou returned to her conversation with Pike. "You could have shared your message by subspace, Captain. So why is your ship now in orbit behind mine?"

Her question made Pike visibly uncomfortable. *"To paraphrase the admiral, my ship is here to make sure you obey his orders—and, if you fail or refuse, to carry them out myself."*

"And what, pray tell, *are* Admiral Anderson's orders?"

Pike swallowed before he answered. *"To bombard the Juggernaut with phasers and photon torpedoes, and to continue our attack until every trace of the vessel is obliterated."*

She was appalled and didn't try to hide it. "Detonate photon torpedoes on the surface of a populated planet? Captain, do you and the admiral have any idea the sort of collateral damage that would cause? Even a limited barrage could strip away this planet's atmosphere."

The muscles in Pike's jaw tensed as he considered his reply.

"The admiral was very clear, Captain."

"But the colony—!"

"—is to be considered expendable," Pike said. *"By order of Starfleet Command."*

Just saying the word "expendable" in relation to sentient lives made Pike sick to his stomach. He had always understood that his oath of service meant he would, at times, be called upon to act as a soldier. But at heart he was an explorer, a scientist, a dreamer—not a cold-blooded killer.

He intuited from the horror on Georgiou's face that she felt the same way. *"What do you mean, 'expendable,' Captain? We came here to help these people, not incinerate them."*

Pike turned his chair just enough to see his first officer, Commander Una, at the edge of his vision. "Number One, send Starfleet's sensor analysis to the *Shenzhou*."

"Aye, sir," Una said, then delegated the order with nods to science officer Lieutenant Spock and communications officer Garison.

"Have a look at what Starfleet found in your scans," Pike said to Georgiou. "Evidence that the ship you and the locals call the Juggernaut has a massive stardrive. That beast is warp-capable, and if it has half the power Starfleet thinks it does, it could pose a threat not just to the colony on Sirsa III, but to populated planets in neighboring systems."

"So we're going to condemn hundreds of thousands of innocent lives based on nothing more than a hypothetical danger? That strikes me as premature and reactionary."

"Tell that to the eight hundred thousand colonists on Teratus V. Or the four million who make their home on Corratus Prime. Or the Regulans—their homeworld is less than ten light-years from here, and it has a population of over a billion."

Georgiou's mien darkened with defiance. *"This isn't some abstract numbers game."*

"Sometimes it is," Pike said. "I don't like it any more than you do, but this is the cold, hard reality we have to live with." Swiveling his command chair again, he said to Garison, "Send the *Shenzhou* the verified orders from Admiral Anderson." Returning to Georgiou, Pike put on his most apologetic manner. "I don't mean to be callous about this, Captain, but we're picking up some troubling power readings from the Juggernaut. If we don't act now, we might lose our best chance to stop this thing before it gets started."

"Hang on," Georgiou said, turning away to confer with one of her officers. When she looked back at Pike, she seemed more hopeful. *"What if there was a way to complete the mission without jeopardizing the colonists and ecosystem of Sirsa III?"*

Intrigued, Pike leaned forward. "I'm listening."

"We use tractor beams to haul the Juggernaut off the surface, away from the planet. Then we destroy it in space."

He tried to visualize that tactic and was plagued with doubts about it. He shot a sidelong look at Una and Spock. "Do we have enough power to tow something that massive out of a gravity well?"

"Neither of our ships alone could do it," Una said. "But together? Maybe."

Spock's brow lifted, telegraphing his fascination with the idea. "We would have to match the frequency of our tractor beam with that of the *Shenzhou*, in order to avoid gravitational shearing that would disrupt both our holds on the Juggernaut. It would also pose a significant risk of overloading both ships' impulse drives unless—"

"Unless we tie in the power from our warp engines," Georgiou cut in, *"and balance the loads through our dilithium matrices."*

Her suggestion elicited a nod of approval from Spock. "A viable proposal."

That was good enough for Pike. "All right, I'm game. How soon can we give this a go?"

"We'll need a few minutes to run the cross-patch between the warp and impulse systems," Una said, turning toward her console. "Relaying the orders to engineering now."

"I will calculate the optimal angle and frequency for the tractor beams," Spock said.

Pike enjoyed a small surge of pride as he watched his officers swing into action. He hoped Georgiou's people were as reliable as his. "Stand by, Captain," he said to her. "We'll send over the specs for the dual tractor beam in a few seconds."

"We'll be ready. My engineers have already set our warp-impulse patch."

Worst-case scenarios paraded through Pike's imagination. "Captain, if, for whatever reason, this plan doesn't actually work—"

"We'll burn that bridge when we come to it," Georgiou said.

Spock looked up from the sciences console. "Specs ready and sent to the *Shenzhou*."

"Good work, Mister Spock. Number One, where do we stand on the cross-patch?"

Una conferred discreetly with the engineering officer, then faced Pike. "Ready."

"All right, everyone. Brace yourselves. This could get bumpy." Pike added to Spock, "Patch in backup power and target tractor beam."

The half-Vulcan science officer keyed in the commands, reporting as he went along. "Warp power tied in. Combined output balancing. Coordinates set." He faced Pike. "Ready, sir."

Pike asked Georgiou, "Ready, Captain?"

"Relinquishing control of our tractor beam to your science officer . . . now. Good luck."

"Same to you, Captain. *Enterprise* out." As the main viewscreen reverted to an image of the *Shenzhou* ahead of the *Enterprise* in orbit, Pike said, "Mister Spock, engage tractor beam."

A low-frequency hum resonated through the hull of the *Enterprise* as the tractor beam activated, charged with more power than it had ever emitted before. It sounded to Pike as if the ship were a bell that had been struck, and now only the lingering memory of vibration remained.

On the main viewscreen, a pale blue beam streaked from the saucer of the *Shenzhou*, down into the atmosphere of Sirsa III, converging with the *Enterprise*'s beam as it met its target.

"Status," Pike said. "Do we have hold of the Juggernaut?"

Spock adjusted the settings on his console. "Both beams have reached the target." He creased his brow in apparent frustration. "We are having difficulty confirming a tractor lock."

Pike threw a look at Una, who leaned over a hooded sensor display to gather more information. "The Juggernaut is barely moving."

Though Pike had come to this world with orders to destroy the Juggernaut where he found it, he desperately wanted Georgiou's plan to work. "Can we increase power?"

"Power is already at maximum," Spock said. "Any increase will overload the mains."

Garison interjected, "Sir? Captain Georgiou is asking us to stand down."

Pike felt his shoulders slump with disappointment. "Tractor beam off," he said to Spock. Then, to Garison, "Put *Shenzhou* on-screen."

Georgiou's lean, attractive face once again filled the viewscreen. *"Captain, our scans indicate there's either a compound in the Juggernaut's hull, or an energy field around it, that makes it resistant to our tractor beams."*

"How resistant? Is it bouncing them off?"

"*Not quite. But it is definitely one slippery fish.*"

"Point taken," Pike said. "Can we compensate by adjusting the beams' frequency? Or finding a little extra juice?"

Georgiou shook her head. "*My science officer studied the Juggernaut up close. He says its hull is quite dense, and has ablative qualities that will make it hard to penetrate.*"

That was not the news Pike had hoped to hear. "Well, if we can't tow it away from the planet, and we can't slice it up with phasers, then we have no other choice but to return to the orders we already have in hand."

"*Captain,*" Georgiou pleaded, "*we still have time to find another way.*"

"No, Captain, I'm afraid we don't. You said it yourself: tractor beams and phasers are both off the table. Which means we have only one card left to play." He resigned himself to the inevitable. "It's time to find out how that thing does against a spread of photon torpedoes."

How had everything gone wrong so quickly? Burnham stood, aghast at the rapid decline of the *Shenzhou*'s partnership with the *Enterprise*. A solution had seemed at hand, an answer based in logic and restraint—but at the first sign of impediment all hope was cast aside. This was everything she had feared Starfleet would be when she had first been courted to its service by Sarek and Captain Georgiou: reactionary, shortsighted, blinded by a knee-jerk impulse to seek security at the expense of knowledge.

Then the advice of Sarek echoed in her memory: *If that is what you find, it is up to you to change it for the better.* For six years she had devoted herself to that idea. In that time, Captain Georgiou had never given her cause to put it into practice. Now Captain Pike was doing just that.

Georgiou stood in front of the command chair, making her case to Pike's shimmering holographic avatar. "Captain, I thought I'd made it clear that a torpedo bombardment of the surface was not an acceptable outcome."

"You made your opinion clear," Pike said, *"but your personal preference doesn't change the order from Admiral Anderson. We tried things your way, and it didn't work. Now we have to proceed with the best option we have left."*

His intransigence stoked Georgiou's temper. "A torpedo barrage on the planet's surface might be the simplest option, but that does not make it the *best* one." She moderated her tone to one less strident. "Please, we have time to explore alternatives. Join us, and maybe we can still find a solution that doesn't come with mass casualties."

Pike's resistance hardened. *"The problem with your appeal is the word 'maybe.' There's too much at stake here for me to disobey orders based on a vague hope."* To one of his bridge officers the *Enterprise*'s captain said, *"Move us into firing position."* Then, to Georgiou he added, *"You can either assist in the completion of our mission, or you can stand down. It's all the same to me."*

Without muting the channel, Georgiou said, "Detmer, bring us about and put us into the *Enterprise*'s firing solution, point-blank range. Ops, all power to dorsal shields. Mister Gant, arm all weapons and lock on to the *Enterprise*'s targeting sensors."

Her flurry of orders left Pike fuming. *"Captain? What the hell are you doing?"*

"Whatever I have to," Georgiou said. "If you want to bombard a populated and defenseless Federation colony, you'll have to go through me, my crew, and my ship to do it." Returning to her command chair, she snapped at Oliveira, "Comms off."

Pike's hologram flickered and vanished before he could protest.

This was precisely the scenario Burnham had hoped the captain would find a way to avoid. Now she and the rest of the *Shenzhou*'s crew were in it—over the line with no easy way back. The forward viewscreen filled for a moment with the spectacle of the underside of the *Enterprise* looming large and precariously close—and then, as the *Shenzhou* slipped beneath its sister ship, the *Enterprise* passed out of view above the *Shenzhou*'s saucer, which obstructed any direct line of sight from the *Shenzhou*'s underslung bridge module to the *Enterprise*.

Burnham's mind raced as the captain doled out combat orders. *There must be some way to defuse this before it goes any further.* Once shots were exchanged, there would be almost no hope of a brokered resolution. Burnham knew that whatever she was going to do, it had to be done now. *If only we had an actual plan of action to suggest as an alternative.* She reflected on all that she had seen of the Juggernaut during her mission to the planet's surface. *There has to be a way to get inside. To coax the hull into opening an aperture. If we could do that, Pike might listen to reason.* She interrupted Georgiou's battle preparations: "Captain, I have a plan to—"

"Not now, Number One. Focus on getting our shields back to full."

"Sir, if I'm correct, we might persuade Captain Pike to—"

"He's done talking, Number One. And so am I. Now get those shields up!"

Vexed by the captain's dismissal, Burnham searched her console for options. Cycling through the command systems at her disposal, she found one that offered a glimmer of hope: a command-confirmation subchannel remained in place between the *Shenzhou*'s tractor-beam control system and the sciences console on the bridge of the *Enterprise*.

Burnham worked quickly to take advantage of her discovery. She isolated the subchannel and placed it under her exclusive control. Next she rendered it invisible to the *Shenzhou*'s communications and security systems by patching it directly to the ship's primary subspace transceiver circuit. Now she would be able to use the subchannel as a private conduit to send an e-comm message directly to the *Enterprise*'s science officer.

It was a long shot. Burnham had known Lieutenant Spock when they both were children, but it had been many years since they had seen or even spoken to each other in passing. She had no idea what he might really think of her, or if he would even accept her transmission. If he were a by-the-book officer, he might report her attempted communication to his superiors, who would be just as likely to review it as to simply order the subchannel terminated without reading what she'd had to say. And even if he accepted her message, would he be inclined to trust her enough to risk challenging his own chain of command to deliver her missive to Pike?

Let's hope he judges that the "logical" thing to do. Burnham composed her message as swiftly as she was able, pausing only a few times momentarily to satisfy the captain's request for improvements in the *Shenzhou*'s shield emitter output.

As she neared the end of her e-comm, Gant announced from tactical, "*Enterprise* is charging phasers and targeting our engines."

From the helm, Detmer asked, "Evasive turn, Captain?"

"Hold." Georgiou's voice was as firm as steel. "This is where we make our stand."

There was no more time for Burnham to fine-tune her message. She sent it in a single burst transmission to the *Enterprise*—and hoped in silence that her gamble on the goodwill of Spock, son of Sarek and Amanda, had not been made in vain.

9

Ensign Lao Shin's words echoed in Pike's ears, an invitation to calamity: "Ready to fire, sir."

Pike was torn between patriotism and pride. The former made him balk at the notion of opening fire on another Starfleet crew, especially one that was making a stand on principle; the latter left him stewing in anger at being made to look the fool by having his bluff called. But was it a bluff? He had fully intended to make good on his promise to fire when this confrontation began. After all, if he was willing to sacrifice more than three hundred thousand civilians, what difference would a few hundred more lives make? But that had been when the only lives at stake were mere abstractions to him, people he had never met or seen. Now, faced with the prospect of taking lives at point-blank range by destroying a ship of the line, Pike found himself sick at the idea of taking his place in history's dark hall of fame—the one reserved for mass murderers who were "only following orders."

His silence filled the bridge with a palpable unease. So many eyes were on him, awaiting his order to begin the carnage they all clearly dreaded. The only member of the bridge crew not judging him was Lieutenant Spock, whose attention seemed riveted to the hooded sensor display at his station. Hoping to procrastinate just a moment longer before triggering Armageddon, Pike asked his science officer, "Something I should know, Mister Spock?"

Spock looked up, then stood still. His expression and silence betrayed his confusion. After a few seconds of thought, Spock left his post to approach Pike's command chair. As he did so, Commander Una moved to intercept him. They arrived together at Pike's side.

Una confronted Spock. "Why did you leave your post, Lieutenant?"

Though Spock acknowledged Una's presence, he spoke directly to Pike, his voice hushed. "Captain, I request that we postpone the attack."

Pike took a stern tack, though he was secretly hopeful that Spock could give him a plausible reason to stand down. "On what grounds, Mister Spock?"

"I just received a clandestine communication from the first officer of the *Shenzhou*."

That rankled Una. "Clandestine? By what means, Mister Spock?"

"The command-confirmation subchannel linking my station with the *Shenzhou*'s tractor beam system. A rather ingenious contrivance, considering its impromptu nature."

"You two can draw me a diagram later," Pike said. "What did her message say?"

"She believes she has a plan for neutralizing the Juggernaut's offensive capabilities before its next attack." Spock paused to note Una's suspicious demeanor, then continued, "To accomplish this objective, she wants me to ask you for two things: a three-hour grace period in which to act . . . and my assistance."

The second item led Pike to emulate his first officer's wariness. "*Your* help?"

"Yes, sir. She was most specific."

Una and Pike exchanged looks of concern, and she read it correctly as her cue to take over the questioning of Spock. "Why is she asking for *you*?"

"I did not have an opportunity to inquire. Our communication was somewhat one-sided."

There was an evasiveness to Spock's manner that told Pike something was amiss with this situation, and he couldn't embrace the opportunity it provided until he knew exactly what he was getting himself, his crew, and his ship into. "Time for full disclosure, Mister Spock. Who is the *Shenzhou*'s XO to you?"

"Her name is Michael Burnham," Spock said. "She is . . . a friend of my family."

Pike was confused. "How well do you know her?"

"She is a few years older than I am, so we rarely moved in the same social or academic circles. If not for her connection to my parents, I would barely know of her at all."

Having more facts had not made the matter any clearer to Pike. "Never mind the trip down memory lane, then. The big question is, can we trust her?"

"The alternative," Spock said, "would be to sacrifice the lives of more than three hundred sixty thousand sentient beings, and destroy the ecosystem of a healthy planet, when they might otherwise have been saved. If there is a chance that Lieutenant Burnham's plan might work, I think that as Starfleet officers we have a duty to attempt it before resorting to drastic measures."

"He makes a good point," Una said. "If we can fix this mess by loaning Spock to the *Shenzhou*'s XO for a few hours, that sounds like a best-case scenario."

Pike gave her his canniest side-eye. "Easy for you to say, Number One. You aren't the one who'll have to answer to

Admiral Anderson if this goes wrong." He asked Spock, "Are you up for this, Lieutenant?"

"Yes, sir." There was no hesitation in Spock's answer. No pride, either.

"Very well. Grab whatever gear you'll need, then get to the transporter room. As soon as we clear all this with Captain Georgiou, we'll beam you over to the *Shenzhou*."

"Understood, Captain." Spock nodded once to Una, then headed for the turbolift.

As soon as the science officer had departed, Pike beckoned Una to lean closer so he could confide in her without the rest of the crew overhearing. "This is the last reprieve I can give to Georgiou and her crew. If this Burnham can't knock out the Juggernaut in three hours, we have no choice but to proceed as ordered. Is that understood, Number One?"

"Absolutely, Captain. But I trust Spock to get this done."

"I hope you're right," Pike said. "Your faith in him is the only reason I'm taking this risk." He leaned away from her and straightened his posture in the center seat. "Garison, open a channel to the *Shenzhou*." To himself he muttered, "Time for me to eat some humble pie."

Through the ready room's door panel speaker, Burnham heard Captain Georgiou say in a stern voice, *"Come."* The door slid open, admitting Burnham to the captain's sanctum.

With the *Shenzhou* and the *Enterprise* both returned to standard orbits, the aft-facing viewports of the ready room afforded an excellent head-on view of the *Constitution*-class starship, which now was only a few kilometers behind the *Shenzhou*. Below it sprawled the bluish-white orb of Sirsa III, and above it yawned an endless darkness salted with stars.

The door closed. Burnham turned to her right, toward Georgiou's desk. There the captain sat, hands folded in front of her. Her countenance was grave. She lifted her gaze to assess Burnham as she approached, and only once the acting first officer halted in front of her desk did the captain secure their meeting from the bridge crew's insatiable curiosity by uttering two simple words: "Computer. Privacy." The transparent-aluminum panels of the ready room's doors frosted an opaque white, and sound-canceling pulses resonated through it.

Not a good sign, Burnham realized.

Georgiou shook her head. "I honestly don't know what to say to you right now. On the one hand, maybe I ought to thank you for giving us an alternative to a violent showdown with the *Enterprise*. On the other, I'm sorely tempted to give your job to Saru and have you court-martialed for insubordination. Can you give me any good reasons why I shouldn't?"

"As you said, I helped prevent a potentially deadly conflict with another Starfleet vessel and crew. And if you wish to check the bridge's security logs, I think you will find that I did try to present my plan to you first."

The captain's eyes narrowed. "And you think that excuses what you did? Has it occurred to you, Number One, that there might be any number of situations in which a commanding officer might not be open to your suggestions?"

The question was a rhetorical trap, one to which Burnham was obliged to submit. She masked her annoyance as she replied, "Of course."

"And do you think having your suggestion refused entitles you to act upon it anyway? Because I'm having trouble recalling any part of Starfleet's regulations that empowers first officers to supplant their commanding officers' judgment with their own."

Burnham saw that she needed to shift the narrative frame of the captain's inquiry. "Would it improve your perception of the matter if I explained that I merely sought to employ an information-warfare tactic in order to enable your opponent to stand down without losing face?"

It was obvious Georgiou was not yet persuaded, but her interest was snared. "Explain."

"Captain Pike is a young commanding officer," Burnham said, "and a proud one. Given that he was acting on orders from our mutual superiors, his pride as a commanding officer was bound up in his success or failure in the execution of those orders. He could not stand down just because you opposed him; to do so would have undermined his authority. So I presented him with an alternative scenario, one that he could propose to you, and in so doing recover the proactive role in the negotiation. I enabled Pike to avoid embarrassment, by helping him offer you an alternative to combat that I knew you would find acceptable. It was, in my opinion, the most logical resolution to a most unfortunate confrontation."

The captain weighed that argument while holding Burnham in place with her unyielding stare. It often seemed to Burnham that Georgiou would have made an excellent poker player, if not for the captain's general aversion to games.

"That'll work for my log," Georgiou said. "Though if anyone ever asks, this meeting never happened. Is that clear?"

"Perfectly, Captain."

Georgiou reclined her chair and crossed her legs. "So, was it just coincidence that the *Enterprise* officer you chose as your back channel was Spock, son of Sarek?"

"It was a fortunate happenstance that his console was the one linked to our systems."

"But that doesn't explain why you asked for him specifically to work with you, does it?"

Burnham answered with an evasive truth. "I asked for his assistance because I think he is the best qualified officer available to assist me."

"Based on what criteria?"

Does the captain think I have ulterior motives? It was hard for Burnham not to feel as if she were on trial. "I need an investigative partner," she said. "One whose training, mental discipline, and foundations in logic are comparable to, and compatible with, my own."

"Why not Pike's first officer? I hear his Number One is no slouch, in any regard."

A polite nod of demurral. "While I have the utmost respect for Commander Una and her Illyrian mental conditioning, I think I will find it easier to build a working relationship quickly with someone of a more . . . *Vulcan* temperament."

"I see." Georgiou stood and circled her desk to stand in front of Burnham. "I'm going to take your word for this, Michael, because we don't have a lot of time. If I approve this meeting of the minds, are you sure you can find a solution in under three hours?"

"No," Burnham said, unwilling to lie to her captain and friend. "But I *am* certain that thousands of innocent lives will be lost if we do *not* attempt this."

Georgiou's grim resolve turned to a look of quiet hope

in the face of impossible odds. "All right, then. Good talk, Number One." She lifted her chin toward the door. "Get to work."

"Aye, sir." Burnham accepted the informal dismissal and escaped to the bridge, then to the turbolift, before Georgiou had time to reconsider.

Burnham headed for the transporter room, where her next official duty would be to welcome to the *Shenzhou* the one person in the galaxy she had hoped never to see again, and who would now be coming aboard at her invitation.

I get the distinct impression this constitutes a working definition of irony.

10

A golden shimmer and a mellifluous droning washed away the familiar gray confines of the *Enterprise*'s transporter room and delivered Spock to its counterpart inside the *Shenzhou*. He noticed immediately that the two compartments were laid out very differently. Whereas the *Enterprise*'s transporter room consisted of a dais with six energizer pads in front of the console, on the *Shenzhou* the energizer pads were larger and mounted on a curved bulkhead behind a semicircular dais. Also of note to Spock was the darker ambience of the *Shenzhou*'s transporter room and its more spacious nature.

The transporter operator left the room as soon as the materialization sequence was completed. Standing in front of the console was a sole officer, a human woman whose blue utility uniform sported piping and side panels of command gold and was adorned by a lieutenant's rank insignia. She greeted Spock with a polite dip of her chin. "Lieutenant Spock. Welcome aboard the *Shenzhou*."

"Thank you." He stepped off the dais into the empty space between them.

She met him halfway and offered him her hand. "Thank you for coming."

They shook hands for less than a second, her brown

fingers contrasting with Spock's pale digits. He had learned from a young age to minimize unnecessary physical contact with others, because it carried an elevated risk of triggering his touch-based Vulcan telepathy. Even though Spock was half-human, he had inherited powerful psionic talents from his Vulcan father, Sarek. Consequently, the danger of accidental telepathic contact was greater for Spock than it was for even some full-blooded Vulcans. It was a talent he took great care not to advertise or abuse.

He folded his hands behind his back. "How may I be of service, Lieutenant?"

"Please," Burnham said, "you can call me Michael. Or if that's too familiar—"

"I think it would be best if we kept our association professional," Spock said.

His suggestion made Burnham self-conscious. Then her human mannerisms shifted, and her affect took on an almost Vulcan coldness. "As you prefer, Mister Spock." She gestured toward the room's exit. "Follow me, please."

He fell in at her side as they left the transporter room and strolled the corridors of the *Shenzhou*. Once again Spock noted marked differences in the interior of the *Walker*-class ship from that of the *Enterprise*. Aboard the *Shenzhou* the grays were darker, and the bulkheads' orientations more angular. It was clear to him that the two ships had been designed and constructed in different eras, according to very different aesthetic standards. Such drastic changes in a short span of time were not unusual among the humans of Earth, though it had proved a constant source of bemusement among their Vulcan and Andorian allies.

Awkward silence filled the spaces between Spock and Burnham while they walked. The human woman turned a wary look Spock's way. "How is your father, Mister Spock?"

How was he to answer without prevarication? "I am told he is well."

"You're told? You mean by Amanda?"

"By my mother, yes." It taxed Spock's hard-won emotional control not to betray how deeply it bothered him to hear Burnham refer to his mother in so familiar a manner.

Burnham seemed confused by Spock's elision. "So you've not spoken with Sarek?"

"Not in four years, ten months, and seventeen days."

"Ah." She halted and beckoned Spock toward a turbolift as she pressed the call button. They waited only a few seconds before a lift car arrived, and the doors slid apart. She motioned him inside, stepped in behind him, then said to the computer, "Science lab four."

The doors closed, and the lift car shot into motion with hardly any sensation of movement. Spock noted the profusion of display screens that ringed the top of the lift car, and the complexity of the interface screens placed at eye level. He preferred the austerity of the *Enterprise*'s turbolifts, with their dearth of distractions and an optional control handle.

Burnham's inquiry nagged at him, though it taxed his logic to ascertain why. He put aside any consideration of his motives and asked her, "When did you last speak with Sarek?"

The first officer rolled her eyes. "Not as long ago as you did . . . but it's been a while."

"I see. . . . And Amanda?"

"Even longer." That was all Burnham said, and her tone made it clear that was all she intended to say on that subject. The turbolift halted, and she led him out onto another deck of the *Shenzhou*'s saucer, then into one of its curving outer corridors. "This way."

Hoping to elicit some sense of what she had in store for

him, he said, "May I ask, Lieutenant, why you requested my assistance specifically?"

She looked askance at Spock. "I hope you won't misinterpret this as a boast or as racism born of a stereotype . . . but I'm reasonably sure you're the only person on both our ships who might be able to keep up with me once I get started on this."

Spock nodded. He required no explanation from Burnham; he knew of her family history, her youth and education on Vulcan, and the groundbreaking circumstances of her admittance to the Vulcan Science Academy. She possessed an unusual degree of mental conditioning for a human; it was unlikely that any of her shipmates truly deserved to be called her peers.

"Very well. Your message to me on the *Enterprise* indicated that you had developed a plan for infiltrating the Juggernaut. Is that what you've asked me here to evaluate?"

Suddenly, Burnham's affect turned sheepish. "Um, not exactly."

"I do not understand."

"When I said I had a way inside the Juggernaut . . . I might have overstated the matter."

Spock raised one eyebrow in subtle condemnation. "You lied?"

"I exaggerated." She stopped and keyed in a code that opened the door to a superbly well-equipped research lab, then tried to placate Spock with a crooked smile. "What do you want me to say? I'm kind of making this up as I go." She gestured toward the lab. "Shall we?"

He followed her inside, wondering every step of the way what his rigid taskmaster of a father had ever seen in this impetuous, irreverent human woman.

—

Never before in his life had Saru seen such a profusion of documentation that imparted so little information. When he considered that nearly all of his adult life had been spent in Starfleet, his dismay only deepened. Few organizations embraced the mind-numbing drudgery of bureaucracy with the zeal of a technocratic military exploration agency, but apparently the combination of Federation governmental administration and the private corporation behind the colonization of Sirsa III had put to shame the inveterate paper-pushers of Starfleet Command.

All these words for naught . . . it reads like verbal camouflage.

He began to hope he might be near the end of the colony's application paper trail when an incoming message popped up on his console. In the scant delay between when he received the message and when he opened it, Ensign Connor appeared at his side to say, "I just sent you the next round of files on the Sirsa III planetary survey."

Saru fixed the young human man with a weary glare. "Forgive me, Yeoman, but did you say 'next'? Are you sure you didn't mean to say 'last'?"

"No, I said 'next,' sir. There are two more still to be sent from Earth."

"Of course there are. Carry on, Yeoman." Saru shook his head at his console while Connor headed aft, toward the captain's ready room. *Clearly, someone at Starfleet Command hates me and has waited until now to exact their vengeance.*

The jungle of red tape and triplicate survey data proliferated across Saru's console. There was an almost hypnotic quality to its repetitions—an effect achieved, he realized, by the use of automated survey drones to gather the legally required data about the planet. Unlike manually generated surveys, which were subject to random tiny shifts in such details as flight path or velocity, repeated scans by auto-mated drones were often nearly perfect in their elimination of unnecessary variables. It created a uniformity to related data sets. Saru appreciated that.

His eyes snapped open and his head jerked back—a sud-den waking from the soporific lull of bland sensor data. As soon as Saru realized what had just happened, he felt shame and wanted to retreat and seek cover—his species' instinc-tual response. He fought against it and straightened his posture. *Perhaps no one noticed.*

He cast furtive glances around the bridge in search of accusatory stares. All was well to port side . . . but when he glanced to starboard, he was met by the black eyes of Lieutenant Frel glasch Negg, the ship's lone Tellarite crew member. Negg cracked an arrogant smirk. "Something spook you, sir?"

It felt imperative to Saru to deny the implied accusation. "I have no idea what you're talking about." Only after he'd spoken did he realize his response had drawn attention to his exchange with Negg that hadn't existed before. *Damn.*

From the aft engineering station, Ensign Britch Weeton quipped, "Are we keeping you awake, sir? Should we work more quietly?"

His professionalism impugned, Saru turned to con-front the engineering officer. "In case you have forgotten, Ensign Weeton, I am no longer just the senior science of-ficer of this ship. I am now also third-in-command of this vessel—and, in either case, your superior officer. Facts that you and your would-be fellow jesters would be well advised to remember."

It was a heavy-handed approach to such a minor bit of ribbing, but it achieved Saru's desired outcome: now everyone's focus was on Weeton and his verbal gaffe. The ensign withered quickly from the heat of the bridge crew's collective attention and turned back toward his console to take refuge in his work. Seconds later, everyone else did the same.

Saru breathed a quiet sigh of relief. *Too close. Have to drink more of that—what did they call it in the mess?* He searched his memory. *Ah, yes. Coffee. Definitely need more of that.*

Poring over the new documents, Saru noted movement in his peripheral vision—someone coming toward him. He turned to meet the arrival of Ensign Januzzi. "Yes, Ensign?"

The shaved-headed human allayed Saru's apprehension with a kind smile. "Sir. Everything's five by five on the life-support station. I wanted to see if there was anything I could do to help you go through all this new intel Connor dumped on you."

"Well, I—yes, actually." Saru relaxed, grateful for the offer of help. "If it would be convenient, I could transfer the latest batch of files to your station for analysis."

Januzzi nodded. "It'd be my pleasure, sir."

"Thank you, Ensign." As he keyed in the command to send the files to Januzzi's duty station, he added, "We're looking for an explanation as to how the planetary survey missed all signs of the Juggernaut's presence under the seabed, as well as any other suspect anomalies."

"Understood, sir. Should I alert you as soon as I find something, or would you prefer a more complete analysis before I make my report?"

"Notify me at once if you find anything that gives you cause for alarm or suspicion."

"Yes, sir." Januzzi returned to his duty station and set himself to work with an intensity that Saru found admirable. In the months since Januzzi had transferred aboard, Saru had noticed how quickly the young officer had grown popular among his shipmates. At first Saru had chalked it up to the man's habit of volunteering to assist fellow bridge officers with seemingly mundane tasks or to cover their duty shifts whenever they needed time off. But the more that Saru had observed Januzzi's interactions with other *Shenzhou* crew, including enlisted personnel, the more he had come to admire the man's genuine affection for others.

It occurs to me, Saru thought, *that I have never heard Januzzi speak in derision or envy of a crewmate. If that is a true representation of his inner self, he is a rare person, indeed.*

He set his mind back to work on the mound of raw data with which he had been deluged. It was not reasonable to attempt to compare such huge data sets manually. He programmed a filter to identify points of diversion in the behavior and logged results of the survey drones. As it ran, he wondered how much deviation from one scan to the next would be considered within normal parameters. Starfleet's own survey protocols tended to be more exacting than—

An alert warbled on Saru's console. He paused the filter's comparison analysis. Then he stared, dumbstruck, at the absurdly implausible result it had flagged.

He was considering his next course of action when Januzzi stood from his own post and crossed the bridge at a quick step to stand beside him. "Sir, I think I found something."

"Let me guess, Ensign: an excess of data commonality—"

"—centered on the exact location where the Juggernaut was found," Januzzi said, simultaneously finishing and confirming Saru's damning observation.

Strings of telemetry from what were supposed to have been three separate drone passes were superimposed over one another on Saru's screen. While the flight recorder data from the drone was ever so minutely different on each fly-over, its sensor sweeps had somehow yielded fully identical data sets—something that, given the realities of molecular decay and shifts in water currents and temperatures, should have been impossible. But unless someone had searched for this kind of data artifact, it would likely have gone unnoticed in perpetuity.

But there it was. As plain to see as sunlight penetrating the depths of a cave.

Januzzi leaned in and spoke more softly. "Sir, would I be correct to say that the data strings we've highlighted look a lot like tampering?"

"Yes, Ensign, I think you would be." He turned and faced Januzzi. "How would you feel about helping me locate evidence to confirm this?"

"Whatever you need, sir."

Saru liked this man more with each passing minute. "Then let's get to work, Mister Januzzi. If I'm correct, we have a conspiracy to expose."

The more time Burnham spent in Spock's presence, the more she disliked him. The son of Sarek of Vulcan and Amanda Grayson of Earth seemed to relish contradicting Burnham and undermining her hypotheses. It was not a behavior that Burnham found endearing.

"Much of your information appears to be speculative, at best," Spock said. "I doubt it would be possible to draw a defensible conclusion based on such limited data."

Condescending and judgmental, just like his father,

Burnham fumed, while at the same time struggling to maintain a neutral façade for Spock's benefit. "We've analyzed the signals being sent from the Juggernaut. Though some of its output appears to be correlated to its launch of attack drones, other, repeating portions of its sonic emissions don't seem to bear any relation to its past, current, or upcoming actions."

"At best, an unsupported supposition," Spock said. "At worst, a possibly fatal error."

She wanted to throttle him—a reaction whose ferocity surprised her. It was rare for anyone to get under Burnham's skin. Ever since her youth on Vulcan she had cultivated a patience and a reservoir of calm rarely enjoyed by Terran humans. But something about Spock—his way of speaking, his near-perfect air of detachment—drove Burnham to distraction. He seemed to embody so effortlessly all that she had so long struggled to become, and it vexed her.

She called up a series of audio waveform images on one of the science lab's viewscreens. "Can we agree, at least, that these signals all started subsequent to the Arcadia Explorer's drilling accident in relation to the Juggernaut?"

"I remain unconvinced that the incident was, in fact, an accident," Spock said. "The odds of an encounter between the drilling platform and the Juggernaut occurring purely at random this early in the drilling rig's operational life-span are extremely remote."

How many times would this ice-blooded Vulcan—*half-Vulcan*—make her rephrase the same question? "Will you concede that the emission of these signals from the Juggernaut was subsequent to the most recent incident with the Arcadia Explorer, regardless of its nature?"

If the *Enterprise*'s science officer was aware that he was

annoying Burnham, he did an excellent job of concealing his awareness. "I will so stipulate, yes."

"Hallelujah," Burnham grumbled. She side-eyed Spock. "It's a Terran expression—"

"I am aware of its meaning, and of its apparent relevance to our exchange."

Even when he tried to be agreeable and forthcoming, he made Burnham furious. Determined not to let him derail her deductive process, she resorted to her long-ago Vulcan education to purge her mind of emotional undertows, so that logic could give order to her thoughts upon a serene surface composed of reason. "Mister Spock, are you aware of the work conducted over the past several decades by Doctor Egot Huln of Denobula, concerning the use of infrasonic pulses as a means of influencing behavior in sapient humanoids?"

"I am. I found many of Doctor Huln's theories quite provocative."

"As did I. Recall, please, Doctor Huln's proposition concerning the use of infrasonic signals to attract primitive humanoids for xenoanthropological testing. Did not the signal waveform that he postulated as being potentially the most efficacious match that emitted by the Juggernaut, to within three-thousandths of a frequency?"

"It did."

"And were not the period and amplitude hypothesized by Doctor Huln markedly similar to those employed by the Juggernaut?"

"They were," Spock said. "Though I feel compelled to note that similar frequencies, as well as other identifying factors, have been shown to occur in nature."

Burnham took a breath, partly to cool her ire, but also to give Spock time to register her dissent. "In nature,

Mister Spock? Need I remind you this is not some pulsar, nor some quasi-aware planetoid using tectonic vibration to control its ecosphere. This is a starship of unknown alien origin and design. For a synthetic construct to emit such pulses—"

"You are assuming it to be synthetic," Spock cut in. "Long-range scouts have reported encountering space-faring life-forms whose physiology gives them the appearance of uncrewed starships. Pending the outcome of a more thorough investigation of the Juggernaut, it might be premature to declare it a synthetic construct rather than one of biomechanoid origin."

If I break his nose, will he question whether it's really broken? "For the purpose of our discussion, let's put aside for now the question of the Juggernaut's true nature. Would you concur that its emission of these signals comports with the majority of the postulates put forth by Doctor Huln in his treatise on infrasonic control of humanoid psychology?"

"I would."

Finally, some progress. Burnham wondered whether Spock's resistance to her ideas, and his penchant for sandbagging her efforts to move their exploration forward, was rooted somehow in their peculiar shared history as it concerned his parents. She was tempted to ask, but she feared that broaching the subject directly would only alienate him further, and bolster his rationale for treating her own logic as somehow suspect. Satisfied to build on what little common ground they had established so far, she asked, "If we accept Huln's propositions as valid, what course of action would that suggest we take with regard to the Juggernaut?"

Her question rendered Spock silent for several seconds. He considered the data displayed on the lab's multitude of viewscreens; he pondered the equations and waveforms on the workstation screen he shared with Burnham. "A closer investigation might be warranted."

"To put it another way," Burnham said, "I think we should accept their invitation. You and me, just the two of us."

Her proposition seemed to confound Spock. "I do not understand."

"We beam down to the Juggernaut, pool our experience and efforts, and find a way to gain access to the ship's interior. I have some ideas how we might accomplish that, but—"

Spock silenced her with a raised hand. "You said earlier that you had no plan."

"No, I said I might have overstated the degree to which I had one. In the brief time that you and I have been comparing notes, I feel as if I've made a number of breakthroughs on a subconscious level. Now I'd like for us to beam down together and put them to the test."

The son of Sarek raised an eyebrow at her. "Your methods are most unorthodox."

Burnham couldn't help but smile. "Flattery will get you everywhere, Mister Spock." She quick-stepped toward the door, unable to constrain her enthusiasm for a mission of exploration. "Well? C'mon!" She tapped her wrist, an ancient Terran gesture meant to signal impatience, one of the few things she remembered from early childhood on Earth. "The clock's ticking, Mister Spock, and people are waiting for us to save the day—not to mention their *lives*."

"Sir, I think I have something," Januzzi said, breaking Saru's concentration. Saru turned to face the ensign as he approached Saru's duty station, which stood to starboard behind the captain's chair. "Can you call up the new files I just downloaded from Earth?"

"I should certainly think I could," Saru said, accessing the documents from the ship's main computer. He checked the files' metadata and opened the ones with the most recent download and analysis timestamps. "Rather prodigious documents," he noted.

Januzzi tilted his head in what Saru perceived as a gesture of acquiescence. "That's because they're the original, uncompressed sensor data from the planetary survey."

His revelation transformed Saru's enthusiasm to trepidation. "By what means did you obtain this data, Mister Januzzi?"

A faux-humble shrug. "I might have appealed to a contact at Starfleet Intelligence to remotely access the memory cores inside the probes, which are currently undergoing refit and refueling at the Kayo Mining Consortium's maintenance station in the Ishanee system."

Saru became paralyzed with indecision. This was crucial intelligence, the sort of data that might illuminate otherwise occulted facts. Alas, Januzzi's admission that it might have been acquired by extralegal means left Saru in an ethical quandary. Illegally obtained information was the poisoned fruit of a tainted search, inadmissible in a legal proceeding—but its tactical value to the *Shenzhou*'s ongoing operations might serve to aid its mission and save numerous lives.

Rules of evidence are the JAG's problem, he decided. *The mission comes first.*

"Walk me through what you've found, Mister Januzzi."

Januzzi called up a number of work files he had created, using the new sensor data and the colony's previously submitted files as resources for comparison. "First, notice that the areas we flagged earlier yield very different results when checked against the original logs. In the master files, the data shows the expected variations on each of the three flybys."

"Yes, continue."

"But there's more. Lots more." Januzzi switched the data to display a wider area of the planet's surface. "There were anomalies in other regions, too. I've isolated them for you."

Saru felt as if he were being set up to miss something. "What am I meant to see?"

"I'm not entirely sure, to be honest. My specialty at the Academy was astrophysics." He regarded the sensor data with a good-natured frown. "This is a bit out of my bailiwick."

"I understand." Saru resumed scrutinizing the sensor imagery. "Fascinating. I had no idea that civilian sensor technology had become this sophisticated. Its depth and resolution are—"

A detail in the image all but leaped from his screen, it was so prominent. He applied a series of filters to confirm what he had found. "Oh, my. That's remarkable." He keyed in a series of commands to automate a repetition of the work he had just done, on the other regions of the data that Januzzi had flagged as having been altered. As the computer worked, Saru confided to Januzzi, "If the consortium's modifications of their sensor logs all were made for the same reason, this will be a most serious matter you've brought to light."

"That *we've* brought to light. . . . Sir."

Diligent, efficient, and quick to share credit—Januzzi continued to impress Saru. "Quite correct, Ensign." His console beeped to indicate it had finished its task. "Let's see what we—" Words abandoned Saru as he stared at truths unearthed from the original sensor logs. All his suspicions lay confirmed. "Would you like to know what we've found, Mister Januzzi?"

"Very much, sir."

"Evidence of a primitive civilization." Saru pointed out the pockets of data. "One that encircled the tropical latitudes of this world's land masses more than nine million years ago."

"Nine million?" Januzzi concentrated. "Wasn't that roughly the same length of time that Commander Johar said the Juggernaut had been under the seabed?"

Saru centered the sensor imagery on the coordinates where the Juggernaut had been found. "Yes, Ensign. Those numbers do appear to correlate—though we must take care not to presume a causal relationship between them, absent any evidence of such. That said—" He magnified the image. "Nine million years ago, the Juggernaut would have been standing on dry land, in the midst of one of the densest population clusters of the planet's previous inhabitants."

"That seems unlikely to be a coincidence," Januzzi said.

"I am inclined to concur. Now, given the limitations of the probes' sensors, I could forgive the Kayo Mining Consortium for having mistaken the Juggernaut for an anomalous deposit of duranium and other exotic compounds considered valuable for starship hull manufacturing." He tapped the readings related to the lost cities. "But their tampering with the logs to hide the evidence of these alien settlements . . . that I cannot and will not condone."

Januzzi's affect turned somber. "So, what do we do now, sir?"

Saru closed the documents and entered new orders into his console. "We transmit all our data and findings to Captain Georgiou and to Admiral Anderson at Starfleet Command. The rest"—he sent the damning message with a single tap—"is above our pay grade."

11

Few offenses angered Christopher Pike as profoundly as being lied to. He couldn't help but interpret it as a slight; it was an insult to his intelligence for someone to assume he wouldn't find out, and a show of disrespect for his authority as a starship commander. It didn't matter whether the prevaricator was enlisted, commissioned, civilian, or—in the case of Governor Gretchen Kolova—elected. If anything, Kolova's position as the leader of the Sirsa III colony meant that Pike expected her to uphold a higher standard.

Kolova looked back at him from the right side of the *Enterprise* bridge's main viewscreen, and Captain Georgiou's grim expression filled the left side of the split image. In spite of the accusations Pike and Georgiou had leveled at Kolova when they told her what Saru and Januzzi had found in the original planetary survey data, the governor carried herself with an unrepentant air. *"What do you expect me to say, Captains?"*

Pike was in the mood for a confrontation. "Why don't we start, Governor, with why you concealed this evidence of a prior civilization?"

"That wasn't my call," Kolova said. *"The decision to modify the sensor data was made by the executive board of the Kayo Mining Consortium."*

Her evasion stoked Georgiou's wrath. *"But you were more than happy to go along with it, weren't you, Governor?"*

Kolova maintained a stoic front. *"I didn't know about it when I accepted their appointment as the colony's governor. By the time I and the other colonists learned the sensor logs had been altered, most of us were bound by strict nondisclosure contracts with Kayo."*

"Nondisclosure contracts?" Pike wondered for a cynical moment what century he was living in. "Governor, you withheld evidence of a serious crime. Are you really going to try to justify it by claiming you were silenced by a business agreement?"

Before the governor could answer, Georgiou added, *"Who, besides you, knew about the falsified data? Anyone who knew of this fraud and failed to report it could be criminally liable."*

The captains' double-barreled rhetorical assault prompted Kolova to put on a strained smile. *"In the absence of a subpoena delivered by a duly appointed agent of a civilian court with appropriate jurisdiction, I will not give you names with which to expand your persecution. Second, before you start demanding access to my administration's files and deposing my citizens, I'd suggest you obtain a warrant from the Federation's colonial court."*

Her challenge made all of the *Enterprise*'s bridge officers look up from their respective duty stations to stare at the viewscreen, as if to collectively ask, *Did she really just say that?*

Pike felt the weight of his crew's attention, and he noted also the steely quality that had manifested in Georgiou's eyes. To her he said, "Do you want to take this, or shall I?"

"Let me," Georgiou said. *"Governor Kolova. I don't know*

where you received your legal education, but it seems to me you might have skipped a few chapters pertaining to Federation colonial law. First, because your local law-enforcement authorities have to be considered as possibly corrupted by the same scandal as your administration, your colony's right to police its own offenses is liable to immediate suspension, at the discretion of the ranking Federation authority in the sector—which, unfortunately for you, is me.

"*Second, the Federation's attorney general is, even as we speak, determining whether she will prosecute KMC—and you, and anyone else on Sirsa III who knew about this—for conspiracy to defraud the Federation.*

"*Third, you don't seem to appreciate how grave an offense this is. This wasn't merely a matter of concealing the presence of valuable exploitable resources, though that appears to have played a role in KMC's actions. Your patrons, and subsequently you and anyone else who knew about this, engaged in a pattern of deception to hide the discovery of an extinct alien culture, as well as a previously unknown type of alien starship. Any of you found guilty as accomplices or accessories after the fact might be facing up to ten years in a penal colony.*"

That litany disturbed Kolova's façade. The governor swallowed hard, blinked once. "*If it comes to that, Captains, I would have no choice but to nullify this colony's charter and declare it an independent world, one no longer subject to Federation law.*"

This time, Pike decided to be the bearer of bad news. "I wouldn't recommend that, Governor. Casting off your obligations to the Federation would also mean surrendering the few protections it offers you. For instance, planting your personal flag on a world still classified as a Federation possession would make you invaders—and obligate me and Captain Georgiou to escalate a military response." He

noted a subtly accusatory look from Georgiou, and was reminded that less than an hour had passed since he had been
on the verge of eradicating all life on the planet's surface
without any warning to its residents. Pushing back against
the bitter irony of his position, he said to Kolova, "I think
it's safe to say that's an outcome none of us want."

Kolova acknowledged his warning with a slow nod,
then forced her chin upward once more in a hollow imita-
tion of pride. *"How, then, are we to proceed?"*

"Captain Georgiou and I still need to deal with your
Juggernaut problem. While we're doing that, I'd sug-
gest you prepare your colonists and yourself to abandon
Sirsa III."

"Why?"

Georgiou replied, *"Because, even if by some miracle you
escape prosecution, the Federation will want to document the
remains of the extinct indigenous culture, and the Council
will likely demand an all-new xenoarcheological survey—
one that will require all potential cultural contaminants,
such as you, your colonists, and all your infrastructure, be
removed."*

At last Kolova seemed to resign herself to defeat. *"Very
well, then. I hope you'll forgive me if I at least try to lodge an
appeal for mercy with the Council before they render judgment."*

"Be my guest," Pike said. "Just be sure you pack your
bags while you're doing it."

If the governor had a retort for that, she kept it to herself as she closed her end of the three-way channel. That
left Pike and Georgiou to confer, captain to captain. He
checked the ship's chrono. "Time's slipping away, Captain."

*"Is it? By my reckoning, Burnham still has over two and a
half hours."*

Pike nodded. "Barely that. But if I find out she has no plan to neutralize the Juggernaut, I want you to know I intend to proceed with the orders I have in hand."

"*Yes,*" Georgiou said. "*You've made that quite clear.*" She checked something off-screen. "*I've just been informed Burnham and Spock are beaming down in two minutes. Trust me when I tell you not to underestimate her. She can be quite resourceful.*"

"I could say the same of Spock." Pike recalled a detail from the *Shenzhou*'s briefing about the hidden native civilization. "Your second officer speculated that the planet's indigenous culture went extinct around the same time the Juggernaut went dormant. Did he find any reason to think the two events were connected?"

"*Not yet. But perhaps we might each consider sending an officer down to the planet to look into it. If there is a link, it might yield some kind of clue to help us stop the Juggernaut.*"

It was a reasonable suggestion. Pike glanced to his right and caught his first officer's eye. He saw that she was keen to snag that assignment. He faced Georgiou. "I can spare my first officer, if you have a mission site in mind."

"*The remains of a densely populated settlement lies buried in a cave complex along the coastline closest to the Juggernaut,*" Georgiou said. "*Lieutenant Saru suggests we start any investigation there.*"

"Works for me," Pike said. "Send the coordinates to my transporter chief. I'll have Commander Una meet your man on the surface in ten minutes. *Enterprise* out."

Chief Garison closed the channel as Pike turned to face Una. "Be careful down there, Number One. I've learned a lot of things the hard way in Starfleet—one of them being: extinct civilizations sometimes aren't."

"Your concern is noted, Captain." As Una passed his

chair on her way to the turbolift, she lowered her voice to add with a playful smile, "If I see any ghosts, I'll let you know."

The shimmering golden veil of the transporter dissipated, delivering Spock and Burnham to the back of the Juggernaut. The massive vessel had drifted closer to the shoreline, which appeared as little more than a hairline sketch interrupting the perfection of the horizon.

A stiff gale baptized Burnham with saltwater mist. She winced, palmed the moisture from her face, then reached for her tricorder and switched it on. A few paces away, Spock was already consulting his tricorder and ambling slowly toward the narrow end of the alien vessel. Cycling through sensor modes, he asked, "What are we looking for?"

"An ingress point," Burnham said. "The hull is made of a smart metal that opens and closes without leaving a seam. That was how it launched the drones earlier."

Spock adjusted his tricorder. "I see now what you described as the prevalence of symmetry in the ship's exterior. The tendency manifests even at very small scales, suggesting it might have been grown using biomechanoid materials in a fractal matrix."

"That was my thought, as well," Burnham said. "I had the chance to work with some experimental biomech templates at the Vulcan Science Academy, and they produced textures similar to these." She lowered her tricorder. "I wasn't aware that biomech was on the curriculum at Starfleet Academy these days."

"It isn't." Spock continued to gather tricorder readings. "I do my best to stay apprised of recent advances in a variety of scientific disciplines."

Burnham nodded. "Sensible." She resumed scanning with her tricorder, but she felt distracted. Stealing a look in Spock's direction, she inquired, "If your interests tend toward cutting-edge science, why choose Starfleet?"

His eyebrows lifted in a dignified approximation of surprise. "Starfleet is one of the premier scientific research and exploration entities in—"

"Sorry," she interrupted. "Please don't misunderstand. I'm well aware of Starfleet's bona fides. What I meant to ask was, why choose Starfleet over the Vulcan Science Academy? I'd heard you were offered admission, but turned it down."

Only after she asked the question did Burnham feel self-conscious about it. She had been unable to restrain her curiosity regarding Spock's estrangement from Sarek and his troubled relationship with Amanda, but as she watched him grapple in silence with what she presumed were difficult emotions, she feared she had pushed too far into a private matter.

He frowned for only a moment, but it was enough to warn Burnham she had struck a nerve. "My application to the Vulcan Science Academy was tendered by my father. Though their invitation honored me, I had by that time already elected to seek a Starfleet commission." His focus turned inward. "A decision to which my father took great exception."

"I see."

It sounded like an empty platitude, but Burnham felt as if she truly understood Spock's dilemma. Sarek was a formidable personality, one unaccustomed to being refused by those from whom he expected fealty.

Spock resumed his scanning. "I was given to understand that you graduated with highest honors from the Vulcan Science Academy."

"I did." She followed him as he turned his steps toward the opposite end of the vessel.

"With such credentials, you could have pursued a promising career on Vulcan, in academia, or in scientific research. Yet you also chose to join Starfleet. Why?"

She was unsure how much of the truth to share with him. "Because Sarek told me to."

The whole truth, as ever, was far more complicated. Sarek and Amanda had served as Burnham's foster family after the deaths of her parents when she was a young child just starting her education on Vulcan. Never in all the years that they had looked after her had they asked for her gratitude; all Sarek had ever wanted from Burnham was her dutiful obedience. After she had finished her studies at the Vulcan Science Academy, and having been denied a position with the Vulcan Expeditionary Group, she had acquiesced to Sarek's insistence that she accept a commission from Starfleet instead. He had told her that he hoped it might help her reconnect with her humanity—though why a Vulcan mentor would desire that for his protégée, Burnham could not imagine.

Since then she had hidden her discomfort at living and working among non-Vulcans—just as she had concealed her lingering resentment at Sarek for effectively casting her out of the only world that had ever made any sense to her.

But now she was here with Spock, the much-lauded scion of the great Ambassador Sarek, the heir to one of the most ancient and respected family dynasties on Vulcan, and all she could think about was, *What could possibly have driven him to spurn everything I wish I had?*

Spock seemed equally befuddled by her. "Did acceding to Sarek's request—"

"It was more of a demand," Burnham corrected.

He pressed on. "Did your compliance earn you Sarek's approval?"

She almost laughed, until her Vulcan conditioning diminished her response to a taut half smile. "I am not sure anything anyone has ever done has met with Sarek's approval." Suddenly concerned she might have offended Spock, she added, "Present company excluded, of course."

"Not as much as one might suppose," Spock said. "He has never understood why I would want to live and work among non-Vulcans, and in particular among humans." His thick brows knitted together as he noticed something on his tricorder display, then he quickened his steps.

Burnham picked up her pace to stay alongside Spock. "Have you ever considered requesting a transfer to one of the new, all-Vulcan Starfleet crews?"

"Such as the one on the *Intrepid*?" He shook his head. "No." Then he stopped and trained his piercing gaze on her. "Have you?"

"I've thought about it," she lied, not wanting to admit that her inquiry about a transfer to the *Intrepid* had been coldly rebuffed. Even so, her fear that Georgiou harbored doubts about her readiness to serve as the *Shenzhou*'s first officer had her thinking of trying her luck with the next all-Vulcan crew, which was being assembled for the *Starship Persepolis*.

Walking again, Spock split his attention between Burnham and the path ahead. "I doubt either of us would be welcomed among Vulcan crews. As quick as they are to profess the wisdom of IDIC, they remain in many ways quite provincial."

It pained Burnham to admit to herself that Spock was likely correct. IDIC—the Vulcan philosophy that extolled the virtue of Infinite Diversity in Infinite Combinations—all too often was honored in its breach rather than its obser-vance. *If someone as famous as Spock, son of Sarek, thinks he'd be* persona non grata *on an all-Vulcan ship, what chance will I ever have?*

She rebelled against a swell of desperation and com-pelled her mind into emotional silence. It took all of her Vulcan conditioning to purge her psyche of its toxic brew of regret, guilt, anger, and so many other intermingled feelings that defied definition, but when it was done, the blessed quiet of logic was her reward.

Once more Spock quickened his pace. Burnham matched his stride. "What are we moving toward in such a hurry, Mister Spock?"

"If I am correct," he said, checking his tricorder, "I might have found the ingress point you seek. I have no idea how it might function, or if there is any way for us to make use of it, but now that you have shown me the pattern, I can confirm your suspicion: it is there."

"Outstanding," Burnham said. "Let's go see what's in-side this thing."

After the blissful song and seclusion of the transporter beam faded away, Saru was left with only the far-off hush of waves breaking against a rocky shore, and the whispering of the wind across a terrifyingly open sprawl of grassland and dunes. He had beamed down alone from the *Shenzhou*. At the time the beam-down site had seemed to be a matter of little importance, but as he regarded the vast and empty coastline, he began to feel exposed. To a Kelpien, stand-ing alone in the open was tantamount to suicide. It felt to Saru as if he were begging some unseen alien predator to devour him.

He tightened his grip on his phaser and listened for the padding of paws across sand, or the susurrus of a legless horror slithering through the yellowed grass. To most other sapient bipeds such sounds were barely audible; to a Kelpien they were clarion cries of danger.

His heightened senses fixed upon a sonorous droning. Insects? An avian call? Within half a second Saru relaxed as he recognized the pitch and oscillation of a post-2253 Starfleet personnel transporter's annular confinement beam disrupting the local atmosphere just a few meters from where he was standing. Not wanting to give a misleading impression to his colleague, Saru removed his hand from his phaser. He stood at attention while he waited for the golden scintillation of the beam to resolve into the familiar shape of a humanoid female wearing a pale beige turtleneck tunic, black trousers, tall boots, and a small backpack. As the energy surrounding her dissipated, he saw that she was tall for her species, dark-haired, and wore insignia that identified her as a commander.

Only after the last remnants of the beam had vanished did Saru see her clearly. She turned just enough to face him, and she met his formal at-attention pose with a disarming smile. "You must be Lieutenant Saru," she said, offering him her hand in friendship.

He relaxed and shook her hand. "You must be Commander Una."

"In the flesh." She let go of his hand.

Then she regarded him with a curious double take. He wondered why until he realized that it was his own fault. "My apologies, Commander. I didn't mean to stare."

"It's all right. It's nice to be found interesting." A coy look. "Might I ask why?"

Having been caught out, he felt obliged to explain

himself. "If I might speak candidly?" Reassured by her nod of assent, he continued. "When first I saw you, I perceived you to be human. But then, when you met my gaze . . . I felt that you were not like most Terran humans. You share many of their physiological identifiers, yet you do not seem to be one of them." He feared he had said too much or maybe even given offense. "But perhaps I'm mistaken."

"No, your senses do you credit," Una said. "My biology is human, but I was born and raised on Illyria, in accordance with their traditions."

Upon hearing her explanation, Saru understood and was relieved to learn his instincts remained as keen as ever. "An Illyrian," he said. "That explains it. Mentally disciplined, pacifist by nature, vegetarian—those and microgestures specific to your culture explain why you don't project the 'apex-predator' vibe that I feel from so many other humanoids."

His comments seemed to both flatter and embarrass Una. "Yes, I've heard that before. From Vulcans, for one example. And from the Choblik." She bowed her head by the slightest degree. "I take it as the highest of compliments, and offer you my thanks."

"You are more than welcome, Commander." It was a rare thing for Saru to feel an instant kinship with anyone other than another Kelpien, but he felt it for Una. She reminded him of the small team of Starfleet officers who had rescued him from certain death on his homeworld many years earlier. They, too, had given off the vibe of "evolved beings," a quality of their essential nature that had made them fascinating to him: sentient creatures who possessed the attributes of an apex predator, but also the empathy and compassion of a fellow prey animal. Just as their assurances had done so long ago, Una's kind overtures put Saru at ease.

He gestured toward her tricorder. "Commander, did you have a chance to review my report on the suppressed evidence of a primitive indigenous civilization here on Sirsa III?"

"I did," Una said. "I was impressed you could compile something so detailed and so eloquent in so brief a time. It's clear to me why you're not just the *Shenzhou*'s senior science officer but also its second officer: skill sets and discipline such as yours are rare, indeed."

If she were Kelpien, I would fall in love with her.

"Most kind of you to say, Commander." He lifted his own tricorder and verified their position, and the bearing to their destination. With a westward wave, he said, "The entrance to the cave complex is fewer than two hundred meters in this direction. Shall we proceed?"

"With all dispatch," Una said. She started walking, and Saru stayed by her side.

Together they navigated a narrow path through a rocky cliff face that ran the length of the peninsula. As the space around them closed in, Saru felt his anxiety start to rise. Just as it was nerve-racking for him to be in a wide-open place, it was troubling to move in overly confined areas. If an attack were to come, to where would he flee? Where could he take cover? The nadir of a canyon was just as dangerous a place to be as the middle of a desolate plain.

Perhaps sensing his growing unease, Una took the lead and made a point of looking back every dozen steps to check on Saru. She asked, "How do you like serving on the *Shenzhou*?"

"It's an amazing ship, despite its age," Saru said. He was grateful for the distraction of small talk. "And Captain Georgiou is a remarkable commanding officer."

Una nodded as she looked back. "Yes, her reputation precedes her." Ten steps later, she asked, "Are you the only Kelpien in Starfleet?"

"So far as I know, yes. My people, alas, tend to be risk averse." He felt a twinge of shame as he considered the shortcomings of his species. "But I hope to change that one day."

"I sympathize," Una said. "It can be hard to feel like an outsider even among one's shipmates. Especially for people like you and me—creatures of peace, surrounded by those whose natural instincts drive them toward violence."

It felt to Saru almost as if she were reading his mind. "Yes! It's excruciating at times to be a scientist, an *explorer*, in a culture dominated, in however benign a fashion, by soldiers. So many times I've dreamed of—"

His threat ganglia danced to life, emerging in a mad dance above his ears. Fear constricted his throat and arrested him in midstep. His sense of peril had been triggered by a scent of something with blood on its breath, the scrape of claws against rock in the shadows, a trembling of muscles tensed to strike . . .

Una stopped, turned back, and studied Saru. She noted the waggling of his threat ganglia but said nothing. Instead she listened. Tasted the air, which had cooled in the shaded canyon. When she threw an inquisitive glance at Saru, he darted his eyes upward and to his right. With almost glacial slowness, Una nodded her understanding.

Then she was a blur. She pivoted about-face, snatched a stone from the path, and hurled it up into the surrounding jagged outcroppings of rock. Her projectile found its mark: a creature hissed, then growled as it skittered into retreat, pelting Una and Saru with dislodged pebbles as it fled.

Within seconds its foul scents were gone from Saru's sensitive nostrils, and the sound of its scrabbling flight over the rocks faded into the distance. His ganglia retracted, calm once more.

Saru exhaled a breath he had held by reflex. Una set her hand upon his shoulder, in a manner gentle and encouraging. "Thanks for the warning. I'd have missed it. Are you all right?"

"Yes, Commander. I am fine. Thank you."

"Glad to hear it. How much farther to the cave mouth?"

He checked his tricorder. "Twelve point six meters, on the right."

"Then we'd best get moving." Una resumed walking, and Saru moved forward to walk at her side. This woman of peace was also a born defender, and her example inspired Saru to emulate her, in both confidence and calm. Among Kelpiens there was no honor greater than to be known as a defender of one's clan. Una made Saru feel as if he, too, could become a protector.

Less than a minute later, the ragged entrance to the cave complex gaped open on their right, its maw an invitation to descend into an underworld of darkness. Where some might see a dangerous warren of shadows, Saru saw an environment that finally reminded him of home. He had to remind himself then that this was not Kelpia. There was no telling what devils lurked within this unfamiliar dark.

Una, however, continued inside without missing a step, and without a single look back.

Saru had no choice but to follow her. *Nothing good can come of this,* his fear told him, but he ignored it and pushed onward. Because those were his orders, and because the only thing worse than going into that darkness with Una would be remaining outside of it without her.

Spock kneeled on the aft section of the Juggernaut's ebon hull, beside a patch that was smoother than anything else around it. It was almost glasslike, faithfully reflective, and cool to the touch. He looked toward Burnham. "Have you found the corresponding pad?"

She was down on one knee several meters from him, pressing her right palm against a patch of smoothed hull identical to the one in front of Spock. "I have it."

A chilly breeze flung salt water into Spock's eyes. He winced and shook off the disagreeable sensation. Though half of his heritage was human, he had never appreciated the allure of vast oceans such as those found on Earth and many other Class-M planets. His formative years had been spent in the harsh desert climes of Vulcan, a red world whose environment ranked among the least forgiving of those known to have incubated intelligent life.

Burnham checked her tricorder, which she had set for constant sensor recording. "The oval region between us is the only unique feature on the dorsal hull of this ship."

"Intriguing," Spock said. He appreciated Burnham's restraint; many of his human shipmates on the *Enterprise*— with the exception of Commander Una, of course—would likely have made an unsupported supposition and stated that the oval region between himself and Burnham was the vessel's only unique, unmirrored element. But Burnham had been educated on Vulcan; she knew that they had not yet reviewed a high-resolution map of the Juggernaut's underside, and consequently had made no assumptions about it. Thinking he might test her logic, he speculated aloud, "It is possible the oval has a twin on the underside of this ship."

"Possible, yes," Burnham said, "but we have no evidence for that, and no convenient means of access even should that prove to be the case. For now, the logical course of action would be to explore the potential represented by this feature."

It was exactly the answer for which Spock had hoped. Yet he remained at a loss for an idea concerning how to proceed. "If this does function as some sort of portal to the ship's interior, there seems to be no interface for its control. At least, none on the exterior."

"I'm not so certain of that, Mister Spock." She ran her hands over the hull's surface. "Based on its reaction to the drill head striking its hull, and its subsequent attack on New Astana, it seems reasonable to conclude that the Juggernaut has external sensory capability. Therefore, if this is a kind of airlock or other means of accessing the ship's interior, it would make sense for it to have an external interface of some kind."

"Not necessarily," Spock said. "If this vessel had come here with a crew, would they not have departed after their mission, whatever it might have been, had concluded? Does not its continued presence suggest that it was sent here without crew or passengers, perhaps to perform some limited function, and then be abandoned?"

Burnham turned pensive as she considered his argument. "I see your point. And I will concede that this feature we've found might prove to be nothing more than the launch aperture of an even larger form of weapon than the drones, or perhaps even nothing of note whatsoever. But consider this, Mister Spock: the apertures that opened for the drones vanished without a seam. That suggests to me that this feature we've found would not exist unless the makers of this vessel wanted it to be found. And why would they want it to be found? That in turn implies that they hoped this planet's native inhabitants would seek out the Juggernaut—and this entrance point."

"To what end?" Spock asked, his curiosity aroused.

He was mildly disappointed when Burnham shrugged. "I don't know yet. But I mean to find out." She pawed at the smooth patch in front of her, then looked toward Spock. "Are you pressing your hand against yours?"

"Not at the moment. Do you wish me to?"

"Please," Burnham said. "This is a long shot, but I recall something I was taught as a child on Vulcan: at a bare minimum, the sensory capacity required for space travel is—"

"Tactile," Spock said, his own memory of early teachings jogged by Burnham's cue. He put his hand to the smooth patch in front of him and mimicked the spread of Burnham's digits. At once he felt a firm but shifting pressure under his palm. "A haptic interface," he noted. He regarded Burnham with a new level of respect. "How did you know?"

"I suspect this entry point was designed to be accessible to the lowest common denominator," she said. "And the ship's symmetry, which extends to these two panels, made me think its control interfaces might have been geared toward a pair of respondents."

"Or toward a single operator with an arm span of several meters," Spock offered.

She arched one eyebrow, in a manner that reminded Spock of his father's chosen form of silent rebuke. "A valid analysis, if not a particularly helpful one."

Even her criticism sounds as if it comes from my father, Spock thought.

He felt another series of shifting pressures under his palm. "The interface is working again. The sensation is similar to dull pinpricks rolling against my palm and then subsiding."

"I'm feeling the same thing over here," Burnham said. "Pay attention to every detail. Number of pressure points. The order in which they appear. Their position, duration, and location. Their temperature—I'm feeling some that are hot, some that are icy."

Once she began guiding him, he appreciated the complexity of the interface. "It is not unlike the systems created by your people to make textual information accessible by the blind, combined with those developed by the Andorians."

"Yes, I'd noticed that, too. Now concentrate. Tell me everything you're feeling."

He recited details as he became aware of their patterns, and Burnham did the same. Within a few minutes of back-and-forth, they experienced a simultaneous epiphany:

"It's a challenge-and-response system," they said to each other.

Burnham nodded, then closed her eyes to concentrate. "I'm getting complex numbers over here, if I'm reading this correctly. The early iterations were made to set a baseline. To teach us the number system. Now I'm being fed massive integers."

Spock closed his eyes and trained all of his mental acuity on the haptic panel beneath his hand. "Yes. And I am being given a small set of simple equations. A different set roughly every thirty seconds." Concentrating more intently, he realized, "All the numbers I receive are primes."

"Then what are these longer strings I—" Burnham sighed, partly in relief but also, it seemed, in self-criticism.

"Of course. Factorization by prime numbers. The key to entry is to prove not only fundamental mathematical literacy, but also the ability to parse their haptic matrix." She tensed. "Hang on, I'm getting a new number."

"And I am getting a new set of simplified equations," Spock said.

It took Burnham only a few seconds to interpret the new information. "The challenge number is thirty-four thousand, five hundred sixty-eight."

"In which case the factorization by primes would be two to the third power times twenty-nine, times one hundred forty-nine," Spock said, reading the tactile formulae under his hand. "I have found the matching equation. I am going to apply pressure to it."

He pushed the string of dots corresponding to the correct factorization sequence. They retreated into the hull and left no trace of their presence behind—

The great oval between Spock and Burnham dilated open. It made almost no sound as it swirled apart from its center, the smart metal retreating into itself to reveal a ramp leading down to an antechamber with a long corridor on its far side, both illuminated in sickly green light.

Spock looked at Burnham. "What do we do now?"

"Get inside before it closes," she said, scrambling over its threshold without so much as a single tricorder scan to deduce what might lurk within.

Spock followed her inside without question or hesitation. They moved together into the antechamber, which had many features that reminded Spock of an airlock, though once again he was at a loss to find anything that resembled a conventional interface. A series of alien symbols had been etched around the interior edge of the entrance. The compartment's inner portal opposite the entrance was already open, which suggested they were intended to move deeper inside the ship, on a straight line toward its distant bow.

He lifted his tricorder and checked its ongoing scan mode. "No life signs inside the vessel," he said. "Though I detect a mild surge in energy readings around us, which might—"

The oval exterior hatchway spiraled shut. As the last pinhole of light at its center went out, and the alien symbols around it flashed with crimson energy, it took all of Spock's hard-learned Vulcan conditioning to suppress a natural fear response.

Burnham, however, evinced a more human reaction to their predicament. She frowned at the bulkhead where the portal had been and muttered under her breath, "Shit." It took her a moment to restore her pretense of logical control. "It appears our direction has been chosen for us, Mister Spock." She stepped past him and led the way inside the Juggernaut. "So, like it or not . . . into the heart of darkness we go."

12

Gant and a team of five security officers from the *Shenzhou* materialized from a transporter beam on the edge of the circular plaza at the center of New Astana. Several meters away, another six-person security team beamed down from the *Enterprise*. Gant and his team from the *Shenzhou* wore dark blue Starfleet utility jumpsuit uniforms with black trim, while the *Enterprise* team sported pale gold or light blue jerseys over black trousers—a new uniform style that so far had been issued exclusively to the crews of Starfleet's vaunted *Constitution*-class starships.

The leader of the *Enterprise*'s landing party approached Gant. His counterpart was a tall, slender woman with pale skin and short, slicked-close dark blond hair. As they arrived at a respectable distance for a conversation, Gant spoke first. "Lieutenant Kamran Gant, senior tactical officer, *U.S.S. Shenzhou.*"

"Lieutenant Elena Donnelly, deputy chief of security, *U.S.S. Enterprise.*" She shook his hand quickly, then cast a worried look around the otherwise empty plaza. "I thought a squad of local law enforcement was supposed to meet us."

Gant made his own anxious survey of the empty streets and building fronts marked by closed doors. "That was my understanding. Looks like the colonists didn't get the memo." He snapped an order over his shoulder to one of his own people. "Goldsmith, run a tricorder scan. Get me a twenty on the colonists—especially the governor." He tried to reassure Donnelly with feigned confidence. "If they're here, we'll know soon enough."

Donnelly surveyed the windows and looked toward the surrounding rooftops. "I have no doubt they're here. Right now I'm just wondering how well armed they are."

"Substantially, I'd guess," Gant said. "The Kayo Mining Consortium played fast and loose with the laws and regulations on this rock. It's a good bet everyone's armed."

The *Enterprise*'s deputy security chief looked disgruntled. "Wonderful."

Chief Petty Officer Goldsmith sidled up to show them the results of his scans. "Sirs? We're surrounded, and not just by people cowering inside their prefab houses. We're reading several dozen armed people on the rooftops, and more out of sight behind corners."

Feigning amusement, Gant raised his voice to mock and goad the colonists into showing themselves. "What the—? A *surprise party*? Whose idea was this? You crazy scamps. You know how much I *hate* surprises." He drew his phaser. "I mean, I *really* hate 'em."

The rest of his landing party followed his lead and brandished their phasers. The group from the *Enterprise* waited for Donnelly to draw her weapon, then they did the same.

Donnelly lowered her voice to ask Gant, "Now what?"

"We do what we came here to do—and hope the colonists don't make an issue of it. Everyone, set phasers on heavy stun." Gant led the two parties toward the nearby Executive Complex, a drab block of a building whose only flourishes of style resided in the columns atop its short flight of steps and the tall, narrow windows that lined its façade. The two security teams fanned out as they advanced on the government building. By the time they reached its steps, they were almost a single rank, twelve bodies across, climbing the steps in wary unison.

Then came a man's voice from the shadows behind the columns: "That's far enough."

Gant and the others halted. He strained to see the person who had spoken, but the shade ahead was too deep to pierce. "Who are we talking to?"

"Not important," said the gravel-voiced sentry. "This building's transport-shielded, and you're surrounded. Take one more step up those stairs, and we'll put you down." A blast of charged plasma streaked out of the darkness and left a scorch across the steps in front of Gant. "That's the only warning you'll get. Now I suggest you turn back and return to your ships."

Donnelly raised her voice to answer the threat. "Sorry, that's not an option. We've been sent here with clear orders: to arrest Governor Kolova and her senior advisers, as well as anyone suspected of participating in the planetary survey fraud. We have a warrant from the colonial court. Unless you stand down you'll be facing charges of obstruction, and you might end up charged as accessories after the fact. Do you understand?"

Another blaster pulse scored a diagonal black streak across the steps in front of Donnelly. The gruff voice from the dark shouted, "What I understand is we have cover, and you twelve are standing in the wide open. Now, go back to your ships before this gets ugly."

Gant pulled out his communicator and flipped it open, while keeping his phaser at the ready in his other hand. "Lieutenant Gant to Chief Le Fevre. Chief, do you copy?"

He was answered by Cameron Le Fevre, the capital's chief of police. *"I read you."*

"Chief, my shipmates and our colleagues from the *Enterprise* are facing stiff resistance at the entrance to the Executive Complex. We could use some backup out here."

"Look up and behind you," Le Fevre said.

The two landing parties pivoted slowly about, then looked up to see a team of colonial law enforcement perched along a roof's edge—all of whom were aiming long-barrel blaster rifles at them. In the center of their formation was Chief Le Fevre, manning his own rifle.

"I think you'd best do as the governor's man tells you, Lieutenant."

All around the landing parties there was movement. Shapes emerged from patches of shadow, from around corners, over the edges of rooftops—all of them armed. Gant could see at a glance that he and his Starfleet colleagues were outnumbered at least thirty to one on the ground.

He put away his communicator and turned back toward the man in the shadows atop the steps. "This doesn't have to go sideways, for any of us. Just tell us what you want."

"We want you to go back to your ships," said Gravel Voice, "stop that alien Juggernaut from wiping out our planet . . . and then we want you to go."

His demand incensed Donnelly. "Are you kidding? First you threaten us, then you want us to save your asses. And once we do, you want us to just walk away and forget about all the crimes that led us here in the first place?"

"Our capital is still burning from the last attack!" Gravel shouted. "We see the news! The Juggernaut's moving closer by the hour. It's heading right for us, and you people are doing nothing! Instead of stopping that thing, you're harassing *us*! Where the hell are *your* priorities?"

Out of the gathering twilight came a shimmering blur—a bottle that smashed at the feet of an *Enterprise* security guard, who quick-stepped backward and pointed his phaser back the way the bottle had come. His finger tensed in front of his weapon's trigger—

"Hold your fire, Mister Gupta," Donnelly said, clearly just as committed to avoiding a riot as Gant was. To the mysterious figure atop the stairs, she continued, "I assure you, we're doing everything we can to stop the Juggernaut, but you—"

A blaster shot tore through her left shoulder. The hit spun her about-face as it knocked her to the ground. As she fell, a storm of charged plasma rained down on the landing parties.

Incoming fire of a potentially lethal nature meant the rules of engagement had just changed. Around Gant, his men and Donnelly's laid down overlapping fields of wide-angle suppressing phaser fire, forcing their attackers back under cover. He grabbed Donnelly, threw her over his shoulder, then added his own phaser blasts to those blanketing the top of the stairs. "Go forward!" he hollered over the shrieking of weapons fire. "Get to the columns!"

He had no idea how many hostiles awaited them at the top of the stairs, but that was a problem he'd face when he got there. For now, he needed to get his team out of the crossfire.

By the time they reached the top step, they found only a handful of armed civilians lying stunned—but the entrance to the complex, as well as all its windows, had been barricaded with blast shields. To either side of him, his and Donnelly's teams divided into pairs and took up positions behind the architectural columns. Most of their phasers' emitter crystals were on the verge of overheating from having sustained so lengthy a barrage, so they were forced to duck and weather the latest incoming barrage of blaster pulses without responding in kind.

Gant set down Donnelly, who was conscious and clearly in great pain. "Hang on," he told her, flipping open his communicator. "Time to call in the big guns." He tuned the communicator to its ship-to-shore channel. "Gant to *Shenzhou*! Do you read me?"

Captain Georgiou answered. *"This is* Shenzhou. *Go ahead, Gant."*

"Captain," Gant said, "this op is one-hundred percent FUBAR."

A magnified optical sensor view of the battle in New Astana was not the best vantage point, in Pike's opinion. It could be difficult to know what was really going on based on an almost straight-down perspective, but the image of the street fight that currently filled the *Enterprise* bridge's main viewscreen was clear and detailed enough that he saw the shot that felled Lieutenant Donnelly, and the intercepted comm signals that Garison was routing through the overhead speakers enabled Pike to hear most of the pandemonium as it erupted.

As soon as Donnelly hit the ground, Pike's thumb was on his armrest's intraship comm. "Bridge to security! Get riot teams to transporter rooms one and two, on the double!"

His navigator and acting first officer, Lieutenant Yoshi Ohara, swiveled away from his post at the forward console to face Pike. "Captain, are you sure you want to risk escalating the situation? Captain Georgiou said—"

"She isn't responsible for the lives of my landing party, Lieutenant. I am."

"Aye, sir," Ohara said, returning to his duties without pressing the point.

On the viewscreen, a swarm of bodies pressed in upon the Executive Complex. Blaster pulses crisscrossed with phaser beams, and missed shots and ricochets quickly clouded the area with smoke. Impatience drove Pike to clench his fists as he watched the battle inch toward becoming a slaughter. He thumbed open another intraship channel. "Transporter room, have you beamed down reinforcements yet?"

"Negative," said Chief Pitcairn. *"The locals have activated a scattering field. We can't get a clear lock within two kilometers of the center of the capital."*

"Which means we can't beam our people up, either."

"Affirmative, sir."

"Beam down our reinforcements outside the scattering field. They should still be able to reach the combat area in less than six minutes."

"Aye, sir. Setting new coordinates. Commencing transport in thirty seconds."

Pike closed the channel with a jab of his thumb, then muttered, "What a damned mess."

Garison swiveled his chair away from the communications console. "Sir, I'm intercepting chatter between the *Shenzhou* and her landing party."

"On speakers," Pike said. He leaned forward and listened with intense focus.

The voice over the comm was one of Georgiou's officers, a man. *"Repeat, we're surrounded and taking heavy fire. Request fire support and medical assistance."*

"Acknowledged," Georgiou said. *"Sit tight and stand by for protocol Theta."*

Pike faced Garison. "Hail the *Shenzhou*." It took just a switch-flip, and Garison nodded in confirmation, cuing

Pike to speak. "Captain Georgiou, this is the *Enterprise*. Be advised, I am sending in reinforcements. They're beaming down beyond the scattering field, but—"

"Belay that order if you can, Captain," Georgiou said. *"Or tell your backup teams to stand down and wait for my signal to move in."*

Georgiou's warning made him sit up—she was about to do something unorthodox. "Why?" he asked. "What are you going to do?"

Her voice was as cold as death. *"I'm going to handle this."*

He opened the channel to the transporter room. "Chief, hold that transport!"

"Caught me in the nick of time, sir," Pitcairn said. *"Holding transport, aye."*

The image on the viewscreen flared with an electric-blue glow. It bathed every street, rooftop, and exposed surface within two kilometers of the center of the colony's capital. Though the pulse lasted for less than two seconds, when it faded everyone in view lay sprawled and unmoving. Pike turned his chair toward the sensor console, which was being monitored by Ensign Navah Wolfe of the sciences department. "Wolfe! What just happened down there?"

The petite dark-haired woman checked her data readouts. "The *Shenzhou* fired a five-percent-power, wide-dispersal phaser pulse into the colony's capital. Just enough to stun everyone in the area—and to neutralize the scattering field."

Georgiou's voice filtered down from the overhead speakers. "Enterprise, *this is* Shenzhou. *The crisis in the capital has been contained, and you are clear to beam down reinforcements. Also, please send in additional medical personnel, if you can spare them."*

"Understood, *Shenzhou*," Pike said. "And might I add, Captain, that's one hell of an effective crowd-control tactic you've got there."

"It might not be pretty," Georgiou said, *"but it gets the job done."*

"Copy that. *Enterprise* out." He reopened his internal channel. "Transporter room, the scattering field is down. Revert to original coordinates, beam down reinforcements, then stand by to beam up wounded before dispatching medical teams to the surface."

"Understood, bridge," Pitcairn said.

On many levels, Pike still felt he didn't understand Captain Georgiou, but now he was sure he knew at least one thing about her: she was both pragmatic and restrained. Those were admirable qualities in a person to whom had been entrusted the power to mete out life and death. Knowing she possessed such virtues would make it all the more difficult for him to overrule her when Burnham's mission to the Juggernaut failed, and the time came to carry out Starfleet's order to blast Sirsa III into an orb of radioactive molten glass for the good of the galaxy.

Difficult, but not impossible.

Georgiou had her principles . . . but Pike had his orders.

And when death's hour came round at last, that would be all that mattered.

13

Burnham stole forward through the wide oval passage inside the Juggernaut, prowling like a thief through a deserted mansion and expecting to be apprehended at any moment. Spock walked beside her, his posture straighter, his manner betraying not a hint of anxiety at their surroundings.

The interior of the Juggernaut exhibited the same propensity for symmetry that she and Spock had noted on its outer hull. Its bulkheads gave her the impression of something grown rather than manufactured and assembled. They were marked by a fine vertical ribbing, and at regular intervals the passage was encroached upon by thicker ribs whose purpose appeared to be structural. Eeriest of all was the bioluminescence that suffused the Juggernaut's interior. It had come to life seconds after the exterior hatchway had sealed itself behind them. Now everything glowed with teal radiance, including the decks and overheads. The absence of directional light and shadow felt surreal to Burnham.

Spock lifted his tricorder and adjusted its settings. Its semimusical oscillations resounded down the long passageway ahead of them. "Now that we are inside, I am able to make a more detailed assessment of the Juggernaut's internal functions," he said. "If I am not mistaken, this vessel is biomechanoid in nature." He lowered his tricorder and re-garded the ship around them with a newfound admiration. "A living machine. Fascinating."

"It is," Burnham said, while trying to conceal the genu-ine excitement coursing through her as she contemplated what eons-old mysteries lay ahead for her and Spock to uncover. She pulled her communicator from her hip and flipped it open. "Burnham to *Shenzhou*." After a few sec-onds without a reply, she tried again. "Burnham to *Shen-zhou*: Do you read me?"

"It is likely," Spock said, "that the same compounds that occluded our ability to scan the Juggernaut's inner workings from the outside now impede our ability to trans-mit a signal."

"So it would seem." She flipped shut the grille of her communicator and tucked it away. "We have this marvel of antiquity all to ourselves, Mister Spock."

He paused, so she stopped and faced him. He regarded her with wary curiosity. "You speak as if our present status is the result of fortune or favor. Might I suggest an alternative interpretation of our circumstances?"

She tried not to take his proposal as a rebuke. "By all means."

"Unless we locate and identify a means of escape from this vessel, it will very likely become our shared tomb. In just over two hours, our captains will be bound by a Starfleet directive to destroy this ship, regardless of whether we are still on board."

She gestured aft. "We can always go back the way we came."

He shook his head. "There was no interface inside the first hatchway. At least, none of a similar nature to the one we used to gain access. I would posit that the hatch we exploited was always meant to permit passage in only one direction."

"You're saying you think we're trapped."

"I have considered the possibility," Spock said. He seemed about to continue when a low groaning reverberated through the deck and bulkheads. As the deep moaning rose and fell in both volume and pitch, the ship's interior bioluminescence shifted from teal to tangerine, and then back to a deeper blue-green, verging on turquoise. Spock recovered his composure. "At the very least, I think we should prepare for the likelihood that the feat which facilitated our entry will not in any way earn us our freedom."

"Why do you say that?" Aware of the dwindling time remaining, and eager to press onward, Burnham resumed walking. "And why did you refer to what we did as a 'feat'?"

He answered as he walked beside her. "The very nature of the test at the hatchway concerns me. As a means of securing a ship against intrusion, it leaves much to be desired. But if it is just a simple test of mathematical knowledge and pattern interpretation, it would be a logical first obstacle for those whom the Juggernaut, or its makers, wish to test."

"That would track with my hypothesis that the Juggernaut's subsonic pulses were intended as a form of invitation," Burnham said, thinking aloud.

"Agreed," Spock said. "But that raises the question: An invitation to what? Abduction? Experimentation? Genocide?"

Burnham had no idea what answer would satisfy Spock. "I don't know. But I'm relatively certain the only way we'll find out is to push on and see where this leads."

He cocked one eyebrow in disdain. "With all respect, I think your reasoning on this matter verges upon the fatalistic." He shot an accusatory sidelong look her way. "Are you always so willing to let yourself be manipulated by the will of others?"

"Well, Lieutenant junior-grade Spock, for what it's worth, I'm happy to resist your efforts at manipulating my command decisions. To be honest, I blame myself for them." She skewered him with a look. "On account of my failure to impress upon you that you're addressing a superior officer."

"An 'appeal to authority' is a form of logical fallacy," he said dryly.

"The invocation of superior rank is not an 'appeal to authority' fallacy."

"Normally, no. Given our present situation, however, an exception might be in order."

Burnham felt her patience bleed away and her most toxic emotions stir. This was the sort of verbal flensing she had been forced to suffer for years as a child and adolescent enrolled in the Vulcan Learning Center of ShiKahr. She was in no mood to relive those days.

"Do me a favor, Mister Spock. Keep your idle observations to—"

A crackling ball of lightning popped into existence in front of them. It lingered at eye level, bobbing by only the slightest measure as it hovered in place. As Burnham stepped toward it, Spock checked his tricorder. "A hologram." He checked his readings. "Its photonic matrix is fused with a number of shaped force fields to give it a tangible presence."

"Don't tell me," Burnham cut in. "It's *fascinating.*" Spock said nothing in response, but he could not help but appear mildly put out.

Tendrils of energy danced around the sphere, then leaped toward Burnham and Spock. Before either of them could retreat, the orb seemed to probe their communicators and tricorders with its sparking slender tentacles. The devices it touched gave off bursts of static and atonal noises, and the displays on the tricorders went haywire as all their indicator lights flashed in what appeared to be random sequences.

Then the tendrils vanished, and once more the orb hovered. As it pulsed, deep percussive *thump*s shook the deck under her feet, in time with the orb's changes.

Burnham's communicator beeped twice, the alert for an incoming signal. She lifted it and flipped it open. "Burnham here."

A masculine voice emanated from her communicator's speaker, and the orb's intensity and coloration varied in synchronicity with the words. *"Follow me."*

Without waiting for an agreement or even an acknowledgment, the lightning orb floated away, as if to guide them ahead toward the front of the vessel. Every few seconds the orb pulsed, and another *thump* registered through the bulkheads and deck.

Spock faced her. "Orders, sir?"

"You heard our pal Thumper," she said, setting off in pursuit. "Follow it."

"We can't stay here," Bowen told the governor and her advisers. "No matter how secure you think this bunker of yours is, Starfleet will find a way in. If you're still here when they do, you'll be trapped." He turned all his focus to Ishii, the governor's chief of staff. "You know I'm right. The best shot any of us have is to kick on the sensor blinds and keep moving."

Ishii frowned, exacerbating the worry lines on his forehead. "It's a problem of optics, Mister Bowen. If we run, it will only make us look guilty."

"You *are* guilty," Chandra said from his seat on Bowen's left, breaking a long silence. "We *all* are. Which is why we need to bolt, while we still can."

Omalu, who sat to Bowen's right, nodded vigorously. "Yes. This. Time to run."

Governor Kolova remained resolute. "Run to where?" she asked. "We don't have enough transport ships to evac more than a few hundred of the colonists." She aimed a withering stare at Ishii. "And don't you even think of telling me to flee the planet and leave these people behind."

"The alternative," said her science adviser, "is to stay and die with them."

"If that's the case," Kolova said, "then goddammit, Medina, that's what we're going to do." She palmed sweat from her forehead and wiped her hand dry on her shirt. "We need to get those Starfleet clowns to stop wasting their time on us, and get them to focus on the Juggernaut."

Around the bunker, a dozen faces went slack as they realized the group's collective argument had come full circle without any of its points of contention having been resolved.

Bowen was frustrated beyond belief, and his annoyance colored his retort. "How the hell are we supposed to do that? This is Starfleet we're talking about. Handling more than one crisis at a time is what they do. Unlike half the people Kayo installed in your cabinet, Starfleet officers know how to walk and chew gum at the same time."

"In situations such as this," Kolova said, "the problem is always one of motivation. We know that Starfleet's personnel are eminently capable. So what we need to do is adjust their priorities until they align with our own."

Nervous looks between Omalu and Chandra made it clear to Bowen that they didn't like where the governor was going with that train of thought; he was fairly sure he wasn't going to like it, either. "I don't suppose you'd care to elaborate on that last point, would you?"

"Not yet. Let's just say I have a few notions I'm kicking around." Kolova poked an index finger with a perfectly manicured nail against Ishii's chest. "But we'll need time and resources."

Ishii regarded the map of the city projected on the bunker's situation table. "If you mean what I think you do, then Mister Bowen is right—we'll need to abandon this bunker. We have a limited cache of weapons here, but we're far shorter on personnel." A shrug of surrender. "If you really want to take a stand, you'll need to recruit."

"We have the constabulary," Kolova said.

"Most of whom were stunned and captured five minutes ago," Medina said. "And in another five minutes, the Starfleet security teams sent down here to arrest us are going to open this bunker's door with some kind of military-grade master key. At that point, if we're still in here, we can try to resist, but one photon grenade lobbed through that door, and we're done."

Bowen could see that Kolova was vacillating, unable to choose between a futile last stand and a desperate if temporary flight from justice. He knew he didn't have time to wait for her to reason it out on her own, and neither did anyone else who was trapped in the bunker with her. "Madam Governor, if we go now, we can take shelter in the deep maintenance passages connected to your city's infrastructure. Down here," he said, pointing at the city schematics, "beneath the water mains, near the waste processors. Make that our base of operations, and we'll be able to move anywhere in the city within minutes. Then we can plan a real tactical response, and set up fallback points to drag out the chase when they come after us."

Kolova looked for advice from Ishii, who said, "It's a sound strategy, Madam Governor."

At last she seemed swayed. "Let's move out. Leave anything nonessential. Prioritize weapons and water." Reacting to a questioning look from one of her bureaucratic underlings, she added, "This mess won't last more than a day, if that. Either Starfleet stops the Juggernaut, or else it kills us all. Either way, this seems like a good time to travel light."

The mound of rocks blocking the passage to the deepest caverns disintegrated at a rate of roughly half a meter per second as Saru and Una bombarded it with steady blasts from their phasers. It had taken a few minutes to cut their way past the obstruction—a task made necessary by the presence of minerals in the local bedrock that interfered with the integrity of transporter signals. Consequently, the air in the ancient tunnel had grown oppressively warm, as well as humid, thanks to the vaporization of water trapped in the rocks.

Saru loosened the collar of his jumpsuit to get more air to his throat spiracles, but he kept his phaser hand steady and his finger on the trigger. When he chanced a look in Una's direction, he was surprised to find her showing no reaction to the increasing heat or humidity. It was as if nothing could affect her unless she wanted it to. *A most enviable gift,* Saru thought.

The last few meters of fallen rock crumbled, revealing a fathomless darkness on the other side. Based on the plethora of echoes Saru heard of his and Una's activity, he surmised the open space ahead must be vast. Una ceased fire, so Saru did the same. He lowered his weapon as Una tucked hers back onto her belt, and then she kneeled down and shrugged off her backpack. From a small pocket on its side she pulled a replacement power cell for her phaser and proceeded to swap it for the nearly depleted one in her weapon. As she worked, she asked Saru, "Did you bring a spare power cell?"

"I did, as per Starfleet landing party protocol."

"This might be a good time to make the switch."

"Yes, sir." He retrieved his phaser's backup power pack from his belt and exchanged it with the one from his weapon. As he did, he saw that he had expended more of its charge than he had thought. "Do you expect to face resistance inside the cave?"

"I have no expectations whatsoever," Una said. "However, it would be prudent before entering an unsecured and unexplored area to make certain all of our options are ready for use." She stood and fixed her phaser back into place on her hip. Then she opened the top flap of her backpack and removed two pairs of high-tech goggles. She handed one to Saru after he put away his weapon. "Put these on. They'll adjust to suit the environment."

"I don't need them," he said, and tried to hand his pair back. "My people live most of their lives underground. Our vision is optimized for environments such as this."

Una refused to accept his return of the goggles. "Just put them on. As good as your natural sight might be in the dark, these will make it better." Perhaps sensing his reticence, she added, "Trust me, they'll adjust to maximize compatibility with your biology. I promise."

"If you insist." Saru fixed the goggles into place. He noted a few brief pulses from sensors inside the goggles as they identified his species' retinal structure. It was a common feature for general-issue equipment such as this. Because Starfleet personnel hailed from many species, it was an inconvenient reality that not all humanoids' eyes perceived the same range of electromagnetic information or reacted the same way to enhanced-vision technology. For that reason, Starfleet enhanced goggles adjusted their output to best suit the optical physiology of the wearer. Within moments his eyes adjusted to his new holographic view of the cavern.

The color response of the goggles was restricted in Saru's case to a variety of grays and greens, with some nearly white hot spots and a few regions of inky shadow. But the limited palette did nothing to diminish the natural majesty of the space that yawned around him and Una.

Great pillars of stone, formed from fused stalactites and stalagmites, joined the jagged labyrinth of the massive cavern's floor with its distant, pearlescent ceiling. Underground streams snaked through eroded rock formations, or spilled from cracks in the walls, and they all converged in a vast central lake. Superimposed over the image of the cavern was sensor data gathered by the goggles, indicating the direction that Saru was facing, and the approximate distance to whatever object he focused upon. When he strained to see the far end of the cavern, the readout indicated his shadowy would-be destination was more than eleven kilometers away.

He faced Una, who was busy surveying the cavern through her own goggles. The lenses' oval shape gave the human woman's visage an almost insectoid quality that amused Saru. When she noticed his attention, he masked his stare by remarking, "A far superior solution to flares."

"And a less disruptive one." Una started down a gradual slope, on a direct heading for a cluster of what appeared to be artificially shaped stones. "There might be life-forms down here that evolved to exist in the dark. The last thing we want to do is disturb their habitat. Our goal is to make our survey and depart, leaving as little trace of our presence as possible."

Saru refrained from pointing out that he was well aware of Starfleet's policy with regard to survey protocols. It was, after all, just good science to minimize one's impact on the subjects of one's interest. But he also understood that for Starfleet it was about something more than that: it was about respect for all life, and its right to be free of undue external influence. That lesson had been the cornerstone of his education at Starfleet Academy, though he doubted its sanctity.

I'm just glad the Starfleet officers who saved me on Kelpia had the compassion to know when to break that rule.

Within a few minutes he and Una were down in the twisting paths among the towering rocks. Fragments of a long-dead primitive civilization lay strewn about. Everywhere Saru looked he saw blanched bones, crude tools, shards of unknown provenance, and scratches in the timeless stone. The entire cavern, he realized, was a buried maze of ghosts and shadows, an epitaph for a culture reduced to dust and whispers from the farthest reaches of antiquity.

Una slowed her pace. "Curious that so many artifacts and remains should be clustered here, so far below ground." She stopped, lifted her tricorder, and aimed it at a nearby pit. Saru waited while she scanned the deep, circular excavation. The whistling tone of her tricorder returned to them from all directions, not just repeated but amplified. When she finished, the echoes abated until a deathly silence enveloped them. "Multiple layers of oxidized organic compounds suggests this was a funeral pit used for cremations over a period of several hundred years, with the last activity taking place approximately nine million years ago."

"How do you know it's a funeral pit and not a cooking pit?"

"There are bone fragments in the sediment that are consistent with those we have seen elsewhere in the cave. In addition, there appears to be no mechanism for keeping food at a consistent distance from the flames that would have filled this pit, nor anything nearby to which such a mechanism might be secured. All of which suggests that whatever was burned here was most likely subjected directly to the flames. It might have been an altar for burnt offerings of a superstitious nature, but because it would be very difficult for people living in this cavern to dig graves for their dead, I think this was most likely a cremation site."

I should know not to ask uninformed questions. "Most logical, Commander."

She squatted to pick up a piece of what appeared to be a stone tool. "Would you agree that the people who dwelled in this cave likely had not advanced beyond stone-age or perhaps bronze-age technology?"

"I would concur with that assessment, yes."

"Can you think of a reason why they would choose to live here, underground?"

Saru considered that. "They might have evolved from a cave-dwelling species."

"If so, how did they learn to harness fire?" Una stood and regarded the cavern with a worried expression. "Something about this feels wrong to me, Saru."

He inferred her supposition. "You think they were a surface-dwelling species driven underground by the arrival of the Juggernaut, much as my people were driven under-ground by the coming of the *t'rrask*."

"I do. What I don't understand is *why*. This was *not* an advanced culture. So why did the Juggernaut come here? Why did it target them? What purpose would that serve?"

"I don't have enough information to answer that, Commander." Saru gestured toward the path that led deeper into the cavern, toward what looked like an ominous structure of pale stone. "But perhaps if we dig a bit deeper, we might glimpse the heart of this mystery."

"A capital suggestion, Lieutenant. Lead on."

Energized by her approval and invitation, Saru took the lead as they continued their venture into the dark. Out in front was not a natural place for a Kelpien to be—but for the first time in Saru's life, he had started to see the appeal of feeling like a leader.

Darkness, here I come.

14

After nearly thirty years in Starfleet, Philippa Georgiou had learned it was possible for a starship to be lacking nearly anything essential to its operation. It was a rare day on any starship that nothing was said to be in short supply. But it was only after she reached the upper echelons of the command division that she had learned there was one commodity that was always present in abundance on every vessel and in every facility: bad news.

Today's unwanted delivery was arriving courtesy of the *Enterprise*'s commanding officer, whose holographic full-body image shimmered in front of the *Shenzhou*'s forward bridge viewport. *"Our landing parties searched every room in the Executive Complex, and then they spent fifteen minutes cutting their way inside the governor's secure underground bunker. Care to guess what they found?"*

Though weary and annoyed, Georgiou played along. "An empty room?"

"Pretty much," Pike said. *"The governor and her people raided the water rations and weapons lockers before they bugged out, but they were nice enough to leave us a note. Your man Gant tells me it reads, 'Do your jobs, and maybe then we'll talk.'"*

Georgiou massaged her aching temples with the thumb

and middle finger of her right hand. "Exactly the kind of additional complication we don't need right now." She sighed, then asked Pike, "Do we know where Kolova and the other colonists are now?"

"All we know for certain is they aren't in the Complex or the bunker, and they're not out in the streets. But that leaves a lot of private structures all over the capital, not to mention a few hundred kilometers' worth of underground maintenance tunnels."

Engineering officer Weeton looked up from his station. "Captain?" He waited until she acknowledged him before he continued. "If I were them, I'd be underground. It would maximize their mobility and their cover, not to mention give them control over the city's power and other utilities. Plus, with all the metal in the natural rock, and all the power being moved around down there, they'd be pretty well hidden from our sensors."

"Thank you, Mister Weeton." She faced Pike's holographic avatar. "Did you and your people catch that?"

"We got it. And for what it's worth, that was our conclusion, as well. So, the ball's in your court, Captain. How do you wish to proceed?"

Georgiou sat back and folded her hands in front of her chest, with her elbows on the armrests of her command chair. "Our number-one priority is the safety of the colonists. Their governor has fled her post, but seeing as we were about to take her into custody, the burden of providing leadership and security would have been on us all the same. First, we need to secure all communications within the capital, as well as all channels in or out of it."

"Understood," Pike said. *"My people can take care of that. What's next?"*

"My crew will block all subspace signals to or from

the planet's surface. We can't have Kolova agitating other nearby colonies, or bringing in mercenaries to muddle things up. As far as taking her and her accomplices into custody, that has to be a lower priority. As long as they stay hidden and don't complicate matters, I'm content to leave them in peace until we finish dealing with the Juggernaut."

Pike nodded. *"That works for us. As for the Juggernaut, have you received any word yet from your first officer? Or from Lieutenant Spock?"*

It was impossible for Georgiou to hide her dismay. "Not yet."

"Captain, if we don't hear from them by the deadline, you know what we need to do."

"One disaster at a time, Captain. One disaster at a time."

The city below the capital was like a foreign land to Kolova. She had always known that dozens of kilometers of utility passages sprawled beneath the city she called home; that had not prepared her to roam those dim pathways with barely any idea of where she was. As she and a few dozen of her fellow colonists retreated deeper into the city's infrastructure, she had to put her trust in the engineers and mechanics who made their livings in this shadowy undercity.

"How much farther?" she asked Floyd Tanzer, the man at the front of the group.

The broad-shouldered fix-it man answered without looking back. "A ways. Not far."

She chewed on the ambiguity of his assessment. "A ways" had seemed to imply a significant distance, but "not far" negated that interpretation. After careful consideration, all she could say she had learned from that exchange was not to ask Tanzer for updates.

Behind her, the rest of the group marched single file. No one spoke above a whisper. There were few active surveillance devices in the sublevels, but Bowen, the rig foreman, had suggested the group keep a low profile in case Starfleet sent security personnel into the tunnels to stop them. It was a sensible suggestion, though their hushed transit of the tunnels had begun to make Kolova feel like a fugitive on a world where she was supposed to be the head of state.

Who am I kidding? I became a fugitive the moment I fled the bunker. She bit down on her resentment of the Federation and its oh-so-righteous meddling. *We'd have been an independent planet if they hadn't laid prior claim to this rock. But if the Federation didn't want to settle it themselves, why should they get to make the rules for those of us who did?*

There were no obvious answers that Kolova could see. So she stewed in silence and plodded onward through the confines of dark tunnels whose walls were lined with parallel rows of pipes and seemingly endless runs of multicolored optronic cables.

Her mind was still wandering when the claustrophobic passage opened onto a wide platform beneath what looked like a gigantic spherical tank suspended from the ceiling grid of duranium girders high above. Through the metal-grate floor panels of the platform, Kolova saw a deep pit with several layers of crisscrossing pipes. Gathered on the platform were a couple of dozen more colonists, including a handful of officers from the local police force. Everyone waiting on the platform had come with lightweight personal armaments: stun pistols, shock guns, and a few melee weapons. It wouldn't be enough to win a prolonged stand-up fight against the crews of two Starfleet starships, but that had never been Kolova's intention.

The rest of her group from the bunker filed out of the passageway behind her and spread out onto the large platform. As soon as she was sure they all were accounted for, she moved to the center of the platform and raised her voice to be heard over the background rumble and hiss that permeated the undercity. "Thank you all for coming. I'm sure you're all aware that we're facing a pair of threats right now. To be honest, I'm not sure which one I fear more—the alien thing in the sea that's trying to kill us, or the Starfleeters who seem more interested in arresting us than helping us." Turning in a slow circle, she read the nods of agreement in the crowd as a good sign. "I want to make this next point very clear: We did not come down here to hide. We're here to plan our next move, and we need to make it quickly."

A man who looked as if he had spent his life tinkering with gadgets coated in black grease raised his hand, then spoke before Kolova had a chance to realize he was interrupting her. "I sure hope our next move is finding a way off this rock!" The crowd rumbled in concurrence.

"Not an option," Kolova said with as much force as she could muster. "We scrapped our transports to build better cities. *Stronger* cities. So, no—running's not an option for us. Our first task is to figure out what Starfleet's doing about the Juggernaut. If they're dragging their feet, we need to light a fire under them."

One of the police officers, a woman whose name tag read EICHORN, stepped forward. "Governor, I understand why you're emphasizing the need to motivate Starfleet, but I think we need to start talking about what's going to happen to us after all this is over. Legally, I mean."

"Yeah," added Tanzer, the engineer. "Assuming we live, how screwed are we?"

Ishii moved to stand beside Kolova, as if he could physically shield her from criticism. "There's good news and bad news. The bad news is that Starfleet has already acquired a great deal of evidence regarding the presence of an extinct indigenous civilization here on Sirsa III, and that means there's going to be a full investigation by the Federation Council." Groans and profanities rose up like a swelling wave. The chief of staff raised his hands, gesturing for calm. "The good news is that most of their legal wrath is likely to fall upon the Kayo Mining Consortium"—he shared a pessimistic look with Kolova—"and upon myself and the governor. Most of you will not likely face any individual charges."

Grease-man asked, "But we're going to lose the colony, right?"

"Our charter is likely to be revoked, yes," Ishii said. "But that doesn't mean we don't have alternatives. Most of you could just stay put while the Federation installs a new interim colonial government. They might ask you to draw up your own charter, or they might hand you off to another sponsor. But if you stay, you'll have to find new ways to make a living if you want more than a subsistence lifestyle, because all mining ops will be suspended pending a new planetary survey by Starfleet and the Federation Colonial Authority."

Eichorn was a portrait of dismay. "What if we defect? Get some other power to raise its flag on this rock? I bet the Orions would love a shot at all this mineral wealth."

"Sure they would," Bowen said. "As long as you don't mind living like a serf under the tender mercies of an Orion merchant prince. Me? I'll take a rain check on that."

"As would I," added Bowen's right-hand gal Omalu. "I would rather spend ten years in a Federation penal colony than live for one year as an Orion's peon."

Kolova felt the meeting slipping off subject, and she was determined not to let that happen, not with so much at stake. "Everyone, stop. The Orions won't plant a flag if doing so means open war with the Federation, so just forget about that. The hard truth is that if we live through this, I'm probably going to a penal colony. I will do everything I can to make sure none of you goes with me. But first we have to survive long enough for that to be an issue." She pointed at Tanzer. "Is this the safest part of the undercity?"

"Define 'safest.'"

"When the Juggernaut sends its next attack and starts blowing holes in everything, is this where you would want to be?"

"All things being equal, I'd rather be on a different planet."

She cowed him with a glare. "Well, you're stuck on this one with the rest of us, so get your goddamned head in the game. When the shit hits the fan, where's the safest place for us all to be? Here? Or somewhere else?"

Grease-man intervened. "Madam Governor? If I knew the world was ending topside, I'd want to be as far below the auxiliary reservoir as I could get. Tons of metal and thermo-concrete down there, and millions of gallons of water. Good barrier against blast effects and radiation."

That worked for Kolova. "You know how to get there from here?"

"Yes, ma'am."

"Then you're on point, Mister . . . ?"

"Tassin. Roy Tassin."

"Lead on, Mister Tassin." Kolova ushered everyone into motion. "The world's about to catch fire, and I want to be well away from the flames when it does."

Fine tendrils of lightning danced between the radiant sphere and the softly glowing overhead of the Juggernaut's central passageway. At each thick-ribbed interval, the crackling sphere dropped and spun, throwing off sparks as it ducked beneath the protruding structural supports. Then, on the other side, it would bob upward once more to skirt the ceiling, all the while teasing it and the lower portions of the oval corridor with luminous jolts of electricity.

Following a few paces behind the orb, Spock could not help but compare his and Burnham's following of the orb to a fish being tempted by the shine of a lure.

At his side, Burnham remained fixated upon the holographic entity, which she had persisted in calling "Thumper," on account of the powerful, low-frequency pulses it emitted in synchronicity with its momentary increases in brightness. Spock wondered whether it might hold some special fascination for her because of her human neurophysiology, one that eluded his predominantly Vulcan mind. He observed her discreetly for a moment before he spoke.

"May I ask a question?"

She split her attention between Spock and the orb, which at least reassured him that she wasn't entirely under some form of hypnotic control. "Ask away."

"Why do you think the Juggernaut dispatched this hologram to us?" He tilted his head toward the passageway ahead of them. "There do not appear to be any intersec-

tions or diversions for us to consider, so it is unlikely to
have been intended as a guide."

His observation seemed to intrigue her. "Do *you* have a
hypothesis?"

"Perhaps. It manifested shortly after I began to question the wisdom of pushing deeper inside the vessel." He
regarded the bobbing orb with dispassion. "I believe it to
be a distraction."

"You might be right," Burnham said. "But in the interest of full disclosure, I've been committed to exploring the
inside of this thing from the moment I saw it. And since
we're on a rather tight deadline, I would've insisted on continuing forward, orb or no orb."

He respected her honesty, as well as her tenacity and
clarity of purpose. Shortly after the orb cleared its next
inverse hurdle, it halted and traveled in a circle against
the ceiling. Spock and Burnham stepped underneath it
and gazed upward. "What is it doing?" Burnham wondered.

"Perhaps it—" The orb vanished in a flash of light, taking Spock's train of thought with it.

Then he felt a vibration in the deck, the kind that resonated throughout his body—and only too late did he pin-
point its source, behind them: "Sir!"

Burnham looked back in time to see the passageway
constrict behind them, just beyond the structural support
rib. She extended her arm in front of Spock and ushered
him half a step away from the sudden obstruction. It solidi-
fied with hardly a sound.

"Well," Burnham said, "I guess forward really is our
only option now." She started to walk onward, only to
pause when her foot struck another barrier. Surprise and
a momentary flicker of anger animated her features as she

recoiled from the next segment rib. Then she reached out and ran her hand across what was now revealed to be a bulkhead adorned by a two-dimensional holographic image of the corridor they had expected to see continuing onward.

"A holographic *trompe l'oeil*," Spock said. "A crude but effective deception."

"More than just a deception, Spock." Burnham knocked on the image. "A trap. And a solid one, at that." She took out her communicator and flipped open its grille. "Burnham to *Shenzhou*. Do you read me, *Shenzhou*? . . . Burnham to *Enterprise*. Please respond." She listened for a few seconds, then put away the device. "Nothing, not even static."

Spock nodded. "It would seem the Juggernaut intends for us to either remain here indefinitely, or to engineer our own means of escape."

"A reasonable assumption," Burnham said. "Though I have to wonder what—"

A piercing tone assaulted Spock's ears.

He winced at the pain, purely out of reflex. Next to him, Burnham gritted her teeth and clapped her hands to her ears, but she remained in agony. The sound came from everywhere at once—the bulkheads, the overhead, from ahead and behind. Covering his own highly sensitive ears did Spock no good. He lowered his hands and reached for his tricorder.

Burnham spoke to him, but he couldn't hear what she was saying. Then he saw blood trickle from her ears and her nostrils—and he felt warm sensations issuing from his own nose and ears. He palmed dark green blood from his upper lip.

Whatever was generating this terrible sound, it had been weaponized to penetrate flesh and bone—and unless he and Burnham found a way to stop it or to escape this chamber in the next sixty seconds, he had no doubt that it would kill them both.

15

The tone was a spike through Burnham's ears, a knife cleaving her thoughts. No matter how hard she focused on the teachings of her Vulcan mentors that pain is a product of the mind, something to be mastered by reason and discipline, all those lessons abandoned her now. All she knew in the world was white-hot agony. It had put her on her knees. Humbled her like a child.

It took every remaining ounce of her Vulcan conditioning to suppress her body's urge to panic. Squinting, she saw Spock reach for his tricorder and struggle with its controls.

She tried to shout over the screeching, "Spock! Do you have a plan?"

He looked at her, his face wrinkled from discomfort and confusion.

Blood issued from her ears, then from her nose. Warm and tacky to the touch, it was proof that her pain was no illusion. Then she saw Spock's ears and nose start to bleed, and she knew the sonic attack was no petty obstacle: it had been designed to kill them.

Forced onto her hands and knees, she crawled toward Spock. He slumped back-first against a bulkhead and landed in a sitting pose on the deck, his legs splayed in front of him. All the way down he continued trying to change the settings on his tricorder. But as soon as he came to rest on the deck, the portable scanning device fell from his left hand, and he pitched over to his right and sprawled across the deck, unconscious.

Pulling herself forward through sheer willpower, Burnham felt as if her skull were cracking apart, its fragments collapsing under the onslaught of that merciless shriek. Her body yearned to succumb, to surrender to the pain and sink into the comfort of black oblivion, but she refused to grant herself that mercy.

Her hand landed on Spock's tricorder. She pulled it closer and strained to focus her eyes on its settings, in the hope of deducing what Spock had been attempting before his collapse. In a glance she understood his plan and knew what had to be done. She tweaked its settings with trembling hands. There would be no time to fine-tune it. It would either work the first time, or else she and Spock would die, here and now.

She activated the high-frequency audio sensor and triggered the noise-canceling wave. Instantly the crushing and piercing sensations in her head abated, and within seconds the hideous shriek had abated to a tremor in the air. It was a simple, direct solution. *Good thing Spock thought of it as quickly as he did. If only I had been a bit quicker—* She put a stop to that line of thinking. *No time now for regret or blame. Stay focused, remember your training.*

Burnham cleaned the blood from her face and used her tricorder to assess her condition. *No lasting damage,* she was relieved to see. *Nothing a few hours in sickbay won't fix.*

She kneeled beside Spock. Using the end of her sleeve, she dabbed the green blood from his chin and upper lip, then from his ears and neck. A quick check of his vital signs with her tricorder revealed that he also had escaped any serious lasting injury, though she suspected he might have a headache for the remainder of the day. She put away her tricorder and tried to rouse him in a firm but gentle manner. "Mister Spock, can you hear me?"

His eyes fluttered open. He did a poor job of masking his pain as he sat up, letting slip a wince that confirmed Burnham's theory about his cranial discomfort. Rubbing the nape of his neck, he said, "I see you finished my noise-canceling wave."

"I did. Once I saw your partial settings, I grasped your intent." She rested her hand on his back to help steady him. "Do you feel ready to stand?"

"I believe so. But I would appreciate your assistance."

She slipped her hands under his armpits and added her strength to his as he got back on his feet. Upright once more, he dusted himself off and smoothed his blue uniform tunic.

"Thank you," he said. "Now, if I am not mistaken, our next challenge"—he raised an eyebrow before he finished—"appears to have been resolved for us." He nodded toward the forward end of the chamber. "The path beckons."

Burnham turned to see that the bulkhead with the hologram had vanished at some point while they had been focused upon each other. The passageway was now open, and it climbed along the back of the Juggernaut in a gentle slope. The only difference she noted was that the luminescence in the corridor ahead ranged in hue from deep gold to burnt orange.

"The color's changed," she said to Spock. "Do you think that's significant?"

"Unknown. It might be a purely aesthetic element—or it could signify increased levels of difficulty and danger." He picked up his tricorder. "The high-frequency tone has ceased." He switched the device back to its default passive-sensor state. "Time is short. We should go."

Troubled by the calamity that had nearly finished them, Burnham paused. "In a moment." She eyed their surroundings with a new degree of suspicion. "This Juggernaut has been on this planet for millions of years. And if, as I suspect, it was sent to lure in members of the indigenous primitive culture in order to test them . . . I have to wonder: Why would it feature a trap that can only be survived through the use of advanced technology? The natives wouldn't have had any."

"No, but we did," Spock said. "The Juggernaut has already demonstrated an ability to adapt and modify its drones to suit their intended prey. It is logical to assume it is equally capable of modifying the challenges it poses within itself, in order to present an appropriate level of difficulty for those who come to it. As I recall, when we first entered, the holographic orb performed what seemed to be an invasive scan of our communicators, tricorders, and phasers."

"So it knows what our equipment can do," Burnham said, following Spock's reasoning. "Now it means to find out what *we* can do."

An unfazed nod from Spock. "So it would seem."

"Never a dull day in Starfleet." She tucked away her tricorder and led Spock into the vermilion passage. "Let's go see how it means to kill us next."

The carvings formed a cathedral of bone and marble. Being rendered in the monochrome of Saru's enhanced goggles did nothing to diminish the majesty of the ancient monument, which had been formed from the fossilized ribs of some gargantuan beast and curved slabs of polished stone.

Unlike the rest of the rocky maze Saru and Una had traversed to reach this place, the floor under the enormous
curving bones was tiled with polished bits of marble and
glass. It lacked the deliberate art of a mosaic, but it was no
less beautiful for its evocation of natural chaos.

"Most remarkable," Una said, her head swiveling from
one point of interest to the next. "None of the other areas
of habitation exhibited this level of sophistication, size, or
detail."

It was a labor for Saru to interrupt his admiration of
the space in order to make some scans of it with his field
tricorder, a slender rectangular frame of burnished metal
around a responsive touchscreen. "The age of this construc-
tion is consistent with the other parts of the settlement
we've examined." He applied some filters and watched the
data shift in real time. "The stone elements are definitely
marble, unlike anything else in this cave. I would surmise
that all of the marble pieces in this structure were obtained
elsewhere."

Una reviewed some scans on her own tricorder, whose
offset beveled edges appeared more prominent in her
smaller hands. "I'm comparing the trace elements and other
chemical markers in the marble to the geological scans
made during the original planetary survey." After a moment, a nod. "The only region that has this kind of marble
is over three hundred kilometers from here. That would
support your hypothesis."

"I wonder if this was part of their settlement before
they encountered the Juggernaut, or if it was something
created later." Saru lowered his tricorder and envied the
xenoarcheologists who would soon be dispatched to this
planet to answer questions such as his, among others. Part
of him wanted to join them . . . but then he felt the irresist-

ible attraction of a galaxy filled with wonders, all awaiting him and the crew of the *Shenzhou*.

A few meters ahead of him, Una stopped, faced a long curved wall of marble, and pointed her tricorder at it. "I think I found something." She returned the device to a pouch on the outside of her pack. "Switch the frequency on your goggles to C-band."

Saru did as Una had directed. In the blink of a filter transition, everything changed. Nearly every centimeter of the enormous wall was decorated with art, images scribed not in pigment but etched directly into the stone. "Why didn't we see this before?"

"Layers of dust and sediment," Una said. "A lot can collect in nine million years."

They drifted in slow steps along the wall, transfixed by the elaborate mural. "These illustrations are more advanced than I would have expected," Saru said. "They demonstrate a keen understanding of parallax, depth of field, and selective focus. Its figures exhibit details beyond the symbolic—I would say this is on par with most cultures' representational periods."

"The style is quite sophisticated," Una said. She pointed out other aspects of the mural. "But what impresses me most is the manner in which these images have been arranged, separated from one another, and placed in relation to one another." She took a step back to review a broader segment of it at once. "This has all the hallmarks of sequential art. I think we're looking at more than a simple mural, Saru—I think this is a graphical narrative."

Looking closer, Saru saw the same thing. "Amazing." It was a struggle to resist his desire to reach out and touch the art, to make contact with this tangible piece of prehistory. "These remind me of the kinds of drawings my people use to document our lives underground. The engravings, the narrative sequencing. It all feels so . . . *familiar*."

Una pointed at a series of images in one corner. "It looks as if it's made to be read starting at the top, from right to left, and then reversing direction with each row." She led Saru to the far end of the mural, and together they started walking its length, back and forth, as they parsed its visual tale. "These early panels seem to describe a surface-dwelling culture," she said.

"Nomads," Saru said. "Hunter-gatherers. Sheltering in forests and caves." He directed Una's attention to a representation of the sun. "Note how the number of dots around it changes. That might suggest years, or generations, or some other unit of time."

"Possibly." The images changed to scenes familiar to most students of sentient history. "The rise of agriculture. The formation of stable cities alongside rivers and sea-coasts." Una gestured toward a depiction of three groups of natives, with each group's helmets demarcated by different symbols. "This might indicate the beginning of trade between different settlements. Or the start of conflict. It's not really clear."

There was nothing ambiguous about the next image in the mural's narrative sequence. It dominated a huge chunk of the graphical real estate on its slab of marble: the Juggernaut, surrounded by pillars of fire or energy reaching into the heavens, and emitting rays that cut down the natives who had gathered around it. "I suppose that rules out any notion that the Juggernaut came in peace," Saru said.

"It certainly doesn't paint the vessel in a forgiving light." They moved together to the next marble slab, on which had been inscribed an image of pairs of natives lined up to enter the Juggernaut through a single opening on its dorsal hull, while it lay half-buried on a beach.

Then the two officers arrived at the last slab in the mural, its final image: an epitaph for a species and its culture. In the center of the image was the Juggernaut, sending out beams and curling waves of energy, all of which seemed to lay waste to the landscape by tearing it asunder and setting it ablaze. A tiny handful of natives—their helmets a jumble of mismatched symbols—were depicted huddled in the darkness deep below the ground, inside a shelter that bore a striking similarity to the bone cathedral in which Saru and Una now stood.

Gazing in horror at the image of a world in flames, Saru felt his species' gift for sensing impending doom make his tongue taste like tin and set his pulse racing. "That is not good."

Una's wide eyes betrayed the same grim understanding. "No," she said in a hushed voice. "That's not good at all."

"Cave paintings don't exactly constitute hard evidence of the Juggernaut's origin," Georgiou said, having weighed Saru and Una's report against Starfleet's unforgiving criteria for intelligence analysis. "However, given your estimations of their age, and the specificity of their graphical content, I'm willing to concede they merit further study."

"Thank you, Captain," Saru replied over the audio-only channel. *"We've discovered another set of illustrations on the exterior of this underground temple. It's not yet clear if their narrative is related to the one about the Juggernaut, but we need more time to study them."*

Georgiou reclined behind her desk in her ready room. "How much longer do you need?"

"It's unclear, Captain," Saru said. *"Commander Una and I both feel there is much to learn from this site, but we understand that only mission-critical intel is desired at this time."* There were muffled sounds of conversation as he conferred privately with Una. *"We should be able to complete our survey of this temple within the hour."*

"Very well." Georgiou let her eyes wander from one item to another as she swiveled toward the wall of partitioned shelves behind her desk. Each piece of note was housed in its own angled nook. Geodes, small sculptures, and other artifacts both natural and artificial she had collected from worlds throughout the explored galaxy surrounded a tall central nook occupied by an alien artist's colorful statue of a warrior-priest. Gazing upon them, she calmed her tempest of conflicting thoughts. "You have exactly one hour, Mister Saru. Then you need to leave those caves and get back to the surface for beam-up."

"Understood, Captain. Thank you. Saru out."

She was at least thankful for the change in his demeanor. For the first time since she had told him that he had been passed over for the first officer's billet, he sounded as if he might actually be excited about something. More than that, he sounded as if, perhaps, he might actually be having fun. *Heavens, I hope so,* she prayed to whatever power might listen.

Georgiou turned back toward her desk and rested her chin on the fisted column of her arm. To her left, on a small table set against the bulkhead separating her ready room from the bridge, was an antique turntable, complete with a vinyl disc bearing an analog audio recording cut by one needle and waiting to be read by another. The restored antique had been a gift from her ex-husband, Nikos; it and her surname were the only things he had ever given her that she hadn't discarded in their divorce, both retained in the name of sentimentality.

Perched on the deep sill that fronted her ready room's aft-facing viewport was an antique telescope. *From this low orbit, I could probably take the Juggernaut's measure with my own eyes,* she reflected.

Impatient for signs of progress, she used the panel on her desk to open a channel to the main cargo hold. "Georgiou to Commander Johar."

"This is Johar," said the chief engineer. *"What can I do for you, Captain?"*

"How goes your analysis of the probe debris?"

"Slowly, I'm afraid. We're mapping out its circuit pathways, but I can't really claim to know yet how this thing works. But we might have a bit of good news."

"I'm all ears, Commander."

"We've been investigating a number of unusual trace compounds in the drone's hull that we also detected in the Juggernaut's hull. There are some beaucoup strange elements in there, ma'am. Including a few not found naturally on this planet, or on more than a handful of others."

That sounded promising. "Any chance you could narrow down *which* other world might have been the source of those elements?"

Johar's mood brightened. *"A very good chance, Captain. But I could answer that for you a great deal faster if I had the help I needed from the sciences division. To be precise, I'd love it if someone would light a fire under the asses of our astrophysics, exogeology, and xenohistory experts. If I had them working this from all sides at once—"*

"Say no more," Georgiou said. She started composing an order on her desktop terminal. "I'm sending out a directive to sciences and to Oliveira to allocate to you and your team any and all personnel and resources you deem necessary."

She imagined she could hear Johar pumping his fist in a pantomime of victory. *"Thank you, Captain. We'll have something actionable for you inside of an hour, I'm sure of it."*

"I hope you're right," Georgiou said, "because if we get caught with our pants down when the next drone attack comes, there's a serious risk we might all end up dead. So whatever angle you're working, make sure it includes a plan to neutralize or destroy those drones."

"Understood, Captain. We're on it. Johar out."

The channel closed with a soft click, and once more Georgiou felt isolated in her ready room. Time was bleeding away, yet she felt paralyzed. What more could she do? It was the great paradox of command. Her role was to set objectives, define goals, and let her people work. But once that was done, there was often little she could do but sit back and wait to see whether the dominos she set to falling landed as intended or went askew.

The chrono on her desktop reminded her that Burnham and Lieutenant Spock from the *Enterprise* now had less than two hours to unlock the mysteries of the Juggernaut. The two of them had either passed out of communications range or were having their comm signals blocked now that they were inside the Juggernaut. None of the myriad technical tricks normally employed by communications officer Fan had been able to raise the duo. Whatever they might have found or encountered inside the Juggernaut, it would remain known only to them unless and until they found some means to restore contact with the *Shenzhou* and the *Enterprise*.

Georgiou stood and stepped out from behind her desk. She walked over to the turntable—a device she had once heard her grandfather refer to by its colloquial nickname of a "record player"—and let her hand hover over its activation switch. The analog playback device was delicate, but the vinyl discs from which it replicated sound were downright fragile. Feeling a need for its warm, natural tones in the cold, gray sterility of her ready room, she turned it on.

One touch was all it took. The device activated and followed a precise routine. The flat turntable began to rotate at a speed of thirty-three and one-third revolutions per minute. As it achieved its proper velocity, its arm—a fluid-balanced polymer rod whose angular head housed a precision-cut diamond needle—lifted from its cradle at the side of the machine and swung out to hover above the outer edge of the vinyl disc. Then, with slow grace, it dropped into position. The needle found smooth blank space at the disc's edge and glided across it, into a steady, continuous, inward-turning groove almost too narrow to see with the naked eye.

From the device's built-in speaker came a soft crackling— the interference of dust against the needle—and a low hum, a resonance of the turntable's own motor.

And then there was music.

The bright metallic shimmer of cymbals. A tinkling of piano strings struck by tiny key hammers. The voice of a trumpet and the wailing of a saxophone. Sensual thumps of rhythm from a stand-up bass. All fusing into a sophisticated melody—this was jazz. A vintage recording of Miles Davis and Sonny Rollins, a performance captured over three hundred years earlier.

And it sounded as if it were happening for the first time, there in her ready room.

Apart from live performance, vinyl analog recordings were Georgiou's favorite way to enjoy music. Rich, warm, and so eerily present—that was the enduring appeal of

analog media, the bizarre magic that gave them such ca-
chet among aficionados of jazz and classical music. She had
never heard a single digitized recording that had affected
her quite so profoundly.

This was how Georgiou freed herself of thoughts that
refused to find resolution or order. The music helped her
mind make strange connections, discover untapped possibilities, and just learn to process information in unexpected
ways. Alone with the solace of jazz, she could allow her
mind to go blank and make room for new ideas to flourish.

Or, if that failed, it was her one comfort in, and escape
from, a job and a universe she had started to believe really
meant to be the death of her.

But not today, she promised herself. *Not here . . . and not
today.*

16

Soon after Spock and Burnham had moved ahead from the Juggernaut's first deathtrap, its holographic sprite reappeared to keep their attention fixed in a forward direction. At least, that was the purpose Spock inferred from the orb's presence and behavior. It did not seem to offer helpful cues to warn of their trials or point the way past them. It merely existed, a technological will-o'-the-wisp to coax them deeper into the shadows—until it rebounded off another closed portal in front of them, again disguised with a holographic image of the corridor beyond.

Then a portal spiraled closed behind them, its final pinhole melting without a trace into the smart metal of the Juggernaut's hull. Spock regarded their predicament with dry detachment. "It would appear our next test is imminent."

Burnham eyed the bulkheads around them, and then the overhead. "I have to confess a measure of curiosity. Which will it present first: the riddle, or the threat?"

The hologram on the closed portal ahead of them switched off, revealing a pair of user interfaces at either end of its flattened oval frame. The two panels were similar in configuration to the ones Spock and Burnham had used on the exterior of the vessel, in order to gain entry. "It would appear the riddle has been presented," he said. He moved toward the blank panel on the right, and Burnham put herself in front of its counterpart on the left.

She dragged her palm across the flank of her uniform, leaving behind a sheen of sweat. "Is it just me," she said, "or is it quickly getting warmer in here?"

Spock had not immediately noticed the upward shift in temperature, as it was still well within what he considered a comfortable range, but once aware of it, he felt it acutely. "You are not incorrect. The temperature has increased." He retrieved his tricorder from its half-pocket holster on his belt and checked the device's running sensor logs. "To be precise, the temperature inside this compartment has risen by six point one degrees Celsius since the portal behind us closed. Current temperature is twenty-eight degrees. If the rate of ambient thermal increase remains consistent, we can expect it to rise approximately six degrees per minute."

"Now we know the threat. Let's get to work on the riddle." She positioned her palm above her smooth panel, and waited until Spock did the same. "On the count of three." He nodded his understanding, so she started her count. "One. Two. Three."

In unison they pressed their hands to the interface panels.

Percussive noise assaulted Spock's ears. It was so loud that he felt the pressure of displaced air on his skin with each bass beat, and the higher-pitched tones were painful to hear. The effect was agonizing cacophony. He pulled his hand from his panel, and the compartment went silent. Burnham removed her hand from her panel. "Are you all right?"

"I am," he said, masking his discomfort. "I was unprepared for that level of volume. I had hoped that removing my hand might reduce it by some measure."

Burnham shook her head. "Looks like it's designed to be all or nothing." She put her hand back above her panel. "Ready to try again?" She waited until he affirmed his readiness with a nod, then she counted, "One. Two. Three."

Their hands both pressed down, and the concentration-shattering din resumed. Spock closed his eyes and focused on the panel under his palm. His sense of time melted away while he felt raised shapes manifest on the smart-metal surface—ovals linked by radiating lines to dots and tiny triangles and squares. "The surface under my hand is manifesting shapes," he shouted over the noise to Burnham.

"I feel them too," she hollered back. "Simple at first. But getting more complex."

"I am noticing the same pattern." The deafening clamor made him wince. Was its purpose to test their ability to focus in spite of distraction? It seemed possible, but did the heat not already serve that function? He forced past the noise to give his full attention to the shapes, and to a matrix of hexagons that appeared on the portal's holographic surface. Each new shape was reproduced inside its own hexagon after it melted from the smart-metal panel.

He looked over at Burnham, whose face was beaded with sweat that pasted her stylish forelock of dark hair to her forehead. "Are you all right?"

"I'd feel better if it were a dry heat," she shouted over the noise, which continued to pummel them from either side. "Do you know what these symbols mean?"

Spock searched for significance in the arrangement of the symbols in the hexagons. "The symbols do not fall into uniform rows or columns. They form clusters and branches—some parallel to others, some distinct and separated from the rest." His voice grew hoarse from shouting as the air became hotter. "I do not believe it represents any kind of simple mathematical progression." To his surprise, his observations went unremarked by Burnham.

He checked on the *Shenzhou*'s first officer. She seemed on the verge of wilting as the temperature passed what Spock realized must be close to forty-six degrees Celsius—a not-unusual level of heat on Vulcan. He knew Burnham had spent most of her life acclimating to such heat, but it had been years since she had endured it on a regular basis, and her human physiology was unlikely to deliver her peak performance under such conditions for much longer.

"Burnham!" he called to her. Weakly, she lifted her head to look at him. "Do not succumb to the heat. We must both remain conscious and in contact with the panels in order to complete this test."

"I'm trying, Spock, but this alien oven has me beat."

He was about to offer some platitude intended to bolster her spirit, but her words sparked a moment of sudden connection in his thoughts. *Yes,* he realized, *that's it. It must be.*

"Stay with me," he told Burnham. "I need you to pay attention to the rhythm on your side of the compartment."

She blinked, then squinted at him. "The what? Why?"

"The tempo," Spock said. "The rhythm issuing from your side of the compartment is not the same as the one on mine. If I am correct, I believe the time signatures in each percussive pattern hold a key to the solution of this challenge."

Burnham nodded, then closed her eyes. She tapped her foot on the deck to map out one portion of the pattern playing behind her, and she drummed her free index finger against her leg to track the other side of the rhythm. Spock closed his eyes and listened to his side's pattern. As a trained musician, he did not need to tap out the pattern to isolate it in his thoughts.

At the same time he and Burnham opened their eyes and faced each other.

"My side's time signature is two-five," Burnham said.

"Mine is two-three." He faced the growing tree of symbols inside the hexagons on the holographic display over the portal. "We need to match those figures to these." Now Spock felt stymied. "Unfortunately, none of those look like fractions to me."

Burnham looked ready to collapse. "What if they aren't supposed to be?" She sagged forward against the bulkhead, but kept her hand on her panel. "What if we're meant to read the time signatures as whole numbers? Twenty-five and twenty-three?" She threw a lazy wave at the clusters and strings of symbols in the hologram. "Some of those notations aren't that different from the ones we used to solve the prime factorizations at the first hatchway."

"Yes," Spock said, starting to see the logic in the arrangement before him. "Growing from simple to more complex, arranged in branches and clusters—"

Burnham blurted out the answer just as Spock thought of it: "It's the periodic table! Or an alien version of it, anyway. And if they want us to press twenty-five and twenty-three—"

"Then we just need to identify which of these symbols represents the atomic structures of manganese and vanadium, respectively," Spock said. "Most logical. Shall we proceed?"

"Please, before I go from medium to well-done."

They lifted their hands from the interface pads and met in front of the oval portal. Burnham touched the symbol for manganese as Spock put his hand to the symbol for vanadium. Both symbols glowed green as the others around them faded away. Then the holographic screen went dark, and the obstruction retreated into its frame, like a fast-melting glacier, to reveal the next leg of the Juggernaut's central passageway ahead, glowing an intense reddish-orange. Cool air washed over Spock and Burnham, bringing the human woman some clearly welcome relief.

Spock took Burnham's arm and helped her over the portal's frame. After a few moments in the cooler environment, Burnham was quick to recover her focus. "Thank you, Mister Spock." She cast a half-amused look at the peril they'd just escaped. "And to think . . . I once laughed at Sarek when he told me music was a vital subject."

"Odd," Spock said. "He often seemed to regard my interest in music as a frivolity."

Burnham trudged forward, toward the next challenge. "If we live through this, let's have the Andorian Imperial Drum Corps honor him with a predawn serenade."

"I have entertained less reasonable suggestions," Spock said as he fell into step beside her, not knowing what they would face next, but confident they would overcome it together.

The last thing Saru wanted was to return to the planet's surface, with its dangerously open spaces, harsh daylight, and free-moving wind full of scents alien yet almost familiar. He had felt nearly at home in the underground caverns, sequestered in the darkness. It had reminded him of his youth on Kelpia, his days of roaming its seemingly endless networks of subterranean passages with his clanmates. Even the pictographic quality of this world's long-extinct natives had fostered fond remembrances. Though he had long been estranged from his people on Kelpia, this excursion had, for too brief a moment, felt like a sort of homecoming.

Lost in his thoughts, he led Una out of the catacombs. The climb had been more taxing than the descent, and had left Una a bit short of breath for conversation. Though Saru could have carried on a spirited monologue for the duration of the return, he had elected to keep his silence. Una comported herself like one who eschewed small talk and pointless chatter. Her stoicism was yet another quality Saru admired.

Soon enough the light of day came into view, a beacon to mark the end of their shared journey. Saru exited the cave entrance first, his gangly legs overstepping the large rocks piled at the cave's mouth. Una stepped onto the rocks as she passed over them, and then she stopped to bask in the warmth of the afternoon sunlight. "Good to be back aboveground," she said.

"I suppose," Saru said, suppressing his urge to regale Una with every stray factoid there was to know about Kelpiens and their preference for dwelling and traveling underground. He lifted his tricorder just enough to call attention to it. "Before I start my analysis on the *Shenzhou*, I will transmit a copy of my data to you for independent confirmation."

Una offered a smile of gratitude. "And I will do the same from the *Enterprise*."

As she reached for her communicator, Saru sought to postpone their separation. "I expect my analysis will take under an hour, provided I receive priority access to the computer."

"That sounds like a reasonable estimate," Una said. She

flipped open the grille of her communicator and was about to activate its ship-to-shore channel.

Saru took a halting step toward Una. "I just wanted to say, Commander, that I have very much enjoyed making your acquaintance." He wondered how much he could confess without turning the moment awkward; he gambled on truthfulness. "I have not always found my Starfleet colleagues easy to understand. My attempts to forge meaningful bonds with them—of friendship, or even just simple camaraderie—have often met with rejection or misunderstanding." Despite the fact that he towered over Una, he felt small as he bowed his head to add, "If only I could change my past, I should very much have liked to have served with you."

She took his hand and favored him with a smile. "I'm going to hold you to that if I ever get a command of my own. Because I, for one, would welcome the privilege of serving with a keen, enlightened mind such as yours, Lieutenant. And let me also say that the feeling is mutual: I, too, have greatly enjoyed meeting you." She let go of his hand and stepped a few meters away from him. "Now let's hope our commanding officers don't get one or both of us killed."

A sardonic wit and a born realist, Saru swooned. *She'd have made a fine Kelpien.*

Una activated her communicator. "Una to *Enterprise.* One to beam up."

"Stand by for transport," a male voice replied over the comm.

A wash of sonorous noise, then a shine of golden energy cocooned Una. The particles danced and swam, and they grew brighter as the image of her faded. Then the coruscating light dissipated along with the doleful whine of the transporter effect, and a swirling gust of warm wind became Saru's only companion in the rocky pass.

He had been sad to see her go, and now he feared what might happen if Georgiou and Pike's confrontation escalated. *What if I never see her again?* he wondered.

Deep breaths. In through his body's countless spiracles, then out through his nostrils. It was not the most efficient means of oxygenating his blood supply, but the practice had been proved to have a calming effect on his species. After several seconds he felt in control of his emotions. Equilibrium had been restored, and with it his hard-won air of dignity.

Can't let the apex predators see one actually having tender feelings, now can one? One sign of weakness and the meat-eaters go for the jugular.

He opened the grille of his communicator, resigned to the resumption of his duties in the company of those who would likely never really appreciate or comprehend his true self. "Saru to *Shenzhou.* One for transport. Energize when ready."

"Acknowledged, Lieutenant," a female officer replied. *"Stand by."*

Within moments he would be safe once again in the comforting embrace of the transporter beam. Its blessing of intangibility would be fleeting, but that made it no less a pleasure for Saru. The first thing that every Kelpien learned was that the essential nature of life and the universe is impermanence: everything changes, and everything ends. Trying to resist that truth is the root of all suffering. Or, as he had learned to phrase it for his Starfleet comrades: *Enjoy what you have while you have it. Because any second now, it, and you, might cease to be.*

As the transporter beam enfolded him, he felt perplexed.

I fail to understand why I am not more popular at social gatherings.

If there was a segment of New Astana's underground infrastructure less accessible or more remote than the pumping station beneath its central reservoir, Gretchen Kolova didn't want to see it. There was precious little free space in the control room, barely enough for her and the other resisters to gather in a standing-room-only capacity. Above them was the forbidding shell of the auxiliary reservoir, itself located near the nadir of an abyss of crisscrossed pipes.

She and her inner circle—which now consisted of her political advisers Ishii and Medina; drilling-rig survivors Bowen, Chandra, and Omalu; ranking police officer Eichorn; Tanzer, the engineer; and Tassin, the mechanic—gathered around the room's main situation table, which had been designed to control the flow and filtration of water resources throughout the city.

"This'll do as a short-term base," Kolova said. Pointing out tunnel junctions on the table's water-system map, she continued, "We'll need to post sentries or intruder-detection devices here, here, and here, and at all the points on sublevel eight, since that's where they'll have to make their first incursion to reach the lower sublevels."

Eichorn studied the map. "I have enough people and gear to get that done."

"Good," Kolova said. "That brings us to our next issue: monitoring the two Starfleet ships in orbit."

Ishii leaned forward, over the table. "Shouldn't we concentrate on putting people in position to move against the Starfleet medical teams already on the surface? We're going to need them as bargaining chips."

Kolova shook her head. "I'd rather not escalate to violence unless we have to. For now I'm willing to play cat and mouse. As long as we evade capture, we can use ourselves as leverage. We tell Starfleet that if they save the colony, we'll come quietly."

"Speak for yourself," Bowen grumbled.

"I'm not proposing we hand ourselves over without taking precautions," Kolova said. "But saving our fellow colonists has to be our chief priority, or else we're nothing but fugitives trying to save our own skins. And I plan on making those Starfleet captains share my priorities." She scanned the faces in the room. "So, how do we monitor the ships?"

"We're not equipped to do more than track their movements in orbit," Medina said. "If we tap into the planetary traffic-control system, we'll at least have a sense of where they are. Beyond that, the system can't tell us much. It lacks tactical components, so we can't know if they're charging weapons or raising shields unless they announce it on an open channel."

Kolova concealed her disappointment. "It's a start," she said.

"It's not enough," Bowen said. "Starfleet almost never uses open channels. If we really want to know what's going on up there, we need to be tapped into their coded frequencies. That's the only way we'll know what the two captains are telling each other, what they're telling Starfleet Command, and what it's telling them."

Tanzer threw some side-eye shade at Bowen. "And how are we supposed to do that? They've got military-grade comms, and all we've got are what Kayo's lowest bidders were willing to provide."

"It's just a difference in processing power and speed,"

Chandra said. "Scrounge up some spare duotronic chip sets, plug them into an FTL array, and then all you need is the software."

Omalu rolled her eyes at her comrade from the rig. "Oh, is that all? Just an operating system for a standard-issue Starfleet-grade communications suite? Why didn't you say so? I'm sure we can just buy that on a set of data cards in the city's central market."

The only person around the table wearing a hopeful expression was Tassin. "I might know someone who can help," he said.

Eager to exploit any good news she could find, Kolova asked, "Who?"

"Her name's Kiva Cross," the greasy mechanic said. "She was a Starfleet comms officer. Trained in code breaking, signals intelligence, and everything in between. She's been a civvy for a few years now, but if anyone can break into Starfleet's comms, it'll be her."

Kolova felt encouraged. "Is she with us here?"

Tassin shook his head. "No, she runs a duotronics repair shop in the Tech Quarter. But she knows me, and I think she might help us if we can make her understand what's at stake."

"All right," Kolova said. "Then we have two objectives for the next thirty minutes. Tassin, go find your friend and bring her back here—I want to talk to her myself."

"On it," Tassin said, and then he slipped through the crowd and hurried up a staircase toward the surface.

Kolova continued as Tassin departed. "Bowen, you and your people recon the hospital. See if the Starfleet docs are spread out or clustered. Bring back sensor readings with detailed floor plans if you can."

"Copy that." Bowen nodded at Omalu and Chandra,

and the trio left together, up the same stairs Tassin had used.

That left only the rudiments of defense to be put into place. Kolova faced Eichorn. "Post your guards and intruder alarms, and be quick. If this all goes south, Starfleet will come for us, and I want to make sure we give them a very warm welcome when they do."

17

It was difficult for Burnham to know whether she could trust her senses, but with each step forward she and Spock took inside the Juggernaut, she imagined she felt the gravity growing stronger. The effect had been subtle at first. Early on, she had attributed the sensation to oddities of footing or a peculiar slant in the deck. And if truth be told, if there was any difference from one step to the next, it was of such a minuscule degree that the difference could be felt only over time. *In other words,* she brooded, *by the time I'm sure, it will be too late.*

Thumper bobbed through the air ahead of her and Spock. It continued to crackle with superfine filaments of lightning. The hue of its electrical corona shifted from one second to the next—from white to golden to violet, then to chartreuse and white again. Whenever Spock's or Burnham's pace flagged, Thumper let out a low beat of reproach. Its latest pulse of criticism was Burnham's fault. She resented the correction but quickened her step.

She asked Spock, "Am I the only one of us growing weary of being tested?"

He accepted her complaint with a show of mild surprise. "I find a small measure of encouragement in its feedback." It took him a moment to register Burnham's probing look and take it as a cue to clarify his remark. "If the Juggernaut's only purpose were to destroy all life on the planet, it would have no logical reason to pose such hurdles."

"True," Burnham said. "It would have just killed us by now. And it still might."

"Perhaps," Spock said. "Though I suspect it would compel us to play a role in our own demise. All of its elements we have encountered so far have been directed toward such an end."

Burnham searched the curved bulkheads of the oval-shaped passageway. They, the deck, and the overhead here all glowed with dull red light. "I wonder," she said, "if all its tests are made to be overcome. After all, why lure us deeper and subject us to new and different threats? What's to be gained by that? Does the Juggernaut itself benefit somehow? Or would putting us through our paces somehow enrich its makers?"

Spock regarded their environs with dignified curiosity. "It might be a form of intelligence test," he said. "One designed to test mental adaptability, problem-solving skills, and the ability to apply esoteric knowledge in uncommon combinations and circumstances."

"Yes, but to what end? Is it sizing us up as potential threats?"

Her question made him stop and think. She halted and faced him. He met her expectant gaze. "Perhaps this is a form of initiation or recruitment. A gauntlet designed to identify those worthy or capable of performing some task or role that requires exceptional ability."

"What role would require the sorts of skills and abilities needed to foil these traps?"

Spock tilted his head. "One that I doubt few intelligent beings would want to fill."

That was a conclusion with which Burnham found no fault. She was about to say as much when the Juggernaut trembled, and a familiar haunting sound reverberated through its bulkheads and deck. Burnham looked upward and listened, trying to differentiate nuances in the din. "Drones," she said. "That's the sound they make when they launch." She held up a hand to forestall Spock's questions until after the noise abated. "Nine point four seconds. That's longer than it took last time, which suggests the Juggernaut just deployed at least seven drones."

Spock pulled out his communicator and flipped open its grille. "Spock to *Enterprise*. Do you read me?" He adjusted his communicator. "Lieutenant Spock to *Shenzhou*, please respond." Silence reigned over the channel. Spock flipped the grille shut and tucked the communicator onto his belt. "I suspected it would be futile, but we were duty bound to try to warn the ships."

"I agree," Burnham said. "Had my reflexes been faster, I'd have made those hails."

Spock glanced upward in a manner that suggested his thoughts were far away, perhaps with his ship and crewmates—a momentary exhibition of sentiment that betrayed his persona of classical Vulcan logic. Burnham couldn't tell if Spock knew his slip of emotionalism had been observed, but he turned away from her and continued walking. She followed and said nothing.

"The continued aggression of the Juggernaut compels me to wonder," Spock said. "If this vessel was somehow linked to the extinction of this planet's indigenous sentient species . . . was that the end of its mission? The fact that it was roused by the drilling rig suggests the Juggernaut might have been designed to carry on a perpetual assignment."

Burnham feared she knew where Spock was going with his line of inquiry, but she had to be certain. "What do you think such a 'perpetual assignment' would look like, Spock?"

"I lack sufficient evidence to form a testable hypothesis. But if the Juggernaut was designed to test peoples rather than worlds . . . who is to say its test of our people would end with the destruction of the colony? If the presence of our respective ships in orbit has made the Juggernaut aware of our culture's interstellar nature, who is to say it will not seek out other colonies and homeworlds and test them by fire, as it is doing to Sirsa III?"

"So you agree with Starfleet—you think we need to sacrifice Sirsa III in order to save other Federation worlds from the Juggernaut?"

A fleeting grimace. "I made no such conclusion. I merely raised the question."

"The question alone is being treated by some at Starfleet Command as sufficient cause to order the annihilation of an entire planetary ecosystem."

If Spock perceived her statement as a challenge, he didn't act that way. "There will always be those who draw conclusions from questions when none are implied. That does not absolve us of the responsibility to ask, or to seek impartial answers."

She took his gentle rebuke in stride. "You're right. It would be irresponsible to ignore the possibility that we've exposed others to the danger of the Juggernaut merely by having made our own existence known to it. Logic demands not only that we collect objective information, but also that we be truthful with ourselves and others about the possible consequences of our actions. Something I promise we will do, in earnest." Walking beside him toward the Juggernaut's ever-heavier core, she snuck a sidelong look and caught his eye. "But first, let's render those queries purely academic by finding some way to sink this thing."

"Ohara," Pike said on the move, pivoting into his command chair and bracing himself for the worst, "what are we looking at?" On the *Enterprise* bridge's main viewscreen, six radiant objects streaked upward through the atmosphere, in two clusters of three. Pike leaned forward, his focus keen upon this new threat. "Garison, hail the *Shenzhou*. Make sure they're seeing this."

Ohara looked back at Pike from the right side of the bridge's two-seat forward console. "New drones from the Juggernaut, sir." Ohara returned his focus to his console readouts. "Faster than the last round that hit the *Shenzhou*. I'm having trouble getting a weapons lock—they've improved their scramblers." Another anxious look over his shoulder at Pike. "Three headed for us, three for the *Shenzhou*, and one about to strafe the colony's capital."

"Shields up," Pike ordered. "Charge all weapons. Helm, take us to higher orbit. I want room to move without hitting atmosphere."

"Aye, sir," Tyler said from the left side of the forward console. "Moving to higher orbit."

Commander Una looked up from the hooded sensor display at her station. "Fifteen seconds to firing range. They're splitting up and locking weapons."

"Increase to half impulse," Pike said. "Ohara, coordinate with the *Shenzhou*. Overlap our firing solutions, create a kill zone between us, and force the drones into it."

"Aye, sir," Ohara said. A nod from him to Garison was all it took to cue the comms officer to set up a dedicated channel between Ohara and his counterpart on the *Shen-zhou.*

Blinding streaks whipped across the main viewscreen. Knowing what was coming, Pike gripped the armrests of his command chair and drew a deep breath—and then the *Enterprise* juddered on the receiving end of a brutal volley of energy blasts. Lights dimmed and consoles flickered. The barrage continued, disrupting the ship's inertial dampers and artificial gravity, leaving Pike feeling momentarily like a feather before trying to launch him from his chair.

He was still recovering his equilibrium as Una demanded, "Damage reports! All decks!" Switching intraship channels with a single touch on her console, she added, "Bridge to sickbay! We need running casualty reports!"

Overlapping replies from several decks and divisions poured from the speakers at Garison's communications console. The chief petty officer scrambled to mute the chaos and route the general-channel traffic onto dedicated circuits for Una's and Pike's convenience.

"Ohara," Pike said, "tactical analysis."

The young navigator seemed to be in a struggle against his own console. "The drones aren't going into the trap. We're trying to corral them, but they're too quick"—he looked back at Pike—"and too smart. I think they knew our play before we did."

Garison pressed his hand to his in-ear transceiver, then adjusted his console's settings. "Distress signals from the planet's surface, sir. The drone buzzing the capital is knocking down entire blocks. At this rate, it could set the whole city on fire in less than twenty minutes."

"Dammit," Pike muttered. "Can we get a torpedo lock?"

Ohara shook his head. "Not at these speeds, sir. And if

we fire blind and let the torpedoes seek their own targets, there's a good chance we'll hit the *Shenzhou*."

Hull-rattling explosions resounded through the *Enterprise*'s spaceframe. The overhead lights fluttered to half brightness, then recovered. Then came a crushing blast that sounded to Pike as if it had erupted just above the dome of the bridge—and a storm of sparks from a ruptured plasma relay rained down on his head.

Pike and his officers swatted burning-hot motes of plasma from their shoulders and heads, racing to prevent the ignition of hair or fabric. Seconds later a gray smoke perfumed with the bitter stench of burnt hair and scorched synthetic fibers filled the air.

"Dorsal shields buckling," Una said. "Starboard shields losing power."

Adrenaline coursed through Pike's veins and impelled him out of his chair. "Helm, roll us over, show the drones our belly. Number One, divert all shield power to the ventral emitters. Tyler, put us above the *Shenzhou*, let her obstruct the drone's access to our topside." He stalked forward to hover behind Ohara's left shoulder. "Set phaser banks one and two for zone coverage, scissor pattern. Fire at—"

Invisible fists of disrupted gravity and momentum hit Pike. Hurled toward the port side of the bridge, Pike was a rag doll, a leaf in a gale—right up until the moment he struck the bulkhead beside the turbolift doors. Every part of him hurt as he picked himself up off the deck, a jumble of aching bones stuck in a bag of bruised meat. "Fire at will! And for the love of the Great Bird of the Galaxy, hit something!"

"Firing," Ohara said. The lieutenant pounded his fists on his console. "Dammit!"

Tyler turned a hangdog look toward Pike. "That was

my fault, sir. I just don't have room to maneuver this close to the *Shenzhou*. I—"

"No apologies," Pike said. "Just solutions. Solve the problem first, tell me how you did it later. Vaporize those drones!"

Una arrived at Pike's side and steadied him as his balance faltered. "Captain, Tyler is right. By using the *Shenzhou* as cover, we're impeding our ability to maneuver, and theirs."

He understood the criticism implied by her analysis: he wasn't just putting his own ship at risk with a questionable tactic, he was endangering another captain's vessel as well. It was never pleasant to admit an error in the heat of battle, but it would be criminal not to correct it. "What do you suggest, Number One?"

"Break orbit," Una said. "If the drones follow us into open space, we can use full-impulse combat maneuvers, and maybe open up enough distance to use torpedoes."

"If we break orbit, we'll be leaving the colony undefended."

"We already are." Una held Pike upright as another barrage from the drones rocked the *Enterprise* and showered the bridge in sparks. "As long as we're on the defensive, we're of no use to the colony or the *Shenzhou*. We need to break away and take this fight to where *we* hold the advantage." Another explosion shook the *Enterprise*. "Unless we go on the offensive now, we might not last long enough to help the colony. Sir."

Retreating, even temporarily to gain a superior position, rubbed Pike the wrong way. But he had spent enough time at the Academy learning the philosophies of war and the logic of tactics to know that Una was right. His crew would have a better chance against the drones if they could wage this battle in the environment best suited to the *Enterprise*.

"Mister Tyler," Pike said, "break orbit, heading two-one-five mark nine. Once we're clear of the planet's gravity, override the safeties and take us to flank impulse. Mister Ohara, keep hitting those drones. I want them mad as hell and on our tail, every step of the way."

It figures, Georgiou lamented. *No sooner do the engineers put my ship back together than the drones start breaking it again.*

She winced as a series of punishing blasts from the drones hammered the *Shenzhou* and left numerous duty stations on her bridge belching black smoke and red-hot phosphors. The acrid stink of burnt circuits was thick in the air, which grew hotter by the minute. *Life-support must be failing,* Georgiou realized. "Gant," she snapped over the chatter of panic streaming from the communications panel, "pick one of the three drones and concentrate all your fire upon it until it's gone. Oliveira, steal every last drop of power you can find for the shields."

Her tactical and operations officers both nodded their understanding as they continued to struggle against the automated onslaught. Outside the three broad viewports at the front of the bridge, streaks of light whipped past, then vanished into the glare of sunlight off the ocean that covered nearly all of the planet's eastern hemisphere.

Three sharp cracks of detonation made the *Shenzhou* lurch and forced Georgiou to white-knuckle her chair's armrests to stop from being hurled halfway across her own bridge.

I wish Michael was here. Only now, in the thick of a firefight and bereft of her first officer's aid, did Georgiou realize just how much she had come to rely upon Burnham's skill at handling the details of combat. *Here's hoping Gant can fill her shoes.*

Jarring shocks batted the *Shenzhou* in one direction after another. Gant frowned as he fought to get ahead of the ship's attackers. "The drones are faster than before," he noted, as if Georgiou hadn't seen the battle's telemetry projected on the port screen. "And they're packing more of a punch. If we don't—" He raised his brow at something on his panel. "Sir, the *Enterprise* is above us. I think they're using us for cover."

If Gant's read of the *Enterprise*'s tactic was correct—and Georgiou suspected it was—then she expected her own ship was about to face a concentrated attack from the opposite side. "Shift power to ventral shields," she said. "Gant, redirect weapons power to our ventral phasers. Set up zone defense and fire at will."

Saru looked up from the XO's post, which he was monitoring during Burnham's absence. "Captain, casualties are mounting in sickbay, but the medical division is running a skeleton crew because of relief efforts on the planet's surface. What should we tell the wounded?"

Georgiou wondered whether Saru knew he had committed a heinous bit of wordplay, then she reasoned the Kelpien was likely not even aware that referring to a medical unit as a "skeleton crew" constituted a poor show of wit. "Do we have any personnel with medical training in other divisions who can be retasked?"

"Searching," Saru said. "Negative. Doctor Nambue took nearly all of the ship's senior medical personnel to the surface. Sickbay is presently being supervised by two paramedics and a dental hygienist."

"Tell them to do their best and to grab something heavy," Georgiou said. "Helm, can we get some distance from—" She halted in midorder as she saw *Enterprise*'s position change on the bridge's main tactical holo. "Gant, what's the Big E doing now?"

"Breaking away from us." Gant checked his data and struggled to hide his mounting alarm. "And heading out of the planet's gravity well." He tilted his head back, as if he were in the throes of an epiphany. "Makes sense, Captain. In open space they'll have the room to make complex maneuvers at full speed. . . . And so would we."

"Follow them," Georgiou told Detmer. To Gant she added, "Link our firing solutions." To the rest of the bridge she declared, "Heads down, eyes open. Time to go to work."

"I've interlinked our targeting computer with the one on the *Enterprise*," said junior tactical officer Ensign Jira Narwani. She adjusted her holographic targeting helmet. "Now get ready to see some serious shit." Her hands seemed to dance in midair as she used the virtual-reality environment created by her helmet to choose targets at the speed of thought and make them the loci of the combined firepower of the *Enterprise* and the *Shenzhou*.

Lancing beams and bolts of energy sliced through one of the drones, which erupted in a greenish fireball and peppered the *Shenzhou*'s forward shields with burning shrapnel.

"One down, two of ours to go," Georgiou noted under her breath. "Helm, as soon as we're free of the planet's gravity, increase to maximum impulse."

Detmer pushed the ship to its full speed, provoking creaks and groans from the battered old spaceframe as she put the ship through turns that would shatter most ships' keels. "We're clear and free to maneuver, Captain."

"Look sharp," Georgiou said. She pointed at a target pictured over the center viewport. "Gant, tractor beam on this one! Push it into that one!" As the tactical officer carried out her order, Georgiou pressed onward. "Helm, hard to starboard, twelve degrees yaw! Crush that drone between our shields and *Enterprise*'s! Ops, angle deflectors for maximum crush!"

In seconds, her orders paid off. Barrages from the *Enterprise* and the *Shenzhou* tore apart one drone, while the tractor beam forced two more into a collision. A fourth drone disintegrated as it was trapped between the invisible energy screens of the two starships, which crackled as they brushed against one another during the high-speed flyby.

"One left," Gant declared. He dedicated himself to the drone's destruction with an intensity Georgiou had never seen from him before. "Just a little closer," he muttered as he fought to get a weapons lock on their last attacker. "That's it, just break left—"

The drone darted right—and was obliterated by a phaser shot from the *Enterprise*.

Gant suppressed an obvious urge to swear, then forced himself back into a semblance of dignity as he reported, "All clear, Captain."

"Helm, put us back in orbit, on the double," Georgiou said. "Gant, neutralize the drone attacking the capital. No extra points for neatness."

"Understood," Gant said.

Oliveira looked back from ops. "Captain, the *Enterprise* is following us back to orbit. They're also scanning for a weapons lock on the last drone."

"This isn't a contest," Georgiou reminded her bridge officers. "I don't care which of our ships eliminates that drone, as long as—"

"Got it!" Gant shouted with a pump of his fist.

So much for the "no I in team" speech, Georgiou decided.

"Secure from red alert," she said, "maintain yellow alert. Mister Saru, collect damage and casualty reports from all decks, then get me new repair estimates from engineering."

The Kelpien responded with a birdlike stiff nod. "Aye, Captain."

Ensign Fan swiveled away from her panel. "Captain, the *Enterprise* is hailing us."

"Patch them in, but keep my forward view clear."

A holographic projection of Captain Pike manifested in front of the *Shenzhou*'s starboard viewport. He looked very much the worse for wear after this latest scuffle with the drones. *"The Juggernaut launched its drones a lot sooner than we'd expected, Captain. And my XO tells me its energy readings are already climbing again, faster than before. Whatever that thing has up its sleeve for its next trick, I don't think we ought to wait to see what it is. The time to frag that monstrosity is right now."*

His insistence on immediate assault shocked Georgiou. "Captain, need I remind you that Lieutenants Spock and Burnham are still inside the Juggernaut?"

"I'm well aware of the sacrifice we'll be making," Pike said. *"And I have no doubt that Mister Spock would approve of the logic behind my decision."*

His tone made Georgiou bristle. "We promised them we would give them three hours to find a solution to this crisis. We still owe them another thirty minutes."

"When we made that promise, we thought we had three hours to spare. Now we know otherwise. If we let the Juggernaut become fully active, we might not be able to stop it—and that's a chance I can't—that I won't—take. I'm going to end this, Captain, before it's too late."

Georgiou stood from her chair to strike her most imperial pose. "I can't let you do that, Captain. Not while there remains even a chance to resolve this without blood-shed."

"*That ship has sailed,*" Pike said. "*Now it's my turn to remind you: I have valid orders in hand from Admiral Anderson, and they supersede your authority as the senior commander. So you can either help me destroy that alien wrecking machine—or I can obliterate you and your ship along with it.*"

With a haughty arch of her brow, she asked, "That's how it's going to be, then?"

"*Sorry, Captain. But that's the way it* has *to be.*"

She lowered her chin, ready to charge headlong into the brewing storm.

"Then I'm afraid we're going to have a problem."

The passageway inside the Juggernaut had reversed directions and sloped downward twice since Burnham and Spock had first entered it. She estimated they had traversed most of the vessel's length with each leg of the journey. Given the angles of their descent at each switchback turn, they were now almost at the core of the alien ship.

Thumper the sparking hologram slipped out of view, past a shallow curve ahead of them. When Burnham and Spock rounded the curve they found their holographic guide had vanished once more, having led them to an open portalway curtained with falling mist. The vapors were tenuous and short-lived, making it possible to see a wide-open compartment on the other side of the entry's threshold. Though the oval corridor in which Burnham and Spock stood glowed a sinister crimson, the chamber ahead shone with hues of iridium blue and imperial violet. The pair slowed their pace as they neared the mist.

"Another test," Burnham said, finding it difficult to mask

her waning patience. "I'm growing tired of being treated like an animal conditioned to perform tricks for its supper."

Spock remained sanguine. "Curious. I find the challenges . . . stimulating."

His blasé attitude toward the Juggernaut's deathtraps stoked Burnham's irritation. "A well-played game of three-level chess is stimulating. This thing is trying to kill us."

"Were that its goal, I should think its methods would be more direct."

"Fine," Burnham conceded, "it's testing us. But if we fail the tests, we'll die." They halted half a meter shy of the mistfall. "Perhaps I'm being overly cautious, but the novelty of this vapor curtain makes me suspicious." She lifted her tricorder and scanned the mist. "Water vapor and traces of unknown compounds. Running a toxicity simulation—" Two short, high-pitched beeps from her tricorder signaled danger. She turned the device to show its results to Spock. "Just as I thought. Those trace compounds will be absorbed through our skin on contact. Once they reach our bloodstreams, we'll suffer acute anoxia and be dead in under ninety seconds."

"A most efficacious poison." Spock hefted his own tricorder and began entering new data. "Assuming you and I are both carrying standard emergency first-aid kits . . . we do not possess the necessary ingredients to formulate an antitoxin to the mist." He wrinkled his brow at something on his tricorder's display. "However, there is another open portalway opposite this one, approximately forty-two point seven meters from our position. And according to this scan, the mist falling in that portalway contains the antitoxin to the one in front of us."

Burnham peered through the falling mist and glimpsed the other open portal, far across the wide-open chamber.

"So all we'd have to do is reach the other portal before the toxin's effects become irreversible." She considered the variables. "Forty-three meters? We should be able to sprint that distance in under ten seconds."

"But assuming we will be physically and perhaps perceptually compromised—"

"Even if we quadruple our time to allow for the debilitating effects of the toxin, we could reach the antitoxin in under forty-five seconds. If we make an effort to hyperoxygenate our blood before stepping through the mist, we should be able to make it."

Spock regarded the vast blue-and-purple chamber with a dubious expression. "If the Juggernaut's past challenges can be trusted to serve as indicators of those to come, I suspect this will prove more complicated than just holding our breath and running in a straight line."

Burnham knew he was right, but refused to acknowledge his observation. "I'm setting my tricorder for a ninety-second countdown, with alerts at thirty and sixty seconds." Once the device was prepped, she poised her index finger above the start button on the touchscreen. "Ready?"

"May I make a suggestion?"

"Of course."

"After we pass through the mist," Spock said, "I suggest we pause to assess the room."

"Sensible, but remember the clock is ticking." She tensed for departure. "Set." As soon as she noted Spock hunched forward, she gave the order: "Go!"

Together they sprang through the wall of mist and stumbled to a halt on the other side. As their boots touched the deck inside the cavernous space, brilliant geometric patterns blazed into view beneath their feet. Whorls and long Fibonacci-style spirals were linked by angular lines that crossed one another to make irregular shapes—some with as few as three sides, others with as many as seven, and numerous variations in between. Different lines pulsed with varied hues ranging from white to yellow to neon green.

Burnham frowned. "Want to bet it's a riddle showing us the only safe way across?"

"I would prefer not to wager on such—" Spock doubled over, his retort superseded by acute pain. He clutched at his abdomen and winced as he fell to his knees like a penitent.

She reached out to comfort him as a prelude to helping him up. "Spock! Are you—"

Agony bloomed inside of her, a black flower of nausea and knifing pangs. Her legs betrayed her, and then she was brought to her knees, humbled beside Spock. Through gritted teeth she forced the words, "No time!"

Soft pings from her tricorder counted off the seconds they were losing to their sudden infirmities. Relief from their shared suffering was just a few seconds away—but for all Burnham knew, the wrong step might prove just as fatal as a delay born of indecision.

She reached out with one hand to steady herself. As it pressed on a trapezoidal shape defined by surrounding white lines, an excruciating jolt of electricity stretched from deck to ceiling, sending fiery pain through her hand, which she yanked back to her side.

Huddled inside a circle that now seemed to be the only safe space in the room, she turned a look of contrition at Spock. "You were right. Good thing we didn't make a break for it."

"Indeed." Spock forced himself to stand. "But unless we find a way to move forward in the next thirty seconds, we are both about to die in this room."

18

"Focus your mind," Spock said. "Pain is an illusion. Acknowledge it, then put it aside."

Burnham turned her thoughts back to her childhood, her formative years spent on Vulcan. She imagined herself back in the concave pods of the Vulcan Learning Center in ShiKahr, her proctors stalking the pathways between the students. As Spock repeated the exhortation to move past pain, she heard the voices of her first instructors echoing in her memory.

The lesson was simple. Putting it into practice was not. Stabbing pains flared in her gut and chest, and with each gasp of pain she let slip, she felt her blood losing precious oxygen.

Spock's calm baritone soothed Burnham's rising panic. "Master your pain."

"I'm trying," she snarled through her clenched jaw. With effort she pulled in a greedy breath, only to feel her lungs burn in response. The core of her being felt as if it were being devoured by fire. *No time for this,* she told herself. *Get up, before it's too late.*

Her body refused to obey. Then she remembered the mantra that so long ago had enabled her to master the Vulcan technique of pain suppression. It was a single line from the poem "Self-Pity" by D. H. Lawrence: *I never saw a wild thing sorry for itself.*

With the words came strength. *Be a wild thing. Get up and fight!*

The pain was still there, but now so was Burnham's hard-won mental discipline, and she honed the edge of her will until it cut through the pain. Trembling but resolute, she stood and faced Spock. "I'm ready. How do we proceed?"

He tested an adjacent shape on the deck with the toe of his boot. Another flash of electricity compelled him to pull his foot back. "Very carefully," he said.

The tricorder on Burnham's hip beeped softly as it counted down the seconds until the poison in their blood asphyxiated them. "We have to move, but to where? What defines a safe step? The shape of a space? The number of sides?"

Spock looked down. "We are both standing in circles," he noted. "There are no other circles on the deck. If a circle represents 'one,' then perhaps two—"

"Would be a teardrop," Burnham cut in, anticipating his idea. "Something two sided." She searched the spread of the deck within stepping distance. "I don't see any."

"Nor do I. Which seems to rule out defining a simple path." Spock grimaced, but he fought to regain his composure, then exhaled slowly. "I am all right," he assured her. He studied the deck with his intense stare. "What was the first thing you observed about this vessel?"

"Symmetry," Burnham said. With that in mind, she surveyed the room again, starting from the point opposite their own, in front of the far portalway that held the antitoxin mist. "Two circles," she said as she saw the shapes on the deck. Then she saw that the room's chaotic design masked a hidden order. "It's a mirror image! On both the x and y axes."

"Perhaps there is no single correct path," Spock said. "So long as we mirror each other's movements across the deck."

"Only one way to find out." Burnham lifted her foot. "On the count of three, put your right foot into the irregular pentagon on your right, and I'll put my left foot into the one on my left. One. Two. Three!" She and Spock each braved a single step out of their respective circles. In tandem they set their feet into the assigned shapes—and no jolt punished them. "So far, so good. I'll call out shapes, you match my stride."

"I will do my best," Spock said.

Seconds bled away as they navigated their way across the room. Burnham struggled to find the least ambiguous shape for each next step, to avoid confusion regarding into which space she intended for Spock to advance. But each step magnified the pain snaking through her body. The toxin was a dark rider in her blood, delivering its message of agony from one extremity to the next, and threatening with each beat of her heart to break down her mental barriers.

They had almost reached the far circles when she heard a crackling bolt to her right. She halted and looked for Spock. He teetered inside his current space, smoke rising from his left foot. "A minor misstep," he called out. Tremors in his voice betrayed his worsening condition as he added, "Call the next step."

"On your left. Irregular hexagon bending toward the center. Left foot first. On two. One. Two!" She stepped forward with her right foot into her mirror-image of the space to which she had sent Spock. Her foot landed a fraction of a second ahead of his, and a searing fork of blue energy lashed out and skewered her from her left clavicle to her right knee. She stumbled as she entered the hexagon and started to drop to one knee.

No! If our movements don't match—!

On the other side of the room, Spock looked back at Burnham as she lost her balance—and he matched her lurch and accidental genuflection with perfect synchronicity. They were close enough for him to ask in a normal speaking voice, "Are you all right?"

"Yes," Burnham lied. "I'm going to put my left hand on the deck and use it to push myself back to standing." She didn't need to direct him to mirror her effort; he did it almost as if it had become instinct to them, as if they had been each other's reflections all their lives.

Back on her feet, Burnham felt her head swim. She could barely breathe, and her vision softened. *Only a few seconds until we're toast,* she realized. They needed to reach the far circles as quickly as possible, but the safest path was going to take too long.

Then logic demands I take the fastest path, not the safest one, Burnham decided.

"Three hops," she said, barely able to make herself heard without breath. "Start on your left leg." She needed to tell him the path, but she was afraid she would lose consciousness first. It took all her strength to draw one more fighting breath. "Five. Three. Six."

"I understand," Spock said, his own voice a gasp. "Ready."

She tensed to spring and looked him in the eye. "Go."

As one they leaped from their matching positions to the nearest pentagons, then to an isosceles triangle. The last step before the final circles was a symmetrical hexagon—

Burnham landed off-balance and had no time to recover. She either had to jump for the exit or splay herself across the floor. Faltering and exhausted, she threw herself at the circle.

She landed short. Spock landed beside her, his footing sure.

Gravity tugged Burnham backward. She windmilled her arms, fighting to force her center of balance forward, but it was of no use. Her left foot shifted backward—and the lightning slammed into her chest, ripping away the last of her breath in a hideous scream.

Then she was in Spock's arms, both of them cocooned in lightning as he pulled her out of the circles and into the antidote mist. Only as they passed through the vaporous threshold did the lightning release them. Spock let go of Burnham, and they tumbled onto the deck. They both lay there for half a minute, letting the healing mist cascade over them.

The sickness and agony within Burnham faded quickly, and she was able to breathe again without pain. She sat up and checked on Spock, who was in the same sorry state she was. "Thank you," Burnham said. "If you hadn't pulled me back—"

"We likely both would have died," Spock said. "After all, the test was built for two."

"Well, thank you anyway."

As the two of them stood, the vessel's holographic orb reappeared in front of them, its surface bristling with intense energies, and the air pulsating from its acoustic emanations.

Burnham frowned at the lure. "Well, look at this. If it isn't our own holographic Virgil, come to lead us down to the next circle of Hell."

"I thought we had dubbed this entity Thumper," Spock said.

Following the bobbing orb down the next stretch of oval corridor, Burnham replied, "That was when I thought it was our guide."

"If it is not that, then what is it?"

"Unless we're careful? A willing accomplice to our murders."

A special brand of quiet tension reigned on the *Shenzhou*'s bridge. More than ten minutes had passed since Georgiou had retired to her ready room to continue her heated discussion with Captain Pike in private. She had set the ready room's door to its privacy mode, and though the compartment was soundproofed, Saru imagined he could feel her anger through the reinforced bulkheads.

As the ranking officer on the bridge, he had chosen to busy himself at his usual station rather than sit idle in the command chair. His motives were, he knew, partly selfish. He had brought back such a wealth of tricorder data from his excursion into the caves that he was unable to resist digging into it, in the hope of unlocking more of Sirsa III's ancient mysteries.

Even immersed in his work, however, he sensed the anxiety on the bridge. Everyone was keenly aware of the *Enterprise* looming outside the center viewport, its state-of-the-art shields and weapons likely more than a match for the decades-old technology of the *Shenzhou*. If Georgiou and Pike failed to reach an accommodation soon—

"Something bad is happening in there," Oliveira said, looking back from her post at the ops station toward the ready room. "This isn't going to end well."

Ensign Detmer, well known for being jumpy under stress, tried to conceal her worry. She snuck a look aft, then asked Oliveira, "What makes you say that?"

Oliveira frowned. "Let's just say I'm getting a bad vibe off this whole situation."

Her pronouncement worsened the already failing morale on the bridge, because her hunches had a knack for proving to be correct. In the face of that, what could Saru say that wouldn't come off as trite?

"Let's have faith in the captain to sort this out," he said, hoping to stifle further grim speculations. "Until then, keep your minds on your duties and remain calm."

His attempt at a pep talk garnered suspicious looks from around the bridge. *A far cry from rousing leadership,* he brooded, *but at least they've ceased gossiping.*

New analysis reports appeared on his console. Deep scans of the cave art had been processed by the ship's computer using filters too intensive to run on a tricorder. Saru found himself confronted with a far greater number of etched illustrations than he had dared to think might be down there, and the newly revealed segments were rich with details—especially the ones that surrounded the drawing of the Juggernaut.

Lieutenant Troke, the *Shenzhou*'s deputy chief of the sciences division under Saru, got up from his console and climbed the steps from his sunken duty station to stand beside Saru's post. Rows of circular metal cybernetic enhancements set into the Tulian's teal-blue face reflected light from Saru's console. "Sir, I've been monitoring your analysis of the cave art. I think you've made a remarkable find."

"That much is obvious, Mister Troke." Saru did his best to be nonchalant when faced with Troke's augmentations. The Tulians, a cousin species to Bolians, had long ago embraced cybernetic technology with a zeal most Federation cultures had yet to emulate, and their casual fusion of organic tissue and high technology still made Saru uneasy at times.

He pointed a long, bony finger at the complex designs that surrounded the image of the Juggernaut. "What do you make of these elements?"

Troke squinted at the enhanced images, then fiddled absentmindedly with the neural coupling that protruded from his left occiptal lobe. "The beams emerging from the vessel appear to form an ordered pattern at their points of intersection, and again at their points of terminus. Can we isolate those points for analysis, sir?"

"Just a moment." Saru keyed in the necessary commands. When only the points and their connecting lines remained, he was struck by an odd notion. "These look familiar somehow."

"I agree," Troke said. "Could it be a form of writing?"

"Doubtful," Saru said. "All available evidence suggests the indigenous people relied upon a form of sequential art to express narrative. We found no evidence that they had developed a phonetic or symbolic written language." He rotated the image and tinkered with manipulating the relationships between the points in three dimensions rather than limiting them to a flat plane. "Could it be a formula?"

Troke shook his head. "There doesn't seem to be enough data for that." His expression brightened. "Maybe it's a molecular structure! Or a map of a single atom."

Saru felt what he could only describe as a flash of insight. "A map!" He restored the original image of the Juggernaut. "What if these lines indicate that the information was being projected by the vessel for the natives to see and record? If that's the case, maybe it was trying to show them where it had come from, in a format they would understand."

Now young Troke nodded. "A constellation map."

"Exactly." Saru straightened with pride and towered over Troke. "Of course, there are numerous variables to consider before we can make effective use of this clue. We need to construct a virtual model of the galaxy as it existed approximately nine million years ago. We'll need to account for stars that have gone supernova in the past nine million years, and rule out those that have formed after that period. We'll also have to correct for the movement of this star system as it orbited the galactic center and chart its drift away from the galactic plane. Then, using its position as a center point, we'll have to search for constellation patterns that would have been visible to the naked eye from this world at that time, and then compare any likely matches against known entities in the Federation Galactic Catalog."

If that list of action items intimidated Troke, he didn't let it show. Instead he smiled and said, "I'll have it ready for you in ten minutes, sir."

"Thank you, Mister Troke."

As the science officer hurried back to his station, Saru's console flashed with an alert of an incoming message on a secondary channel from the *Enterprise*, coded for his personal review. He accepted the signal and was pleased to hear Commander Una's voice through his panel. *"Saru,"* she said, *"I might have good news. I've analyzed the cave art and found new details surrounding the Juggernaut."*

"A possible star chart," Saru said, "provided one can compensate for nine million years of galactic rotation, stellar movement, star formation, and supernovae."

Her excitement abated, but she remained upbeat. *"You already knew?"*

He couldn't help but smile. "Great minds think alike."

Too many bodies stood in a paranoid huddle around the subspace transceiver. Kolova felt the weight of the crowd behind and around her as she loomed over the shoulder of Kiva Cross, the ex-Starfleet officer whom Tassin had cajoled into helping their ad hoc insurgency.

Cross, for her part, seemed oblivious of the pressure in the room. The vaguely Polynesian-looking young woman had put all her focus on the hodgepodge of gadgets she had insisted be hauled down into the bunker to facilitate her efforts.

Watching Cross work without understanding what she was doing made Kolova more anxious. She leaned closer and asked, "Is it working?"

Cross answered in a condescending deadpan, "If you mean, 'Is it recording comm traffic to, from, and between the ships in orbit?' then yes, it's working."

"So what are they saying?"

"No idea." Cross looked up with a bored roll of her eyes. "We're recording encrypted signals. Once we have a few more transmissions in hand, I'll analyze them for cipher patterns."

Her blasé attitude seemed to grate upon Ishii, who asked in his rasp of a voice, "How long will that take?"

A shrug conveyed Cross's disinterest. "Minutes? Hours? Depends how chatty they are."

Bowen leaned in on the other side of Cross and tapped his wrist chrono. "In case it wasn't obvious, we're under a bit of time pressure. So if there's any way you could speed this up—"

"Keep your pants on," Cross said. "This is just foreplay. Once I get a few kiloquads of data, the real fun begins." She tapped a readout on the front of her portable comm console. "At the rate they're flapping their gums, I'll be ready to start cracking any minute now. So chill."

Chandra the engineer poked his head past Bowen to get a better look at Cross's setup. "Nice gear. Is that a Van Muren transceiver with a Ko-Mog subspace amplifier?"

His question earned a look of quiet respect from Cross. "Good eye."

"What's your decryption matrix?"

This time she side-eyed him. "Proprietary." The curtness of her reply deflated what remained of Chandra's curiosity, and he fell back into the anonymous ranks of the crowd.

Kolova, however, remained unsatisfied. "Are you sure you can break their codes?"

"Pretty sure. The *Shenzhou* is sending and receiving real-time holovids. Total data-hogs. Hard as hell to crack. And the *Enterprise* has some newer comm tech. That'll take time."

"None of that sounds encouraging," Kolova said.

"Ain't supposed to be easy." Cross tweaked some settings on her equipment. "One thing working in our favor: Starfleet's like any other big organization—slow to change. All I need is one legacy cipher in the mix and we'll have an in." She pointed at some indicators as they flipped from red to amber. "There we go. A possible vulnerability." She started keying in new commands. "Give me another ten minutes, and we'll know what they said in the comms we've intercepted, and then we'll be able to monitor them in real time."

Kolova clasped her hands on Cross's shoulders. "Well done."

Cross squirmed free of Kolova's grip, clearly resistant to uninvited physical contact. "Just remember that when it comes time to hand out pardons"—she looked up at the governor with dark, accusatory eyes—"or to forget the names of your conspirators."

Was there any more exquisite agony than being forced to wait to deliver good news? Saru stood outside the privacy-frosted doors of Captain Georgiou's ready room, awaiting its reversion to clarity so he could deliver his latest report. His lanky frame felt energized with excitement.

The off-white opacity clouding the doors' window panels melted away, giving Saru a look at the holographically projected forms of Captain Pike and Admiral Anderson, two human men who seemed very much to have been cast from the same mold. Saru pressed the visitor signal next to the doors and waited. After a momentary pause, Georgiou's voice spilled from a speaker above the visitor button: *"Come."*

The doors parted with a soft *swish*, and as Saru entered the ready room the hologram of Admiral Anderson faded like a lost memory. Saru stopped in the middle of the room beside Pike's holographic avatar. Georgiou sat behind her desk, her countenance sullen, her left hand wrapped around her right fist. Saru could not remember the last time he had seen his captain in so dark a mood; his Kelpien senses felt her anger as she said, "Report, Lieutenant."

Her tone inspired Saru to stand almost at attention, further accentuating the height differential between himself and Captain Pike, to say nothing of his advantage over Captain Georgiou. "Lieutenant Troke and I have made a major discovery, based on our analysis of the cave art I documented with Commander Una of the *Enterprise*." He gestured toward the conference table on the opposite side of the ready room from Georgiou's desk. "If I might be permitted to make use of the—"

"Go ahead," Georgiou said. She got up and walked out from behind her desk. "Just make it quick, Saru."

"Of course." He led Georgiou and the Pike hologram to the conference table and switched on its holographic presentation system, which projected images above the table. Then, from the main computer, he accessed the file he and Troke had prepared. A spectral image of a star and planets appeared above the table and ever so slowly began to rotate. "Mister Troke and I believe we have identified the origin point of the Juggernaut, based on evidence already gathered by Mister Johar and his team, cross-referenced with clues the Juggernaut itself provided to this planet's native inhabitants nine million years ago, and which they faithfully recorded."

Pike squinted at the image. *That doesn't look familiar. What are we looking at?*

"The Giunta system," Saru said. "A Class-K main-sequence star with eleven planets that range from rocky to gas giants. It's located in an outer sector of the Alpha Quadrant, on the spinward edge of the Perseus Arm."

"That's pretty far out there," Georgiou said. "Farther than anyone's explored."

"True," Saru said. "But Starfleet has dispatched a large number of automated deep-space probes over the past few decades, mostly for the sake of creating rudimentary star charts. A handful of those probes were also designed for long-range cultural observation. That's how Troke and I came to cross-reference our discovery of the Giunta system with intercepted alien comm traffic which identified that system as the former home of the Turanian Dynasty."

Pike held up a hand. *"Former home?"*

"Yes, sir. All recent scans suggest the system is uninhabited. However, nine million years ago, it was the seat of a major interstellar hegemony, one whose sole remaining legacy is its reputation for tyranny." Saru switched the image above the table to show illustrations of the alien vessel that had triggered their present crisis. "Representations of the vessel we know as the Juggernaut appear to be prevalent in the mythology and history of numerous civilizations located in that sector of the galaxy, according to transmissions intercepted by Starfleet and analyzed by teams at the Daystrom Institute and the Vulcan Science Academy."

Georgiou folded her hands behind her back as she examined the images up close. "How often did these Turanians dispatch Juggernauts to other worlds?"

"Whenever they detected one worth colonizing," Saru said. "The Turanians inducted worlds into their hegemony by sending each planet a Judge—or as we call it, a Juggernaut. If the planet had no intelligent native species, the planet was immediately claimed in the name of the dynasty. But if the planet was inhabited by sapient life-forms . . ."

The next part of his report was difficult for him to deliver without succumbing to emotion; its parallels of the horrors that had shaped his homeworld of Kelpia struck close to his heart. Mustering his resolve, he continued. "They were put to 'the Test,' regardless of their civilization's level of development. It would seem the Turanians did not restrain their labors of empire with anything resembling our Prime Directive."

He updated the image to show panels from the cave art he and Una had documented. "The Test was a series of trials designed to test the intellect and adaptability of potential new subject races. According to the legends, the Judges customized the Test for each new race it encountered. Those that failed the Test were deemed unworthy, and their cultures were exterminated"—he presented the image from the caves, of the Juggernaut laying waste to a broad landscape—"without delay, and without mercy."

A somber nod from Pike preceded his next question. *"And those that passed?"*

"Were offered the chance to submit to the Turanian Dynasty and swear their allegiance—along with seventy-five percent of their culture's output in energy, natural resources, and refined goods, with regular increases expected in each category, in perpetuity. Those who accepted the terms were declared subjects of the dynasty and placed under its control."

Georgiou frowned. "And those who refused? Let me guess." She nodded toward the cave-painting of planetary annihilation. All Saru could do was nod in confirmation.

"Well, that's just great," Pike said. *"Even if Spock and your XO survive whatever that thing has in store for them, what are they supposed to do when it asks them to hand over one of our colonies to some alien empire that doesn't even exist anymore?"*

"It's a question with no right answer," Georgiou said. "Unless the Juggernaut, or Judge, or whatever the hell that thing is, is willing to listen to reason."

"It hasn't seemed to be in a talking mood so far."

"No," Georgiou said, "it hasn't." She sighed. "I just hope that whatever terms the Juggernaut offers Burnham, she doesn't wind up making a choice on behalf of the Federation based on nothing more than her stubborn pride."

"I was just thinking the same thing about Spock."

Saru could not muzzle his disgruntled opinion. "This might not have been the right mission to assign to a pair of Vulcans."

Georgiou scrunched her face in confusion. "Saru . . . Burnham is human."

He shut down the holographic display. "With all due respect, Captain, I remain unconvinced of that assertion."

As Thumper vanished yet again, and the next obstacle became visible, Burnham tensed. Not so much from fear, but from what felt like annoyance. "How many of these tests do we have to pass to reach the core?"

"A question neither of us can answer with certainty," Spock said. "Though my estimation of our position comports with your expectation: we should be very close to the ship's center."

They reached the bottom of a curved slope in the oval passageway and gained their first clear look at the next impediment to their mission. A meter-deep barrier occupied the center of the passage, its core space alive with arcs of fire and flashing blades moving in a variety of directions—some slicing in wide curves, others stabbing into the middle from either side, and large circular blades with fearsome teeth rising up from the deck like deadly half-moons that never broke free of their horizon. Between the blades arced flashes of light in a multitude of colors. The overall effect was at once hypnotic and intimidating.

Burnham stopped a few meters from the deadly dance of blades. "Whoever concocted this has got to be out of their minds." She lifted her tricorder and scanned the barrier. "Blades of titanium. Energized plasma in magnetically controlled arcs. Pulses of high-energy laser light. All in overlapping patterns of coverage." She set the tricorder back to passive mode and returned it to her side. "I was hoping it might be a holographic illusion."

"Such mercy would seem inconsistent with the tests we have endured so far."

"True." She rested her hand on her phaser. "Normally, I'd shoot through this thing. But even with both our phasers at full power, we'd never be able to melt tritanium blades."

Spock nodded. "Yes, most unfortunate. But perhaps not unexpected. Once again, the Juggernaut seems to know not only our strengths, but also our limitations." He scrutinized the bulkheads around them. "However, each challenge has been solvable."

Burnham watched him as he studied the overhead, and then the deck. "What are you looking for? You don't really think they'd give us an on-off switch, do you?"

"Nothing so simple," he said. He took a few steps back the way they had come, and then he squatted to run his fingertips along the edges of a deck plate. "But I refuse to think the makers of this vessel would have brought us this far only to leave us without options."

She eyed the blades and flames with mounting dread. "What if the option is death? What if they mean for one of us to sacrifice ourselves to the trap so the other can pass?"

"That is a possibility," Spock said, "but it would seem inconsistent with their penchant for symmetry. Note that the obstacles we have overcome so far all seem to have been created for two subjects. I suspect this one will prove to—" His fingers found purchase along the edge of the deck plate. "I have something."

Spock pried the plate loose, lifted it off the deck, and set it aside against the bulkhead. Beneath where the plate had rested was an alcove approximately one meter wide, two meters long, and three meters deep. On its forward wall was a ladder; on its side walls were numerous levers, sliders, and large dials, all festooned with alien markings.

Looking over Spock's shoulder, Burnham asked, "A control booth?"

"So it would seem."

Burnham looked around the sunken booth, then back at the barrier of blades, and at once she realized the cruelty of the test's design. "There's only enough room for one person to work in the pit at a time, and whoever's down there won't be able to see the portal."

"A most ingenious trial," Spock said. "One of us will need to act as the observer and report to the other as adjustments are made to the controls."

"Well, I'm glad you're amused." She swung her leg over the edge and found the ladder. As she climbed down into the pit, she said to Spock, "You're the spotter."

"As you wish." After she reached the bottom, he said, "Begin when ready."

She picked a large lever and began reversing its position. It resisted her efforts, and when she had moved it as far as it would go, she had to hold it in place. "Any change?"

"One of the blades on the right has ceased to emerge. But the rate at which the far circular blade rises and falls has increased."

"All right," Burnham said. "Let's see what else we can tweak." Straining as if she were trying to shift the weight of the world, she flipped one toggle. "Now?"

Spock replied, "The plasma arcs have retreated to the edges of the portal, but the vertical slashing blade has increased in frequency. Also, the right-side blade you suppressed before is beginning to resume its pattern."

His observation made Burnham look back at the first lever. It was gradually reverting to its previous position. "Well, this is fun. The controls are geared to reset themselves." She flinched as the toggle she had just flipped snapped violently back to its previous position. "Some faster than others." She adjusted her tricorder to an active sensor mode. "I'm going to record my actions and how long it takes the controls to reset. I need you to interplex your tricorder with mine so we can coordinate our analyses of causes and effects."

"Updating interplex circuit now," Spock said. "Scanning the barrier."

Burnham faced the left wall of controls. "Continuing adjustments. Call out changes as you see them." She forced a large dial through a full counterclockwise turn.

"The forward circular blade has retracted," Spock said. "Laser pulses have increased in frequency and intensity."

"Dammit." Burnham shook her head. "Every function we suppress enhances another."

"That is an accurate assessment," Spock said. "I suggest you continue, as we are running out of time to complete our mission."

"You don't say." She reversed the positions of a row of sliders on the right wall.

After a few seconds, Spock reported, "The center circular blade has retracted, and the plasma arcs have multiplied and overlapped."

One by one, Burnham tested all the controls in the pit, recording the effects and duration of each change. When there were no more levers to move, toggles to flip, or sliders to push, she programmed her tricorder and Spock's to jointly compute the most advantageous configuration, and the most efficient order in which to set it. She reviewed the result with dismay.

"I have bad news," she said.

Spock looked down over the edge of the pit. "Tell me."

"The optimal configuration to create a gap large enough for us to somersault through the barrier will take me nearly a minute to arrange, following a very specific sequence, and adjusting various controls to partial settings. Once the last control is set, the path will be open . . . but only for about four seconds. Just enough time for you to get through."

"And you?"

She shook her head. "I can't climb out of this pit, sprint to the barrier, and jump through before it closes. I'm in good shape, but not that good."

"Is there an alternative setting that would enable—?"

"No, I checked. Any adjustment intended to buy me more time disrupts the equilibrium and causes one of the systems to trigger early, which would prevent you from getting across."

Spock absorbed that, looked at the barrier, then faced Burnham. "I suggest we exchange roles. I might be able to escape from the pit and pass the barrier before it closes."

"No, Spock. I've already memorized the sequence. And as the senior officer, I'm responsible for your life. You're going first, on my mark. Is that understood?"

"Yes, sir."

"Then get ready. Because I'm starting the sequence." She set herself to work executing the complex series of adjustments to the controls in the pit, aware that the moment she let go of each one it began its march back toward doom. One after another, she forced the levers, sliders, dials, and toggles into the configuration the tricorder had told her was their only safe choice.

She moved the last slider into place, three centimeters from its top position. "Go, Spock!"

Burnham sprang toward the pit's ladder. From the corridor above she heard Spock's running steps as he sprinted toward the paused barrier. As she pulled herself over the edge and out of the pit, she saw the soles of Spock's boots as he dived through the empty space between stuttering blades and impeded plasma arcs.

Scrambling for purchase, Burnham fought to get traction, to get off her knees and run. By her second step the blades in the portal were shivering as if with anticipation of taking her life. The plasma was quavering, threatening to slip its magnetic bonds, as she took her third running step. In her head, the precious seconds counted down, and she knew she wasn't going to make it.

But she was committed now; there was nowhere to go but forward.

Her foot landed and she tensed to make her leap forward.

Inside the barrier, the center blade began to rise—

—until Spock reached into the trap and jammed his tricorder into its gears.

Burnham was airborne and passing through the barrier when she heard the grinding of metal and polymer beneath her, the hideous crunch and crackle of a tricorder being chewed into scrap, spitting sparks and shrapnel every which way, peppering her as she passed over.

An arc of plasma lashed out and cut a burn across her left thigh. The barrier's rear blade nicked the tip of her boot and barely missed severing one of her toes.

Then she crashed to the deck, smoldering and bruised, scuffed and sliced, but alive. She looked back at the barrier, once more in full flower, a mesmerizing sculpture of fire and metal locked in a lethal dance.

Then she looked up at Spock. "Risky move, mister. You might've lost an arm."

"It seemed the logical choice." He offered her his hand. Burnham accepted his help, and he pulled her to her feet.

She dusted herself off. "Like father, like son."

Her comment perplexed Spock. "Pardon?"

Only too late did she realize she had broached a subject better left unspoken. She looked away, unable to meet his searching gaze. "Forget I said anything." Eager to abandon her *faux pas*, she resumed walking toward the Juggernaut's core. "Let's just get this done and go home."

Spock said nothing as he followed Burnham on what she hoped was the final leg of their shared journey, but she imagined she could feel his justifiable curiosity hounding her every step.

Sarek was right, Burnham lamented. *I really need to learn the value of silence.*

19

"Get ready to be impressed," Cross said, leading Kolova to immediately lower her expectations instead. The governor-in-exile watched the ex-Starfleeter make a few last-second adjustments to her jumble of tech tucked into a shadowy corner below the city's auxiliary reservoir.

Pale blue beams shot from an emitter mounted on top of Cross's computer. They danced and sparred with one another as they struggled to resolve themselves into recognizable shapes.

Cross tweaked settings on her gear. "I just need a second to sync the audio with the hologram." Nudging dials a few degrees one way or the other, she added, "I had to strip out the color subcarrier data to stabilize the signal after I broke the cipher. But we should have the last full communication between the ships in orbit and whoever they were talking to on Earth."

While the communications expert coaxed the hologram into stability, Kolova glanced over her shoulder. A sea of faces, each a portrait in anticipation, pressed their attention inward.

The palpable tension worsened as Cross continued to finesse the settings of her system. From behind Kolova, Bowen grumbled, "Is this gonna work or not?"

"Loosen the strap on your jock," Cross snapped back. "If you could do this, I wouldn't be here. So do me a favor, and shut up while I'm working." Her fingers struck like lightning as she keyed in a long sequence of commands with terrifying precision. The holographic projector's beams brightened, and she declared, "Make a hole, folks! It's showtime!"

The crowd stepped back from the suddenly coherent projection. Now present in their midst were pale blue ghosts of Captains Georgiou and Pike, and a square-jawed Starfleet admiral.

"Patching in the audio," Cross said. "It's gonna be a bit thin. Best I could do."

She flipped a switch, and the ghosts acquired voices.

"—see what the goddamned problem is," the admiral said, his anger evident in spite of his voice sounding tinny and distant, robbed of its lower frequencies. *"For that matter, I don't understand why you haven't destroyed that thing already."*

Georgiou protested, *"The situation is more nuanced than that. In addition to the risk to the colonists, we've also found new evidence of a previously unreported indigenous civilization from nine million years ago. To lose the chance to study and document—"*

"Hang on, Captain," the admiral said. *"The presence of our colony by far outweighs the archeological value of some obscure pile of bones your science officer dug up. So what makes you think that this 'new evidence' would have any effect on an order I've already given?"*

"I'm just trying to say that the situation is more complex than it—"

"No, Captain, it isn't." The admiral frowned. *"Starfleet Command and the Federation Council are in agreement on*

this: *The Juggernaut absolutely must not be allowed to leave that planet, no matter the cost. That's why we tasked Captain Pike with destroying it.*"

His argument visibly annoyed Georgiou. "*With all respect, sir, my ship was the first to respond to this crisis. And while I respect that Captain Pike has been trusted with command of a* Constitution-*class vessel, the fact is that I have seniority of command.*" She threw a conciliatory look at Pike. "*No offense.*"

"*None taken,*" Pike said, dismissing her worry with a wave and a nod.

"*Be that as it may,*" the admiral said, "*if the Juggernaut gets off Sirsa III, millions of innocent lives will be at risk on worlds in adjacent star systems. The Federation simply can't have a massive alien killing machine running amok within our borders.*"

"*I understand that, sir,*" Georgiou said. "*Which is why two of our officers infiltrated the Juggernaut and are working even now to disable it before it does further damage.*"

The admiral wore a creased mask of doubt. "*Are you sure they'll be able to accomplish that mission? Have you been in contact with them since they went inside?*"

"*We're still waiting to resume contact,*" Georgiou said, "*but I have every—*"

"*Not good enough,*" the admiral cut in. "*There are too many lives on the line to put my trust in long shots, Captain, so let me make this as direct as I can: If that behemoth powers up its stardrive, you are to take any and all measures necessary to destroy it, up to and including the implementation of General Order Twenty-four. And since you've made an issue of your seniority, let me add that ultimate responsibility for accomplishing this mission now rests with you, Captain Georgiou. If the Juggernaut escapes from Sirsa III, and by some miracle you're still alive, rest assured that your career in Starfleet won't be. Do I make myself clear, Captain?"*

"As a bell, Admiral."

"Then I'm glad we've had this little chat. Now stop wasting each other's time and mine, and get to work destroying that thing while you still can. Anderson out."

The admiral's image flickered, then disappeared. Cross paused the hologram's playback. "There's more," she said, "but the autotranscript says it's just a bunch of boring tech stuff." She swiveled her chair away from her consoles to confront Kolova and the crowd. "The thing y'all should be shitting bricks over right now is Admiral Anderson giving them the go-ahead for General Order Twenty-four."

A knot of concern tightened in Kolova's stomach. "Why? What's that?"

Cross rolled her eyes. "Oh, just a few lines in the Starfleet Charter that compel starship commanders and their crews to exterminate all life on a planet by orbital bombardment."

Eyes widened with horror throughout the crowd. Bowen mastered his fear with anger. "Are you serious? Would they really do that?"

"I'm as serious as a warp-core breach," Cross said. "And yeah, they would. They've got a direct order from an admiral and sign-off from the Federation Council. Which means if they don't think they can take the Juggernaut in a fair fight, they've got permission to blast this whole planet—and every last one of us—into radioactive glass, if that's what it takes to kill it." She tapped a fingernail against a screen showing a map of the region around the capital, including the bay where the Juggernaut now floated, just a few kilometers offshore. "And if any of you are wondering, right now we're all sitting at ground zero for maximum glassage. So smoke 'em if you got 'em."

That was the last straw for Kolova. She was done being patient, being meek, playing defense. "Everybody grab a weapon. I don't give a damn what you find, as long as you're armed before we reach the surface."

Her chief of staff wore a worried look. "Why? What are we doing?"

Kolova took a plasma pistol from a stranger standing next to her, and she tucked the weapon into her belt. "If Starfleet plans to put *us* in harm's way, I say we make sure *they* keep some skin in this fight too."

If hours of triage and emergency medicine in the New Astana Medical Center had confirmed anything for Doctor Nambue, it was that it took far less time and expertise to inflict massive casualties than it took to diagnose and treat them. He and the other medical personnel from the *Shenzhou* and the *Enterprise* had been up to their elbows in burn wounds, lacerations, and broken bones for the past two hours, and the parade of wounded civilians had yet to abate.

He sprayed a coating of synthetic skin over a blistered wound on a woman's arm, then put a hypospray to her jugular vein and with a gentle push injected her with a mild dose of analgesic mixed with anti-inflammatory medicine. "You'll be fine," he told her, marshaling his most calming bedside manner. "In a few seconds, the pain will fade away. Lie back and try to rest. A nurse will be by to check on you in a couple of hours." The woman smiled, nodded once, then slipped into blissful unconsciousness.

She has no idea how I much I envy her right now, Nambue

thought as he gathered up his medkit and moved down the line to the next patient waiting for care.

Across the narrow corridor from him, the *Enterprise*'s chief medical officer, Doctor Philip Boyce, hunched over a groaning young man while setting the fellow's broken tibia. "This is gonna smart," Boyce warned him—and then he forced the bone back into alignment with a sharp *snap*. The patient did his best to swallow a scream of pain, while Boyce dug a hypospray from his satchel. "Normally, I'd give you a shot of Tennessee anesthesia, but I've been told the locals frown on my brand of classical medicine." He put the hypo to the man's neck and injected him. "That oughtta take the edge off, son. See you tomorrow."

The two CMOs faced each other, and Nambue tried to endear himself to his curmudgeonly counterpart with a disarming smile. "Busy day."

"Is that what you kids are calling a crapshow these days?" The white-haired physician scowled and shuffled down the hall to his next patient.

Mildly embarrassed but too professional to let it show for long, Nambue moved in the opposite direction, in search of his next patient. There was no shortage. The drones from the Juggernaut had racked up a disconcerting list of dead and wounded in just two incidents, and the automated attackers had inflicted serious damage on the medical center itself. Barely half of the facility was still operational. Only the fact that its most critical areas had been situated underground or on the first floor, in heavily shielded parts of the building, had enabled its staff to go on treating new patients without respite for the past several hours.

Nambue stopped beside a gurney on which lay a rust-haired, freckle-faced teenaged boy whose lower left leg was charred black. "Hello," Nambue said. "I'm Doctor Anton Nambue. Are you in pain right now?"

"No." The boy shook his head.

No pain—that's not good. Nambue activated his tricorder and scanned the youth's injury, though he suspected he already knew what he would find. In a matter of seconds his fears were confirmed. Deep third-degree burns, massive tissue damage, nerve damage, and cellular damage consistent with a high-energy disruptor discharge. He considered soft-pedaling the bad news, then thought better of it. He put away his tricorder. "Son, I have bad news. We need to amputate your lower left leg. You'll have to be fitted for a cybernetic replacement."

"I know," the teen said. "I looked up my symptoms on the comnet while I was waiting."

"Too smart for your own good." Nambue loaded a new ampoule into his hypospray. "This is a broad-spectrum antibiotic. It'll prevent infection from setting in before we get your new leg fitted." He tapped the hypo to the lad's thigh. The drugs were delivered with a soft hiss.

"Thanks, Doc." The boy pointed past Nambue. "Look out!"

Nambue turned—and met the stock of a blaster rifle with his chin.

The world was a soft blur, his chin a beacon of throbbing pain. Floating and falling—he couldn't tell them apart at first. Then he struck the cold tiled floor, and for a moment stretched by his fear he perceived every crack and speckle in the handful of tiles within a few centimeters of his face. Then everything was back in motion, and vertigo took him.

Lights drifted past above him.

No, he told himself, fighting for clarity, *I'm being dragged under them.*

Strong hands held his wrists. Two people pulled him down a flight of stairs. As his feet slammed down onto each step from the one above, Nambue was thankful his attackers were dragging him backward by his wrists and not towing him by his feet. *Probably already have a concussion,* he figured. *No need for major brain damage.*

A semblance of awareness reasserted itself as he was thrown against the back of a freight elevator. Blinking, he realized he was surrounded by other Starfleet personnel— nurses, medical technicians, paramedics, doctors—from both the *Shenzhou* and the *Enterprise.* He saw no sign of their respective security detachments, but to his right, in the corner of the lift, he spied Doctor Spyropoulos, moaning and cursing under his breath. He tried to get the man's attention with a harsh whisper. "Greg! Are you all right?"

"I'm not even supposed to be here," Spyropoulos mumbled. "What the hell is going on? I'm not even a doctor, dammit. I'm just a dentist!"

If not for the glares of warning from the two armed colonists standing over the hostages, Nambue might have taken that moment to give Spyropoulos a brief lecture on the cruel whimsy of a bitch named Irony. *Have to save it for another time,* he decided.

A third man with a blaster rifle stepped inside the lift and said in a Cockney accent to his two comrades, "Guv's waiting. Let's take this lot down." One of his accomplices closed the lift gate, and the other pressed a button to send the car to the deepest sublevel it serviced.

Shadows and distant flickers slipped past outside the lift car as it sank into the darkness beneath the capital. The hospital's sharp perfume of antiseptics and astringent was replaced by the odors of mechanical oil and lubricants, the stench of harsh chemicals and untreated sewage.

By the time the lift halted, Nambue was sure they must be deep underground. Cockney Man opened the gate. His two fellow kidnappers aimed their weapons at Nambue and the others. One of them told the prisoners in a voice of low menace, "Don't do anything stupid."

Cockney and his pals backed out of the lift, then ushered out the prisoners. Nambue did his best to linger near the back of the group, to buy himself time to observe their surroundings. All he saw were endless jungles of pipes large and small, and metal catwalks beneath which lay abyssal plunges into blackness.

The prisoners were marched at a quick pace down a few more flights of steep stairs, until they were herded into a storage area lit by a single light rod on its ceiling, and whose entrance was guarded by more armed men. Through the open door, Nambue heard people talking outside. At least one of them he recognized from the colony's news feeds as the voice of the governor, Gretchen Kolova. The others he didn't know.

"You destroyed their communicators?" Kolova asked.

Another woman replied, "Yes, all except this one. We need it to make our demands."

"Yes, of course. And the transporter scramblers—?"

"All in place," a man answered. "No one's beaming in or out of here, Governor. And we have all the choke points covered. If they send down security teams, we'll be ready."

Another trio of armed guards arrived with a fresh batch of prisoners. Among them was Doctor Boyce, who sported a bloody nose and a split lip, as well as a number of abrasions on his knuckles. The *Enterprise*'s chief surgeon hadn't been taken without a fight. He nodded at Nambue, who replied in kind. Then they turned toward their makeshift cell's entrance as Governor Gretchen Kolova stepped into its frame, holding a Starfleet communicator in her hand.

She flipped open its grille with a flick of her wrist.

"Attention, *Enterprise* and *Shenzhou*. This is Governor Gretchen Kolova. My people and I have been monitoring your communications. We know about your General Order Twenty-four, and that you've been told to consider my planet and my people expendable in your fight against the Juggernaut. Well . . . I just want you to know that my people and I are holding your medical teams hostage until this crisis is resolved. In other words, Captains, if you decide to treat *us* as collateral damage, we'll be taking at least a few of *your* people down with us."

20

Just what this situation needed, Georgiou fumed behind her failing mask of calm. *Another complication.* She did her best to sound unruffled. "Governor, you and your people are in enough trouble already. Adding kidnapping to the charges against you isn't going to help matters."

"I don't see how it can make things worse," Kolova replied over the audio-only channel. *"You're already planning on blasting us all into charcoal in a few minutes. I just want to make sure you get to share some of the pain you're about to inflict."*

One by one, the *Shenzhou*'s bridge officers tried to steal looks at Georgiou to see how their captain would react to this latest crisis. The only one of her officers who kept his focus on his own work was Saru, and the only officer whose opinion Georgiou would actually have cared to know was still trapped inside the Juggernaut. Hoping not to inflame matters further, she told Kolova, "I don't know what you think you heard, Governor, but just because something is an option, that doesn't make it a foregone conclusion. And I assure you, we're doing—"

"—all you can," Kolova interrupted. *"So you keep telling me. It's getting old, Captain."*

"Believe me or don't," Georgiou said, her patience expended. "But this conversation will have to wait until after my crew and I deal with the Juggernaut. *Shenzhou* out." She signaled Ensign Fan with a slashing motion in front of her throat, and Fan closed the comm channel. Freed from Kolova's merry-go-round of empty posturing, Georgiou stood from her command chair to reassert her presence in the center of the bridge. "Mister Gant. On the off chance that we succeed in stopping the Juggernaut and saving the planet, we'll need a tactical response to rescue those hostages."

"How do you want to play it, Captain? Slow and steady, or shock and awe?"

Too many times Georgiou had seen the costs of carelessness. "Let's game out slow and steady," she said. "Maximal rescue with minimal violence."

"Best-case scenario," Gant said, "is we bring down the Juggernaut, and then we talk down Kolova and negotiate a peaceful release of the prisoners."

Georgiou appreciated his willingness to start his speculations from a place of optimism. But she had to consider all possibilities. "And if they decide not to stand down?"

"The first step would be to isolate them." Gant thought for a second. "Box them in. The tighter the space, the better. We have to assume they'd be able to weather at least a short siege. Beneath the city they'll have access to water conduits, maybe even emergency food lockers."

Saru looked up to join the conversation. "Could we not use the transporter to beam in anesthetic gas? If the targets are inside a contained area, such a tactic could be quite effective."

"Maybe," Gant said. "But they're using transporter scramblers. If we want to hit them with tranq gas, we'd have to send in a security team to make a direct assault.

Which is possible, but if the colonists shoot to kill, we could lose a lot of people real fast."

That notion seemed to diminish Saru's enthusiasm for his own proposal. "Oh. No, that won't do. Not at all." He folded his long bony fingers together in a pensive gesture. "What if we devised an automated delivery system, such as a drone, to deliver the gas?"

"If it's remote controlled," Gant said, "the command system would be crippled by the same scrambling field that's blocking our transporters. And as I'm sure you recall, autonomous robotic attack systems—"

"Are prohibited by Federation law," Saru said, finishing the citation. "A most nettlesome restriction, if you ask me."

Ensign Fan turned away from the communications console. "That's what the people of Earth used to think, right up until World War III. Every time I think about those killer 'bots in the streets of Paris, I get a shiver down my spine."

"It's clear this might take a bit more thought," Georgiou said. "Mister Gant, keep looking for new angles on this. In the meantime, let's focus on the Juggernaut. How do we neutralize it without killing the planet?"

Ensign Weeton's nervous voice piped up from the back of the bridge. "Commander Johar just sent up some sensor data. It's from his forensic work on the drones. He says if we can map the fluctuations in the quantum resonance frequency of the Juggernaut's hull material, we might be able to retune our phasers to punch holes in it."

That sounded as if it might almost be helpful. "Give him my thanks," Georgiou said to Weeton, "right after you send that data to Gant, Troke, and Saru." To the science specialists and tactical officer she added, "You three start crunching those numbers. Fan, send Johar's data to the *Enterprise*. Let them work the problem with us."

Three nods of affirmation. Placated by the promise of a new tactic, Georgiou returned to her chair and confronted the image of Sirsa III outside the center viewport. *I know we can solve this . . .* Her hand closed into a fist, channeling her frustration. *If only we have the time.*

As if in mockery of her silent hopes, alerts shrilled on the ops console. Oliveira muted them, then looked over her shoulder at Georgiou, her eyes wide with alarm. "Captain, there's something happening on the surface, and it doesn't look good."

"Specifics, Lieutenant."

"The Juggernaut, Captain." Oliveira projected a magnified holographic image of the vessel over the main viewport. "It's powering up on a level we haven't seen before— weapons, shields, more drones in ready positions, and a major heat bloom from what I'm pretty sure is a stardrive." She updated her readouts, then added, "No idea how soon it'll be ready for lift-off, but at this rate I don't think it'll be more than a matter of minutes."

Georgiou felt the blood drain from her face, replaced by a cold wash of dread. Despite the company of her crew, she suddenly felt very alone.

"Leviathan has awoken," she said under her breath. "Heaven help us all."

"We're out of time," Pike said to his bridge crew. "Number One, sound red alert, battle stations. Mister Tyler, raise shields, charge phaser banks, load all torpedo tubes. Chief Garison, hail Captain Georgiou, right now." Around him, his bridge officers remained cool and professional as the whoop of the red alert siren resounded through the *Enterprise.*

"Power levels inside the Juggernaut are escalating rapidly," Una said, peering into the cerulean glow of her hooded sensor display. "At its current rate of increase, the Juggernaut's energy output will be double the combined power of the *Shenzhou* and the *Enterprise* in less than twenty minutes. Potential maximum output is currently impossible to calculate."

"Whatever Spock and his new friend are doing down there," said navigator Ohara, "it looks like they've really pissed it off."

Garison swiveled toward Pike. "I have Captain Georgiou on channel one."

"On-screen," Pike said. Georgiou's stern features filled the main viewscreen. Pike mirrored her grave expression. "We're out of time, Captain."

"No, not yet. The Juggernaut is powering up, but it's not yet mobile."

"We don't know that," Pike said, growing more emphatic. "It could lift off, or launch more drones, or both, at any second. We might never have a better chance to destroy it."

"If we strike now," Georgiou said, *"even if we succeed, everyone on the surface will be killed, including Mister Spock and my first officer."*

"I don't see that we have any alternative. That thing will be able to overpower us both in a matter of minutes. If we delay our response until after it's mobile, that might be too late."

Someone off-screen relayed a report to Georgiou, who nodded once, then returned her attention to Pike. *"My second officer informs me the Juggernaut's stardrive will not have sufficient power to achieve launch for another fifteen minutes."*

"And in twenty minutes the Juggernaut will be turning our ships into scrap." Pike sprang from his chair, overcome by the need to be in motion, to take action, to *do* something. "You heard the same orders from Admiral Anderson that I did. Our priority is to neutralize the Juggernaut, by any means necessary—even if that means sacrificing the planet or ourselves."

Georgiou remained stoic in the face of his challenge. *"I heard the admiral's orders quite clearly. Including the part where he vested me with operational command of this mission. This is my call to make, Captain, and I've made it. We have fifteen minutes before the Juggernaut's capabilities escalate this conflict to the point of no alternative. I intend to give Burnham and Spock every one of those minutes to accomplish their objective."*

Pike was livid. Decorum demanded he conceal it; duty required him to move past it. But the anger at being forced into inaction burned like a hot coal festering in his belly. "What are we supposed to do in the interim? Stand down?"

"Of course not," Georgiou said. *"We keep looking for a way to penetrate the Juggernaut's hull with our phasers. If the situation on the surface changes, or the Juggernaut lifts off ahead of schedule . . . then we do what we have to, no matter the cost."*

He wanted to believe her, but he found it hard to trust her judgment. "And if we come to the end of this fifteen-minute grace period, and the Juggernaut remains a threat . . . will you keep telling me to give Spock and Burnham more time?"

His question seemed at last to pierce Georgiou's unshakable façade.

"Have your crew set a synchronized fifteen-minute countdown with mine," she said. *"If the Juggernaut remains a*

threat and we haven't heard from Burnham or Spock by the time it expires . . . we'll glass the planet."

At a nod from Pike, Ohara set up the countdown, which appeared in the lower right corner of the main viewscreen. It was the concession Pike had wanted, but now that he had it, he felt nothing but regret.

"I hope you're right about this, Captain."

"Believe me," Georgiou said, her eyes betraying a shimmer of fear, *"so do I."*

21

Tremors of vitality hummed beneath the deck; vibrant colors pulsed behind suddenly translucent bulkheads. It was apparent to Burnham that the Juggernaut had been roused from its eons of slumber. Like a dormant volcano stirred to life, the alien behemoth was alive and gravid with the promise of death and destruction. Ashamed to show emotion in front of Spock, she banished all semblance of fear from her face and voice. "I suspect we are nearly out of time."

He coolly appraised the new aura of menace that infused their surroundings. "Indeed."

Ahead of them bobbed Thumper, its swirls of ribbon-like energy casting off sparks like motes from a bonfire, its steady beat louder and deeper than before. Whatever was invigorating the Juggernaut was increasing the brightness and volume of the holographic lure. It led them down another slope in the passageway, then it paused at a fork where the corridor split into two parallel passages, one on each side of the ship.

"This is new," Burnham said. "Up until now, we've only had one path to follow."

"Intriguing." Spock halted and inspected the protruding thresholds of the diverging paths. He pointed at markings engraved into their outer edges. "We have seen these symbols before. At the first threshold after we entered."

Burnham remembered. "The one that closed behind us. Not an encouraging sign."

"The design of this intersection seems to imply we are meant to part ways. Perhaps if we stay together, we can avoid triggering the mechanism that closes the portal."

"Maybe," Burnham said. "Or perhaps they'll close anyway, and then we'll be unable to finish the last challenge, because we'll both be stuck in the same passage."

Spock considered that. "May I borrow your tricorder?" She handed the device to him. He studied its display, then furrowed his brow. "The hull's signal-blocking compounds are quite concentrated here. If we become sequestered in separate passages, we will be unable to maintain contact with our communicators."

"So we have no way of knowing what's at the end of each corridor," Burnham said. "And no idea what kind of challenges we'll face when we get there." She took back her tricorder and reviewed the automatic map it had compiled of their movements inside the Juggernaut. "If this is correct, then there's a good chance these two passages both lead to the same place." She pondered their predicament. "If the makers of these tests want us to split up, wouldn't it be more logical for the portals to remain open until after we part ways?"

Her question was met by a one-shoulder shrug. "Perhaps. Without knowing the motives and design imperatives of the builders, all I can do is speculate. If you wish to test the paths together, that is your prerogative as the officer in charge."

"Well, I prefer action to inaction, so let's proceed down the starboard passage. We'll step together over the portal's threshold on the count of three. One. Two. Three."

Burnham and Spock synchronized their movements and stepped over the threshold. When they both were on the other side, and the portal remained open behind them, Burnham breathed a quiet sigh of relief. "So far, so good. Let's see where this leads."

With each step they took, the glow infusing the bulkheads changed colors and grew more intense, and a deep thudding noise gave Burnham the uneasy sensation that they were deep in the heart of a living thing, one not pleased to welcome them as invaders. The passage curved outward and then back in, so that as they neared its far end its entrance was no longer visible. At its terminus was a single oval panel recessed into the inner bulkhead.

"End of the line," Burnham said. She put her hand on the oval slab. It was cool and smooth like polished obsidian. After several seconds without a response, she removed her hand. "Nothing." A look around uncovered no other clues. "No markings. No other interface." A weary nod at the oval panel. "Just this."

"And," Spock said, "most likely a mirrored twin at the end of the other passage."

"Let's go see." Burnham led Spock back the way they had come, and then they ventured down the portside passageway. At its end, just as they both had expected, was another oval interface set into the inner bulkhead, to the right of the closed portal. Burnham shook her head. "No line of sight between the interfaces. And with the portals closed, we won't be able to hear each other or send signals." She grimaced at the oval slab. "If this test is like the others, it'll require us to do something in synchronicity, some kind of coordinated action."

"Without the ability to share information, that will be difficult," Spock said, exhibiting his Vulcan knack for understatement. "Setting arbitrary parameters for timing or response will most likely be futile without knowing the nature of the test in advance."

"This is ridiculous," Burnham said. She plodded back toward the intersection. Spock followed her. Several seconds later they were back at the fork in the main corridor. "We can't go back, and if we go forward, we'll be cut off in locked passageways with no way to cooperate."

Above them the ship rumbled with the sounds of great machines going to work. Spock noted it all with what seemed to be perfect detachment, but each new quaking of the vessel reminded Burnham that once it was mobile, their shipmates on the *Shenzhou* and the *Enterprise* would have no choice but to destroy it by any means possible. The only scenario she could think of that didn't end with her and Spock's deaths required them to get past this final obstacle.

But how? After testing them in tandem so many times, why split them apart now?

Dejected, Burnham pressed her palm to her forehead and fought to maintain her last vestiges of emotional control. "This is it," she confessed to Spock. "We're finished."

"We cannot know that for certain. Not until we face the last challenge."

His calmness was maddening. "Are you serious? Once we split up, that's it. We're done, Spock. If we can't communicate, we can't collaborate. If neither of us even knows what the other is looking at, how are we supposed to make the right choice?" She shook her head and let her shoulders slump to signal her admission of defeat. "This might look like a fork in the path, Spock, but that's just a disguise. What this really is? Is a dead end."

22

Burnham's quiet desperation struck Spock as premature. "It is too soon to concede failure," he said, hoping to bolster her morale. "As long as options remain, we have a duty to persevere."

His attempt to mitigate her frustration seemed only to worsen it. "I'd hardly call charging blind into a tandem test a viable option."

"I concur," Spock said. "But that is not what I am suggesting." An ominous pulsing shook the oval corridor, whose bulkheads brightened to yellowish-white. "All of the trials to which the Juggernaut has subjected us have been designed to test knowledge and abilities it knows we possess. I suspect this challenge to be no different."

Her manner was incredulous. "And do you have any idea what ability or knowledge this was designed to test? Because if Starfleet Academy actually has training that addresses *this*, I might finally have reason to regret not having studied there."

"I do not think it was my Starfleet experience that this obstacle means to assess, but rather a talent of a more personal nature." He debated with himself over what would be the most politic way to broach this topic with a non-Vulcan. He knew that Burnham had spent much of her life on his homeworld; perhaps that called for a more direct approach. "You lived among my people for many years. You studied in our learning centers, attended our Science Academy—"

"Get to the point, Spock."

"Many Vulcans have telepathic abilities. Some possess exceptional gifts, while others, such as myself, are primarily touch-telepaths, with minimal range absent physical contact."

Her apprehension became revulsion. "Tell me you're not suggesting—"

"A mind-meld," Spock said. "It would enable me to maintain a tenuous link with your mind after we split up into the parallel corridors."

Burnham paced and shook her head, as if in denial. "No, there has to be another way."

"I do not believe there is. At least, none that are viable in the limited time we have left."

Her anger gave way to fear. "What about a less-invasive approach? Maybe you could read my mind without the meld. Or send me telepathic suggestions."

Spock shook his head. "My talents are not strong enough. Perhaps, with more training, I might affect a weak mind from a short distance. But your mind was disciplined on Vulcan, and we will be separated by over a dozen meters. Those complications, coupled with the complexity of the puzzles favored by the Juggernaut, suggest we will need a strong psionic bond if this plan is to succeed. For me to create and maintain such a bond, you must join me in the mind-meld."

His argument left Burnham in a state of distress. "No. I just—I can't. Just . . . no."

"I understand feeling a measure of resistance to the proposal," Spock said, thinking he might reason with her.

"The mind-meld is an extremely intimate form of mental communion, not something to be entered into lightly. But given the severity of our crisis, and the fact that we are not so much strangers to each other as—"

"That's part of—" She cut herself off, as if there was a terrible truth waiting to break free of her, one she refused to let go. "Look, I know what a mind-meld is."

Her defensiveness aroused his curiosity. "Have you been part of a mind-meld before?"

Burnham turned away from him, as if fighting to preserve some shred of privacy in spite of their close quarters and shared jeopardy. Then she faced him, her demeanor still unsettled but clearly doing her best to present a rational front. "It's a subject I'd rather not discuss."

"Why not? Forgive me for prying, but under the circumstances, I feel I must."

She closed her eyes, and only afterward did Spock realize she had done it to conceal her involuntary wince at his question. With her eyes still shut, she said, "The memory has . . . painful associations for me, Mister Spock. Sensations I'd much prefer not to relive."

A shift in the Juggernaut sent them both stumbling toward the same bulkhead, and Spock caught Burnham just before she would have made impact. The vessel righted itself and jostled them again, all the while increasing its ambient roar of ancient machinery surging back to full capacity. Spock made sure Burnham had her balance, then let her go. "With all respect, what you want is no longer relevant. You and I need to reach the core of this vessel if we are to complete our mission, and a mind-meld appears to be our only remaining means of doing so. If we do not, we and many other people are going to die."

Burnham clenched her fists and gritted her teeth, as if she

were in physical pain. "I know what you're saying is true," she said, her voice strained. "I know it's logical. But dammit, Spock . . . I just *can't*. I can't open my mind like that."

She looked at him; tears shone in her dark eyes. "I'm sorry."

He wanted to absolve her of blame, to tell her she owed him no apology, owed the world no remorse. But beneath his Vulcan logic, the part of Spock that was human knew he could not. Despite all of Burnham's many admirable qualities, her failure to master her fear was about to spell not only her doom and his, but those of their shipmates and over three hundred thousand civilians, as well as an entire planet—and that was a crime of weakness Spock could not forgive.

The countdown timer projected onto the center viewport of *Shenzhou*'s bridge flipped from 12:00 to 11:59. Georgiou wiped the sweat from her palms across the pant legs of her uniform. She felt acutely aware of time's passage, as if it were a weight pressing on her chest. Outside the transparent-aluminum viewport, Sirsa III looked placid, with its blanket of clouds wrapped around the vast expanse of open ocean that dominated more than half its surface. Absent a miracle, all of that beauty was minutes away from being consumed by fire.

Denial had enabled Georgiou to postpone the inevitable, but the time for delay was over. She stood from her command chair and moved to stand over Gant's and Narwani's duty stations. "Mister Gant, what is the status of our shields?"

"Back to full power, Captain. Damage-control teams report all major systems restored."

"Good. Energize shield emitters, have them ready for quick response."

Gant nodded. "Already done."

"Then start charging all phasers, and instruct the torpedo bays to load all tubes and to prepare for fast loads and snap shots." She tried not to show her unease at addressing Narwani, whose VR helmet made her look to Georgiou like a human with a snail for a head. "Plot a firing solution for a full-power bombardment of the Juggernaut. Be prepared to adjust that solution on the fly if the vessel becomes mobile."

Narwani's small nod was magnified by the mass of her metallic helmet. "Aye, sir."

Pivoting back to Gant, Georgiou continued, "If the Juggernaut shows signs of movement, target torpedoes in a tight spread. Direct hits are the goal, but don't let the perfect be the enemy of the good. When it comes to photon torpedoes, close is often good enough to do real damage."

This time Gant balked. "Are you sure you want to risk torpedoes, Captain? In the planet's atmosphere, I mean?" He looked toward Narwani as if expecting support, but found only his own reflection in the gleaming metal of her VR helmet.

"I understand your reservations, Mister Gant," Georgiou said, "but this has to be done."

Saru stepped away from his station to stand near Georgiou. "Does it? Are we sure?"

"Yes, Saru, *we* are." A slow turn confirmed what Georgiou already suspected: every member of her bridge crew was watching her exchange with Gant and Saru, their faces taut with anxiety at the prospect of committing ecocide and mass homicide in the name of duty. She raised her voice as she returned to the middle of the bridge. "Listen up. We have been given explicit orders by Starfleet Command. These are some of the most difficult orders I have ever received. But they are lawful, and they were not issued carelessly or out of malice. I have done all that I can to prevent this outcome, to find a better way . . . but sometimes bad solutions are the only ones we have left. So when that countdown ends, if the Juggernaut remains a threat, I expect every one of you to do your part to ensure that it is destroyed, no matter the cost."

Far from galvanizing her officers, her address seemed only to deepen their concerns. Troke, usually content to avoid drawing attention to himself, stood from his post. "Captain, I don't question the need to confront a threat such as the Juggernaut. But to obliterate an entire planet . . . I would consider that a crime against science."

"As would I," Saru said. "Excusing ecocide in the name of tactical advantage offends me as a scientist, and as a Starfleet officer. It betrays every value the Academy taught us to revere."

The mounting resistance started to trouble Georgiou. "We have a duty to—"

"To who?" interrupted Ensign Fan. "Starfleet? What about to our shipmates being held hostage down there? What about Doctor Nambue? And Lieutenant Burnham?"

Oliveira said, "What about the colonists? Three hundred sixty *thousand* civilians."

Detmer added, "That's a lot of collateral damage to have on our collective conscience."

It galled Georgiou to be put in the position of defending the very tactic she had fought so hard against, but there was no more time for moral equivocation. "You all know what's at stake if the Juggernaut gets off that planet," she said, her manner quiet but grave. "You heard me have this very same argument with Captain Pike. And you probably all know I made this case to Admiral Anderson. I was over-ruled, every time. And I didn't like it any more than you do now."

Exhausted, she rested her hands on the back of her command chair and bowed her head while she collected her breath and her thoughts. "I joined Starfleet for the same reasons many of you did. All my life, I've thought of myself as a scientist first, an explorer second, and a diplomat when I needed to be. But we don't always get to choose the role we play. The price of serving in Starfleet is that there are times when we need to be *soldiers*. That's why each of you wears a uniform. It's more than just a piece of clothing. It has to be *earned*. To wear it is to tell the universe that you are part of something greater than yourself. The reason we all wear the *same* uniform is to remind us that we've all sworn to put aside our egos—our wants, our needs, our personal beliefs—and faithfully carry out all lawful orders given to us, no matter how terrible they might be. That is the burden we all vowed to accept."

A dark melancholy settled over the bridge of the *Shenzhou*.

No one met Georgiou's steely gaze; no one raised their voice in protest.

One by one, her officers turned back toward their consoles and resumed their duties. The last to abandon his stand of principle was Saru, but even he remained respectfully mute as he returned to his console.

From the tactical station, Gant said in a subdued voice, "Phasers charging. Torpedo room reports all tubes loaded, all teams standing by for fast action and snap fire."

"Well done, Mister Gant. Ensign Narwani, coordinate our attack with the *Enterprise*, to maximize the impact of our combined firing solutions."

"Aye, Captain," Narwani said, her voice filtered through her helmet's speaker.

As Georgiou took her place once more in the center seat, Saru approached and stood beside her chair. "Captain," he said, his voice discreetly quiet, "I want you to know that I intend to note my objections to these orders in my official log."

"I would expect nothing less," Georgiou said, secretly proud of Saru for not being willing to surrender his principles without protest. All the same, caution was in order. "But when you do, you should keep in mind the millions of lives that will be jeopardized if we fail to act here and now. It's a numbers game, Saru." She glanced at the countdown as it shrank from 10:00 to 09:59 and continued to diminish. "And ours are running out."

Saru frowned at the countdown timer, then returned to his post.

Alone in the center of the bridge with only her conscience for company, Georgiou hoped that in spite of the distance between them, Burnham might hear her silent plea:

This is it, Michael. Time to do or die. Please don't let us down.

Three minutes of silence had felt like forever. Stalled with Spock at the fork in the passage, all Burnham could think about was how profoundly disappointed Sarek would be if he knew what she had just done—or, to be more precise, what she had just refused to do, out of fear.

Spock, in typical Vulcan fashion, had not pressed his case or even said a word since her refusal of his invitation to a mind-meld. *Repression masquerading as courtesy,* Burnham stewed, secretly ashamed that she was committing the same emotional fraud, masking guilt with anger. All her thoughts for the past three minutes had been evasions, distractions to keep her from facing the intractable logic of Spock's proposal. A mind-meld represented their best chance for overcoming the Juggernaut's next and hopefully final obstacle.

Why does that have to be the solution? she raged. When she imagined some coldly rational artificial intelligence guiding the creation of the Juggernaut's challenges, she could conceive of it accessing their tricorders, and through them learning of their respective species—including the Vulcan talent for psionics. Perhaps the test had been intended only to gauge the strength and precision of Spock's telepathy, as a metric by which to judge the potential of his species. After all, nothing the Juggernaut could have gleaned from their tricorders could have betrayed how passionately Burnham would resist the suggestion of a meld.

No, that's just icing on the cake, she brooded.

So many memories, so much pain . . . all of it tucked away, into parts of Burnham's mind she had hoped never to visit again. But she knew what a mind-meld could do, knew what it would mean to reopen old emotional wounds. It would take her to parts of herself she had hoped never to confront again. To the alien shores of her childhood and adolescent selves.

But what's the alternative? Give up? Let thousands of innocents die because I don't want to show my wounded inner child to the man I've measured myself against for most of my life?

She imagined what Georgiou would say if she saw her like this.

"Get over yourself." That's what Philippa would say. Burnham conjured the disapproval she knew would infuse

the captain's words. *"You're a Starfleet officer. Act like one."* Bitter tears stung Burnham's eyes. *Putting my pain ahead of others' lives. She'd be so ashamed of me.*

Her rational mind retorted, *You're ashamed of yourself. So do something about it.*

Burnham sleeved the tears from her eyes and face, then turned toward Spock. "You're right," she said. "A mind-meld is the only way. I apologize for my reluctance."

"No apology is necessary," Spock said. "A meld is not to be undertaken in haste."

She was grateful for his understanding, and she suspected a word of caution was also in order. "I should say up front that you might find a meld with me to be . . . difficult."

"I might offer you the same warning."

Burnham waved off his caveat. "I'm not talking about the volatility of emotions. Those I was taught to control long ago. What you need to know is that my previous experience with the meld was linked to a trauma—one that continues to haunt me despite years of guided meditation. You might not be prepared for the intensity of that experience."

If Spock was concerned by her admonition, he didn't show it. "I am prepared to contend with, and hold in confidence, any secrets you harbor. But I would be remiss if I did not counsel you with regard to my own emotional turmoil. Rather than mitigate the violence of my Vulcan emotions, the human side of my nature seems to have amplified them. Even if you think you know what it means to meld with a Vulcan mind, this experience might prove very different."

That's not what I expected, Burnham thought, and for a moment she wondered whether going ahead with the meld might be a mistake. Then she recalled all the lives that were in danger of being lost forever if her courage failed. *If the risk in front of me was a charge into enemy disruptor fire, I'd have acted already. Time to stop living in fear.*

She drew a deep breath. "I'm ready. Let's begin."

"We should sit," Spock said, gesturing toward the deck.

They both squatted, then sat facing each other, both of them cross-legged, their knees almost touching. He leaned toward her, and she reciprocated. As he looked into her eyes, she felt her pulse start to race, and beads of sweat traced chaotic paths down the back of her neck.

His baritone was as calm as a windless sea. "Are you ready?"

Her only honorable response was a lie.

"Yes."

23

"My mind to your mind . . ."

Burnham had to let her barriers fall. Spock's fingertips were points of warmth upon her cheeks, against her
temples. He held her face in both his hands, the pressure of
his fingers as delicate as the shy exploration of his telepathy.
Not even joined yet, and I feel his reluctance. It surprised her
to think that Spock feared melding with her as much as she
did with him.

To fight the meld would only prolong the pain. Surrender was the quickest route to peace. Yet her subconscious
resisted, erected barricades, fogged the path to unity.

Spock's voice was steady and sure, a beacon of courage
on which Burnham could focus. "My mind to your mind.
Our thoughts are merging . . ."

Time slowed, like molten glass cooling and becoming
trapped in one shape. The shifting of colors inside the bulkheads of the Juggernaut stopped; the tides of Burnham's
respiration grew so deep that their roar became endless, like
the breath of an abyss. Then the distractions of the world
around her and Spock dimmed and faded away, lost and
forgotten, figments of shadow.

"Our thoughts are one."

She heard his assurance inside her own thoughts, in his

voice as well as her own. Here in this uncreated womb of thought, Sarek's estranged son and surrogate daughter confronted each other without barriers to candor, bereft of the armor of ego and lies, stripped of the comforts of isolation. *"To form a lasting telepathic bond,"* he explained to her, *"we must trust one another."*

"I understand," she said, knowing even as she had thought the words that she wasn't sure she had such faith left in her—and that Spock now knew that as certainly as she did.

Then came the fusion, and deception became an impossibility.

His mind and hers became a single entity, a blended consciousness. He gifted all his pain to her, and she shared her lifetime of hurts in kind. She lived his life, and he dwelled in hers.

"Half-breed!" the other children yell, and Burnham feels her cheeks flush with the heat of shame and anger. "You're no more Vulcan than a Tellarite!" They are only words. Burnham knows she shouldn't let them affect her emotions, but they do. She is an embarrassment to her father, Sarek. Just by existing she has sullied the ancient and powerful dynasty of their family.

Exiled early to bed by his parents, Spock can't suppress his urge to eavesdrop on their conversation. Doctari Alpha, the remote science outpost on which they've lived for the last year, is full of antiquated hardware and software. The communication system is no exception. Despite his tender youth, Spock has taught himself to bypass the comms' parental lockouts. From his tiny room he taps into their quarters' communications subsystem. It takes him only a few moments to access the sonic receivers in the family room, where his parents argue in hushed voices.

"*Are you kidding me? We're already packed!*" Father is furious. "*Whether we're here or on the transport, she'll be watching the supernova on a viewscreen.*"

Mother does her best not to sound upset, but her calm pretense falters. "*She knows how hard I worked on this project. How much I care about it.*"

"*You saying you changed your mind? You want to stay? Because until yesterday, you were fine with leaving on tonight's transport.*"

"*I was willing to* accept *it,*" Mother says. "*It's not the same thing.*"

"*So? What's changed?*"

"*She changed.*" Mother pauses to rein in her anger. "*She's old enough to know the difference between just seeing a vid and being part of a moment in history.*"

"*If we miss tonight's transport, we're stuck here another week.*"

"*Calvin,* please. *You didn't see the look in her eyes when she asked to stay. She* wants *this experience. Don't take this away from her. And really—what difference does a week make?*"

The silence between them is fraught with unspoken resentments. Spock imagines he can almost hear their contest of wills in the conversational lull. Father resigns from the argument with a sigh. "*Fine. If being here for the supernova means that much to her, we'll stay.*"

Alone in his room, it's all Spock can do to contain his joy. He fights the urge to jump and whoop in celebration, and instead logs out of the comm system. Then he scrambles back into his bunk. He cocoons himself with bedcovers in the nick of time: He hears his bedroom door slide open a few centimeters, just enough to admit a sliver of light. His parents hover outside the door.

"She's already asleep," Father whispers. "We'll tell her in the morning."

The door slides shut. Under the covers, Spock smiles in anticipation—but only because he doesn't know that when he sees the supernova of Beta Volanis in three days' time, he will witness it alone, through a fish-eyed lens of tear-stained eyes.

The next morning explosions and alarms wake Spock. He rushes to his bedroom door and opens it to find his path blocked by fallen debris and hot smoke. His family's quarters are shattered and aflame. In the midst of the fire, his parents lie slain, their corpses charred and broken.

Firefighters in hazmat suits break through the wreckage. Spock wails with grief, reaching in futility toward his parents, as paramedics spirit him away from the blaze, to safety.

Lying in the infirmary, Spock weeps until his eyes burn and his strength is spent. He gleans from muted conversations all around him that the outpost was attacked without warning by a Klingon starship. Casualties at the outpost are heavy, and the Klingons have escaped.

This is my fault, he realizes. *If we'd left last night, like Father wanted, he and Mother would be alive. We'd be together. I could've watched the supernova on the transport. But I made them stay. They died because of me.*

Orphaned and grieving, Spock confronts a cruel truth:

Regret, by definition, always comes too late.

Burnham reels from the adrenaline of landing a punch on a taller, older Vulcan boy. The youth lands hard, stunned by the blow not just because of the strength behind it, but for the naked admission of savagery it represents. The momentary pleasure that came from lashing out, from knocking down the older boy, fades in an instant as Burnham sees the fear—no, the *revulsion*—in the eyes of her victim and all his friends as they retreat from her.

When Father hears, he will think as they do.

He will say I am not a Vulcan.

Arriving for the first day of instruction at the Vulcan Learning Center in the planet's capital city of ShiKahr, Spock is taken aback by the open hostility he finds in the faces of the Vulcan children. They glare at him as if he is an infection that has violated the sanctity of their school.

He notes their disdain as they eye him and mouth the word "human" as if it were a vulgarity; by the end of his first hour in the Learning Center, he has come to believe that it is. During the few rest intervals that break up the daylong program of teachings at the VLC, none of the other students deign to speak to Spock, even though he wears the same plain cassock and has made his mother cut his bangs in the classic Vulcan style.

From his first day, he knows the truth that no one will say out loud: no matter how hard he tries to fit in on Vulcan, he will never be accepted by his peers. To them he will always be an oddity, a freak, an alien imposition upon their cultural purity.

He will always be alone.

A child of nearly eight years, Burnham embraces the trembling body of I-Chaya, her pet *sehlat*. His wounds, sustained defending her from a *le-matya* in the Llangon mountains outside ShiKahr, are grievous. She has known the noble animal companion her entire life. She cannot imagine a home without his rumbling purr, his clumsy lumbering bulk disturbing small pieces of furniture, his strangely silken fur warding her from the chills of winter winds . . .

But there is no denying the reality of this moment.

I-Chaya is dying.

Burnham has just returned with a healer from a nearby village. The healer has examined I-Chaya and made his prognosis. All his medicine can do now is prolong I-Chaya's suffering.

It would be unseemly for Burnham to cry. She is Vulcan.

"Release him," she tells the healer. "It is fitting he dies with peace and dignity." As the healer prepares his hypospray, Burnham's adult cousin Selek watches while she whispers her farewell to I-Chaya, with her thanks for his courage, his loyalty, and his sacrifice.

Burnham's face is blank and her eyes dry as the healer injects I-Chaya with a dose of powerful sedative. The glaze of pain and confusion departs from the *sehlat*'s eyes, and then Burnham watches his last spark of life dim and go dark.

Selek reminds her on the journey home that she made the logical decision. The merciful choice. She knows these things are true. But all she wants in that moment is to hold her beloved pet and weep until her well of grief runs dry— the one solace a Vulcan will never allow.

Amanda grips Spock by his shoulders and looks him in the eye. "Don't listen to the other children. Just because they're Vulcan and you're human, that doesn't give them any right to judge you. Do you understand what I'm telling you?"

Spock nods. He is so alone, so frightened. The universe seems to have no end of people who wish to do him harm, to see him excluded, and he doesn't understand why. All he knows is that he has lost nearly everything and everyone he loves; now this harsh place is all he has left. He can't give up, not ever. He has come too far. To surrender now would mean—

A bear hug, tighter than any he has ever felt. Amanda enfolds him in her sinewy arms and the gauzy fabric of her desert robes. Spock feels as if he could vanish into that embrace, disappear inside the feather-light folds of Amanda's robe and never return. Hidden in her arms, he feels safe at last; treasured beyond all comparison.

For the first time in years, he feels *loved*.

Burnham wants to wither and vanish from sight as Sarek glowers at her. "A place awaited you at the Vulcan Science Academy. Why throw that away to apply to Starfleet Academy?"

She refuses to let fear color her reply. "I desire to experience more of the universe than would be possible as a member of Vulcan academia."

"Preposterous," Sarek says. "There is nowhere that Starfleet goes, no mystery of science or philosophy that it explores, that the VSA does not."

"Perhaps," Burnham says. "But as a fellow of the VSA, all of my travels and discoveries would be made in the company and context of Vulcans. As a member of Starfleet, I will have access to the perspectives of a great many more species and philosophies. It is that broadness of experience that I desire."

"You would deny your birthright in the name of novelty," Sarek says. "Most illogical."

Burnham speaks without thinking: "You would elevate tradition and societal approval over the expansion of knowledge. If anything deserves to be called 'illogical,' it is that."

Sarek's expression never changes, but he lifts his chin.

It is a subtle cue, but enough of a reaction for Burnham to realize she has insulted her father more heinously than she had intended. It is too late now to retract words spoken in haste. All she can do is watch her father turn his back on her and walk away, leaving her to wonder if they will ever speak civil words to each other again.

Days melted into weeks that bled into months that flooded into years. Through it all, two lives flowed as one: Spock's and Burnham's memories became a river that carried them both from their earliest moments of cognition, down through the decades . . .

Observing the fusion of identities from a psionic redoubt in his metaconscious, a part of Spock struggled not to seethe with envy.

All his life he had yearned for his father's mentorship, only to find nothing beyond Sarek's taciturn disapproval; now he lived in Burnham's memories and realized she had spent her youth being tutored and guided through Vulcan life and education by Sarek's steady hand.

Since his youngest days Spock had wanted to rebel against the emotional stilting of Vulcan customs and show his mother how deeply he loved her, but every time he had come close to revealing his feelings to her, something had stopped him. When he had been young, it had been Sarek, or his peers, or his instructors who had forced him to deny his love for his mother. But from adolescence onward, he realized to his enduring regret, it had been he alone who bore the blame. Not since his earliest childhood had Spock known the comfort of his mother's embrace. Burnham, on the other hand, had ended up the focus of all of Amanda's maternal instincts, yet she barely seemed to appreciate how precious that gift truly was.

It was enough to stir the fires of anger in his Vulcan blood . . .

A shadow of Burnham's psyche lingered outside the telepathic blurring of memories and felt a deep swell of pity for young Spock. She felt his envy, and his rage. They were easy feelings to understand. He had so much respect for his father—it verged dangerously close to worship.

As for the depths of Spock's love for his mother, Burnham was sure they were beyond measure. Yet he had been compelled—cruelly, in Burnham's opinion—to suppress his love for his mother all his life. When she reflected on the unconditional love and devotion she had received from Amanda, she understood at once why it must sting Spock to bear witness to it.

He deserves to know the truth. All of it.

There was a part of her memory that she had walled off many years earlier, with help from Sarek. It was a dark and terrible corner of her mind, a place she preferred never to go. But without this last piece of her puzzle, Spock would never understand Sarek and Amanda's choices. Their actions would haunt him unless he knew what had bonded them to her.

To lower the last of her mental defenses, to expose the most vulnerable aspect of her mind to a stranger, went against everything Sarek had ever taught her.

But it wasn't some stranger with whom she needed

to connect. This was Spock, Sarek and Amanda's beloved son—and everything she had experienced of his life in their first few moments of connection told her that if anyone would be able to understand, it would be him.

Making a leap of faith, she let her last walls of defense crumble.

Pain and confusion are all that Spock knows. He struggles to remember.

Everything had flashed, then gone dark. Thunder rolled—no, an explosion. A bomb had detonated. Walls of fire had devoured the slow and the unsuspecting, and then there had been nothing left but the agonized cries of the wounded and the keening of the bereft.

Above Spock a holographic display filled with equations blinks on and off. Its lessons had felt so important just moments earlier. Now it is just another broken machine.

Spock looks down at his brown hand. It is caked in red blood, shaking—no, twitching. His vision is stained now with crimson, and the ferric tang of iron-based blood fills his mouth. Frightened and in need of comfort, for salvation, he searches the darkness around him—the wreckage of the Vulcan Learning Center. The bodies of slain children lay strewn about, some of them dead in spite of heroic acts of sacrifice by the proctors, many of whom also lay dead throughout the facility. Smoke drifts through the shattered building.

Consciousness stutters. Reality comes in flashes, broken and perplexing.

Then Spock hovers above himself—looking down at his body, but it is Burnham's frail form, skinny and dark, her hair cut in the Vulcan style . . . and her face caked in blood, her flesh burned. The explosion has caved in part of the back of her skull.

Darkness intrudes. A momentary gap stretches out . . .

An icy cold blackness engulfs Spock, an oblivion unlike any he has ever felt. It is an erasure of self, an obliteration of his being. He knows he should be terrified, but it came on so swiftly that he had no time to realize—

"Please," Amanda begs, her voice cracking with fear and desperation, "bring her back. I don't care what it takes. Bring her back."

A flash of reality, looking down from the ceiling. Sarek and Amanda kneel beside Burnham's—beside Spock's—broken body. Sarek gently presses the fingertips of one hand to her face. "My mind to your mind," he intones, "my thoughts to your thoughts . . ."

Spock sees the strain of effort on Sarek's face, the agony of using his psionic gifts for something more taxing than has ever been asked of him before—

And then Spock—no, Burnham—gasps and bolts upright, alive, jolted back into consciousness by Sarek's sheer force of psychic will restarting her autonomic functions. She springs past Sarek, into the safe harbor of Amanda's embrace. Spock is mesmerized by Sarek's stern mask of weary concern and Amanda's tearful countenance of relief and gratitude, until he slips once more into the shallows of unconsciousness.

Spock retreated mentally from the meld, just by a degree, to process Burnham's revelation. As a youth he had heard of the bombing, referred to on Vulcan at the time only as "the Incident." He had known that many adults and children had been hurt in the blast, and that his parents had been there in the aftermath. But until this moment he had never known that Burnham herself had actually died for nearly three minutes, or that Sarek had revived her with a mind-meld.

No wonder she resisted the meld, he realized. *Linked to a trauma, indeed.*

A familiar but unexpected voice called to him: "Spock."

He turned to confront a flood of light—and silhouetted within it, a spectral image of Sarek. Spock shielded his eyes with his hand, but it did not help. "Father?"

Sarek extended his hand toward Spock.

"Come, my son. Our time is short, and there is much to do."

Confused but unable to decline, Spock followed Sarek into the light.

Burnham didn't know where the *katric* shade of Sarek had led her, but she stepped through the curtain of light to find herself facing the mental projection of Spock. She cocked an eyebrow at him. "So, are we in your head or mine right now?"

Sarek answered, "Neither. Both. You are melded. You are one." He regarded the pair with a disapproving stare. "And yet trust eludes you both."

Spock reached out and waved a hand through the ghostly form of Sarek. "Your mind is not actually present. And yet you are the true essence of Sarek."

"A *katric* echo," Burnham said. "Left behind after he revived me from brain death." She circled the *katra* ghost. "I don't think even he expected this would be a side effect of saving me."

"Fascinating," Spock said, studying the ghost with an

admixture of curiosity and horror. "Part of his essence lives now in your mind." He asked the Sarek *katra* echo, "Why have you brought us here?"

The Sarek echo folded his hands together, then let the sleeves of his robe come together to conceal his hands. "To urge you both to let go of any envy or mistrust you might bear each other because of your respective relationships to me. You need each other right now—not just to survive your present ordeal, but to come to terms with who you are, as individuals."

"But I have questions," Spock said.

"As do I," Burnham added.

Sarek shook his head. "There is no time. You must finish what you set out to do, while you still can. But know that through your meld, you have both gained from the other the answers to the questions that plague you—even if they are not yet consciously evident. When your minds are ready, the proper truths will be revealed. I promise you."

"I understand," Spock said

Burnham wondered how the half-Vulcan could take any such assurance, even one from his own father's *katra* echo, at face value. But when Sarek faced her, all she could do was parrot Spock's response. "I understand, Sarek."

"Then it is time to go forward," Sarek said. "Awaken."

Spock and Burnham opened their eyes, each seeing the other and themselves through a shared perspective. They were one mind in two bodies, two identities fused into a single persona. They raised their right hands in unison; flexed and drummed their fingers on open air in synchronicity.

"The meld is holding," they said to each other. "But we must act quickly."

They stood and turned toward the separate corridors. Stepping forward, they parted but remained united, each aware of all the other saw and felt. Moving with the grace of the choreographed they passed their respective portals' thresholds—and as they had expected, the portals irised closed behind them. They were cut off from each other now, with no path left to walk but forward to the oval consoles. Their breathing quickened with their steps; time was not their ally. The farther apart they moved, the more tenuous their link might become.

Burnham-Spock arrived at the ends of the corridors. Still acting in concert, they each placed their right hand upon the oval panel set into the bulkhead beside their closed portal. With the dual contacts, the panels came alive, once again employing a haptic interface. Dots, lines, and shapes manifested, then receded, leaving behind only the memories of their contact.

Beneath Burnham's hand there appeared only a single amalgam of shapes, which together formed a complex symbol—perhaps a word or a concept. It did not resemble the glyphs they had encountered earlier, the ones that had been used to express numerals and mathematical concepts. Whatever this was, it was more symbolic, more abstract.

Under Spock's palm there appeared a variety of such forms, rising and falling in sequence, then repeating. Each form was different from the others, and lasted for only a moment, which made it difficult to identify and compare to the single form upon which Burnham now concentrated. And then Spock felt it—the match for the symbol in Burnham's mind. He pressed against it, selecting it as he had selected choices on the Juggernaut's other haptic panels.

The oval interface went smooth and cold.

The portals in front of Spock-Burnham spiraled open

from their centers, revealing a vast spherical chamber with multiple ring-shaped levels surrounding a radiant metallic orb suspended by unseen forces. The mind-linked pair advanced together into the brightly lit space.

A galvanic prickling of their skin made the hairs on their forearms and the napes of their necks stand up. Then they heard a familiar pulsating rhythm—and Thumper, their holographic guide, appeared once more, orbiting the central sphere like a red dwarf star trapped in the orbit of a golden giant. The outer walls of the space were packed with delicate constructions of crystal and hairlike metallic filaments, all of them blazing with creeping tendrils of white-hot plasma. Power and menace were palpable qualities inside the sphere chamber.

Burnham and Spock were several meters apart on the equatorial ring level, the largest and widest one. Three levels stood above them at regular intervals of just over two meters, and three more lay beneath them, each separated from its neighbors by the same distance.

Shimmering on the surface of the great sphere were slowly drifting images of the colony's capital city, the *Shenzhou*, and the *Enterprise*.

Spock-Burnham turned to face each other. As they shared a thought, Spock raised one eyebrow, and Burnham cracked a lopsided half smile.

Welcome to the core.

24

Pike registered the flash of incoming fire a fraction of a second before it rocked the *Enterprise*. He gripped the armrests of his command chair until the ship's inertial dampers dissipated the turbulence. "The Juggernaut's packing a hell of a punch," he said to his bridge crew.

"Brace for another volley," Una said. She grabbed the edges of her console and hung on as another barrage raced up out of the planet's atmosphere to pummel the *Enterprise*'s shields. "Multiple hits on our ventral shields. All of them holding."

On the main viewscreen, a trio of reddish bolts slammed into the *Shenzhou*, momentarily illuminating its cocoon of energy shielding—and revealing the dimples forced into that bubble by the Juggernaut's attack. The flares of impact faded, and the *Shenzhou* seemed none the worse for the encounter. Meanwhile, in the lower corner of the viewscreen, the final few minutes of the countdown ticked away, diminishing Pike's sense of hope with every passing second.

Ohara looked over his shoulder at Pike. "Sir? Those last few salvos from the Juggernaut were all over the place, in terms of frequency and power level. I think it's testing our shields, looking for the best way to punch a hole in them."

"That's only fair, since we're looking to do the same thing."

Una declared, "Incoming!"

Pike opened an intraship channel. "All decks, brace for impact!"

A vermilion blast filled the viewscreen. The ship heaved and rolled to starboard, almost throwing Pike from his chair as it sent the rest of his crew sprawling while the overhead lights flickered like strobes. When the *Enterprise* settled at last, smoke curled from the circuit relays beneath a bank of consoles on the port side.

"Mister Singh," Pike said, "check that panel, on the double."

"Aye, sir," the engineering officer said, then scrambled back to his station to pull the ventilation grate off the base of his console to inspect the damage within.

At the forward console, Tyler and Ohara hurried back to their posts. Ohara checked his readouts. "Captain, that last hit was almost perfectly tuned to punch through our shields. The next one might go straight through the saucer."

"Then we'd best not get hit," Pike said. "Tyler, initiate evasive maneuvers. Ohara, adjust our firing solutions— we'll have to target the Juggernaut while we stay on the move."

"Aye, Captain," Ohara said. "But if I might offer a suggestion?"

"I'm listening."

"We should fire now, before the Juggernaut goes mobile. If we're at evasive when it starts to maneuver, that's going to make it a lot harder to hit."

"You didn't train for this job because it was supposed to be easy," Pike said. "That said, your idea has merit."

Una looked up from the sensor display, her manner aggrieved. "Captain, permit me to remind you that Mister Spock—"

"—and Lieutenant Burnham are still inside the Juggernaut," Pike said. "I'm well aware of the situation, Number One." He nodded at the countdown as it flipped from 03:00 to 02:59. "Just as I'm aware we're running out of time, and out of options."

Chief Garison silenced an alert on the communications panel, then listened to a message piped through his ear-mounted transceiver. "Captain, a message from Commander Barry."

"Put her on speakers, Chief."

Garison patched in the intraship channel, and the voice of chief engineer Caitlin Barry issued from the overhead speakers. *"Good news, Captain! The* Shenzhou's *chief engineer and I made a breakthrough regarding the Juggernaut's power signature and hull composition."*

"What kind of breakthrough?"

"The kind that would take an hour to explain, but only ten minutes to exploit by recalibrating the phasers. If we're right, we should be able to punch some holes in that thing without having to use torpedoes."

"Which means we don't have to destroy the planet in order to save it," Pike said, appreciating the importance of the news. "Good work. Now get ready for the bad news. We don't have ten minutes. We might not even have five. So work quickly."

"One small catch," Barry said. *"We need to take the phasers offline to recalibrate them. Which means you can't fight back until the fixes are done."*

"In that case," Pike said, "work *very* quickly. Bridge out."

On the viewscreen, another streak of fire from the Juggernaut hammered the *Shenzhou*. When the glare abated, the old workhorse of a starship was still intact, but Pike had no doubt its crew had been shaken to their core. Then the *Shenzhou* broke from its orbital pattern and emulated the *Enterprise*'s evasive maneuvers.

In the bottom of the viewscreen, the countdown ticked away: 02:15 . . . 02:14 . . .

A red signal flashed on Ohara's console. The navigator announced, "Phasers offline for recalibration. Torpedoes standing by."

Pike took a deep breath and hoped he hadn't just condemned his crew to death in the name of hope. "Just over two minutes to Armageddon," he muttered, "and we've got front-row seats. . . . Lucky us."

The Voice of the Juggernaut came from every direction and it boomed like thunder, rattling the teeth in Burnham's jaw with every word: "WELCOME. LONG HAVE YOU BEEN EXPECTED. MANY AGES HAVE PASSED WHILE WE WAITED FOR YOU TO PASS THE TRIBULATION."

Pained by the Voice's volume, Burnham and Spock both pressed their hands over their ears. Spock replied in a normal speaking voice, "Who or what are you?"

"I . . . AM THE JUDGE."

Burnham did not like the sound of that. "On whose authority do you judge us?"

"I WAS SENT TO EVALUATE THIS WORLD AND ITS PEOPLES ON BEHALF OF THE TURANIAN DYNASTY. YOU HAVE PROVED YOUR WORTHINESS TO SERVE AS SUBJECTS AND SOLDIERS. ARE YOU PREPARED TO PLEDGE YOUR LOYALTY ON BEHALF OF THIS WORLD?"

Just as Burnham was about to make a declaration of a

far more vulgar variety, she heard Spock's thoughts interrupt her own, a lingering effect of their fading mind-meld.
«*Do not reply in haste,*» he cautioned her. «*I once read a
paper about the Turanian Dynasty that was published by the
Daystrom Institute. Their empire has been extinct for millions
of years.*»

His memory jogged hers. *Yes, I read a similar report
produced by the Raxan Foundation.* She regarded the ominous scintillating sphere that hovered before them. *We're
being asked to pledge our loyalty to something that no longer
exists. How do we handle this?*

«*I am uncertain. Attempting to explain the circumstances
might trigger any of a number of programmed responses that
could prove more dire than the one we now confront.*»

"I AWAIT YOUR ANSWER," the Voice said. "DO YOU PLEDGE
YOUR LOYALTY, AND THAT OF THIS WORLD, TO THE EVERLASTING
GLORY OF THE TURANIAN DYNASTY?"

*Not so everlasting, as it turns out. But its choice of words
strikes me as a bad sign.*

«*I concur. However, it seems impatient for a reply.*»

We need more information, Burnham decided. "What
would be the consequences of accepting your request? The
terms of our subjection, as it were?"

"IT IS NOT YOUR PLACE TO ASK QUESTIONS. PLEDGE YOUR
LOYALTY, OR DO NOT. CHOOSE."

Spock asked, "What happens if we decline to make such
a pledge?"

"YOUR TIME TO DECIDE IS ALMOST EXPIRED. CHOOSE."

"What happens if we make no choice at all?"

The Voice thundered even louder, "CHOOSE."

Burnham shot a look of dismay at Spock. *Not wired for
negotiation, is it?*

«*The range of its interactivity does appear to be sharply*

limited, and in a most authoritarian fashion. It seems we must make our decision based on incomplete information.»

The Voice remained singular in its focus: "CHOOSE."

A weary sigh left Burnham feeling empty and exhausted.

And to think . . . this day started out so well.

25

One blow after another punished the *Shenzhou*, and it was all Saru could do to remain upright on the bridge. He gripped the sides of his console, but his height and higher center of balance made him more susceptible than his shipmates to fluctuations in the ship's artificial gravity and inertial damping. "The intervals between salvos are decreasing," he called out to Georgiou.

The captain looked frazzled—a rare state for her. Locks of her black hair had come loose and now framed her face, which glistened with sweat. "Continue evasive maneuvers," she said. "Increase to half impulse. Divert power from nonessential systems to the shields, and keep our base frequencies on a random cycle. If we're too slow to change, the Juggernaut will punch us full of holes."

Around the bridge, senses were sharp, and reactions came fast.

Gant was the first to report. "Engineering teams still recalibrating the phasers."

Another hit rattled the ship and instilled Georgiou's voice with fresh urgency. "How long until we can return fire?"

"Best guess?" Gant said. "Six minutes."

Detmer snapped, "Six minutes? How long does it take to transmit new phaser specs?"

Her outburst motivated Narwani to turn from her console and retort through her VR helmet's speaker at maximum volume, "It's not a damned software update! The engineers have to *manually* recalibrate the collimating lenses on *every* emitter to make them fire in a new frequency range. If you think you can do better—!"

"Enough!" Georgiou shouted. "Mind your posts!"

Rebuked, the *Shenzhou*'s bridge officers returned to the tasks in front of them. Another barrage from the Juggernaut sent everyone staggering portside and set the lights and displays to flickering. Panicked voices spilled from speakers at the communications console, with more coming in faster than Ensign Fan could mute them.

"Successive attacks exhibit increasing power," Saru said.

From ops, Oliveira added, "Shields are holding—but at this rate, not for long."

"Saru, Oliveira: Coordinate firefighters and damage-control teams. Keep us in this fight for as long as you can. Sacrifice nonessential compartments and personnel if necessary."

It was a grim command, one that made Saru balk. It was not the first time Georgiou had asked him in a combat situation to be pragmatic to the point of being cold-blooded, but there had not been many such instances. It was not a stance she adopted cavalierly. He waited until he heard Oliveira acknowledge the order, and then he echoed her response of "Aye, Captain."

"Movement," Narwani declared from the auxiliary tactical station. "The Juggernaut is increasing power to its thrusters and navigational systems."

Gant checked his console, then faced Georgiou. "Confirmed, Captain. The Juggernaut has initiated its launch sequence. It's going mobile."

Saru looked at the holographic overlay on the main viewport. The countdown in the lower right corner ticked away its final seconds: 00:02 . . . 00:01 . . . 00:00.

"Right on time," Georgiou said. "Ops, magnify our view of the Juggernaut."

Oliveira keyed in the command. The image projected atop the center viewport showed the Juggernaut rising out of the ocean on Sirsa III. Aquatic vegetation and sea froth spilled from its gleaming, insectlike hull, whose black contours shimmered with a rainbow of colors as it climbed skyward and accelerated toward its rendezvous with the *Shenzhou* and the *Enterprise*.

Crimson pulses streaked from the Juggernaut's bow and then diverged—two heading toward the *Shenzhou*, and two others aimed at the *Enterprise*.

"Brace for impact," Georgiou said.

The twin blasts struck with terrifying force. The bridge's overhead lights went dark, and sparks rained down on the bridge crew. Saru swatted burning phosphors from his shoulders and the back of his neck. "Forward shields buckling, Captain."

"Steal power from anywhere you can," Georgiou said, "but keep those shields up!"

Sweating bullets at the back of the bridge, engineering officer Weeton asked, "How long until we can fight back?"

Cool and matter-of-fact, Gant said, "Four minutes, ten seconds."

That didn't seem to quiet Weeton's anxiety. "Then let's use torpedoes!"

"We're not cooking off this planet's atmosphere," Georgiou said, "not unless there's no other way." Another round of fire from the Juggernaut blew out the life-support station and filled the bridge with bitter smoke. The captain winced at the new damage, but she remained resolute. "Our job is to hold the line. Come blood, come fire, come hell itself—we draw the line *here*."

Her courage proved contagious. Around the bridge, chins were raised, shoulders were squared against the approaching storm. No one was backing down. Not today.

At the aft engineering station, Weeton worked like a whirling dervish. "Patching reserve batteries into the shield grid," he said as he keyed in commands.

Georgiou smiled. "That's the spirit. Look alive, people! *This* is why we're here!"

Saru's chest swelled with pride and fighting spirit—and then he beheld the dark majesty of the Juggernaut, a monster of a ship many times the *Shenzhou*'s size, ascending to take its vengeance upon them . . . and then his natural instinct to flee and hide asserted itself.

He drew a sharp breath, clenched his jaw, and remembered his Starfleet training.

No, he told himself. *I am not a slave to my biology. I am not prey unless I choose to be.*

Every fiber in his Kelpien body told him to abandon ship and hide somewhere distant and dark until the threat had passed.

All that stood between him and an act of shameless flight were four years of Starfleet Academy training and the love he had come to feel for this ship, its captain, and its crew. He locked his hands around the edges of his console, and repeated his captain's words to himself until he believed them: *Come blood, come fire, come hell itself—we draw the line* here.

When his breathing slowed, and he no longer feared he would run, he knew that what the captain had said next was now also his truth: *This is why I am here.*

Then came the next round of detonations against the *Shenzhou*'s shields, and all Saru could do was hang on and pray that his courage lasted longer than the battle.

There was no time left for subtlety, so Burnham resorted to direct confrontation. "Judge," she said to the disembodied voice of thunder that spoke for the Juggernaut, "the Dynasty you represent no longer exists. It collapsed nearly nine million years ago. It is *extinct*."

"YOU MUST CHOOSE."

Burnham felt her shoulders slump, an involuntary admission of defeat. She looked to Spock for encouragement, but found only his preternatural calm and neutrality. "This has to be the worst-programmed artificial intelligence in history," she said.

"Its intransigence might be deliberate," Spock said. "Past candidates might have resorted to any number of rhetorical strategies to outwit its intended function. What we find to be a confounding simplicity its makers might have considered an operational imperative."

Fleeting images projected on the central sphere of the core depicted the *Shenzhou* and the *Enterprise* enduring increasingly severe attacks by the Juggernaut. Burnham winced at each flash of energy that struck the shields of either vessel, because she knew all too well what they meant for the people inside.

"We have to do something," she said. "And soon, before this thing pulverizes our ships."

"All we can do is give it one of the two answers it has declared acceptable." Spock regarded the scenes of battle without apparent emotion. "If we refuse, it is likely to mark us as enemies of its Dynasty. But if we accept its invitation . . ."

She completed his thought process out loud: "It might see us as allies, or at least as its own subjects. Which would negate its need to continue its attack."

Spock nodded. "Perhaps. At the very least, it seems worth trying."

Burnham raised her voice. "Hear us, Judge! We accept the invitation of the Turanian Dynasty. On behalf of our people, we consent to be your subjects."

Her declaration was answered by a change in the colors that surrounded her and Spock. The banks of fine metal and crystal shone a brilliant green, as did the decks, the bulkheads, and the overheads. Around the core, other portals spiraled open, and the few holographic images that had depicted the capital of New Astana and other settlements of the Sirsa III colony shifted to represent new vantages of the *Shenzhou* and the *Enterprise*.

"YOUR WORLD IS NOW, AND EVERMORE SHALL BE, UNDER THE BANNER OF THE TURANIAN DYNASTY. AS A SUBJECT WORLD, YOU WILL BE KEPT INFORMED OF YOUR EXPECTED TITHES TO THE DYNASTY. IN RETURN, YOU WILL ENJOY OUR PROTECTION—AS WE WILL NOW DEMONSTRATE BY DESTROYING THE TWO THREAT VESSELS CURRENTLY IN ORBIT."

"Those aren't threat vessels," Burnham said, "they—"

"THE VESSELS ARE OF UNKNOWN ORIGIN, AND HAVE DEMON-STRATED HOSTILE INTENTIONS. FOR THE GOOD OF THIS WORLD AND ITS PEOPLE, THE HOSTILE VESSELS WILL BE DESTROYED."

Aggravated and enervated, Burnham sighed and rubbed her eyes. "So much for de-escalation through surrender." When she looked at Spock, he remained maddeningly serene. "It's hopeless," she said. "There's no reasoning with this thing."

"On the contrary," Spock said. "If we have accomplished nothing else, we have persuaded the Juggernaut that the colonists are not its enemy. Since protecting them was the core objective of our shared mission, one could argue that we have succeeded."

"Except for the fact that the Juggernaut is about to destroy both our ships."

Spock acknowledged her criticism with a small nod. "Yes. Most unfortunate."

His penchant for understatement appalled her. *"Unfortunate?"*

The deck pitched and heaved as the Juggernaut accelerated through the planet's atmosphere. Around the core chamber's middle level, holographic images of flight telemetry and tactical information appeared, all of them updating with terrifying speed.

Burnham concentrated and hoped that some remnant of her telepathic link to Spock was still active, because she didn't want the Juggernaut to hear what she needed to say.

Spock . . . can you still hear my thoughts? Please answer me if you can.

«Our contact persists, but not for much longer.»

We need to stop the Juggernaut before it destroys our ships. Even if what we do means we die with the Juggernaut, we have a duty not to just stand by and let it kill our shipmates.

«I agree. Our first objective should be to commandeer control using the interfaces around us. If that fails, our next imperative should be sabotage, by any means.»

Then let's get to it. I'll take consoles to the left. You take the ones to the right.

Burnham and Spock split up. They moved down the rows of holographic displays until they each arrived at one that seemed tactical in purpose. She reached up to see which, if any, of its settings she could adjust—and a painful electrical shock made her pull back her hand.

Undeterred, Spock tried to access the nearest interface to him. He, too, received a jolt of electricity for his trouble.

The pair regrouped and let their foreheads touch.

Maybe we can use my tricorder to disrupt the force fields.

«*Perhaps, though it is unlikely to be able to generate sufficient energy to negate even a small area of the force field for more than a second. However, it might enable us to identify some other vulnerability in the systems around the core.*»

Burnham lifted her tricorder and started scanning the force fields being generated inside the Juggernaut's core. She was dismayed to see that, just as Spock had predicted, they were far too powerful to be negated, even for a moment, by the output of a single tricorder. Even worse, the image it compiled of overlapping defense fields inside the core chamber presented no clear weakness for them to exploit. She returned the tricorder to its passive sensing mode and shook her head at Spock. *No weak spots, no chance of breaking through with a tricorder.*

«*Could we shoot through with our phasers?*»

I'd doubt it. Maybe if we both hit the same point at full power with an extended burst. But what do we target? Frag the wrong bit, and we'll waste our last option.

Spock moved to the ring's inner railing and looked down. «*Under ideal circumstances, I would propose we target that.*»

Burnham joined him at the railing and followed his gaze. Below the spinning sphere was an aperture glowing with white light. *A power source,* she realized. *That'll do nicely. And it'll have the bonus of giving us quick and relatively painless deaths. But there are at least six layers of energy shielding between us and that. Our phasers will run cold before we hit it.*

«*As I feared. Then we are faced with yet another test by*

*the Juggernaut: salve our feelings of guilt by taking futile ac-
tion . . . or do nothing and bear mute witness to the deaths of
our crewmates.»*

The pointless choice filled Burnham with frustration
and sorrow. "This is what you Academy-trained officers call
a *Kobayashi Maru*, isn't it?"

Spock answered with slow nod. "That scenario and ours
share distinct similarities."

26

A hacking cough left Georgiou nearly doubled over. The bridge of the *Shenzhou* was thick with smoke, and the Juggernaut's assault drowned out the steady stream of damage reports flooding Fan's and Oliveira's consoles. Fighting for breath, Georgiou raised her hoarse voice above the din. "Helm, go to full impulse! Roll to starboard!"

Detmer did her best to push their decades-old *Walker*-class starship through the brutal maneuver, but halfway through the rolling turn funereal groans from the space-frame swallowed the whining of the impulse engines and the Juggernaut's relentless blasts.

"Aft shields failing!" Gant shouted over the battle noise. "I can shift their power to other sections, but we can't take any more hits on the aft quarter!"

"Do it," Georgiou said, adjusting her tactics on the fly. "Detmer, come about and cut across the Juggernaut's field of fire. Whatever you do, keep them in front of us! Weeton, help Gant angle the rest of our shields for maximum forward defense!"

"On it," Weeton said, his hands a blur of action across his wraparound console.

Georgiou was about to order a kamikaze run at the Juggernaut, when Saru announced, "Phasers back online! All banks charging!"

Ensign Fan looked up from the communications panel, her face bright with hope. "*Enterprise* confirms its phasers are ready to fire! They're locking on to the Juggernaut now!"

"Helm, break to port!" Georgiou snapped. "Watch for crossfire!"

There was a fierce glee in Gant's eyes as he declared, "Target locked!"

"Fire at will," Georgiou said. "And keep firing until that thing goes down."

"Copy that!" Gant pressed his index finger to his panel's firing control. Outside the center viewport, a fierce storm of energy pulses erupted from the *Shenzhou*'s numerous phaser batteries. The barrage tore holes in the Juggernaut's shields, which crackled into view like a tattered bubble of sickly green light. Then a pair of steady blue beams from the *Enterprise* pierced the green cocoon, sliced into the goliath, and flensed off large pieces of its hull.

The fearsome power of the *Constitution*-class starship's state-of-the-art weaponry drew a gasp from Oliveira. "My God," she said. "The new type-ten phaser banks can do *that*?"

"And a lot more," Georgiou said, succumbing to a small twinge of envy.

Flashes of red lit up Narwani's auxiliary tactical station. She swiveled toward Gant, who listened to her report and then swung into action as he reported, "The Juggernaut's accelerating into a new attack run. Its weapons are increasing power and locking on—"

Horrific roars of detonation and collision shook the bridge crew and left half of them sprawled on the deck. Darkness swallowed them for half a second. Emergency lights snapped on, their weak orange glow casting pitch-black shadows and emphasizing the pall of smoke lingering over the bridge. Georgiou clawed her way back into her command chair. "Gant, reacquire target and continue firing. Helm, protect our six. Go head-to-head with that thing if you have to."

Through the viewport, Georgiou saw a salvo from the Juggernaut strafe the *Enterprise*'s port warp nacelle and its pylon—until the *Enterprise* retaliated with a shot from its aft phaser bank and cut a long, brutal gash through the alien vessel's dorsal hull, releasing a spew of gases, ignited plasma, and debris.

Georgiou sprang from her chair and pointed at the blazing wound in the Juggernaut's back. "Target that and fire!" She spun toward Gant. "Break its back!"

"Aye, sir," Gant said, training all of the *Shenzhou*'s phasers on the vulnerability.

Hope rekindled itself in Georgiou's heart. She turned back toward the viewport. "Saru! Can our sensors see inside that thing yet?"

"Only limited areas," Saru said. "But as we strip off more of the hull—"

"Keep scanning," Georgiou said. "Look for any sign of Burnham or Spock. If we can get a comm signal, or a transporter lock, do it!"

"That will be extremely—" He abandoned his protest when Georgiou shot a sharp look his way. Chastened, he nodded. "I will continue scanning."

Another fusillade from the Juggernaut hammered the *Shenzhou*, and Georgiou saw the alien dreadnought punch a burning hole through the *Enterprise*'s saucer. This beast was never going to surrender. The only way this bare-knuckle brawl could end would be with a knockout.

If only Michael and Spock weren't on board, one torpedo could—

The *Enterprise*'s forward phaser banks scissored across the tail section of the Juggernaut. A blinding flash forced Georgiou to shield her eyes. When it faded, she saw the *Enterprise* had severed a piece of the Juggernaut's tail several dozen meters long.

Oliveira announced, "The Juggernaut's shields are down!"

Georgiou seized the moment: "Target its stardrive and fire!"

Gant unleashed the *Shenzhou*'s phasers as Detmer swooped under and around the Juggernaut's belly. From above, the *Enterprise* skewered the monstrous vessel with three phaser beams. Georgiou was about to crow with excitement—then came a wild storm of green energy blasts from the Juggernaut, a mad flurry that engulfed the *Shenzhou* and the *Enterprise*.

Consoles went black and spat sparks. The impulse engines' high whines of strain became falling groans, and the *Shenzhou* listed to port, its inertial dampers and artificial gravity both in flux, hurling personnel in all directions.

Georgiou clung to an arm of her command chair as the artificial gravity failed. Around her the duty stations of the bridge went dark. Outside the center viewport she saw a dizzying slow spin-and-tumble of stars: the *Shenzhou* was adrift and in a chaotic roll.

Even worse, for a moment the *Enterprise* passed into view—and it, too, was rolling and yawing on more than one axis. Its running lights were off, and just like the *Shenzhou* it was on a trajectory that would, within minutes, send it screaming through Sirsa III's upper atmosphere.

One more shot is all it would take to finish either of us,

Georgiou realized. *Which means if we don't restore main power before that thing fires again . . . we're all as good as dead.*

It was a waking nightmare. Burnham felt trapped as she and Spock watched holographic images of the *Shenzhou* and the *Enterprise* being battered in their fight against the Juggernaut, while the two of them stood in the alien vessel's nerve center, powerless to do anything to help their ships. Even worse, she found it hard to root for the Starfleet vessels to win; every hit they struck against the Juggernaut threatened to kill her and Spock.

Spock, for his part, calmly adjusted the frequency and gain of his communicator, whose signal he was boosting with the subspace transceiver built into Burnham's tricorder. "Still no response to my automated distress beacon," he said, seemingly oblivious of the battle transpiring around them. "It would appear the Juggernaut's hull and shields, though compromised, are still sufficient to obstruct a clear comm signal."

"I don't know whether to feel protected or trapped right now," Burnham said.

"I fail to see the value in ascribing a subjective—"

He lost the thread of his pedantic rebuttal as the *Shenzhou* and the *Enterprise* drilled through the Juggernaut's shields and hull in a stunning counterattack. Then the *Enterprise* carved off a section of the Juggernaut's tail, and the ring-shaped deck beneath them trembled as the alien vessel shook from numerous secondary explosions that set all the holovids in the sphere chamber to flickering. Even after the images stabilized, Burnham saw they had lost some of their resolution. *Finally! About time our side landed a solid—*

Her elation ceased as she witnessed the Juggernaut's crushing retaliation: a mad barrage that knocked both Federation starships off their headings and left them dark and tumbling.

"They're adrift," Spock said. "One more hit—"

Burnham's tricorder chirped at her. She lifted it to glance at its display—and her eyes widened at the news it offered. Its passive sensors had detected a vital change in the chamber around them. "Mister Spock," she said, lowering the tricorder back to her hip, "the force fields inside this compartment . . . are offline."

In unison, they both looked over the railing, toward the shining power source below. Then they regarded each other. Burnham drew her phaser, and Spock did the same.

"Set for overload," she said, sabotaging its power cell, "twenty seconds to critical."

Spock disengaged the safety components of his own weapon. "Set."

"And drop," Burnham said.

Spock lobbed his weapon over the railing. She threw hers into the delicate—and now undefended—machinery surrounding the core. All that remained was the obvious last step.

"Run!" Burnham shouted, already on the move.

Whether out of hesitation, deference to seniority, or some notion of chivalry, Spock let her lead the way out of the core chamber. They sprinted back the way they had come, past empty alcoves where just minutes earlier they had braved deadly riddles and puzzles—

Then came the detonation.

Louder than anything Burnham had ever heard, she felt it in her gut, in her bones. The sonic force of it threw her and Spock forward and dropped them facedown on the deck, which quaked with the aftershocks of the critical blow they had just struck to the Juggernaut's brain.

All the colors faded from the bulkheads in the oval passageway, and then the last embers of weak, sallow light faded entirely, leaving Burnham and Spock in the dark, with the glow from her tricorder display their only illumination.

"Is that it?" Burnham wondered aloud. "Did we kill it? Is this mess finally over?"

Before Spock could venture an opinion, the passageway sealed itself on either side of them with what appeared to be emergency bulkheads. The gargantuan vessel groaned like a dying beast. Next the artificial gravity cut out, leaving Spock and Burnham afloat in zero *g*—and then a terrible roar resounded through the ship as gravity reasserted itself and slammed the pair against one of the emergency bulkheads.

"I could be wrong," Spock said through gritted teeth, "but I don't think this is over."

Pinned by the growing force of acceleration, Burnham knew she might be about to speak her last words. She chose them without sentiment or regret.

"You are *such* a Vulcan."

"Thank you," Spock said through a clenched jaw. "Most kind."

"There's been an explosion inside the Juggernaut," Una said, parsing new data as it scrolled across the *Enterprise*'s sensor readout. "Near the ship's core."

Pike swung his chair toward her. "Secondary damage from our attack?"

"Negative. The energy profile is consistent with the

discharge from a type-two phaser overload." She stood and faced her captain, and tried to control her elation. "Sir, I think Spock and Lieutenant Burnham are still alive in there!"

Pike looked at the image of the alien vessel on the fritzing main viewscreen. "It hasn't fired since that last mad salvo. Ohara, get me a deep scan. Is it dead, or just *playing* dead?"

Ohara coaxed data from his scorched half of the forward console. "No charge to its weapons. Shields are down. Stardrive and main power are offline." He looked back with a grin. "I think we got it, sir."

The captain smiled. "I think Spock and Burnham get the credit for this one." He turned back toward Una. "Number One, do we have a lock on either of them inside the Juggernaut?"

"Negative," Una said. "Scanning for—" New data churned a sick feeling in her gut. "Captain, the Juggernaut is still inside the planet's gravity well—and it's in free fall!"

Around the bridge, everyone wore the same look of horror. Ohara blurted, "From this altitude? It'll hit the planet like a one-hundred-fifty-gigaton bomb!"

Tyler looked almost sick at the conn. "It'll cook off the atmosphere in a flash." He stared in shock at the falling Juggernaut on the viewscreen. "It'll kill the whole planet."

"Not today, it won't," Pike said. He thumbed open a channel from his chair's armrest. "Engineering! Get me main power and tractor beams in the next thirty seconds."

Commander Barry started to protest, *"But, sir, we—"*

"I'm not *asking*. Get it done. Bridge out." Pike stood and stepped forward. "Mister Tyler: pursuit course. Use thrusters if you have to." He pointed at the Juggernaut. "We're going after it. And we're going to stop it—even if it's the last thing we ever do."

27

"Do we have impulse power or not?" Georgiou strained to hear chief engineer Johar's response through the static on the *Shenzhou*'s comms. "Johar, repeat your last!"

After a loud crackle of noise, Johar's voice broke through: *"Affirmative, bridge! Half impulse power restored. Working on the other half now!"*

"Good work. Bridge out." Georgiou closed the channel with a tap on her chair's armrest control panel as she said to Gant, "Divert all power to the tractor beam."

"Charging tractor beam," Gant confirmed. "Scanning for a target lock."

Georgiou tensed as she saw a corona of fire form ahead of the Juggernaut as it plunged into Sirsa III's upper atmosphere. "Detmer, time to intercept?"

The helm officer answered as she guided the *Shenzhou* into position behind the falling alien vessel. "Ten seconds to optimal tractor-beam range."

"Be ready to switch to full reverse as soon as we have a grip on that thing."

Detmer kept her eyes on the Juggernaut outside the viewport. "Aye, Captain."

"Ops," Georgiou said, "can we get a transporter lock on Spock or Burnham?"

Oliveira shook her head. "Negative. They're still too deep inside."

"Then they'll just have to hang on 'til the ride's over," Gant said. "Captain, tractor beam is charged and ready— but I have to ask: If it didn't work before, why would it work now?"

Georgiou deflected the query with a look to Saru, who replied, "Because the damage we and the *Enterprise* inflicted on the Juggernaut tore away some of its ablative hull plating." He used his console to project a magnified image of the Juggernaut over the main viewport, complete with computer-drawn annotations of the damage. "Its exposed spaceframe and infrastructure will give our tractor beams 'handholds,' if you will." Another tap on his panel highlighted specific points on the Juggernaut's exterior. "These are the best points for traction and control." To Georgiou he added, "Transmitting my data to *Enterprise* now."

"Well done, Saru," Georgiou said. "Gant, engage tractor beam on my mark!"

Ensign Fan touched her wraparound comms headset, then reported, "Captain, *Enterprise* confirms they have the tractor-beam coordinates. Ready to engage on your command."

"Engage tractor beam," Georgiou said. "Full reverse thrust!"

A pale blue beam of tractor force leaped from the *Shenzhou* to the Juggernaut. The instant it made contact, the *Shenzhou* lurched, and its spaceframe creaked and howled in protest. Through the viewport Georgiou saw a second beam, this one from the *Enterprise*, take hold of the alien ship. But even with both ships pulling in concert, the Juggernaut continued to plunge toward the planet, its dead mass now a potential kinetic bomb wreathed in flames.

Georgiou thumbed open her channel to engineering. "Johar! We need more power!"

"The impulse reactor's pushing critical! We—" The chief engineer's next words were lost amid a clamor of bangs followed by screams and shouting voices. After a wet cough, Johar continued, *"Integrity field failing, cracks forming in the starboard warp pylon. Hull breaches in lower engineering, and—"* Then came a muffled sound of explosion, and the channel went quiet.

Ahead of the *Shenzhou*, the nimbus of fire surrounding the Juggernaut grew in size and brightness, to the point where the massive vessel within was almost impossible to see. On tactical monitors around the bridge, Georgiou saw the *Enterprise* falter and vent plasma from its port warp nacelle. In a few more moments, it and the *Shenzhou* would both be pulled into the atmosphere along with the Juggernaut.

There was no time to wait for engineering to contain its cascade of disasters. "Ops," Georgiou said, "patch in all our reserves!"

"Already done," Oliveira said. "I've tapped everything that isn't engines, the integrity field, or the tractor beam. There just isn't enough—"

Dark sections of Oliveira's and Detmer's consoles surged back to life. Detmer sat up as she declared, "Full impulse power back online! Increasing reverse thrust to maximum!"

Another engineering miracle courtesy of Mister Johar, Georgiou thought with relief.

"Partial main power restored," Oliveira added. "Reinforcing the tractor beam and the structural integrity system!"

It took all of Georgiou's restraint not to spring from

her command chair. "Give it all we've got! If there's even a drop of main power we can send to the impulse engines—"

"Doing it now," said Weeton. "Main impulse core is at one hundred four percent of rated capacity and holding!"

Saru, who had not said a word while fighting to maintain the ship's tractor lock on the Juggernaut, declared in a proud voice: "Juggernaut's descent is slowing!" Outside the main viewport, the cone of fire surrounding the Juggernaut dissipated, revealing the two tractor beams still hanging on to its ravaged hull. "Descent halted!" A tense silence settled over the *Shenzhou*'s bridge crew as they waited for Saru's next words: "Reversal under way!"

Wild cheers and applause filled the bridge. At the forward consoles Detmer and Oliveira shook hands, Troke and Fan left their stations to hug each other, and when Georgiou looked over her shoulder, she was fairly certain she saw Weeton pump his fist in celebration. Georgiou tended to discourage her officers from strong displays of emotion on the bridge, but in this case she decided they most definitely had earned it. She even permitted herself a brief smile.

Outside the ship, the Juggernaut remained secure in the grip of the two tractor beams as it was towed out of the planet's atmosphere and clear of its gravity well. After it had been removed to what Saru considered a safe distance from the planet, it was released.

Not a bad day's work, Georgiou decided. "Ensign Fan, hail the *Enterprise*."

"Aye, Captain." A second later Fan added, "I have Captain Pike for you, sir."

"Patch him through." Georgiou waited until Pike's holographic image appeared in front of the center viewport. "Congratulations, Captain. A hell of a save."

Pike looked weary but in good spirits. *"Same to you,*

Captain. We couldn't have done it without the intel from your Lieutenant Saru. How's your ship holding up?"

"It's had better days. Yours?"

"Nothing a week at Starbase 7 won't fix. Give us about half an hour to put out a few fires, and we'll be ready to go back to the planet to deal with our little colonial problem."

"Sounds like a plan."

Fan interrupted, "Captain? We're being hailed on the emergency channel. It's Lieutenant Burnham!"

"Patch them in so Captain Pike can hear them." Georgiou waited until Fan gave her a nod to indicate the transmissions had been merged. "Number One, do you read me?"

Burnham's voice sounded far away over the comm. *"Aye, Captain."*

Pike asked, *"Burnham? Is Lieutenant Spock with you?"*

Spock replied, *"Yes, Captain, I am here."*

Georgiou didn't try to hide her relief. "Are you two all right? Do you need medical assistance?"

"We're fine, Captain," Burnham said. *"We're moving closer to the nearest hull breach to make it possible for one of you to get a transporter lock on us."*

Saru chimed in, "I have their signal, Captain. If they continue in their present direction for another seventeen point three meters, we can beam them out."

"Did you copy that, Number One?"

"Aye, sir. Seventeen point three meters."

"We look forward to your return. *Shenzhou* out." Georgiou cued Fan to close the channel. Pike's image faded away, and then Georgiou turned her attention to Saru. "As soon as you have a clear signal from Burnham and Spock, relay their coordinates to the transporter room."

"Aye, Captain."

Georgiou settled into her command chair and stared in wonder at the defeated Juggernaut. She felt a great relief at not only having prevented it from annihilating the colony on Sirsa III, but at having managed to preserve even a part of it for scientific study. In spite of all the trouble it had caused, it was still an artifact of a culture nine million years extinct, and though it was gravely damaged, there was no telling what insights might be gleaned from forensic analysis of its inner workings, not to mention its "slippery" hull plating.

It would have been a terrible shame to destroy it.

There were still unpleasant tasks left to be done—not the least of which would be ending the hostage crisis on the planet and arresting Governor Kolova and her conspirators, followed by the collection of evidence for the fraud case against the colony's corporate sponsor . . . but the part of Georgiou that was a scientist and an explorer was already thinking ahead to plumbing the secrets of this amazing, eons-old vessel from a dead empire.

She thumbed open a channel to engineering. "Bridge to Commander Johar."

"This is Johar. Go ahead, Captain."

"How long would it take to put together a forensic engineering team to explore the remains of the Juggernaut?"

Something on Johar's side of the channel went *boom* and was followed by a choir of panicked shouts and alien profanities. *"Good question,"* Johar said. *"Can I get back to you on that* after *I put out the fire on deck ten?"*

"Of course. Take your time."

"Thank you, sir. Engineering out."

Dark and eerily silent, the oval passageway terminated at a flat emergency bulkhead. Burnham touched it, expecting it to be cold since there was nothing on the other side but the vacuum of space. Instead, the surface her hand found was the same temperature as the air inside the corridor. "I will admit this much admiration for the Turanians," she said to Spock. "Their engineering and materials science were exceptional."

"Indeed." Spock's angular cheekbones and brow ridges cast deep shadows that gave his face a diabolical cast—an unfortunate consequence of Burnham's tricorder's display being their only light source inside the crippled Juggernaut. "I shall be most curious to see what the Starfleet Corps of Engineers learns about this vessel in the years to come."

"As will I." Burnham didn't know what to say next to Spock. In the space of just a few hours they had gone from being all but strangers to telepathic intimates. The abruptness of that transition continued to unsettle her, and though the last traces of their mind-meld had faded, she felt as if she owed him more than a perfunctory farewell. "Spock . . . I just wanted to—"

Her communicator beeped twice. She pulled it from her hip and flipped open its grille. "Burnham here."

"Lieutenant, this is Chief Newitsky on the Shenzhou. *Are you ready for transport?"*

"Stand by for my signal, *Shenzhou.*" She closed her communicator with a flip of her wrist. "Sorry," she said to Spock. "As I was saying, I—"

Spock's communicator beeped. He lifted it from his hip and opened its grille with a flick of his thumb. "Spock here."

"Lieutenant Spock! This is Chief Pitcairn. Are you—"

"Stand by for my signal, Chief." He closed his communicator, then faced Burnham. "You were saying?"

The interruptions had only amplified the awkwardness

Burnham felt, but there were things she needed to say to Spock before they parted ways. But where to begin?

With the truth.

Her confession proved more difficult to express than she had expected. "I think . . . I've misjudged you, in some respects. I'm not sure who or what I expected you to be, but . . ."

"I understand." Spock's deep voice took on a soothing timbre. "Now that we have melded, there are no secrets between us. It would be pointless for us to prevaricate or to hide behind empty courtesies." On a more somber note, he added, "We misjudged each other."

Burnham found it liberating to be able to confront the truth in the open. "I'm sorry that I let my envy prejudice my opinion of you. When I was young, living on Vulcan as a ward of your parents . . . all I ever heard about was you. *Your* achievements. *Your* accolades. Nothing I did ever seemed good enough to please Sarek."

"A feeling I know all too well."

"I know that *now*. But until today, I'd thought I was Sarek's greatest disappointment."

"Unlikely," Spock said. "I am quite certain he has reserved that distinction for me."

It was a sentiment spoken in jest, but Burnham felt the lingering pain behind Spock's words—not just out of empathy, but out of experience. More troubling to her was her awareness of his anger, an emotion she knew he would deny. "You still resent me, don't you?"

He reacted to her question by hanging his head in shame. "I find it . . . difficult . . . to accept many aspects of your past relationship with my parents."

"It bothers you that Sarek melded with me to save my life."

"Yes." Spock's brow creased, and his manner became uneasy. "You know how private an experience a mind-meld is. It is often practiced among only the closest of friends and the most intimate of partners. Most parents and children never share the meld, nor do most siblings or other kin. And yet you carry a *katric* echo of my father in your psyche. . . . You have had the privilege of knowing my father's mind in a way I likely never will." He turned to face Burnham, and now she saw an even deeper anguish in his troubled gaze. "But worse than that is the fact that it was my *mother* who insisted upon Sarek's melding with you, to save your life. In my entire life, I have never felt a moment of such passionate devotion from her. Yet you and her seem to have formed a bond of great intensity and affection. I cannot explain it."

"I can." Burnham noted Spock's surprise at her assertion. It was clear to her that an aftereffect of their meld was that he had been slow to restore his emotional barriers. *I might be seeing a side of him no one else ever has—or ever will.* She softened her tone and did her best to project compassion without condescension. "First, you need to know that Sarek would never have risked melding with me to save my life had Amanda not demanded it. He cared for me, yes. Even felt a sense of responsibility to me after my parents died. But one thing I know for certain because of my meld with him: Sarek has never loved me, and will never love me, the way that he loves *you*. He will never take the same pride in my accomplishments, never feel the same admiration for my career milestones, as he does for yours. And I know—he has never expressed any of this to you. And he probably never will. If I had to guess, I'd say that someday very long from now he will regret these omissions of affection. But I assure you, I *know* this to be true. And because you've melded with me, you know it, as well."

She reached out and took Spock's hand. The gesture seemed to confound him, but he did not try to pull his hand away. Burnham stepped closer to him and looked up until their eyes met. "As for Amanda . . . I've felt your love for her, and your alienation from her. I know you think you had to separate yourself from her, because that was Vulcan custom. And you wanted so much to be the son your father expected you to be. . . . But the affection that Amanda felt for me, the attachment she formed with me—those were never really about me. When I was a child, I thought they were. But now I know better. It was a classic case of human emotional transference, Spock. All the love and affection and attention she so desperately wanted to shower on you, she gave to me instead, because I could accept it, and you couldn't. Not because I deserved it, Spock, but because the love she felt was too strong for her to hold in. Every moment of devotion she gave to me . . . was really meant for you, Spock. It was always meant for you."

Her confession seemed to infuse Spock with an air of quiet dignity, as if a lifetime of questions that had long undermined his logic had at last been put to rest. He raised his right hand to her in the classic Vulcan salute. "Live long and prosper, Michael Burnham."

She returned the salute and felt for a moment as if she had found the brother she had never known she had always wanted. "Peace and long life, Spock."

They stepped back from each other, raised their communicators, and opened them.

"Spock to *Enterprise*. One to beam up. Energize."

Burnham watched the golden light of a transporter

beam enfold Spock and vanish him in a dazzle of light and a siren's song of white noise.

She opened her communicator with a flick of her wrist. "Burnham to *Shenzhou*. One to beam up. Energize."

Time to go home.

28

After the literal fires inside the *Shenzhou* had been extinguished, Georgiou dispatched more than forty of her security personnel to join forty-odd more from the *Enterprise* in dealing with the figurative fire on the planet's surface. She had expected that her people would face a prolonged struggle in the underground tunnels of New Astana. Instead, the combined force had been met with a surprise: a peaceful and orderly surrender.

Less than ten minutes after beaming her people down, Lieutenant Kressel, her security officer in charge, reported that Governor Kolova and a few dozen of her accomplices were all in custody. Not a shot had been fired. No hostages had been harmed. Their demands had been met, Governor Kolova had said, when the Juggernaut was neutralized.

When the news reached the *Shenzhou*'s bridge, Georgiou had overheard Gant mutter to Narwani, "Well, *that* was anticlimactic."

"And you thought our good luck had run out," Narwani had said, the voice filter of her VR helmet blurring the line between sincerity and sarcasm.

Now, just a few minutes later, Georgiou stood in the central plaza of New Astana and watched dusk settle on the colonial capital. Around her, security personnel from her ship and the *Enterprise* escorted civilian prisoners to designated beam-out points or, for those averse to being moved via matter transmission, into recently arrived shuttlecraft. Blue-shirted medical crewmen from the *Enterprise* parted from their white-uniformed counterparts from the *Shenzhou*, all of them visibly relieved to have recovered their freedom.

From amid the crowd emerged Captain Pike. He spotted Georgiou and crossed the plaza to greet her with a smile on his face and his hand outstretched. "A pleasure to make your proper acquaintance at last, Captain."

She shook his hand. "Likewise, Captain." She let go of his hand and gestured at the scene around him. "Not how I thought this would go."

"Never look a gift horse in the mouth," Pike said. "Any crisis that can be resolved without violence is—" He abandoned his train of thought as a pair of *Enterprise* nurses passed him and Georgiou. The two women carried a stretcher, on which was sprawled a civilian man whose face was a swollen mass of blue and purple over broken teeth stained with blood. "Whoa. What the hell happened to *him*?"

"When the colonists surrendered, one of the hostages went off on him."

Pike looked shocked. "One of our medics did that?"

"A dentist, actually."

"Oh. That makes sense." Understanding once again became confusion. "Hold on. What was a dentist doing on a landing party?"

Georgiou sighed and shook her head. "I have no idea."

The *Enterprise*'s captain surveyed the city. "Admiral Anderson says there's a group of large colony transports on their way from Marus III. Should be here in a few days. With a little luck, they'll have the rest of the colonists packed and off the surface in under a month."

"It's a shame they need to be displaced," Georgiou said.

"It is," Pike said. "But if Kolova and her top people take the fall, and it looks like they will, most of these folks will be able to come back after a proper cultural survey's been done." He frowned. "Most of them will never know how close they came to nearly losing everything."

"That's probably true for all of us, at one time or another," Georgiou said.

Her observation seemed only to deepen Pike's somber mood. "Maybe. But it's one thing to accept the fragility of a single life, or even a handful of lives. It's something else to think about losing a whole planet." He looked up at the darkening violet sky. "It seems so permanent. Almost eternal. So we take it for granted. We get careless. We forget how easy it can be to lose something so beautiful."

"Even worse," Georgiou said, "is to watch people put something so precious at risk for nothing more than greed. Bad enough to damage a world out of ignorance. But to do it willfully, in spite of knowing the truth . . . that's a breed of selfishness I just can't understand."

Pike's solemnity turned to melancholy. "How can it be, after all that the human race went through on Earth in the last few centuries, that some people still haven't learned there are more important things in life than financial gain?"

Georgiou recognized the kind of hurt that lurked behind Pike's thwarted idealism. His was the soul of an explorer who had been forced too many times to shed blood and lose people under his command. His soul wounds, she imagined, were likely quite similar to her own. She hoped he could share her solace in good-natured cynicism.

"Looking back on my lifetime of travels," she said to

him, "I am forced to conclude the universe has only two true constants: entropy and selfishness."

As she had hoped, her observation drew a half smile from Pike. "Don't give up hope," he said. "Selfishness will go away once the universe runs out of sentient beings."

"I'm not so sure." She noted the incredulity in his sidelong glance, and added, "Trust me, Captain. Selfishness always seems to find a way."

29

None of the other diners in the *Enterprise*'s officers' mess had seemed to notice that Spock had not touched his *plo-meek* soup in nearly a quarter of an hour. He sat alone at a table in the corner of the room, spoon in hand, eyes down-cast. Had anyone cared to spare him more than a moment's attention, they might have thought he was staring at his soup. In fact, his focus lay far beyond the plain white bowl on a tray; his thoughts were light-years distant, on Vulcan, and decades into his own past, reflecting on a childhood he had never fully understood until now.

I had never been so arrogant as to think I understood my parents, he ruminated. *But to realize I had misjudged them so unfairly . . . is troubling. On what other matters have I let my personal experiences cloud my logic? Who else have I judged and found wanting in some respect, without taking the time to truly know them?*

He paused his reflections when he perceived the ap-proach of Commander Una. She carried a tray on which was set a plate of vegetarian casserole and a mug of steam-ing green tea whose gentle aroma Spock detected as Una sat down across from him. He set down his spoon as he greeted her. "Good afternoon, Commander."

"Mister Spock. You're looking well."

"Most kind."

Una dug into her lunch and savored the first bite with closed eyes. After a sip of tea to clear her palate, she noted his half-full bowl of soup. "Not as hungry as you thought?"

Spock set the tray aside. "Apparently not."

"Are you feeling all right?"

"To the best of my knowledge, I am in good health."

She reacted to his answer with mock suspicion, then smiled and resumed her own lunch. Between bites she said, "I read your report about the trials inside the Juggernaut. It sounds as if we're lucky to still have you with us."

Recollecting the events of the previous day, Spock found he did not share Una's opinion. "I do not think luck was a relevant variable. If you read my post-mission analysis—"

"I read it," Una cut in, exercising the privilege that came with her rank and billet. "Pretty compelling stuff." She fixed him with a searching stare. He wondered for a moment whether she had deduced somehow that he had omitted from his report any mention of the Juggernaut's final challenge, or of the mind-meld that had been required to overcome it. Then Una sat back and smiled at him. "You seem different since you got back."

Her assertion aroused Spock's curiosity. "In what regard?"

"You seem . . . I don't know. Older? No—calmer than you did before." She tilted her head as she continued to study him and collect her thoughts. "You present yourself in a way that feels more centered. Better balanced." Her smile broadened to a grin. "You have gravitas now."

He cocked one eyebrow as he contemplated the ways in which he might interpret her remarks. He found it acceptable that most such permutations yielded positive impressions. With a polite lowering of his chin, he said, "Thank you, Commander."

"So," Una said, "do I have Lieutenant Burnham to thank for this transformation?"

"I will admit that getting to know her proved, for me, to be a path to self-knowledge."

"How so?" Una's question sounded more like friendly interest than a debriefing.

Spock steepled his fingers in front of himself while he considered his reply. "There is an irony, I think, in the way that our lives have mirrored each other. She is a human who has strived since childhood to live by the codes of Vulcan stoicism, whereas I, a Vulcan—"

"Half-Vulcan," Una corrected.

He pressed on without acknowledging her verbal edit. "I have long chafed against the limitations of Vulcan philosophy and social custom. All those things I turned my back upon by leaving Vulcan, she embraced by going to school there for over a dozen years. And yet . . . we both have found our way here, to Starfleet. And, for one brief moment, to each other."

Perhaps sensing the personal nature of the unfolding conversation, Una leaned closer across the table and lowered her voice. "What kind of a connection did you find with her?"

He answered quietly. "As I told the captain yesterday, she is a friend of my family. What I did not say was that she was, for many years, a ward of my parents. Though it is embarrassing for me to admit this, a sibling rivalry, of sorts, had long existed between us." He paused and remembered those bitter, lonely times in his youth. "It is only now, after getting to know her better, that I realized she and I have both, each in our own way, been disappointments to Sarek.

And that we likely will never fulfill the expectations he holds for us."

"Perhaps that's for the best," Una said. "Children should strive to grow beyond their parents, not just try to conclude their unfinished business."

"Most wise, Commander." He stood and picked up his tray. "If you'll excuse me—"

"Won't you stay and eat with me?"

"I regret that I cannot. But I will see you tomorrow morning on the bridge."

A forgiving smile. "See you then."

He nodded in recognition of her polite release, and then he returned his tray and bowl of half-eaten soup to the matter reclamator in the mess hall's bulkhead. No one else noted him as he passed by on his way out, nor did anyone pay him any mind as he walked alone and silent through the corridors of the *Enterprise*.

He returned to his quarters, and after he was inside he locked the door. Behind his new and improved mask of logic, he was plagued by his unquiet mind. He had admitted to Una the strange connection that he and Burnham had shared in Sarek . . . but he had been unable to broach the painful topic of his mother, and the long-buried feelings that the mind-meld with Burnham had resurrected and inflamed.

I have never regretted disappointing my father, Spock brooded. *But to know that I caused my mother such pain by shutting her out, by obeying my father when he told me to deny, even to myself, the boundless quality of my love for her . . . I cannot forgive him for that. How can I?*

He remembered the mind-meld, Burnham's memories of being cradled in Amanda's protective embrace—and in that moment he knew the sting of envy.

What I would not have given, he realized, *what I would not give even now, to feel the courage in my mother's love that Michael got to know for so long . . .*

His Vulcan indoctrination reasserted itself with cold, intractable vengeance. *This is not our way,* he castigated himself. *A Vulcan does not wallow in emotion, in nostalgia. To fixate upon the past is neither productive nor logical.*

It took all of his mental training, all of his discipline, to deny the truth he had been shown. With terrible effort but no admission of regret, he did what he had so long ago been conditioned to do, and buried all of Burnham's memories of Amanda.

Because it needs to be done.

Because this is our way.

Because I . . . am a Vulcan.

30

Brevity and menace. That was what Burnham read between the lines of the captain's summons. The order had come in writing: *Report to my ready room at 14:30.* No explanation. No agenda. Just a simple order, a place and a time. The rest Georgiou had left to Burnham's imagination.

Don't anticipate, Burnham told herself as the turbolift carried her to the *Shenzhou*'s bridge. *Expect nothing. Ground yourself in the now. Commit to nothing but the truth.*

Her attempt to comfort herself with Vulcan mantras learned in childhood proved less than successful. As the lift car neared the bridge, Burnham felt her stomach clench, as if the organ could literally tie itself in knots through nothing more than the misdirected force of anxiety.

She's going to demote me. Burnham tried to ignore the nagging voice of her insecurities. Did her best to hold her chin high and project poise and confidence. But her mind had become a sea of doubts, one in which she now felt adrift.

The lift doors parted. Burnham stepped onto the *Shenzhou*'s bridge. Outside the main viewport stretched the curve of Sirsa III's northern hemisphere. Around the spacious underslung command deck worked teams of engineers and computer technicians. They labored in small groups, rebuilding consoles damaged or destroyed during the fight against the Juggernaut.

Ensign Weeton, the bridge's engineering liaison, supervised the repairs; Lieutenant Saru had the conn. The Kelpien second officer looked up and noted Burnham's arrival. As ever, Saru's leathery visage was a cipher, betraying nothing of his inner state. Without a word to Burnham or anyone else, he turned his attention to a report on a slate handed to him by Ensign Connor.

Burnham turned right and made her way along the aft upper level of the bridge to the ready room's entrance. She checked the ship's chrono. It was 14:29. The captain was a stickler for precision when it came to punctuality. Arriving early for a scheduled meeting was just as likely to earn one a rebuke as showing up late. Counting down the final seconds, Burnham tried to tune out the sour bile creeping up her throat and the nauseated sensation in her gut.

The chrono flipped to 14:30, and Burnham pressed the visitor signal. Right away she had the captain's response, via the door's comm speaker: *"Come."*

Georgiou's invitation caused the doors in front of Burnham to part. Burnham stepped inside the ready room, then pivoted to her right. She heard the doors close behind her as she walked to within a stride of the captain's desk. "You asked to see me, Captain."

"I did." Georgiou tented her hands in front of her, then reclined her chair a few degrees. "Computer: privacy." At once the transparent panels in the ready room's doors frosted an opaque off-white—a change that heightened Burnham's mounting concern about this meeting.

The captain studied Burnham, but said nothing for several seconds. Then she glanced at the holographic display projected above part of her desk. "I read your after-action report. I have to say, it makes an impression. Alien riddles and deathtraps, all while racing against a deadline. Had I not corroborated your report with Mister Spock's, I might have dismissed yours as being a touch self-serving. But his account supports yours—and in a few cases, gives you credit that you refused to give yourself." She sat forward and turned off her holovid terminal. "But I think you know as well as I do that I didn't ask you here to debrief you about your op on the Juggernaut."

Don't anticipate. Don't assume. Don't volunteer.

"Might I ask then, Captain, precisely what you *do* wish to discuss?"

"The sequence of events that led up to your mission on the Juggernaut," Georgiou said. "Specifically, the moment you decided to step outside of the chain of command and open a back channel to Mister Spock on the *Enterprise*."

"I thought we had already spoken about this."

"We did. We're going to talk about it again. What were you thinking when you made that decision? And were you aware that you were subverting the chain of command?"

The adversarial shift in the conversation suited Burnham; at least now she knew why she was here and what to expect. "I assessed the situation on the bridge at that time as being overly emotional," she said, "and based on your actions and those of Captain Pike, I thought it likely to result in a violent escalation that could result in one Starfleet vessel firing upon another. Establishing contact with an officer of a cooler disposition on the *Enterprise* seemed warranted. Given the potential repercussions that might have resulted from such a conflict, I judged that my transgression would in fact constitute the least serious breakdown of military order and morale."

"Interesting," Georgiou said. "Now let me ask you this:

Why contact Spock? Was it merely a matter of convenience, as you said, because a subchannel to his duty station had been left active? Couldn't you then have used that same channel to hail Commander Una? She's well known to have a calm and rational manner."

It was a reasonable point, one for which Burnham had only the weakest refutation. "My decision to reach out to Spock was driven, at least in part, by time pressure. That said, I will concede that I was partial to contacting Spock because of our tenuous familial connection. Though it would be a mistake to have described us as 'close,' I had hoped that the shared elements in our personal histories might facilitate a quick establishment of trust."

The captain nodded slowly. "A reasonable justification, I suppose." She narrowed her stare. "But it would be quite a stretch to describe your actions as regulations compliant."

"True." Sensing that it would not be long before Georgiou steered the conversation toward the bad news Burnham knew was waiting at its end, she chose to meet the storm head-on. "Permission to speak freely, Captain?"

"I've never been able to stop you before," Georgiou said. "Why start now?"

Burnham ignored the captain's sarcasm for the sake of expediency. "Sarek persuaded me to accept a Starfleet commission at a time when I was ready to just give up, go back to Earth, and vanish. I'd be willing to bet he used more than his share of influence to get you to accept me aboard the *Shenzhou*."

"You'd win that bet. What's your point?"

It felt dangerous to bare her feelings, but Burnham knew she had gone too far to turn back. "Sarek believed that after all the years I'd lived on Vulcan, immersed in their culture and customs, that it would be in my best interest to live and work among humans and other species. To put it mildly, I disagreed. More than once—and even a few times recently—I've wondered whether I'd be more comfortable serving on a ship like the *Intrepid*."

"One with an all-Vulcan crew," Georgiou said. "You think they'd have you?"

There was no point in lying when it was clear Georgiou already knew the answer. "No," Burnham said. "As much as I might wish to be among them . . . the truth is that I would not be welcome there. Not like I am here." She confronted the truth that had been haunting her. "I've come to understand that Sarek was right. Or at least, not wrong. I do belong here.

"But I'll understand if you don't think I should be your first officer. I know that I violated the chain of command by engaging in unauthorized communications, and I am prepared to accept the disciplinary consequences of my actions. In my defense I will say only that I sought to prevent violence, injury, and loss of life. Though if I were questioned under oath, I would have to confess that under similar circumstances, I would do it again."

"I sure as hell hope so," Georgiou said. "In fact, I'm counting on it."

Baffled by the captain's response, Burnham creased her brow. "Captain?"

"I want a strong first officer who will keep me grounded—who won't be afraid to challenge me for the right reasons." Georgiou stood and walked around her desk to stand with Burnham. "Michael, I've known for quite some time that you belong here on the *Shenzhou*. I've also known that Starfleet needs officers like you, and that in your own way *you* need Starfleet. Your Vulcan education, tempered by a refresher course in your own humanity, has made you an amazing officer. You still have a lot to learn . . . but there is no one else I would rather have as my Number One."

The shock of good news left Burnham at a momentary loss for words.

"I'm not being demoted?"

"Not today, Number One. I've already informed Starfleet Command of your promotion." She shook Burnham's hand and smiled. "Congratulations, Lieutenant Commander Burnham."

"Thank you, Captain," Burnham said, savoring both her achievement and the ungracious realization of her promotion's best fringe benefit:

This is going to drive Saru insane.

Acknowledgments

My thanks go out to my wife, Kara, for her support during the months I spent writing this book. This job proved to be a longer and more complex undertaking than I had expected it to be. Also deserving of my gratitude are my esteemed editors, Margaret Clark and Ed Schlesinger, as well as CBS Television licensing guru and my good friend, John Van Citters.

Let me single out for special thanks my sister-from-another-mister Kirsten Beyer, who earned a staff writer position at *Star Trek: Discovery* in early 2016, and whose support was instrumental in helping me land this sweet gig. It has been an honor and a pleasure to work with her during the development and refinement of this story. You're the best, Miss K.

This story originated in a request from *Star Trek: Discovery* cocreator Bryan Fuller, who asked me to craft a tale that would feature both the *Shenzhou* and the *Enterprise* commanded by Captain Pike—and put Michael Burnham and Spock together. Thanks for the idea, Bryan!

I would also like to thank a few of my fellow *Star Trek* authors. John Jackson Miller helped me get a handle on this story at a time when I couldn't figure out how to make it fly. Dayton Ward and James Swallow helped me develop a lot of the material that was needed to flesh out the crews and settings of this new corner of Gene Roddenberry's universe. I could not have wished for better, more enthusiastic, or more imaginative creative partners.

Here's hoping that you, gentle reader, do not judge our efforts to have been in vain.

Until next time, live long and prosper.

About the Author

David Mack wants you to buy his novel *The Midnight Front*.
Learn more on his official website:
davidmack.pro
Or follow him on Twitter:
@DavidAlanMack